Deception

Betrayed Hearts

Terence L. Taylor

ISBN: 978-1-963949-25-4 (Paperback)

ISBN: 978-1-963949-26-1 (Hardcover)

Printed in the United States of America

Prologue

My name is Cyn, and my life's narrative could easily be mistaken for a play Shakespeare forgot to write—filled with as much tragedy, deception, and betrayal. At the tender age of twelve, the streets became my reluctant home, schooling me in lessons of survival, love's false promises, and the sting of betrayal. In those early years, amidst the backdrop of abandonment and abuse, I learned that affection could be a guise, and trust was often misplaced.

This story is more than a mere recounting of past events; it's a revelation of the scars and veils that time has woven over my heart. It delves into the heartache of deceit, the cold touch of betrayal, and the quest for a love that seemed as elusive as the morning mist.

Each chapter of my journey unfolded like scenes from a grand, yet somber play, where the roles of lover and deceiver blurred, leaving me to untangle the truth from beautifully crafted lies. My life was not my own, but a series of acts determined by those who claimed to love me, only to leave me more lost in the labyrinth of their deception.

Yet, standing here, I am not the villain of this tale but its survivor. Bearing witness to the strength that lies in a heart once betrayed, I've learned the power of truth, the importance of genuine connections, and the bravery required to open oneself to love again—even when past wounds whisper warnings to guard your heart.

As you journey through these pages, remember that the experiences laid bare are not solely mine but reflect a universal truth of human connection, where we are all actors on the stage of life, seeking authenticity in a world often shrouded in deception.

Chapter One

Our first date at Palisades was a truly special experience, and the breathtaking views of Elliott Bay marina from the romantic and classic restaurant tucked away at the base on Magnolia hill in Seattle certainly added to the ambiance. Downtown was a backdrop in the distance. The Space Needle stood alone, its majestic silhouette outlined against the sky. We were second in line at the hostess station, the sound of hushed conversations drifting through the air. Two twenty-somethings, arm-in-arm, followed behind. The young lady's hair and make-up were impeccable, revealing that she was hoping for a more thrilling evening. She whispered disapprovingly of her date's choice of restaurants, "There are only old people here."

The hostess transferred a senior couple to a young brunette, who guided them off to their seats.

My date stepped forward, and I witnessed the confidence in his stance as he gave his name and the time of the reservation. Her eyes quickly checked the register, and the polite smile slowly melted into a look of discomfort. She tightened her lips into a thin line. Her face reddened. "Sorry to delay you. Would you? Could you allow me a few seconds? I'll be right back." Pushing hair from her face, she hastily departed from the podium. My mind was running wildly as I tried to make sense of what could've happened to cause the alarm on her face. I was already nervous, and the young lady's hasty retreat raised my levels of discomfort. *Was there a prior disagreement that could explain her abrupt departure?* Three other couples join behind us. I dreaded the long absence of the hostess. She was gone for what seemed like an eternity. She returned and walked towards me, a radiant smile playing on her lips. In her hands, she held a magnificent bouquet of long-stem red roses.

The fragrance that emanated from them was intoxicating, filling the area with a sweet, floral aroma. In that moment, time seemed to stand still. *Oh, my heavens.* With tears of happiness welling in my eyes, I looked at her, my voice choked with emotion. I turned to my amour, Thank you, I whispered, unable to find words that could capture the depth of my appreciation.

It was as though they had crowned me Miss America. The restaurant critic behind us playfully joined in my joy, pinching her boyfriend's arm. Startled, he cried out in a shrill voice, massaging his arm with a puzzled frown, and asked, "What made you do that?" She ignored his inquiry and murmured softly, "Those are lovely." I hoped her date got the message.

I felt the rising heat of awkwardness as I stuttered to convey my thanks. The effervescent hostess grinned and said, "This way, please. I'll take you to your table." My date gestured for me to walk in front of him. As we passed the diners, heads turned, and eyes followed. Looking up, my gaze unintentionally met the wise eyes of an elderly woman. She smiled broadly and clapped loudly, soon joined by the infectious sound of others clapping. We walked through a gauntlet of cheers and applause on our way to the table. I was sure my face was bright red, though I couldn't see it myself.

Our hostess, Kellie, moved her hands with a flourish, like a showgirl, pointing towards our table. Her face full of delight, she asked, "Is this a significant occasion?"

I was uncomfortable with all the attention and grasped for words. My date answered, "Yes," his face beaming with a dazzling smile. What girl wouldn't succumb to its charms? "I'm celebrating my first date with this beautiful lady, and I'm aiming to make the evening as magical and special as possible."

Kellie clasped her hand over her heart. "That is so sweet," she said, her voice like a soft melody. "Tyler will take care of you. Please let us know if there is anything else you need. Have a wonderful evening."

"Wow, that's really impressive. Thank you, I'm genuinely touched by your generosity."

"I'm just glad that you liked them. Besides, as I told our hostess, I'm grateful for the opportunity to have dinner with you. Despite only having known each other for a short time, I find your vivacity and compassion to be truly captivating. I was immediately drawn to you at the conference. Your gestures and laughter with your associates caught my attention, and I knew I had to have dinner with you."

"Just like that?" I asked, snapping my fingers.

"Hmm, now that I think about it," He snapped his fingers. "Yes."

Nervously, I responded, "Thank you." *Water.* I gulped it as soon as he pulled the pitcher away. Requesting one more. Self-talking. *Okay, calm yourself, Cyn.*

Tyler cheerfully greeted us as she introduced herself as our server. "Is there anything I can get you to drink?"

I ordered a tall glass of iced tea with a slice of lemon. He ordered a Macallan 15. I inhaled the sweet fragrance of the flowers before placing them on the table. The evening was off to a wonderful start, and it filled my heart with joy. It's a pleasure to have a man attentive to all the details. His thoughtful gift overwhelmed me, and I couldn't find the words to express my gratitude properly. "I wasn't expecting anything that grand." "Why?" he had to ask. His eyes were soft and innocent. He said to me, "This evening is an introduction to getting to know you. My desires are that we communicate and enjoy ourselves. Life becomes complex when we place expectations on interactions. To properly know and understand—truly appreciate a woman—a man should take his time to learn and appreciate her heart, mind, body, and soul. The key to love is earning my lady's love, devotion, and admiration."

Whoa. I exhaled. "So, you have no expectations?"

He smirked. "No." He subtly shook his head. "I hope to be straight with you. I am truly captivated by your charm and grace. This evening is an introduction to future engagements—I hope." He continued, "I believe romance is a lost art. To me, roses symbolize a woman's soul—the hue of red, fire, and power to consume or spellbind like a candle's flame: soft, luminous, glowing, and tranquil. It's powerful yet delicate, and its fragrance is an aroma that tantalizes the senses. If mishandled, one will feel the painful prick of her scorn. Thus, to avoid its barb, a man must be respectful of how he treats and cares for it, just like he should for a woman. If one does those things right, he'll enjoy its———lustrous beauty and radiant light. All too often, men like to take a rose at the height of its beauty and selfishly cut it off and keep it for themselves. Over time, they ignore it, and the beauty withers away. We should never take the beauty of a woman for granted but nurture and appreciate it. A properly cared-for rose maintains its vivaciousness and strength throughout a woman's life, and she returns her gratitude tenfold."

Hmm, how poetic, Mister Romeo, I'm in.... "Wow, those are beautiful words. Why is a man with such a firm grasp of love single?"

He chuckled. "Life and love have a lot of moving pieces, and it's all a matter of perspective, and I believe in universal timing. Love is a quest; you meet people every day. You, like me, I'm certain, have had your share of dates. However, — and I'm not saying I'm the man for you—but you connect when you meet that perfect person for you. Thus, I may have my visions, but my remaining single simply means that I haven't found the right woman yet. However, we should leave the bulk of the conversation for another time. We'll learn as we go."

I was experiencing first-date butterflies. Looking for a distraction, I picked up the menu. Thinking about what to order, hoping not to be judged by my dinner choice, I peeped up from the menu, inhaled deeply, and looked into his eyes. He had a tranquil glow, soft like the light of the candle, with enough warmth from the flame and a tinge of arrogance to warn of cautions; the innocent blaze can start a fire. But his polite mannerisms enhanced the ambiance, and I felt comfortable—attracted to his presence. I was concerned that my trepidation made me appear awkward. I'd been out of the dating game for two years after ending a two-year emotionally unrewarding relationship and throwing myself into completing my residency. In that relationship, we kind of fell out of love, leading me to question my appearance, wondering if I'd lost my ability to please a man.

There was nothing I wouldn't have done for him… in the beginning. I questioned my appeal to a man as we drifted apart. Initially, I thought it was me failing him in the relationship. He and I came together while we both started our first year of med school. We found hanging on to each other academically fulfilling.

He was a attractive man; I would call him a genius. He was taller than me, with unkempt blonde hair and amber eyes. He preferred the outdoors and spent more time hiking around the Puget Sound area than studying. He didn't really need as much time practicing and studying as I did. It all came so easily to him. It's as though he was born into the profession. I remember pushing him to use his gift to excel in the medical profession and maybe support struggling classmates. I appealed him to think of all his future accomplishments. "You have a gift that will help you do great things in this profession. Use it." However, he was like a teenager more interested in hiking trails, mountains, rivers, lakes, and streams. I guess I was the nag in the relationship, constantly pushing him out in front of me… maybe hoping he'd drag me along. Not that I'm dumb. I was jealous that it came so easily to him, and I wanted him to share his magic. The arrival of our dinner interrupted my thoughts.

He barely touched his steak while I devoured my Dungeness crab-stuffed colossal prawns. He sat back in his seat with a look of amusement, poised with his drink raised, which triggered a heart-racing moment of self-doubt. *Dear God, he's going to think I'm a pig.* Pushing my plate aside, I leaned forth. "You didn't touch your dinner. Is something wrong?"

"No, no, it was great. How about yours?"

"It was delicious. But you barely touched yours." I was curious about what was behind this man's subconscious curtain and asked, "Do you mind sharing your thoughts?"

He responded, looking at my empty glass, "I will—you mind if I get you a refill?"

I smiled, thinking the last thing I needed was more pressure on my bladder. While I was trying to coax him to share his thoughts, I was doing my best to read his body language, wondering what triggered the sparkle in his eyes. I emboldened myself to relax and have some fun with him. Thinking creatively, *two can play the game of attraction, mister.* I seductively put the straw to my lips, toying it with my tongue, slowly placing my lips around the straw.

Glancing at him for effect, then back to the straw, humming my pleasure, pulling the sweet, soft liquid into my mouth. Wow, this was really stepping outside of my norm. I haven't felt sexy in a long while. I still had a little game in me.

During my play of seduction, I suddenly felt the need to pee. I feigned comfort trying to hold back my internal dam from bursting. Finally, my amour reached for my hand, about to share his thoughts, "I'm sorry, I didn't mean to make you nervous with my admiration. I'm distracted by the radiance of your beauty."

Damn, he's charming. I pressed my legs tight, not wanting to leave the table. The air between us grew thick with anticipation, each second stretching longer than the last, weaving a silence that pulsed with unspoken yearnings and curious desires. Then, breaking through the tension with a voice soft yet laden with emotion, he uttered, "And I just want you…"

"Excuse me." I felt the first warning pulse of an impending burst. *Excellent timing, Cynthya.* I fast-walked to the bathroom, doing my best not to break into a full sprint.

As I made my way back to the table, a wave of relief washed over me, only to be quickly overshadowed by a sight I hadn't anticipated. He was deep in conversation with the server, whose smile radiated a warmth that seemed all too familiar.

The moment she caught sight of me, her hand swiftly retracted from his—an action that did little to quell the storm brewing within me. I found myself grappling with a surge of jealousy, a feeling I would normally dismiss as utterly irrational. Yet, the image before me spoke volumes; it's one thing to step away from a man poised to whisper sweet nothings, but entirely another to return to find him intertwined with another, her smile as bright as daylight. No woman ever wishes to witness her date's hands clasped with another's, regardless of the circumstances. As I stood there, her blue eyes met mine, shimmering with an unspoken narrative.

"How is everything?" she asked as I sat.

"Wonderful," I replied disdainfully.

"Excellent!" Her face was a mask of innocence. "May I bring dessert menus?"

I declined the offer. But Mister Charming said yes, inviting me to share the "Trio of crème brûlée." Sounds delicious. My mouth watered, so I said yes. But the thought of adding additional pounds to my ass made me consider a resounding no. However, this was a date, and I should enjoy all of it… including the dessert.

The warm and alluring fire of conversation he was about to start before my jaunt seemed to have passed. I want him to pick up where he left off. "So, you were saying?" He chuckled, asking me if I was okay. I assured him that all was well. *Now retake my hand, you fool, and finish what you were going to say.*

However, the moment of deep conversation shifted. Perhaps his talk with the waitress had distracted his thoughts. He asked, "So tell me more about you."

I gave an appreciative smirk. His question jolted me. What do I tell him? What's the proper dating conversation etiquette? I contemplated his request. Other than work, I have little to say. All I could think was to share openly, reflecting on my past relationship. I told him, "I'm a simple woman. I have my career, for which I busted my butt. I had a few life hiccups—but who doesn't? I will not share those on the first date. However, my life has worked out to my satisfaction. The medical profession is perfect for me. I'm a heart person. Which means I enjoy pleasing and taking care of others. I'm very close to my family and friends." He raised a curious brow.

Our waitress returned with dessert just in time to save me from going overboard about myself. The two spoons lay positioned, waiting for us to dip into the enticing dish. "That looks deliciously inviting. But I better not."

The hours leading up to this evening were spent in a flurry of anticipation and excitement, meticulously searching for the perfect dress that would strike the delicate balance between conservative allure and captivating beauty.

The unanimous choice, heralded by Lexi and Gina, was a stunning black ensemble that seemed to tick all the right boxes: sleeveless, with a midi length that spoke of elegance, a halter neck tie closure that added a touch of sophistication, and a daring low back that promised a hint of intrigue. The dress's pièce de résistance, a thigh-high slit up the left leg, flirted with the boundaries of boldness. Initially, I harbored reservations about its audacity—was it too much? Yet, the way it embraced and flattered the curves of my hips and ass, areas I often scrutinized, left me feeling nothing short of breathtaking.

Despite its perfection, a shadow of reluctance lingered; the dress, as beautiful as it was, underscored my insecurities about my figure. Now, as dessert was being offered, the temptation of its sinful sweetness seemed like it would only exacerbate my concerns, intensifying my self-consciousness about my ass. Hence, I was reluctant, caught in the moment, worried that succumbing to the allure of dessert would betray my efforts to present myself in the best light.

However, my kind amour coaxed me, "Ah, come on. Please share it with me." He leaned forward, his eyes darting left and right as if preparing to share a confidential secret. In a hushed tone that hinted at conspiracy, he whispered, "This is very important. I need us to keep this just between us." My curiosity piqued, I leaned in, my voice tinged with mock seriousness, "What?" He moved even closer, the corners of his mouth twitching with a suppressed smile. "I promise not to tell anyone. It'll be just our little secret," he murmured, a playful glint in his eyes. "Even your friends won't know we indulged in dessert." The solemnity of his vow, juxtaposed with the triviality of the secret, was both absurd and endearing, turning the moment into a shared joke, a tiny bubble of complicity amidst the evening's ambiance. "You better not." I chided, picking up the spoon to share the sinful decadence.

My mind told me, *loosen up, Cyn.* Thus, I decided to have my fun, toying with the spoon, taking a small scoop, raising it to my mouth, slowly parting my lips, and savoring its sweet, smooth sensation with my tongue. I hum, rolling my tongue across my lips, teasing him to share. I whispered seductively, "Now, mister, share your thoughts with me, or else." I wanted to drink more of his thrilling romance, just as the hot coffee sat between us.

He said, "I was admiring you and studying the night. I was thinking after dinner—but the perfect moment has passed."

"Why has it passed? We're still here."

"It was a beautiful sunset when we sat down. I had hoped to take a walk and enjoy the beauty of the night. However, the perfect opportunity appears to have passed. It looks like pending rain.

"That was a very nice thought." I wanted the evening to continue for a while. I daringly suggested, "Great, let's go for a walk." I smiled as he fumbled for words, flabbergasted, saying that we were ill-equipped for the rain and would get wet. He looked so adorable at that moment. I asked if he was afraid of getting damp.

"No!"

I jibed, "Yes, you are."

"I mean… ah, I mean, no, I'm not afraid, but I'm looking at you and thinking I wouldn't want to ruin that sexy outfit. I'm okay with another time."

I challenged, raising my coffee and taking a sip, looking over the brim. The more comfortable I got, the cheekier I became. "I may not be wearing this sexy outfit another time. Who knows what may befall us tomorrow? Besides, I'm a seize-the-moment kind of girl."

"Well, let's check your flowers with the hostess, and you're on." The server returned with the bill. He'd been a marvelous man, and I wanted to express my gratitude for reaching for the check. I don't want it taken for granted that a man will pay. But, unfortunately, he grabbed it before I did. "Please… allow me. I respect your ability to pay, but let's be old-fashioned this evening."

I pondered his statement, curious about the definition of old fashion. Then, resting my face on my hand, I asked, "Define your version of old fashion for me."

Long silence. This is where I learn if he's just using words or if there's a meaning behind them. He reached for my barely touched coffee across the table, asking, "Do you mind? It's cold."

I raised a brow, curious if this was a delaying tactic, as he searched for the right words. "Not at all, please." He took a sip of coffee. Staring into my eyes with a heave of air, he said, "Old fashion is when a man appreciates the honor of a woman: her beauty. It means respecting you as my equal, not as my competitor. Though we have unique differences, I know the planet would be bleak without a woman's prettification, attention to detail, and adornments of colors, styles, and class. The world would be navy blue and battleship gray if left up to men. The date was my request. Therefore, I chose the honor of paying. Unless you're planning this to be the last date."

Clearing my throat, I was speechless. I stood up and curtsied. "By all means, my kind gentleman." He rose and complimented me with a gentleman's bow. I like it when a man doesn't take himself too seriously and appreciates the little joys in life. Outside, a stiff wind blew. He gave me a look of apprehension. I asked, "Are you ready to change your mind? Perhaps afraid of the rain, getting wet and melting away like Frosty the Snowman? Or is it sugar? I forget." He said to me he was more concerned about me. I replied, "I'm a big girl. I am not worried about a few water particles in the air."

He laughed and said, "I don't want to be blamed for your sniffles later. Thus forcing me to bring you hot soup—not that I would mind."

I laughed. "I think I'd make the house call bringing you hot soup and various other necessary prescriptions." A tingle of intrigue rushed through my body from the warm grasp of his hand. I know this was our first date, but taking ahold of his hand felt so natural. We strolled along to the marina admiring the array of boats: large and small sails, medium and giant pleasure crafts to rich-man massive. Unexpectedly, a streak of lightning crackles across the sky, followed by a thunderous boom—the precursor to a torrential downfall. I shrieked in surprise—I was expecting more of a mist— as the chilly raindrops fell relentlessly from the clouds. I cried out, "No, this can't be." Though I was adept at running in my heels, I didn't want to take any risk that would send me face-first to the ground. I pressed close to him, absorbing his warmth, and buried my head close.

We were soaked in a matter of seconds. *So much for being the courageous girl...* We made our way to the valet stand, looking like drenched pups crawling out of the dark. The young blonde whisked away the wet strands of hair dangling from underneath his hood. He hesitated before taking the ticket. "You know… we have umbrellas inside, right?" I smirked and replied, "Thanks, bud." I felt like a chaotic mess, with my hair matted and damp.

My dress was heavy with water, clinging to my skin. If things couldn't be any worse, sudden winds were so cold my nipples throbbed fully erect, and my teeth chattered like an old-fashioned telegraph machine. *"Brilliant idea, Cynthya, daring a man to a walk in the chilling rain."*

As the black BMW glided forward like a majestic lion, its headlights cast a warm glow on the rain-slicked pavement. The patter of the raindrops against its polished exterior was like music to my ears, but it was the deep rumble of its engine that truly captivated me. It spoke of power, confidence, and sophistication. I couldn't help but smile as I watched the young kid behind the wheel, his face beaming with pride as he revved the engine before stepping out of the car.

My amour, always the gentleman, handed the kid a generous tip before opening the passenger door for me. As I stepped inside, I was struck by the lavish leather seats, and I couldn't help but feel a little self-conscious about my own soaked appearance. But then I heard his soft voice, barely above a whisper, as he gestured for me to take a seat. "Please," he said with a smile. As he closed the door behind me, I felt a warm and comforting sense of security, as though I was right where I belonged.

The engine purred as he rolled out of the parking lot. As soon as he turned on the heater, I let out a grateful sigh, appreciating the warmth that enveloped me. The heated seats were an added comfort, and I found myself relaxing into their embrace. Glancing over at him, I smiled, my expression silently conveying my thanks for his thoughtfulness. When he asked if I was okay with listening to some old-school music, I nodded eagerly, welcoming the nostalgic melodies that promised to fill the car.

With a flick of his thumb on the steering wheel, the radio panel came to life, and the smooth and sultry voice of Barry White filled the car. The song, *Can't Get Enough of Your Love*, sent shivers down my spine. It was as if the music was made for this moment, this drive. As we glided down the road, the car's movements were so fluid, so effortless. The heated seats provided a cozy and comforting embrace for my body, and the warm air enveloped me in a soothing embrace. I could feel myself slipping into a state of deep relaxation, and I knew it would be a struggle to stay awake for the rest of the long drive to Gina's house. But for now, I was content to bask in the warmth of the moment, lost in the magic of the music and the company of the man beside me. The city lights blurred past us, twinkling like distant stars, as I found myself moving subtly to the rhythm of the song.

My body relaxed to where I was falling asleep. My lips craved a loving kiss, but that would be too forward of me. "Thank you for the evening. I apologize for the downpour."

He chuckled. "I'll have to go shopping tomorrow."

"For what?"

He smiled. "I don't know… maybe I'll get an umbrella and towels to keep in the trunk for random walks in torrential rains."

I mocked, "Not funny, mister. Besides, you triggered the thought of taking a moonlight stroll. I only accommodated you." My mind was longing for him to take my hand. I tried to reach for him but stopped myself. Too soon. I didn't want to give in to a moment I could later regret by violating my never-promises— *Never-ever engage in sex on a first date. Never rush into a relationship.*

Bruce Springsteen's slow intro to *Fire* melted me away. "Excellent selections," I cooed, though they were songs I'd never really listened to. But I loved their titillating vibes. I had pegged him as a fan of various rap music genres, assuming his playlist would be a plethora of rap. However, it was the saxophone interlude in Maxi Priest's *The Art of Seduction* that finally overcame my efforts to stay awake. The stimulating playlist won out, and as my eyes grew heavy, I drifted off to sleep.

Chapter Two

I awoke as the car slowly rolled to a stop in front of Gina's house. Gina and I had established a rule: always return to one another's home after a first date. This was for safety, to avoid any overly persistent suitors, and, most importantly, to share the juicy details of our evenings. Gratefully, I thanked him for a wonderful night but declined his offer to walk me to the door. I didn't want him to leave the comfort of the car, feeling I had already made quite an impression on him that evening. Moreover, I wanted to sidestep an awkward, prolonged goodbye at the door. Given my long-standing lack of intimacy, even a simple kiss might lead to an unintended escalation of emotions, especially on Gina's porch. So, I chose to spare myself the disappointment rather than him.

Usually, I'd be the one staying awake for Gina to arrive at my place. But tonight, it was her turn to eagerly wait for my stories. As she opened the door, her initial delight quickly turned to concern when she saw me shivering and drenched. "Why are you wet?" she asked, her mind racing with all the things that might have gone wrong. Before I could even respond, "What happened to you?" she demanded, ushering me inside swiftly. No sooner had she tucked me in than she was out the door in her boxers and midriff shirt, marching determinedly toward his car. It was as if she and the car were performing a coordinated dance; him reversing in a hurry and Gina, all five-foot-four of her, striding right up to his vehicle. My friend can be quite over-reactive, and that's an understatement.

It took a while to soothe her and calm her concerns. I mentioned that the situation was partly my own doing, as I had suggested—dared—going for a walk after dinner. This left her looking puzzled and slightly concerned, wondering about the choice to walk in such weather and at night. Sensing the need to change the topic and address my discomfort, I quickly excused myself, mentioning my desire for a hot shower.

"Oooh, one of those kinds of walks?" As I headed into the bathroom, I answered, "Not in the slightest." Slamming the door and stripping off my killer dress that I had bought for tonight's occasion, I turned on the shower, and the water burst from the spa showerhead. I stepped into the glass enclosure, appreciating the warm pulsating jets rolling down my naked, sex-starved body. I closed my eyes, remembering the last track played on the car's radio, *The Art of Seduction*. Another curious hum briefly ignited my suspicious thoughts.

I glided my hands over my lathered body, biting my lower lip, trying to quell my desire to take self-indulgent liberty. My hand slid from breast to stomach, slowly touching my clit. Oh, God, I'm so horny the mere touch ignites my sensation. I tried to deter the temptation, moving away and washing my legs. But my lust beckoned me back to my pleasure zone, teasing, passing over my clit. I craved an orgasm but feared my scream of pleasure would reverberate through the walls. Then, just as I was about to engage my Gloria (our girls' code for vagina), I was interrupted by a hard knock on the door. Gina asked if I was okay. "Hurry! I want to hear the wicked details about the date."

I grabbed the shower handle, wrenching it to cold. I squealed from the shock, quickly extinguishing my internal wildfire. "Yes! I'm okay." I had just stunned my body, going from hard-on arousal to dead-stop numbness in seconds.

Gina sat on the sofa with her legs crossed, sipping a glass of wine. A cup of tea was on the table for me. I sat at the opposite end. Her devious mind churned with curiosity as she asked, "Okay, so?" waiting for erotic details.

Playing naïve, I responded, "So? So what?"

"Come on, Cyn, you know what! Tell me what happened— why were you all messed up?"

I huffed, pretending I was about to reveal the sordid details of our evening. "Okay, I'll tell you. But it's not what you think."

"How do you know what I'm thinking?" she countered.

I rolled my eyes at her rhetorical question.

I explained that we had arrived at the restaurant right before the sunset. The sun gave way to a splendid full moon. I dared him to brave the elements and take a walk with me. He changed his mind at the sight of the rain, the droplets cascading down like a light curtain. I persuaded him to take the risk. The sound of the rain crashing against the pavement was a surprise interruption to my plans.

Gina grumbled, "Girl, it was too cold to go walking at night." I was too tired to keep up the charade of the lustful events that had taken place.

My self-denials of satisfaction had drained me. My body yearned for sleep. "I'm too tired to tell you the rest. Let's save the rest for brunch with the girls tomorrow."

After our sophomore year of college, instead of joining a sorority, the four of us, Gina, Courtnee, Lexi, and I made a pact to always honor each other and set aside Sundays for brunch at Salty's on Alki. We all got tattoos of an adorable little mouse embracing a shamrock on our right ankles with all our names in a circle. The only excuse not to attend our meetings was death; not boyfriends, future husbands, or kid drama could prevent us from keeping this tradition, a tradition we've cherished even through our rigorous med school and residency. Gina snapped her fingers, jolting me back to reality – the reality that I was too exhausted to indulge her curiosity about my evening with Mr. Romantic. So, off to bed I went, leaving her craving the spicy details.

Chapter Three

Though we all lived just a stone's throw from each other on the east side and were heading to the same quaint corner of West Seattle, we each took our separate cars. This had become one of our group's unspoken and inexplicable Sunday habits. By a silent consensus that had never been formally agreed upon, I seemed to have become the designated driver. This role had me rounding everyone up and ensuring they got home safely after our joyous gatherings, inevitably leading to the comically inconvenient task of car retrieval the next morning. We sat in the back corner next to the window. These Sunday get-togethers were precious moments for all of us. We committed to continue keeping this tradition alive. At that time, the only one of us to have gotten married was Courtnee.

Today's topic was last night's date. Gina laid the groundwork, laughing, barely able to contain her exaggeration. She talked about how I showed up drenched at her door. "As soon as I opened the door, her hair was frizzy. She was shaking and crying like a puppy," she gave a demonstration while whimpering and bending her wrists into the shape of dog paws. This led to hysterical laughter aimed straight at me. She explained how she initially thought he had wronged me. All the attention now turned toward me, urging me to take up the story from where Gina left off, persuading me to tell them the sordid details of our night. Lexi was concerned about other details of the evening, asking brusquely, "Is he a good kisser?"

"We didn't kiss Lex. It was our first date."

Rolling her eyes, she responded, "Lame."

I told them how he had the hostess present me with a beautiful bouquet of roses upon our arrival, they all swooned at the romantic gesture. As I recounted my story, I suddenly remembered that I had forgotten the flowers, and a wave of guilt hit me. Lexi gave a villainous coo, rolling her eyes back and forth, animating, sticking her middle finger down her throat, gagging on her laughter.

I glared at Lexi through narrowed eyes, conveying my disapproval of her deplorable behavior, telling her that she was appalling. She responded, "But you're a prude." More laughter followed. She asked, "For what purpose are you saving that thing? The second coming of Jesus?" I pursed my lips together and shot her a stern look, silently begging her to stop. My friends could be so embarrassing with their malicious words and contemptuous opinions. In their wild, salacious minds, they had concluded that we ventured outside, had sex, and got caught in the rain. Lexi asked, "If he was so romantic, how come things didn't go further?" Dear God, it was man-bashing time. "You know, all that men ever want is sex. And when a guy is that nice, he's trying to guarantee some same-night—"

"Lexi! Please."

If only they knew the closest I came to sex was in the shower. Even then, I denied myself the pleasure. Gina asked about our plans for the next date. "Ah," my mind went blank. It was just dawning on me. There was no mention of a second date. Self-doubt took over. Maybe there wasn't to be a subsequent date. I defended our evening.

The charming restaurant, the wonderful dinner—even the fateful walk in the rain—all of that made me feel special. "I'm okay," I lied, "if I don't see him again. It was our first date, and the night wasn't about lovemaking, you guys. Why can't we leave it at the fact that I had a charming man take me to dinner? He dropped me off at Gina's afterward. End of story."

Lexi asked, "So you're saying this man—handsome as you say—had you in his car soaking wet and didn't make any excuse to get you out of that soggy dress, aka panties?" She held her hands up, signaling quotation. "Maybe suggesting you go to his place?"

Courtnee added, "Or maybe the reason was because he had it waiting somewhere else for him, and he was saving Cyn for later." That touched a nerve, but I played it off like it was no big deal. However, by this point, I was feeling a little humiliated by my friends.

I asked, "Why are you guys—ladies—always saying that all men want is sex? Then you beat him up for not trying to get in my pants the first night."

Lexi nodded to Courtnee, "Definitely a sign of another woman." She sniffed the air like a bloodhound, saying, "Guys are dogs, and all they want is p.u.s.s.y. And you know his dick was hard, and he didn't try to get some? There are two options." She holds up two fingers. "He is gay—and that's okay. Or he got OPW." A Lexi-ism. I chose not to fully clarify. Just that the W stands for waiting. I visually threw daggers at Lexi. She smiled, blowing a kiss, saying in her honey-sweet voice. "I love you, Cyn."

Though I love my friends dearly—and understanding us fully requires being part of our group—our banter, deeply rooted in affection, can sometimes highlight their contradictions. I must concede that, perhaps buried within our complex female psyche, there's a part of us that paradoxically hopes a guy will propose sex on the first date, providing us the opportunity to politely decline. Thus, we judge a guy to see if he's an understanding man and respects our request or a selfish asshole trying to push his agenda. A wise woman knows which one to leave alone.

When one of us started a relationship, we all took a moment to appreciate the joy of it, yet couldn't help but feel envious. We found ourselves peering through the cracks to find his imperfections, voicing our criticisms of his mistakes.

Amidst these dynamics stands Gina, undeniably a gorgeous woman with an amazing personality. She boasts a stunning, well-toned physique, emerald eyes, and glossy raven hair—a testament to her timeless beauty and charm that captivate everyone around her. Sadly, she has a tendency to be exceedingly demanding. Hence, her relationships usually don't last too long. Courtnee proudly wears her wedding ring.

There's not much to elaborate on that. Her shoulder-length red hair and light blue eyes complement her tall, slim figure—the "average white girl" look that Lexi describes for her. Stephen and she wed shortly after college, and they've been married ever since. His face is an expressionless mask as he moves through life, never veering from what's considered socially acceptable. He's tall with dark hair that's rapidly receding from the top. He has a bushy mustache and a shy expression that makes him seem boring, but he's a talented engineer for Boeing.

We're not sure if the connection between them is romantic love or just a mutual need for companionship. Courtnee is always trying to brighten everyone's mood with her infectious smile. I—we—believe she could certainly do better. But she resolutely states she's committed to her marriage for life. Lexi, the outspoken, independent gal, has been in a relationship with Marcus, a pro football cornerback. That boy is tall and good-looking. They have been together for nine months, and their relationship seems to be blossoming into something more permanent.

Rain pelted the windows. I knew the puns were coming. And it was Lexi. "Hey Cyn, it's raining. We should all go for a walk… and, you know, [get wet]." Riotous laughter.

I was miffed, biting my lower lip. Hmm, a devious thought came to mind. Why not? This is my chance for revenge against these wenches. "Novel idea, Lex. Let's go."

Smiles faded. Courtnee stuttered, "Go? Go where?"

I responded, "Outside, and as Lex said, 'get us wet.' It's a dare."

Lexi quickly voiced her objection. "Have you lost your mind? It's raining. Freezing your ass off in the rain, that's your thing. I just got my hair done. I'm not going outside without an umbrella, a warm overcoat, and my hot man holding me tight."

I responded adoringly, "It's a dare, my dear… we have to go."

Courtnee looked to Lexi, then to me, "You're not serious, are you, Cyn? I. I. I don't… we didn't come prepared for a dare. Take it back, Cyn. We can do this some other time, like in the summer, when it's hot, very hot. And I'm wearing a bikini. In Hawaii or some other warm place."

We had played dare since our junior year in high school, resulting in wild and crazy antics. We're now grown women, and we still issue the occasional outlandish juvenile challenges. Our covenant—once a dare was declared, all must oblige. Our timid and lovable Courtnee reminded us, "Guys, look. We're wearing dresses and heels, not suitable for walking in or dancing in—did I say rain?" I moved from the table, ready to lead the challenge. Courtnee beckoned Gina to say something. Knowing she had started it, Gina joined reluctantly, simultaneously shaking her head. Courtnee followed wearily. I understood Gina was complying because she thought I was bluffing. Lexi, on the other hand, protested, saying, "No. No. Shit, no, Cyn."

I delighted in making Lexi squirm for her quips. "Sweetie, you suggested it. I believe your exact words were 'getting wet.'"

She sat with her arms folded. "Cyn, you know what I meant."

"No, dear. I do not. How can we possibly get wet in here? Shall we pour pitchers of water over ourselves?"

The three of us stood, waiting for Lexi to surrender. She maintained her defiance staunchly, shaking her head. After what seemed an eternity, she rolled her eyes before relenting. "Fine," she spat out, marching past us. "Let's go, bitches. Just remember you started this, Cyn. Payback is going to be in my favor."

"Oh, Lex, I look forward to your future dare. Just remember, it's a group activity." That's the thing about us—we never know which off-the-cuff remark will generate a challenge that leads to outlandish things. Today's challenge turned out to be fun because we hadn't done something this crazy in a long time. I hadn't planned anything before stepping out into the torrential rain.

Outside, we locked arms, walking down the sidewalk. "Shit! The rain is drizzling and cold." Lexi stammered her protest, "Fu... fu... fk, it's cold. We shouldn't be doing this; we're going to get sick."

From what I could discern, Gina had just set a new standard for craziness with her wildness. She shouted, "Into the water! Dare!"

Lexi shouted back, "What?" Seattle's water is frigid even when it's eighty degrees outside. Now, with the temperature at fifty-three degrees and the rain coming down in a light drizzle, we peeled off our heels and felt the cold, biting chill of the icy water as part of the spirit of our challenges. "I hate you guys," Lexi yelled, joining us. I could only imagine what people must have thought, seeing four women dressed to the nines wading into the water like teenagers. Okay, maybe we were a little insane.

As we walked back to the valet, we clung tightly to one another, our teeth chattering from the cold. As soon as the car arrived, the three of them piled into the backseat, their laughter echoing in the air.

Shouting, "We need heat," Gina belted out, "Girl, when are you going to get a car with seat warmers?"

Courtnee choked out with laughter, "Yeah, like a big, massive BMW."

Gina exclaimed, "Thanks a lot, Cyn. My buzz is gone. Who has backup booze?" Lexi and Courtnee both produced flasks. Shit. I was in trouble. It would be one hell of a drive home with these crazy gals laughing and giggling insanely the whole way. If only they'd pass out. But I wasn't that lucky. Instead, I was treated to a drunken rendition of Madonna's *Like a Virgin,* with my name inserted in the chorus with emphasis on 'touched for the very first time.' Each Sunday, everyone would agree not to have more than two drinks. That was the one oath they could never keep.

I called Courtnee's husband to meet us at my house to pick up his plastered wife. Lexi's boyfriend Marcus wasn't so easy to convince, questioning why I couldn't just drop her at home. From the back seat, Lexi yelled, "Marcus! Come and get me, babe. I love you."

Marcus responded, "You guys seem a little twisted," his tone mixing concern and disbelief. "You sure you can't just bring her home? I'm kind of busy right now." I remained silent. After a long pause, he exhaled deeply, "Fine. I'll see y'all in a minute." Their off-key wailing and the passing of flasks filled the car for the entire drive home.

Stephen arrived shortly after we reached my place. He was greeted by his inebriated wife slurring her speech, trying to explain her condition in a way that only a drunken mind could, "Cyn has a boy-man. Friend. And didn't get to have no sex. And Lexi said we should get us some wet. Cause Cyn is dry. Bone dry, babe. Dry like dust in the wind. You know, like those little tornado things we see when we drive through the desert. Yep, she's that kind of dry." She blew some fictitious dust from her palm.

Red-faced, Stephen told her, "Okay, bone dry. I get it."

She slapped his arm playfully. "You know how when she ain't been gettin' none…" she whispered as if confiding a secret. "You know, the sex." Stephen frowned, looking at me apologetically. She grabbed his chin, forcing his face to hers, "Then Cyn…"

"Sweetheart, I get it," he interjected.

"Wait, babe, you didn't let me finish."

"I got it, honey."

"Good. Let's go home and get you some sex." Stumbling backward, she winked with a thumbs up. "Yeah, I'm going to ride his ass like a buff…a cow-horse, boy-man. Ain't I, babe?" She resisted his attempt to lead her away, pushing his hand off. "Hey buddy, don't get excited." He threw up his hands, walking to the door. "Hey, mister! You leaving me?" She staggered after him, sliding along the wall. As they reached the door, the doorbell rang, and they walked past Marcus, who was now entering the scene.

"My man is here!" Lexi yelled. "Hey, babe." Marcus, wearing a gold chain, black running pants, and a white snug-fit shirt that hugged the contours of his muscular body, looked at me, perplexed, fending off Lexi.

"What the hell, babe? Why? What? Why would you get into the ocean? Did you notice it's cold—and raining?" He glanced at me, then at Gina as she walked out of the bathroom, toweling her hair as if we were responsible for Lexi's drunken state. He shook his head. "Y'all are crazy."

Lexi, evidently aroused, was rubbing her hands on his chest. "Marcus!" she shouted. Then, lowering her voice to a purr, she continued, "Come on, let's go home."

Marcus, concerned about his seats, asked, "You got a towel I can use?"

"We don't need no towel. You're not getting it in the car," Lexi snapped, snapping her fingers and pointing toward the door. "Marcus. Come. You got work to do." He huffed and followed her. As they left, she yelled over her shoulder, "Love you, Cyn," just as Marcus closed the door.

With everyone gone, I had a serious moment alone with Gina, sharing my guilt about leaving the flowers at the restaurant and how the date ended with no suggestions for another. *Maybe daring him to walk in the rain was too much, perhaps a turn-off.* Or maybe he's looking for a less adventurous and spontaneous woman—though I certainly didn't wish it to be a dousing retreat from a joyful walk. "God, I hate dating," Gina replied indifferently. She's used to blowing guys off after a first date. "It's okay. You're an awesome woman. And if he doesn't call, who cares? He can't be that special." She saw my dejection and offered reassurance to lift my spirits. "Trust me, he'll call." Embracing me, she said, "Thank you for bringing us home."

Chapter Four

I t had been a week since our first date. No phone call, no text. Just as I accepted there wouldn't be a second meeting, my cell phone rang at 4:45 p.m. on Friday. I answered. My tone was flat—an obvious expression of my dissatisfaction as he waited this long to call me. Sure, I could have called him, but that would be me engaging in a hapless pursuit, in need of reassurances to stall my feelings of rejection. He did say that he's been super busy with work and travel.

With a wry smile, I thought to myself, *Alright, Mr. Charmer.* His attempt at pleasantries was appreciated, but his explanation was far from sufficient. *They don't have cell phone coverage, or were you traveling to a primitive land where phones don't exist?* A follow-up call would have been a polite gesture. *Hey, I enjoyed your company,* or *I didn't enjoy your company,* or *let's just be friends* would have been nice. But not to wait a week. I sensed a wave of vulnerability washing over me. He asked if I would meet him at Daniel's in Bellevue this evening. One compromise I don't make is accepting last-minute "work me into your plans" invitations.

I firmly replied, "No." The room was filled with a long and tense silence. A thought crept into my mind that perhaps some stories the girls were telling about him had an element of truth to them. His call made me feel insignificant, like I was a last-minute addition to his evening plans. Today, I expect a man to plan a date properly with me.

He wasn't accepting no for an answer, again apologizing for his absence. I reconsidered his request, with part of me wanting to say yes and the other side saying no. My no side won. Another pause. I thought he had ended our call. *Shit, did I just play a losing hand of poker?* As I was about to put the phone down, he asked about my Saturday plans. I didn't have any at the moment. "Would you mind going on a hike and picnicking at Snoqualmie Falls?" *Hmm, maybe.*

I liked the idea of a picnic, and enjoying the cascading water at the falls was romantic, but a hint of a long-past date gone wrong gave me trepidation. I was shaken by the thought of going out in nature for a second date. What if he's not a kind man but some lunatic trying to lure me into the woods? *Maybe I should suggest an alternative date. What's wrong with meeting for coffee?* I did my best to harness the anxiety brought on by the thoughts. I couldn't give him an answer. I closed my eyes tightly, struggling with reminders of times past. I liked this man; thus, I had to trust him and pray that God would not fail me a second time should a frantic occasion arise. My long hesitation prompted him to ask, "Is that a bad idea?"

I had envisioned our hike as a tranquil journey through nature, culminating in a picturesque picnic at Snoqualmie, a perfect scene to gingerly step towards trust after being shadowed by betrayal. The proposition felt like a harmonious balance, a chance to cautiously rebuild trust after Hunter's deceit.

As we embarked, my excitement for a mixture of nature's serenity and budding companionship momentarily wavered under a cloud of apprehension. The memory of Hunter's false front, starkly contrasting with the man beside me, momentarily cast a chill. Yet, against the vibrant tapestry of our surroundings, this unease was a faint whisper, reminding me of the vulnerability at stake.

The genuine warmth and the majesty of nature began to melt away my initial hesitations. Our path, more challenging than I had imagined, wove through stunning landscapes and hidden trails, captivating my senses. His laughter blended with the natural chorus around us, creating moments of unadulterated happiness that transcended my simple picnic expectations.

He was keenly attentive, ensuring I navigated every obstacle with ease. Each step we took together, with him carefully leading me over uneven terrain and through narrow paths, felt like a cautious yet hopeful rebuilding of trust. With every supportive gesture and shared discovery, the heavy remnants of past pains lightened, paving the way for a nascent hope.

The grandeur of the outdoors, with its rich colors and the relentless roar of the falls, mirrored the complex journey of opening up to someone new. The hike wasn't just a physical trek but a reflective journey through the healing chambers of my heart.

As the hike transitioned to our romantic picnic, the earlier trials seemed trivial against the mighty sound of Snoqualmie Falls. There, amidst the powerful roar that filled the air, our efforts felt deeply rewarding. The picnic, framed by the majestic falls, was a celebration of our achievements—a perfect harmony of adventure, romance, and gentle steps toward trust.

This moment, filled with laughter and meaningful exchanges against the backdrop of the falls' thunder, solidified the beauty of taking chances and the possibility of new beginnings within nature's magnificent embrace.

Sunday morning dawned all too quickly. The aftermath of our mountainous escapade left me with a soreness so profound, it permeated every muscle—a detail I dared not mention to my friends, fearing the leaps their imaginations might take. After a much-needed shower and picking out an ensemble significantly more comfortable than the one from last weekend, I made my way to meet my lively friends.

As we were getting settled, a tall, handsome, young busser named Brody was clearing the table. Gina nudged me with her elbow and cooed, "Hmm, he's handsome."

I whispered, "He's a baby. Sixteen. Seventeen max."

He cleared his throat, correcting us, "Nineteen, ma'am." I felt my cheeks warm with a blush of embarrassment. *This misjudgment seemed as good a reason as any to excuse myself to grab some food.*

After loading our plates—we loved to eat, especially on Sundays—it was our time to splurge and not care about gaining weight. We settled in for gossip. Lexi was wearing oversized sunglasses, and her attention was focused outside. She was not her usual self. At first, we made nothing of it. She could sometimes be indifferent, especially when her period started. Admiring her Gucci sunglasses, I chided her, "Those are nice. Are the lights too bright?"

Gina, sitting across the table to her left, noticed she was wearing heavy makeup, which was far from the norm for Lexi. "Damn girl, you piled on the makeup today."

Lexi placed her elbow on the table, resting her head on her hand. I asked if she was okay. She nodded her head slowly. I noticed she winced in pain. By now, we'd usually all be laughing hysterically, discussing something that happened, said, or heard at the hospital, or ridiculing me about my dating life. Today, however, she wasn't laughing and still wore her glasses. She had only taken one sip of her mimosa. Gina leaned in close, noticing the bruising on the side of her eye. Her voice rose with concern, "What the hell happened?"

Tears streamed down her face, leaving salty trails on her skin. Lexi told us that Marcus had slapped and choked her. Gina's face grew red with rage as she fired off a flurry of questions. "He did what? He hit you? Where is that motherfucker? Did you call the police?" Lexi shook her head. Talking through sobs, she explained that she had dropped him off at Sea-Tac this morning for his flight back to the East Coast.

That ignited Gina's fury to a boiling point. "You what?' she exploded, her tension crackling like a live wire. 'You drove that motherfucker to the airport! Who in the hell does he think he is? I told you, Lexi, he's an arrogant, childish, womanizing fucking jerk.'" He truly was a jealous, selfish little boy who had come into a lot of money overnight and thought the world revolved around him. He wanted autonomy yet kept Lexi in captivity, demanding her presence at his beck and call. Lexi's face contorted in pain as she recounted the events of the previous night when the two had a heated argument.

The drama unfolded when she mentioned a news report she had seen two days before his return to finish his move. The sports reporter had traveled back east seeking more details about why Marcus had rejected the Seattle contract and interviewed him outside a restaurant, his arms wrapped around a tall, sexy blonde. Marcus, an attention-seeker, was more than happy to discuss his 'greatness'. It never crossed his mind that the report would air in Seattle, although knowing Lexi, there was a ninety-nine percent chance she would never see it. But life has a way of highlighting that one percent variable that bites you in the ass.

When she confronted him face-to-face and demanded an explanation for what she had seen, he adamantly denied everything. Upon realizing she had photographic evidence, he switched to Plan B, denying the other woman's significance and accusing Lexi of not supporting his ambitions, condemning her for supposedly using the situation to further her own agenda. He claimed that if her love was strong enough, she would pack her bags and follow him wherever his career took him. The lady, he insisted, was just a devoted fan eager for an autograph and a photo. He had innocently invited her to share a simple drink, he said, which was no different from Lexi being with us every Sunday morning. He even tried to point the finger at us, claiming we were responsible for his infidelity.

She had told us in the past how he would refer to us: "If those bitches you call your 'sisters' weren't so important to you, we wouldn't be having these issues." With an eighty-five million, five-year contract, he saw his career as paramount, more significant than all the work she put into hers, and he believed she didn't need to work at all. He'd share his spiel with her, which she recounted during our previous brunch chats: "I'm putting my mind, heart, and soul into our future. If you love me, you'd be there with me." She had challenged him, asking if he needed her so badly, why hadn't he compromised and accepted the contract in Seattle? But Marcus's love for money was no secret; he would have taken an East Coast offer for a dollar more. The conversation turned violent after she told him she wasn't a groupie willing to chase him across the country and suggested they end their relationship. His response was to deflect and cast her as the villain, insinuating that she wanted to end things because she had found someone new.

Marcus was deft at spinning the accusation back on Lexi, demanding to know the name of the man she was supposedly seeing behind his back. "I know it's true, bitch. You're a hot-ass woman, and I know damn well guys are hitting on you all the time. You're probably using those ho's you call your girlfriends as a front for hooking up with some guy. So, don't lie to me, telling me you're always with those bitch-ass girlfriends of yours. That bullshit doesn't work on me," he had said. In a spiteful outburst, he belittled her intimacy skills: "I hope you're better in bed with them than with me because babe... you might be beautiful—but you're not that hot in bed—and frankly, you're not doing that great of a job."

She countered, saying, "If that's the case, go back east and let your followers give you the 'good-fucking' as you call it. I need a man in my life, not some little boy who thinks that catching a football makes him superior to me. I don't need this shit from you, Marcus. I am a damn powerful woman. Speaking bout underachieving in the bedroom, I don't need a childish asshole's lil dick that can't make it past ten minutes to affirm me as a woman—unlike you, I don't cheat. Never have and never will.

However, I tell you one thing: you can't hump on the east coast and expect to come home and get laid on the west coast. It doesn't work that way, not with me." She'd bested him in the argument, leaving him to his primitive male reaction, slapping her, then knocking her to the floor. He was a powerful professional used to throwing men three times her size to the ground.

Marcus' anger had taken him too far, and he quickly realized it. He asked for her forgiveness over and over, his voice frantic and apologetic as he helped her stand up. She slapped him, yelling, "You son-of-a-bitch! No motherfucker has ever hit me." He looked at her with sorrowful eyes, telling her how sorry he was and proclaiming his undying love. His voice was laden with emotion as he swore he never meant to hurt her and that he would never do it again. He must have repeated "I'm so sorry, babe," a million times, his voice imbued with remorse. After an hour of yelling and venting, her fury began to dissolve under the weight of his persistent admissions that he had wronged her.

Finally, after intense groveling, she gave in, accepting his apology, which led to sex. I'm sure Marcus equated sex with forgiveness. Many men think that when a woman succumbs to her emotions, it's a trade-off for the pain felt in her heart. But it does not solve the problem. We capitulate not because we are less hurt physically but because we are more wounded internally. We crave closeness and the reassurance that we are worthy of love.

Gina's adrenaline-fueled wrath was like an overly protective mother chastising Lexi's decision. "You. You fucked that son-of-a-bitch after he did this to you? He's lucky his goddamn ass is on a plane." Gina's aggressive denunciations pelted Lexi's already wounded spirit like barbs. "He's not getting away with this shit, I promise you." I attempted to calm her down, asking her to speak more softly. But it was to no avail.

Lexi snapped, "Gina, will you just shut up? Just shut up! You're so intent on being faultless as if you've never encountered a man's violence before."

Gina recoiled. "I don't know what you're talking about. I wouldn't let a man slap my face, then spread my legs to reward him for beating my ass." Lexi glared at Gina, her eyes brimming with tears and fury, arms tightly crossed over her chest as she rocked back and forth, seemingly trying to contain her rage. The air was thick with tension. They exchanged charged looks. Gina mumbled under her breath, "You know I'm right."

Lexi rolled her eyes, warning Gina, "You can't always be the one trying to watch over us, dictating how we should live. Who to sleep with, who not to sleep with."

Gina pushed back, "Don't turn this into me dictating your life. I'm not the one you're angry at. You know damn well he should be behind bars right now." Gina slapped the back of her right hand into her left palm emphatically. "Just look at your face. Why are you defending this nig—this man?"

Courtnee attempted to bring some levity to the situation, suggesting that they let the issue go so we could enjoy our brunch. Huffing with displeasure, Gina shot Lexi a look full of disdain.

That was the tipping point; Lexi had had enough. Her body shook with contained rage before she exploded. She slammed her palm onto the table, her voice reverberating against the windows.

"What the fuck, Gina? You're criticizing me for having sex with my man? Why aren't you dating?"

"First off, he's not a man—he's a little football punk. And I'm single by choice. But if I were in a relationship, I can guarantee you my partner wouldn't dare lay a hand on me. I'd kick his ass myself and then call the cops, which is exactly what you should've done," Gina shot back.

"Bullshit, Gina! You always act like this tough-bitch, pretending to be stronger, smarter, and better than us. You're so busy managing our lives, too scared to even entertain a relationship yourself. It's easy for you to criticize when you don't know shit about your own life," Lexi countered, imitating Gina's head shake.

Mimicking Gina's assertive tone, Lexi shot back sharply, "No man would do that to me. You cycle through a new man every six months. They're not around long enough for you to give a shit. Because you're as volatile as a storm, and no man will put up with your nonsense," her voice dripping with sarcasm.

"Don't attack me, Lexi. It's Marcus who should be the focus of your anger, the one who considers himself a divine gift to women. He thinks he's a man because of his wealth, but in truth, he's just an overpaid juvenile parading as an adult, seeking thrills in every city he lands. And you? You welcome him with open arms, blind to any potential harm he might carry with him. You're angry with him, not me," Gina countered fiercely.

I tugged at Lexi, enveloping her in a firm hug, then reached for Gina's hand, trying to bridge the gap between them and redirect the conversation.

Courtnee wrapped her arms around Gina, but it was fruitless. Lexi bellowed, "No! No, Cyn, this is bullshit. She's guilting me because I was intimate with my man. This is my life, and I don't need her—or you or Courtnee—judging me."

Our gentle and soft-spoken Courtnee whispered, "Lexi… I haven't—I wouldn't ever look down on you. I'm sorry Maurice hurt you."

Lexi's jaw clenched, and her eyes flashed with anger. "His name is Marcus—"

Gina cut in, sparing Courtnee from Lexi's wrath. "I'm not trying to make you feel bad. I'm saying I love you and hate to see someone hitting you, then you going to bed with him as if it's some tacit approval. It's like you're saying it's okay for him to mistreat you. That's not acceptable to me."

Lexi's lips quivered as she pressed them together. I attempted once more to calm the storm between my friends. Lexi fired back, "You know what, Gina? Go ahead, show off like you're some kind of saint while I deal with my mess. You're so resilient. So impeccable. Everything about you just screams perfection. You'd never let a man disrespect you, right?" Lexi shot back, her voice heavy with bitterness and anger.

"You damn right, I wouldn't."

Lexi tilted her head, her hair cascading over her shoulder. "Really? I could do without your judgmental, sanctimonious tone, Gina."

"I don't have an attitude. You're blaming me for caring about you? Fine. Whatever you choose to do with your—abusive, infantile man is your business." A heavy hush descended upon the room—a much-needed respite. Each moment dragged on, the weighty silence looming over us. I silently hoped for a ceasefire.

But Lexi shattered the stillness. "Gina. I'm sick of hearing what you'd do in my shoes. At least he didn't rape me." Courtnee and I exchanged glances, shock written all over our faces. What? Gina's glacial stare could have frozen the room solid. Lexi held her gaze firmly. "No history of abuse, right?"

"That's right!"

There was a prolonged silence as Lexi glared at Gina, her eyes a cauldron of unspoken words. Then she broke the silence with a heavy burden in her voice, "That's right? You remember coming to my apartment, our third year of med school, with your top ripped and your pants torn away? You remember the black eye, Gina? The busted lip? The bruises around your neck, crying, telling me how he choked you out and raped you? I saw his fingerprints on your neck. You talk to me about Marcus giving me a disease. You didn't even see a doctor, fearing they'd call the cops. You had no idea what he might have left inside of you. But you begged—made me promise—not to tell anyone. Do you remember that night, Gina? The night a guy beat the shit out of you and stuck his cock inside of you?"

I mumbled a hard plea through clenched teeth. "Lexi! Please lower your voice. You're embarrassing her—us." My appeal for decorum had no effect.

The atmosphere was electric, charged as if a hand grenade had been lobbed into the room. Lexi continued, her voice rising with the tumult of the revelation. "You even made excuses for him, protecting his goddamn medical career. And who took care of your ass? Me!" She thumped her chest. "I was the one who babysat you, making excuses for a month while you healed, pretending nothing happened, waking up in the middle of the night to your screams. I was the one sitting beside you at night, comforting you. You refused to even tell me his name, choosing to defend a creep you met at a party, valuing his life over your own. And now? Now, Gina, you judge me for sleeping with my man? At least I did it willingly. You can go to hell."

Taking a deep breath, I glanced around the restaurant at the nosy diners pretending to eat while their ears strained to eavesdrop. Following Lexi's disclosure, Gina sat devastated, her arms folded tightly across her chest, visibly struggling to maintain her composure. Each word from Lexi seemed to strike her with the force of a physical blow, leaving marks that only the heart could feel. Her eyes shimmered with the effort to restrain tears, signaling the depth of her pain. It was as though Lexi had reached deep within her, cruelly twisting her heart. The atmosphere was heavy with tension, and I feared this harsh exchange might irreversibly fracture their cherished friendship.

I took Lexi's and Gina's hands again, squeezing them tightly, whispering, "Come on, ladies, we're drawing too much attention."

Our eternal optimist, Courtnee, rose to her feet with her phone in hand, mustering a facade of cheerfulness. "Happy picture time, girls!" she announced, as if the tension slicing through the air could simply be paused for a snapshot. Her suggestion landed awkwardly, almost jarringly out of sync with the mood of our embattled friends.

Lexi scoffed, her emotions raw and turbulent, as she pushed past me to stand. "Put the damn phone away. I'm going home," she declared, her voice a mix of anger and hurt. With a defiant gesture, she tossed her credit card onto the table. "Brunch is on me," she announced, her tone laced with bitterness. Casting a scornful glance at Gina, she rolled her eyes, her frustration palpable. Then, with a whirl of emotion, she stormed out, leaving a wake of silence behind her.

We remained uncomfortably silent and deflated, trying to process the bombshell Lexi had dropped. Gina wiped away tears of anger, humiliation, and a sense of betrayal. Courtnee and I exchanged looks, silently deliberating on who should stay with Gina and who should follow Lexi. I chose to chase after Lexi, moving quickly but discreetly. Catching up with her outside as she handed her ticket to the lot attendant, I implored, "Lex… what's going on? Don't leave like this. I'm sorry you're hurting, and now Gina's hurting. Please, talk to me."

The attendant trotted off into the rain to retrieve her car. Lexi, growing impatient, muttered, "To hell with this," and started after him.

"Lexi, wait… let's talk before you go," I yelled.

Without so much as a backward glance, she responded, "Forget it, Cyn. Leave it. Leave me alone." She snatched the keys from the attendant and sped away. *Shit.* I went back inside. Courtnee was consoling Gina as best she could. Approaching the table, I began, "Gi—"

"That bitch," she murmured, brushing past me with a turmoil of emotions in her wake. We're sisters in every sense of the word and have never kept secrets, or so I believed until today. My ego was tinged with jealousy, momentarily overshadowing my concern. I found myself wondering why Gina had confided in Lexi and not me. How could such a harrowing secret have been kept from me—and from everyone else? Both Courtnee and I were reeling. I exhaled a long sigh of frustration.

"Cyn, that was quite a display. Should we reach out to them?" Courtnee asked tentatively.

"No, God, no. Let's give them some space to cool down," I said, feeling the weight of recent events pressing down on me. "Besides, you know how stubborn they can be. Right now, the best thing might be to head home. I'm just overwhelmed by all this."

"I know," Courtnee replied, her voice trailing off into silence until we reached the door. "I can't believe someone raped Gina… Did you know about it?"

"No, I did not," I snapped, the revelation still a fresh wound. Astonishingly, only Lexi knew. Gina has always been the pillar of strength among us. It's hard to fathom that she endured such an ordeal. She never backs down and doesn't tolerate any nonsense from men." The groan that escaped me was one of someone trying to reconcile with a new, painful reality. Courtnee's car arrived first.

"You okay, Cyn?" she asked, her eyes searching mine for some steadiness in the upheaval. I nodded numbly, my mind detached and floating in a sea of turmoil. Courtnee pulled me into a tight embrace. "I love my sisters," she whispered, then got into her car. With one last look back, she pulled away, her departure timed with the intensifying rain, as if nature itself echoed the turmoil among friends, her car blending into the gray curtain of the downpour.

I stood there, Lexi's revelation about Gina's rape numbing my senses. Even more astonishing was that Gina had harbored this anguish so privately, confiding in only Lexi. In a way that felt selfish, I was hurt. It seemed she trusted Lexi more than me. I knew, without a doubt, I would have kept her secret sacred. But who was I to judge? Lexi's outburst resonated with a haunting familiarity. I could feel my own suppressed memories clawing their way to the surface. I was hyperventilating, fighting back tears, struggling to keep my nightmares locked away. But the echoed word 'rape' was like an incantation, stirring long-buried demons from their graves, their whispers turning into screams in my mind. "No, no, no," I prayed silently, trying to stave off the resurgence of those dark memories.

The dam I had built to hold back my dreadful past was cracking, threatening to burst. Lexi's disclosure had unwittingly opened a gateway to my own trauma at the same time. Visions of my past assailed me, emerging from the depths of my consciousness with a vengeance. I was livid that the actions of one man had scarred three souls. Marcus, in his villainy, was emblematic of all men who fail to grasp the full impact of their physical and emotional violations. If he hadn't hit Lexi, today would have been another typical happy Sunday, brimming with laughter and bottomless mimosas, ending with me driving my inebriated friends home. That's what I wanted to focus on. But my thoughts were unyielding, and I felt a tightness in my chest as if I were being pulled back through time.

Chapter Five

Hunter James McGowan had recently moved to Seattle from New York to begin his medical residency. I met him at a party given by one of Gina's classmates from her biology class. I always feel like I'm the oddball at parties, while Gina is like a social butterfly on steroids. Her long black hair threaded through the back of a white baseball cap with a purple W lettering, blue shorts, and flip-flops.

"Hey, Gina!" echoed constantly throughout the day as groups vied for her to join their social circles. With a plate laden with a hot dog, ribs, and baked beans, she glided from group to group with a jubilant smile. I, on the other hand, preferred to watch people's behavior while avoiding the frequent dull gossip.

I was famished and had just filled my plate. Wandering around the backyard, I sought a not-so-crowded spot to enjoy my loaded hot dog without the pressure to talk mid-bite. I found a haven by a kid's abandoned swing set. The first bite was divine. Stevie, one of our group and proud of his grilling skills, was the mastermind behind this loaded hot dog. *Kudos, Stevie. Your hot dogs are fabulous.* I thought as I took a big—Miss Piggy—bite. Then, a soft voice inquired from behind, "May I join you?"

What impeccable timing, I mused sarcastically, with my mouth full. Flmmpf, flmmpf, trying to swallow quickly, I mumbled a courteous, "Sure," not wanting to seem rude. *Can't he see I don't want to be disturbed?*

He perched on the edge of the table, encroaching on my moment of solace. "Hi. My name is Hunter. Hunter James McGowan." He extended his hand. *Great, just what I need—why do people, especially guys, insist on talking to you when you're mid-chew? And then add insult to injury by offering a handshake?* As if I wanted to touch anything while eating, I lifted my index finger, signaling for a pause. He chuckled. "The hotdogs are magnificent. I had a couple myself."

After swallowing my tasty morsel, I introduced myself. Hunter's conversation starter revolved around his marvel at the break from the rain. I casually informed him that in Seattle, it's less about rain and more akin to a perpetual misty shroud—a second skin for us locals. His laugh was soft and attractive, not overbearing but genuinely amused.

"You live around here?" he inquired with a tilt of his head.

"Issaquah," I responded, seeing his puzzled look, I elaborated, "It's on the eastside of Seattle, over there," pointing vaguely in the direction as if the city lay just at the fingertip's reach from Ballard.

"Okay, I've only been here two weeks, so I haven't quite gotten the lay of the land yet."

His roots were deeply planted in New York, a place he mentioned with pride and joy. "I'm wrapping up a residency I began there. My family thought it would be beneficial for me to get a change of scenery and maybe gain a better perspective on life. A few phone calls from my dad and voilà, here I am in Seattle. Though I'd heard a lot about the city, it has turned out to be quite different from what I expected."

In response, I nodded and shared my own sense of relief. "I considered myself lucky, actually. I work at the UW Medical Center," I explained. "During medical school, there was always the fear of being matched to a program out of state, far from everything familiar. But somehow, by some grace of God, all four of us managed to stay right here. It was more than I could have hoped for."

Our conversation meandered, with him often circling back to the magnetic allure of his New York home, which led him to ask, "Have you ever ventured outside Seattle?"

The way he asked that question riled me as though I'm some primitive chick who's never left home. I jived saying, "It's my sworn oath to never leave my rainy-often-declared-by-others-as-gloomy-home. I'm sure you've heard about the high suicide rate. It's our fate. We wait for the knock on the door when a gloved hand gives you your dying instructions."

His laughter rung out, unbridled and a touch too loud for my taste. "I'm going to grab another beer. Can I get you one?"

I politely declined, sticking to my usual diet soda and tea preferences. He lingered on the subject with a hint of skepticism. "You don't drink at all, or just not at parties? Or… are you one of those who can't handle their liquor?"

I gave a dismissive smirk. "I don't drink because it's my preference." He nonchalantly shrugged his shoulders, treating my answer as if it were abnormal. He trotted off for his refreshment. I felt relieved, hoping he'd find another place to land. But I wasn't so lucky. He returned with a bottleneck beer, twisting the top off and flicking the cap to the ground—something I found detestable. But it's a party, and you overlook small things like that. He had the build of a jock with soft, enchanting eyes. I have to say he's an attractive—

though not an enchanting—guy. He complimented the curls in my hair and my blue eyes. I blushed at his praises.

Gina abruptly interrupted our conversation, plopping down beside me, and spoke as if she hadn't even noticed Hunter's presence. "Hey girl, why are you sitting over here?" She looked at Hunter. "Oh, I'm sorry." His eyes flicked with delight. He thrust his hand out. "Hunter. Hunter James McGowan." Gina's eyes fluttered, and a frown creased her face, likely pondering the reason behind the full-name introduction. He presented himself as if he were boasting, as if his name bestowed upon him a certain status. That was my initial impression. "Ah, okay, Gina... Nice..." she paused, looking perplexed, "...to meet you." She ignored his extended hand, looking at me for clarity. "Are you having fun?"

"Yeah, I'm fine." She and Hunter locked eyes. He cleared his throat.

A familiar yell cut our chat short. "Hey, Gina!" Her admirers were calling.

"I'll be right back. Nice to meet you, ah, Hunter?" Not waiting for a response, she was off, stopping to tell me, "Cyn, find me when Lexi and Courtnee arrive. Since we're in the area, I want to go to Golden Gardens." I gave her a thumbs-up, watching her disappear into a crowd."That's? That's your friend?" Hunter asked, watching her with drooling admiration.

"Yep. That is my friend. She's a contagious ball of fire."

"She's beautiful—so are you. I was just watching her engagement with everyone. She seems pretty popular."

"None taken," I replied flatly. "And yes, she is quite sociable." It wouldn't have bothered me had he gone and joined the ensemble of those vying for Gina's attention. However, he hung around, swigging beer and scanning the backyard for other opportunities. I guess I was the [un] lucky one.

He told me, "The first couple months in a new city are the worst."

"How so?"

"You know, you don't know anyone or any hot spots or places where all the cool people hang out—not that you have a lot of free time, but events like today are very welcome."

"You found this place."

"Yeah, totally by accident. I discovered it this morning via conversation with a guy posted on a chat board."

"I understand the awkwardness of being the new kid in town. But you have an outstanding personality; you'll have a group of buddies before you know."

Our attention shifted as Lexi made her entrance. As soon as she walked through the gate, she spotted me and called out, "Hey, Cyn!" She and Courtnee made their way over. I sprang to my feet, attempting to juggle my plate and offer them a one-armed hug, but my balancing act faltered. Great. However, it didn't bother me much. Hunter had distracted me to the extent that my appetite had vanished, and the food had cooled off anyway.

I asked my friends, "What took you guys so long?"

Lexi, rolling her eyes, looked at Courtnee, saying, "Miss Thang here spent an hour trying to find the right effing dress while complaining. "My legs are too skinny for these shorts. This dress is too light. People can see my panties. I don't want to wear white to an outdoor party." Then she had to talk to Stephen. "I love you. I won't be too late. Are you sure you don't want to come with us? "Blah. Blah. Blah—dammit, let's go." Lexi shot off into the crowd, protesting, "What the hell are you guys doing standing around eating hot dogs? Where is the music?" And that's all it took for Brandon Davis to crank up the tunes. "Oh Yeah! That's my groove," Lexi shouted.

He gave her a thumbs up. Then, shouting, "I know what you like, Lexi!"

"Hell, yes! Crank _it_ up."

The attention turned to her and Courtnee as they rhythmically rolled their hips to the beat while others, less confident in their dance moves, joined in with an awkward attempt to keep pace. Lexi shouted, "Where are my girls at? Cyn! What the hell? Get over here! Where's Gina?" Gina bounced out of nowhere, hugging Lexi and Courtnee. The three of them danced together. I looked at Hunter. "I think I better join them." He grabbed my hand, asking, "Before you go, do you have plans next weekend? If not, I'd appreciate the company. Maybe show me around the city?" _No._ If only I could be so abrupt. I didn't want to commit my weekend to a guy I just met, plus I was pretty busy. He reassured me, "It'll be a no-strings-attached outing. You know, helping the new kid on the block find his way around. I'm just trying to make friends, and I thought since we just met, touring Seattle would give us a chance to get to know each other—as friends."

I pressed my lips together, caught in contemplation, with a sense of reluctance. "Sure, why not," I thought, considering it might be fun to show the newcomer around town. And above all, I would revisit some charms of Seattle that I've forgotten—or haven't had the time to see. We have many unique places if you know where to look beyond the typical tourist destinations. So, we agreed to meet at the UW's Montlake student parking lot. I told him, "I'll drive."

"Then lunch will be on me. Deal?"

"Deal." I made my way out of my secluded corner and into the boisterous crowd, finally linking up with my girls. We joined in our sacred ritual, dancing together and moving our hips to the enticing rhythm of the music.

My time with Hunter started off innocently enough. Excited to play tour guide, I had picked out a few famous sites I thought he'd appreciate, beginning at Volunteer Park for some tranquility, then on to the bustle of Pike Place Market—a must-see. A ferry jaunt to Bremerton was next, with plans to wrap up our outing with a picnic dinner at Gas Works Park atop the grassy knoll, the perfect spot to watch the sunset.

I arrived ten minutes early. The parking lot was nearly deserted. Hunter arrived ten minutes late, racing into the parking lot in his black Mercedes Roadster, fast rolling next to my little gray Honda. The tinted passenger window glided down. He leaned over, asking, 'You want me to drive? I don't mind.' Translation: Let's show off in my pricey hot sports car. I got it, buddy. But I wasn't impressed by the sheen of your hundred-thousand-dollar car, which I'm sure was a gift from mommy and daddy.

"No. I prefer to drive my rickety ol' gray Honda." Not that my car was rickety or old, but I was paraphrasing the thoughts from the look on his face when I declined his offer.

He got out of his car, slapping the roof. "You're my guide, so let's see some Seattle." I had a strange, uncomfortable feeling about Hunter. But maybe it was just his awkward enthusiasm to make friends. Yet, there was a powerful undercurrent of arrogance. You don't initially see it, but you can tell it's there. However, it was a new friendship. So, I'd let Hunter be himself.

Our drive began with much laughter. Hunter had told jokes about some people he knew back home, explaining his frat house revelries and antics. Mob movies had always been fascinating to me, so I asked him if kids are anything like the ones you see on TV, with accents admiring the local gangster. He laughed hysterically.

"Too much TV, lady. Some of us grew up in normal neighborhoods with a mom and a dad, minus the fat Louis. We have dreams of doing crazy things like, oh, I don't know, becoming doctors and lawyers."

"Ouch. A nice slice of sarcasm." I smiled.

"I didn't offend you, did I?"

I was silent for a few moments and eventually responded, "No. Why would I be offended by having dirt thrown in my face?"

He laughed. "That wasn't my intent. If it's too mordant, I apologize." I nodded my head that it was okay. We arrived at Volunteer Park, one of Seattle's pride and joys. At least it was a favorite of mine. He exited the car with his hands in his pockets and looked around briefly, unimpressed.

"Nice. An interesting little place. Not very many people here. Come to New York, and I'll show you Central Park. You'd be amazed. It's one hell of a park in the middle of a gigantic city."

He looked around as we walked over to what we call the donut, positioned so you can see the Space Needle aligned perfectly through its center. He chuckled, unimpressed. The girls and I had this thing between us we call an 'asshole meter,' one point given for rude, condescending, or impolite remarks. Three for sexual innuendos. Once you reach five, you're deemed an asshole, and the date is effectively over. However, his comment didn't earn a point. But it did stir a bit of irritation. Perhaps our park isn't as grand as Central Park, but it's beautiful and peaceful.

"Have you ever been to the Empire State Building? That's something to marvel at." This guy was really rubbing me the wrong way, and I regretted my earlier politeness. Okay, that's one point, four to go, but I was done at three. "I hadn't planned to pit my city against his beloved New York. If he missed it that much, he should have gone home."

I replied flatly, "No, I haven't traveled back east much. I went to New Hampshire once to visit my aunt."

He showed no interest in what I was saying, instead asking, "Hey, I heard so much about the original Starbucks. Can we go there?"

I gave him a thumbs up. "That's on my tour list. We can go there, grab a coffee, and walk through Pike Place Market with the throngs of tourists." Hunter returned to his amusing anecdotes inside the car until we arrived at the market. I explained that we'd need to park and walk up from the waterfront, which was also on my itinerary.

After enduring an excruciatingly long wait in line with tourists, we finally had our coffees in hand. We meandered through the market, passing by various merchants. "This is a really cool place. I like it," he conceded, showing a glimmer of appreciation for something in my city. But then, almost predictably, he added, "There are so many things I would love to show you in New York."

I inhaled deeply, allowing myself a moment of patience. *Perhaps not an asshole, but certainly an ungrateful jerk.* I couldn't help but feel irritated. New York might be fantastic, but we weren't there—we were in Seattle, my city. I had intended to share the places and experiences that make us who call it home cherish it deeply. However, his obsession seemed solely focused on a future where he could flaunt me through the streets of his New York.

I revived my tolerance and suggested we take a Seattle to Bremerton ferry ride. I pointed out that the ferry terminal was just below and a quick walk. After coming back, we could grab carryout dinner, eat, hang out, and finish the day at Gas Works Park. I could make the route to where it's on the way back to the Montlake parking lot. I checked the ferry schedule on my phone. "Great! The next sailing is in fifteen minutes. If we hurry, we can make it."

"Hey! I heard about the gum wall. I want to leave a piece of gum. You have any?"

"No." *Disgusting*

"That's too bad. We'll have to buy some and come back here. We can leave ours together." The least I hoped to touch the germ-riddled wall, symbolically attaching gum as if we were creating a unique bond. We continued our pace to the terminal, making it just in time to purchase tickets. We made it on board minutes before the ferry was ready to leave. The ferry slowly glided from its berth. I explained to Hunter that we'd cross over, return, visit the Seattle Center, and make our way to Gas Works to catch the sunset.

We walked to the bow of the vessel as it cruised toward Bremerton. I wanted to enjoy the breeze on my face. I had forgotten how much fun it is to ride the ferries. However, I guess it's not as appealing for those who take it to and from work daily. To them, it's just another mode of getting from point A to point B. But how can you not just love Puget Sound, no matter your purpose for taking the ferry? Hunter crept up from behind me, placing his arm around my waist, shouting the morbidly outdated Leonardo DiCaprio Titanic cliché, "I'm the king of the world!" He laughed, thinking himself funny.

Wrong move, buddy. I removed his hands from my waist, telling him this was not that kind of date. He apologized, saying he couldn't resist the temptation of holding me in his arms, insisting it was an innocent gesture. He stood next to me. "It's beautiful out here. What do we do when we get to the other side?"

"Nothing. The trip is about the ride. Something I thought you'd enjoy."

"You were right," he said, a contented look on his face. "I have truly been enjoying it, especially with the anticipation of the sunset you had mentioned." His eyes met mine, carrying a hint of sincerity. "You know, you're a beautiful woman."

"Thank you, Hunter. But I'm not just beautiful—I'm wicked smart. And I plan to be a doctor one day."

He looked at me, his face twisting into an expression of childlike innocence before he grasped my sarcasm. He gazed out into the Sound and said, "This reminds me of a smaller version of…"

Inside, I was screaming, *Don't say it, you ungrateful asshole… Please don't say it!* "…The New York harbor," he finished. "You could spend days there and never see all of it. Maybe, if I'm lucky, you and I will become friends, and I can repay your kindness. We could travel to New York. I'd even pay for your ticket."

I bit back the retort that I would never visit his fabulous city with him. As the ferry slowed, approaching the berth in Bremerton, we watched the cars disembark. "This looks like a delightful city. We should get off and look around," he suggested.

"No, this one is heading back soon. I don't want to miss it," I insisted.

"Isn't there another ferry?" he asked.

"Yes, but I'm getting hungry. I thought we'd grab fish and chips at Ivar's and watch the sunset," I lied, eager to get us back to Seattle and find a reason to conclude our time together.

"Okay, great, I'm looking forward to it," he said, clapping his hands together eagerly.

On the return trip, Hunter seemed more subdued and less critical of Seattle. He stood with both hands on the railing, staring out to sea as if lost in thought. I watched him curiously, pondering what was on his mind. When I tapped his arm to ask if he was okay, he flinched as if I had yanked him from a faraway place. "Are you okay?" I repeated.

"Yeah, I'm fine. Just thinking about the next phases of my life. The things I want to achieve in the next five years. This year is going to fly by, and I want to hit the ground running. Ever since I was a kid, I've gotten what I wanted. My father always said, "Son, there will always be obstacles between you and your successes. Obliterate them. The higher you climb, the less you have to deal with those at the bottom." That's what my grandfather told my dad, and now, my dad has passed it down to me," he shared with a sense of pride.

I found Hunter's family philosophy deeply unsettling. There appeared to be no bounds to his entitlement, and my tolerance was wearing thin with this privileged child.

He continued, reminiscing about being voted the all-league football quarterback champion in high school. "I was good at the game. I played as my dad advised—if there's an obstacle, you run it over." However, his father viewed the sport as a distraction, potentially jeopardizing his future in medicine. He explained that his father had insisted he quit, especially before they played games against the black beasts. "The blood drained from my face at his words. Seeking clarity, I asked, "The Black what?"

"You know, the huge football players, most of them are black. My dad doesn't mean anything by it... they're just, you know, big guys. Beastly," he explained, striking a gorilla-like pose, which only served to enrage me further. "Success, to me, is reaching a level where those beneath you acknowledge your superiority."

Astonished, I challenged him, "So, you believe you're better than everyone else? That includes me?"

He shook his head. "Not exactly. I'm saying work hard, ascend to a level of respect—to be better than the rest, and never stop climbing. Some call it overachieving, but I see it as living life to the fullest. I want a family, a grand home, exotic vacations. With the wealth my family has—and the wealth I'll accumulate—I'll have a wife as beautiful as my mother," he mused, turning to look at me with blind oblivion to the insult his words carried.

Inside, I was fuming, telling myself to keep my composure. *Don't rip his head off. Just stay silent. There's no enlightening his twisted perspective.* He pivoted the conversation to my dating life, to which I responded that I dated infrequently. But I wished to add, "Unlike you, I don't see life in terms of top or bottom. I'm content working with those at all levels, never deeming anyone inferior. I will care for anyone in need—even you in your grand estate—and if I die with little to my name, it will be without regret, for my life's work is to heal, not to amass wealth."

He threw his hands up. "Wait. Just wait a second. I didn't mean that I'm better than anyone else—"

"Please, let's not," I interjected with a forced smile. "I'd rather we didn't delve into this further."

"I'm sorry," he said softly, his voice a mere whisper. We spent the rest of the journey in silence. As we disembarked from the ferry, he tapped my arm gently. "I didn't mean to offend you... I'm still learning how to communicate with those outside my usual circles. I will excel in my profession, but not by stepping on others or thinking I'm better. It's just motivation for me—to push myself to excel."

"Hunter, I'm feeling a little tired. I think we should call it quits," I suggested.

"So, you're upset with me," he surmised.

I sighed, the weight of our activities pressing on me. "No, Hunter, I'm not upset, just emotionally drained and frankly insulted by your ignorance."

"I understand. I'm not really making a good impression on you, am I?" I saw the dejection on his face. Perhaps I had been a little too harsh on him. Maybe there's some truth to it. His societal environment is so different from here in Seattle, with New York's massive and aggressive landscape, where many communities vie for wealth and their place in the hierarchy. Hunter looked at me with pleading eyes. "Cynthya, please forgive me. I didn't mean to insult you. I'm doing my best to adjust. I genuinely apologize." I'm such a softy. I gave him another chance, suggesting we postpone visiting the Seattle Center for another time and go straight to Ivar's. I was getting hungry anyway, and it was nearing sunset. Perfect timing.

The luster of our time together had waned, and we said little during our drive to the restaurant. Hunter reignited our earlier conversation. "I know I keep saying this, but you're gorgeous. I can't see why you're not dating more?" His question cut through the conversation I was having in my own head, questioning why I hadn't ended the trip as I had intended. He wasn't significant enough that I should continue trying to accommodate him. However, I found myself replying that I dated occasionally, but it wasn't a priority in my life. "I go on the occasional dinner or movie date here and there, but nothing serious."

"So, you date for sex?" His question was a jolt, leaving me feeling slapped in the face. How could one continually be so inappropriate? I was doing my best to quell the anger welling up inside me. How could he even make such an offensive insinuation? I turned sharply to him, my eyes burning into his, and asked, "What?"

"I'm not saying you're that type of person. But I've heard—and other guys talk about it all the time—when women say they date casually, it often means they prefer not committing to one person but rather going on random dates to satisfy sexual needs and maybe to enjoy a few free meals. You ladies call it casual dating. We guys... we're starting to understand what that means." He chuckled, under the impression that I would find his comment amusing.

I was gripping the steering wheel, trying to control my temper, pondering the machinations in Hunter's head. Taking deep, calming breaths, I responded to his ill-informed remark with firm politeness. "I'm sorry to disappoint you, Mr. Hunter James McGowan, but I don't do 'sex dates.' The language you say you're learning is a misguided curriculum in ignorance. We women no longer attach ourselves to men to provide for us what we're perfectly capable of obtaining on our own. So, I hope you're not too disappointed. This is not a casual date. It's not a date at all, especially not to— as you so crudely put it— 'cop a free dinner.' I can pay my own way, and I don't need a man—especially you—to give me anything. Not even an orgasm," I said.

He stuttered, "I... I didn't mean to insult you. I was speaking in generalities. I never meant to suggest that you're that kind of girl—" His eyes shifted away from my glare. "Woman," he corrected himself, realizing he had struck a nerve.

"I surrender, understood. I'm sorry if I offended you," he conceded as I sped into the parking lot and slammed the gear into park. I was considering ending this date right then and there. Why hadn't I? Because I was trying to be tolerant. But what I had originally dismissed as naivety now revealed itself as his sheer ignorance. So why was I tolerating this? I couldn't answer that. Maybe part of me was considering being amicable in the face of such unawareness. As we approached the outside order window, Hunter asserted he'd pay.

"Dutch," I stated firmly.

"It's okay, I got it. After all, you've been driving us around," he said, shaking his head. "Look, I know I've said some dumb things today. I'm grateful for your lenience. Let me offer a truce and pay for our meal."

"That's considerate of you, but I'll pay for my own. Thank you," I replied.

"Are you...?" he began.

"Am I what, Hunter?"

"Are you upset?"

"Look, I thought it would be nice to show you around today. I don't want you to feel like you owe me dinner or anything. This is merely a friendly outing. Please understand that."

Contrary to my previous inclinations, I acquiesced to his wish to see the park. We paid for our meals and drove to Gas Works Park.

Chapter Six

I couldn't help but feel peaceful as I watched the sun dip below the horizon. Perched on the edge of Lake Union, Gas Works Park offers a serene escape a stone's throw away from the bustling heart of downtown Seattle. As the city's skyline stretches into the distance, the park itself lies like a verdant oasis, with gentle waves from the lake caressing its shores.

Here, the harmonious rhythm of water lapping against the land provides a tranquil soundtrack to the stunning panorama, contrasting with the urban pulse just a few miles away. I had been so focused on my career in medicine that I had almost forgotten the serene smells of the outdoors here. Even the tension of being with Hunter was slowly ebbing away. Hunter's eyes lit up when he spotted the rusted furnaces as we walked from the parking lot. "What are those over there?"

"It's the remaining relics of a gasification plant," I responded, bracing myself for his reaction. [I cringe] Wait for it. Wait for it. Nothing? Thank God.

Instead, he said, "This is very cool." He took my hand as we walked up the hill.

"Hunter, please," I said, jerking away. How many ways can one say inappropriate? I'll have to travel to New York and learn their definition.

"Thank you, but I can manage on my own," I replied. I laid out the blanket and unpacked our dinner. On the way here, Hunter had insisted we detour to a convenience store so that he could pick up a couple of beers (a six-pack). He twisted off the top, tossing it away carelessly. I retrieved it, admonishing him, "There are families with kids that play here. I'd prefer we consider them and not just toss away the things we don't want. By the way, I don't think they allow beer in the park." *What am I, a babysitter?*

"Oh, I'm sorry, four years of frat behavior, you know?" he said as if it were a badge of honor rather than an excuse for his inconsideration. I imagined he thought someone lesser would come along and pick it up. Seattle was unseasonably warm earlier, so I hadn't anticipated how quickly the temperature would change. I should have known better than to go out without a jacket. Now, regretting my decision, I shivered in my light white and blue sundress as the sun set and the evening air grew cold—a perfect cue to end the date. I told him, "I'm afraid I didn't bring a jacket, and it's getting cold."

"It's okay. You can snuggle next to me," he offered, wrapping his arms around me and pulling me close. *Wrong goddamn move, buddy.* This was too much. He was a total Benson.

"I'm sorry, we'd better go," I said.

"We haven't eaten dinner yet," he remarked as he popped the top on his fourth beer, arching his arm to throw it, catching my scowl, and then tucking it into his pocket. "Do you mind if I finish this before we go?"

After shot-gunning the beer, he admitted he needed a few moments to gain clarity before attempting to drive. "The last thing I need is to be new to Seattle and start practicing medicine with a DUI on my record," he laughed. "Can you imagine the issues I'd have with the medical board?"

Great, now I was responsible for him not getting a DUI. I envisioned being dragged into court as an accomplice. I agreed to sit despite the approaching chill.

My nipples were hard, showing through my dress. Could this get any worse? It was time to get out of here and away from his pompous, New York-loving ass. He opened another beer. "Just one more. I'll be quick." He downed it, and I shook my head in disbelief, signaling that I was done. We walked down the hill and headed back to my car.

As we drove back, silence hung between us, returning to a parking lot that was eerily vacant. He turned to me, "You know I had a great time. Do you mind if we sit in my car and talk for a while? I don't have cable or internet yet, so I dread going home."

"No, Hunter, I'm tired, and I want to go home. I have enjoyed your company as well. We can hang out another time," I said, knowing full well I would never see him again.

"Okay, I understand. Thank you again," he said, his smile too lurid, telling me more than I wished to know, "You are an extremely beautiful woman." I nodded stiffly, holding back nausea. Did he think his flattery would make me reconsider? As soon as he shut the door, I jerked the gear shift into reverse, my desire to flee from the day's exhaustion with Hunter clear in my swift actions. Driving away, a sense of urgency mixed with relief washed over me, each rotation of the tires marking a moment further from the irritant of the date.

As I moved further from the 520 bridge, home was still a 15 minute drive away. The space between us seemed to briefly dull the irritation Hunter had sparked. His recent behavior, inappropriate and unsettling, had tested my limits. Just as I sought a moment of peace in the solitude of the drive, my phone disrupted the quiet. Hunter's name on the screen was a stark reminder that the repercussions of his actions weren't so easily left behind, even with the miles I'd put between us.

What could he possibly want now? I answered begrudgingly, "Hello?"

He sounded upbeat. "Hey, sorry to bother you, but I think I may have left my keys in your car. I thought maybe I dropped them at the park where we were sitting, so I ran back to check before calling you."

"You're back at Gas Works?"

"Yeah. Whew, it's a farther jog than I thought," he panted.

I pulled to the side of the road to search for his keys, finding them under the seat. Irritation coursed through me, regretting ever saying hello to him. Perhaps I was to blame for not ensuring he got into his car before driving off. I told him, with a twinge of guilt, "Yes, they're here. I'll bring them back to you."

"Okay, I'm just going to hang in the park. Would you mind meeting me here? I think I pulled a muscle running back," he said. Great. Saying goodbye to this guy was proving too difficult. He would probably want a lift back to his car. I pounded the steering wheel, mentally chiding myself. *Stop being so damn nice!*

I arrived back at Gas Works at 9:30 PM, wanting nothing more than to hand Hunter his keys and be rid of him for good. I considered tossing them out the window as I drove past, but I couldn't be that cruel. I called his phone—it went to voicemail. Damn it! He knew I was coming.

Why wasn't he here waiting? I called again, and this time, he answered, telling me he was by the railing near the water, stretching his leg. "Would you mind bringing them to me?" he asked. *Fuck!* I couldn't believe him. Fury coursed through me as I slammed the car door, the sound sharply echoing my disbelief at his audacity. I stomped over to meet him. He had his leg propped up on the railing, stretching. *Great, now I have to help him and drive him back,* I thought, rolling my eyes in annoyance. Despite the anger that had driven me to this moment, I cloaked it under a veil of calm, asking if he could walk okay.

"Yeah," he grimaced in pain. "I think I'll be okay." He hopped toward me. "I guess this is not a way to end the first date." *It wasn't a date, you idiot.* I wanted to scream at the top of my lungs, but I allowed him to put his arm around my shoulder to support himself back to the car. "I think I did a pretty good job on myself. I'm pretty certain it's a groin injury." His hand glided down my breast.

"Hey! Would you put your hand there on a guy?" I snapped.

He laughed, "I hope not."

"Then let's pretend I'm one."

"I'm sorry, it was an accident. The last thing I want is to offend my rescuer." Moments later, he leaned on me more heavily. Just as I was about to suggest he continue on his own, he put his weight on me, causing us both to fall. *Enough!* This was it. He could call an ambulance to take him back to his car. I was done. I scrambled to my feet.

"What the fuck is wrong with you?" He pulled me back to the ground, trying to force a kiss. We had a fierce struggle in the grass. "Hunter, what the hell is wrong with you? Stop!" I managed to break free from his grasp, wiping away his disgusting slime. "You've crossed so many boundaries at lightning speed today, and this is the last one you'll ever cross with me. Don't touch me. You certainly don't force a kiss on me, you arrogant bastard. Walk, limp, or crawl to your goddamn car; I'm not driving you."

He stood up quickly, still spewing apologies, saying he had lost his head. "I don't care! Who the hell do you think you are?" I demanded.

"Cynthya, I'm sorry. I'm truly sorry. That was so stupid of me." "You're damn right. It was stupid." His apologies were pathetic rather than persuasive; his flimsy attempt to win his way out of the situation was failing miserably. "You have a warped way of playing around. I'm not some high school chick or sorority girl you can take easy liberties with. I don't play games in parks. I'm done with you." He followed me, his pleas for forgiveness trailing behind as he walked. Remarkably, his limp seemed to have vanished, hinting at a deception not yet fully unveiled.

"Please take me to my car, and I'll pay you for your gas and time. It was disrespectful. I promise I'll never do that again." Overhead, clouds shrouded the moon, casting a warning glow.

I spun around, pointing my finger at him as though I was scolding a child, my tone leaving no room for negotiation. "You, mister, do not touch me. This day, any future interactions with you, all communications with you, are over. That includes driving you to your car. You got that?" His affirmation came not in words but in the form of a sullen nod, his head hanging as low as his spirits. With that, I turned and walked away, my resolve as firm as the steps I took. I was utterly done with that detestable ass.

Suddenly, a powerful impact from behind knocked me to the ground. The force of his grip on my throat was something I've never experienced in my life, rendering me helpless, my lungs heaving, begging for air. My eyes bulged. I struggled to swallow. Tears streamed down my face. I hoarsely pleaded, "Hunter… Please, you're hurting me. Hunter, please don't do this to me." He pulled me into the shadows by the furnaces. He was on top of me in seconds, maintaining his vice grip on my throat. I held his wrist, trying to lessen the clutch. I felt like I was living in a horror movie. The clouds moved away from the moon.

It illuminated Hunter's shadow casting down. In his eyes, I saw pure evil. He applied pressure until I was totally submissive. *I'm going to die.* He Commanded, "You scratch me or scream, you're dead. You are fucking dead. Do you understand?" He had the glazed look of a rabid animal. My eyes rolled up. My hands fell to my side. Then, while holding my throat, he ripped my dress away like it was tissue paper, then tore away my panties so hard the elastic cut into me. All I could think was, *Dear God, please don't let him rape me.* He lessened his grip. Maybe God had intervened, and he came to his senses.

I tried scooting away and got to my feet, poised to run like hell. But the hand of the beast was back around my throat, lifting me off my feet, choking the living hell out of me. He had been toying with me to see if I would follow his command. He was holding my throat tighter. He spoke in a menacing whisper, "I fucking told you what I'd do." He locked his hands on my throat, cutting off my oxygen. My body was convulsing.

He released pressure just as I passed out. He told me, "You get one last chance to live, you fucking slut. I'll choke you out for good the next time." He slammed my head into the ground. "Do you understand me?" he murmured, each word laced with an unmistakable threat. I shook my head as best I could in capitulation. Fear, shock, and confusion controlled me. I felt my heart pounding, each throb echoing like thunder against the walls of my chest.

I accepted that rape… was my fate, and there wasn't anything I could do to stop him from his selfish gratification. He hastily unbuckled his pants, pushing them and his underwear to his knees. Overwhelmed by fear and pain, I tried to speak, my voice emerging as nothing more than a faint, breathless whisper, each word a struggle against the terror that had seized my throat as he fondled my vagina. "Hunter… listen… Hunter, please listen to me. Please don't go inside of me." Oh my god! I cried in horror at the force of his violent intrusion.

In my moment of despair, I questioned God. *With all that I had endured in life, why had this new hell been cast upon me? Why was I Hunter's prey this evening? I had been nothing but nice to him.* Internally, I pleaded with Hunter, my silent appeals echoing unheard in the void of my own mind. *No, you can't do that to me. This is my body. You don't have the right to do what you're doing to me...* He was humping viciously, his vile and disgueting,ug, ug, ug, pushing inside me. Killing my dignity with each revolting thrust. I went limp and accepted my fate. *Dear God, if this is your will, please take me.*

Hunter continued demoralizing me, panting and grunting, pounding me harder until he finally released his disgusting ejaculate inside me. He collapsed with all his weight on top of me, winded by his primitive self-gratification. I was far removed from my body; I wasn't sure if I was dead or alive until he finally rolled off me. The agonizing pain below brought me back to reality. I was repulsed thinking of the sundry problems that followed this torturous event in my life... if I were to survive.

As clarity returned, I curled up into the fetal position, hoping he wouldn't hurt me further. I appealed for inner strength to cry out for help. I'm not on birth control, dear God. I could get... Even worse, he could transfer some dreadful disease to me. Did he think of that? Or maybe he planned to kill me, and it didn't matter. He buckled his pants, and his demeanor switched immediately from that of a crazed madman to one of concern and remorse, murmuring to himself, "Oh my God," as he pulled at his hair. He lamented, "What have I done to you? Please forgive me. You were... you're just so beautiful, and you smelled so good. I... I couldn't control myself. I'm sorry; I can't believe I did something like this. There goes my medical career. My parents are going to disown me for sure this time."

I wasn't coherent enough at that moment to catch, "This time?" Was I not the first victim to suffer his brutality? It felt like he's ripped my vagina. I was too afraid to move or think of the damage he's done to me. His apologies poured out incessantly, a stark contrast to his earlier domineering demeanor.

Each word was heavy with remorse, a torrent of regret that seemed to wash over his previous confidence. He was visibly shaken, the once controlled facade now crumbling under the weight of his emotions. He pulled me to my feet. I was too terrorized to resist him. I pleaded, "Please… just leave me here. I won't say anything if you just go." He ignored my pleas, lifted me up, and carried me, looking about cautiously to ensure no one witnessed his debauchery. I squeaked, "Please don't hurt me anymore. I'm sorry that I upset you today. Just put me down, and I'll go away."

He murmured quietly yet commandingly, "I won't. Be quiet!… I'll take you to my place, and you can shower. Then, I'll do what's right for what I have done to you. I didn't have the right to call this life my own after that. I can almost feel the coldness of the jail cell walls when I think of being there forever. I'm an animal. I'm so ashamed of what I've done."

Never in my life had I been so afraid, my life hanging on the next move of this animal. I was too wounded, too afraid, and too confused to take action. I have already experienced his brutality and his ability to debilitate me. He drove me to his place on Queen Anne. The house he's rented was down a dark, unlit street.

He slipped through the darkness with a predatory stealth, drawing me into a silent, oppressive space. "Why don't I flee?" I chastised myself, yet the cold tendrils of fear rendered me catatonic, unable to act upon the instinct to escape. Each step he took promised a feigned sense of security, and in the depths of my terror, I found myself acquiescing, latching onto the fragile hope that compliance might somehow lead to liberty.

Once inside, he escorted me to the bathroom, tore away the rest of my dress and took a sly grab of my breast. "Here, let me help you to the shower once you're clean. I'll give you one of my shirts and, I will take you home or to the police. Okay?" He turned the water on, sampling the temperature. He was sweating profusely. "Okay, get in." Draped in morbid fear, I followed his commands obediently. Anything to avoid the grip of his hands on my throat again. I stood there, isolated in the cascade of water, yet the warmth did nothing to quell the shivers that wracked my body.

Terror clung to me more stubbornly than the steam, seeping into my very bones, leaving me feeling cold in a way that had nothing to do with temperature. He returned in less than five minutes and ordered me out of the shower. Then cleaned my vagina with a make-shift douche bag. I stood with my arms folded across my breast. I whenced in pain as he sprayed water into me. After he was sure he had cleaned away remnants of his sperm from me, he grabbed a towel and dried me off.

He paced back and forth frantically, each utterance of regret laden with his twisted remorse. His speech, oscillating between self-addressed murmurs and direct declarations to me, revealed his deranged state. "It's not me. It's something—an animal—inside of me." His chestnut blonde hair was matted to his face from sweat, his disheveled appearance mirroring the chaos within.

With unsteady hands, he guided me to the sofa, his voice now softer but still tinged with the remnants of his inner turmoil. He directed me to sit on a blanket, a small gesture of consideration that contrasted starkly with the terror of the past moments.

He handed me the telephone. "Here you go. Call the police. Afterward, I'll call my parents and tell them what I've done tonight and let them know my life is ending. I promise you."

There was so much adrenaline flowing through his body he could snap at any moment. If I dared to flee and failed, he would surely ended my life without hesitation. Despite my pains and loathing, I maintained my composure as best I could, though I wished he would die. I glanced up at him and then at the phone. I wanted nothing he'd touched.

"Please!" he demanded. His shout startled me. I recoiled into a ball on the sofa. With the phone still extended, he told me with force in his voice, "Make your call. I'm ready." My voice was barely audible. "Hunter." Swallowing hard. Just mentioning his name hurt me. "Please… let me go home. Please."

"I won't harm you. But I need you to contact the police so that I can fix myself for what I've done to you. That way, you'll have true—true justice. You deserve it." I knew well that if he genuinely thought his life was over, he'd take mine before taking his own. I declined.

Chapter Seven

y senses returned slowly, and I began negotiating with him, promising not to disclose the rape to anyone. I quickly shut up when he whipped his head; I looked into his malevolent eyes. He continued his preoccupation with self-destruction. He pleaded, "Just help me kill myself?"

I maintained my agenda. "Hunter, I just wanted to go home. Would you… please, I promise not to tell anyone. Just let me go. Could you do that for me? I don't need justice; you have done nothing wrong. We were both on the same life path. I don't want to ruin your career or cause you any pain."

He let out an exasperated sigh."I must do right by you. No man should force a woman to have sex." Thoughts exploded in my mind. *It wasn't sex, you son-of-a-bitch. You raped me.* His gaze was inexorably drawn to the long sword, perched with an air of cold authority on a cradle above the fireplace.

With a mix of reverence and a dark, unsettling intent, he lifted it, his hands revealing a faint tremor of anticipation. As he revealed the glimmering silver blade from its sheath, he caressed it not merely with affection but with a possessive admiration, its lethal beauty shimmering ominously in the dim light. He executed a series of swift, precise movements, each swing of his sword was not just a display of skill but a clear, terrifying demonstration of his control—indicating he was on the brink of an abyss, a descent into the darkest depths of madness, signaling he was ready to drag me into a vortex that could end my life.

"This is real. It's beautiful, isn't it?" he mused, his voice laced with an eerie reverence as he admired the blade, now an extension of his twisted intentions. "My grandfather bought it for me on our first trip to Japan. It's called a Katana, one of the sharpest blades in the world." The admiration he held for the weapon only intensified the terror clawing at my insides.

"The Japanese have an honor code; a warrior would rather die than disgrace his family or allies. They would plunge a sword into their gut, taking their own life. Courageous men." His face became impassive, his voice disconnected, "Very honorable men. They are very brave men. I have always admired that culture." The chasm between his romanticized views and the grim reality before me was stark. His fixation with the sword and what it represented wasn't just unsettling—it added a profound sense of dread to my already heightened horrors.

Forcing aside my fears, I appealed to his self-absorbed rant. I silkened my plea, "Hunter. Listen. Listen to me. Please don't injure yourself. You're a good… person. Look. Things got carried away this evening. "Maybe I," I wanted to puke on my words, "led… you on. I wore that sexy, *now shredded* hot dress just for you today. I knew it would make you want me. "But I pretended I wasn't interested. You know how you say, 'Girls play games?'"

He jumped in agreement as though I had helped him justify his actions. He responded, "Yeah! That's true. I knew you were leading me on. You wanted it, didn't you?" I grimaced in pain, nodding my head. He lowered the weapon to his side. In child-like fashion, he conformed. "Yeah. Yes, it was a beautiful dress. I'm sorry I tore it. Plus, you took me to the store to buy those beers, right? Sometimes I drank too much. You know I really shouldn't do that...." I forced a smile. "I know I shouldn't have taken you there. But it's okay. I'll know better next time we're out." My whole body tensed.

I wascarefully trying to soothe him, choosing my words in an attempt to calm the storm I sensed within him. Yet, despite my efforts, his demeanor took a sudden, dark turn. He watched me with an emotionless gaze, a chilling calm in his voice as he delivered a threat that cut deep, "I can destroy your career, you know that? I've done it before."

A cold shock ran through me at his words, revealing yet another layer of his disturbing character. He wasn't merely making threats; he was admitting to past deeds of manipulation and harm. This man, who was on the path to becoming a doctor, was now threatening to dismantle my life with the same casualness as discussing the weather.

The stark contrast between the healer he was supposed to become and the harm he was capable of inflicting was jarring. More than just exposing his moral bankruptcy, this revelation highlighted the danger of his unpredictability. He had moved beyond violating personal boundaries to menacing my entire professional existence. The fact that he had enacted such threats before, seemingly without remorse or consequence, sent a wave of fear through me.

The realization that he could, and would, act on his sinister intentions left me reeling, struggling to grasp the full extent of his vindictiveness.

Panic clawed at the edges of my mind, but a voice within me urged, *Stay strong. Remain calm. Don't provoke him further. Convince him there's a reason to keep going.* Grasping at straws, I sought to pacify him, to somehow tether him back to a semblance of reason without igniting his wrath. "Hunter... that's unnecessary. What happened tonight will be our pact," I said, my voice steady despite the turmoil swirling within me.

The word 'pact' was chosen to invoke a sense of camaraderie, a shared secret that bonded us uniquely. I hoped it would appeal to whatever fragment of rationality or need for connection he still harbored, making him reconsider his ominous threat. It was a gamble, using language to weave a thread of mutual understanding in the hope it would be strong enough to hold back the tide of his destructive impulses.

As I spoke, I watched his reaction closely, looking for any sign that my words reached him, that they might anchor him to a reality where violence wasn't the answer. It was a desperate bid to navigate the perilous waters of his temper, to find a lifeline that could spare me from the fallout of his actions.

He gave me an expressionless smile, saying nothing. I told him, "Yes, it'll always be between you and me. But you also have to promise me you'll tell no one about us, promise?" He slowly nodded in agreement. He replaced the sword in its original position and walked towards me with his hand extended, saying, "Let's go." The last time he had reached for my hand, I had snatched it away. Not so this time.

He led me from the house to my car, opened the door, and took care to buckle me in. I pulled the shirt as far down my legs as possible. The silence in the car was eeric. I hopped I was being driven to safety, but it was hard to tell what was happening in his unstable mind.

I contemplated jumping from the car, running, and screaming. But what if he caught me? I sat still, watching the changing neighborhood shapes. He was heading toward the U. We were getting close to the parking lot. So many things were going through my head. He could kill me in the parking lot and leave me for discovery by someone else. I saw myself lying on the black asphalt, dead and alone in the cold. I tried to conquer the thoughts, tears flowing, and I tried to muffle my cry. I asked myself, how could all this insanity be so deceiving? How was he able to make it through life?

The day began with an air of adventure as I arrived at the Montlake parking lot, ready to share my hometown's charm with Hunter. What started as a journey filled with promise gradually unraveled, leaving me numb from Hunter's perplexing and erratic behaviors.

Returning to the parking lot, where our day had initially started, now felt like coming full circle, but under vastly different circumstances. Hunter parked his car next to mine, in the same spot he had chosen earlier. This act of returning us to our starting point was not just a physical return but a stark reminder of how far the day had deviated from its innocent beginnings.

After moving me back to my driver's seat, Hunter's departure was notably smooth, executed with a demeanor suggesting he was unfazed by recent events. He drove away with a calmness that seemed to convey certainty of no repercussions for his actions, leaving me alone to grapple with the aftermath. It raised haunting questions about his perception of recent occurrences and whether he harbored a deeper, more calculated motive that I was yet to understand.

Sitting alone in the now quiet parking lot, the disconnect between the day's hopeful start and its tumultuous end was palpable. I was left to ponder the true extent of Hunter's actions and the potential consequences that might follow. The uncertainty of whether this ordeal was truly over, or if Hunter's departure marked the beginning of something more sinister, lingered heavily, a somber reflection on a plan that had promised so much joy.

I stayed in the same spot for the half an hour, eventually, convincing myself it was safe to leave, I summoned the courage to start the engine. The familiar hum of the ignition was both comforting and eerie, a stark contrast to the silence that had enveloped me. As I put the car in gear and pulled away, a surreal sense of detachment washed over me. It was as if I was observing myself from a distance, standing still while the world moved on around me, the sound of my car's tires on the pavement a distant echo in my ears.

My mind was a blur, thoughts racing yet leading nowhere. The physical exhaustion from the day's events, compounded by psychological turmoil, left me feeling utterly spent. As I navigated the empty streets, the journey home felt mechanical, each turn and stop sign a reminder of the autopilot mode I had engaged just to make it through to the safety of home—a safety once taken for granted.

Once, when my friends and I were discussing how we would react to an assault, our hypothetical responses were quite different from reality. I had boldly claimed that my defense would be fierce and brutal, envisioning leaving my attacker with a face marred with painful scratches. I imagined using every ounce of energy to deliver sharp bites, hard punches, powerful kicks, and desperate screams for help. Lexi asserted that no man would ever dare touch her, and Gina echoed this sentiment. At the time, the possibility of such events seemed remote, and we were confident that these dreadful situations would never occur. However, looking back, I feel ashamed for not having the courage to live up to my words.

Upon arriving at my house, the immediate instinct was to rid myself of every trace connected to him. Stepping inside, the door closing behind me marked a boundary between the outside world and my own personal space, yet the intrusion of the night's events seemed to follow me in. In a desperate attempt to reclaim some sense of self, I tore off the shirt I was wearing, the last physical symbol of the assault, and rushed to the kitchen.

My hands landed on the butcher's knife, and with a resolve fueled by anger and a need for catharsis, I began to aggressively slice through the fabric. Each tear of the blade was a silent scream, an assertion of my agency in the face of what had been taken from me.

Reduced to nothing but fragments on the kitchen floor, the destroyed shirt was both a symbol of what I had endured and a small declaration of revenge. I swept up the remains of the shredded shirt, careful not to leave any thread behind. With the rags in hand, I headed outside, my heart pounding with a mixture of fear and determination.

Once outdoors, I placed the rags on the ground, a safe distance from the house. I took a deep breath, and with trembling hands, I lit a match. As the rags began to burn, a sense of grim satisfaction washed over me.

The flickering of the flames and the acrid smell of smoke filled the air. I watched the cloth incinerate. At that moment, I envisioned Hunter's demise. "Die, you pathetic son of a bitch," I whispered to myself.

After ensuring that the fire had consumed all the shreds — not wanting even a single fiber to survive — I returned inside, still clenching the knife, blood dripping from the cut I had sustained while shredding the shirt. After bandaging my wound, I closed and locked the door, pushing the sofa in front of it to add an extra layer of security. This physical barrier, though small, felt like a necessary step to safeguard the sanctity of my space, a space that Hunter had violated in spirit if not in body.

I then entered the bathroom, switched on the shower, and stepped inside. With one hand, I attempted to cleanse my body while gripping the knife tightly. I remained there until the water ran cold. Shaking, I grabbed a towel, dried myself off, and wrapped another around me. Turning off the light, I pressed myself as close to the wall as possible, holding the blade at the ready.

I awoke the next morning, the tension of holding the knife so tightly overnight still lingering in my fingers as I pried them open. I flicked on the light, illuminating my reflection in the mirror. A sharp pain radiated through my throat as I noticed the dark marks of bruises on my neck. Instead of going to the hospital, I decided to rely on my medical knowledge to evaluate my symptoms.

Putting Hunter's attack into words was too difficult for me. I knew I couldn't fabricate a story to prevent the police from getting involved; I couldn't bear to repeat his narrative again. My mind was filled with utter disarray and total humiliation because I had allowed myself to be taken advantage of. My emotions oscillated between the desire to continue living and thoughts of ending my own life. I believed that was the only way to escape the revulsion of that inhuman individual violating my body at his will.

Looking in the mirror, I believed that cutting my wrist might be the way to end my anguish. I held the blade down, pressing it until blood beaded around the knife's edge. If only men understood the pain they inflicted on the people they violated, perhaps they would refrain from such actions. I am a woman, not some piece of flesh to be torn into at will. Why would a man as handsome as Hunter need to force sex on a woman? I've always thought of a rapist as some low-life loser hiding in bushes, attacking women in the darkness.

Though he was a pesky annoyance, never in my lifetime would I have suspected him capable of such heinous behavior. Why? Why?

Why? I snapped, my raging inquiry awakened me from my intent of self-destruction. I forcefully flung the knife, impaling it in the wall. My rage inspired me to call the police.

I wasn't' going to not allow him to get away with what he had done to me. I grabbed the phone and punched in 911. But before I could press send, his threat echoed chillingly in my mind. "I can ruin your career," he had warned, a direct attack on everything I had worked tirelessly to achieve. Paralyzed by the weight of his words and the enormity of my student debt, I felt the scales of justice tilt against me. The privilege he wielded effortlessly was a stark contrast to the struggles that defined my path. I contemplated the long legal journey: me, the victim represented by the state of Washington, against him and his noble family.

His defense attorney loomed large in my imagination, a diabolical strategist skilled in the art of character assassination. I could almost hear the probing questions, the insinuations designed to invert the narrative, painting me, the victim, as the perpetrator. The invasion of my privacy, the public dissection of my past, appeared not as distant possibilities but as imminent certainties.

The weight of his threat, the potential destruction of my career, and the staggering debt that already burdened me made the phone in my hand feel like a leaden anchor. The disparity between our worlds, his unearned ease against my hard-fought gains, resonated with a painful clarity.

In the moment before pressing send, I was besieged by the realization of what lay ahead. This wasn't just a battle for justice; it was a war against my very essence and accomplishments. The prospect of being publicly dragged through a process that could re-victimize me, forcing me to relive the trauma in the most invasive way possible, stopped me cold.

With a heavy heart, I lowered the phone. This decision, made in the depths of my turmoil, was a surrender to the immediate and daunting reality of the ordeal ahead, not to him. It was a decision shaped by a stark assessment of my own resilience against the backdrop of what I stood to lose, a profound acceptance of my immediate reality, a decision made in solitude, reflecting the grim calculus of pursuing justice at too great a personal cost.

Away from work for six weeks, I had time enough for the physical reminders of my ordeal to fade—the pain and bruising around my throat slowly healed. But during my absence, my young patient, Lilly Anne Johnson, passed away. At just six years old, she had faced more than most do in a lifetime, her spirit and resilience outshining her years. She was the bright spot in my routine, a brave little soul who fought hard against her illness.

The staff at the hospital relayed to me how she had frequently asked for me, the 'nice doctor-lady,' wondering when I would return to help her get better. Her innocent questions, now relayed to me in past tense, deepened the guilt that was already consuming me. In betraying her expectations, in not being there, I felt as though I had failed her. Overwhelmed by grief and a sense of responsibility for her unanswered calls for me, I suffered a breakdown. It pushed me further into isolation, and I found myself retreating from the world for another month, struggling to cope with the weight of my absence and the loss of such a young life.

Chapter Eight

A loud, thunderous boom jolted me from my morbid reverie, shattering the fragile tranquility of the moment. A dazzling, white-hot streak of lightning split the sky, casting stark illumination upon the darkened landscape. In that electrifying moment, the realization of why Gina hadn't come to me after she was raped hit hard, like a sudden punch to the gut. I was taken back to the day Hunter came into our lives, the sound of his laughter still ringing in my ears.

I remembered vividly the time when the four of us were dancing, Hunter's unwavering gaze fixated on Gina with an intensity that sent shivers down my spine. Two days after that party, Gina and I had a lengthy conversation over the phone. Her voice greeted me with its usual cheery tone, but I sensed an unspoken curiosity beneath the surface. "Hey!" she exclaimed, "What kind of vibe did you get from the guy at the party?" As I discussed Hunter, I couldn't shake the feeling that Gina had her own reasons for asking, reasons she didn't want to reveal to me. Unbeknownst to me, Gina's subtle curiosity about Hunter would later take on a significance I never anticipated.

My absence, following Hunter's transgression, aligned with the chain reaction of events triggered by Lexi's disclosure. Who would have thought that Gina and I would suffer the same trauma weeks apart? Gina had locked herself away from the world, just as I had. Without a doubt, I knew it was Hunter. Yet, conflicting thoughts raced through my mind. Had he used the same ruse on Gina as he had on me, causing us both to suffer today while he continued unscathed in his medical career?

A month passed in a blur of solitude and introspection, without a word from Gina or Lexi. Then Gina called, her voice low and weary, finally breaking the silence. She was speaking from that edge of emotional rehabilitation—that intricate psychological gap caused by acrimony and conflict, where you're striving to re-establish fractured relationships from the aftermath of friends at odds.

She asked whether Courtnee or I had conversed with Lexi. "No. It looks like everybody needed a break," I replied.

"The affair between her and her man was none of my concern," Gina confessed, her tone carrying a tinge of remorse. There was a moment's silence before she added, "She's no longer here."

"What do you mean she's not here?" My voice trembled with a mix of shock and disbelief as I struggled to comprehend the implications of Gina's revelation.

"She moved to the east coast two weeks ago," Gina's voice was soft, almost apologetic.

"She what? Dammit, why am I suddenly the last to know everything?" Frustration edged into my tone, the feeling of being left out piercing through the fog of my recent isolation.

"Cyn, the weight of my guilt is crushing me," Gina admitted, her voice laden with remorse. "I hesitantly asked Lexi how Marcus had been treating her. She told me he was showering her with kindness and respect. Do you think she was right? Am I just a mega-mama-bear-bitch?"

"No, Gina… you're just a mega-bitch," I said, my words laced with a mix of jest and truth, trying to inject some lightness into our heavy conversation.

Our laughter broke the tension, a brief respite from the storms of despair we'd been navigating. We had managed, for now, to bottle up our genies of grief, quietly hoping they'd remain contained. But the conversation sparked a realization in me. Despite the myriad of unanswered questions still swirling in my mind, I began to see the value in possibly sharing my own ordeal. The guilt of not having intervened when I might have had the chance was overwhelming. Yet, I started to think that maybe, just maybe, by sharing our stories, we could help each other heal.

"Gina…?" I ventured cautiously, sensing there was more she hadn't shared.

"Yes?" Her response came as a forlorn whisper, laced with hesitation.

"Are you able to? Do… you want to? You know… to talk?" The weight of my question seemed to stretch the silence that followed. After a moment, I heard a breathy exhale from her end, a precursor to the silence that followed.

"Gina. Are you there?" My concern grew with her prolonged quietness.

"I'm here." Her voice, strained and weary, finally pierced the quiet, laden with the weight of her unspoken agony. "I'm not in a position to talk about what happened. Even today, the memories haunt me. When Lexi told you all, my heart sank, and I saw his face anew. I relived the events of that day, the brutality of his hand against my face, being demeaned and silenced. Controlled." She paused, the weight of her next words hung in the balance. "That is something you will never understand. And there's more… things I can't yet bring myself to face, let alone speak of." Her voice faltered slightly, hinting at layers of her story yet uncovered. "I will never defile my mouth by mentioning his name. I just pray he's in prison or six feet under. If you truly love me, and if you care about our friendship, please, never bring this up again… Ever!"

"But Gina—" My voice quavered, laden with concern and remorse as I reached out to her, attempting to bridge the emotional distance her revelation had created.

"Please! I have to go." Anger sharpened Gina's tone, betraying her agitation as past events surged to the forefront of her mind. Without another word, she disconnected abruptly, leaving a silence that resonated with the intensity of her emotions. I was left grappling with the sudden void her departure created, a stark reminder of the pain those memories must have inflicted.

Gina hinted at something more, something darker. What further harm did he cause her? The fear that he might have left her pregnant turned into a tangible dread. My heart plunged, acknowledging the complex emotions and decisions she might have faced.

We always championed pro-choice ideals, yet we also harbored dreams of motherhood. Our youthful declarations that we would carry any pregnancy to term, even under traumatic circumstances, now seemed naive in the harsh light of reality. Gina, most of all, had sworn she'd choose death over abortion, making her current silence all the more poignant.

I wrestled with the idea of revealing my own past, wondering if mutual comfort was possible, or if it would only deepen our rift. Would Gina blame me for not stopping Hunter, leading to her current predicament? I counseled myself, fearing that revealing my story might do more harm than good.

Lost in the silence that followed Gina's hasty goodbye, I found myself adrift in a sea of unresolved questions and the burden of untold truths. His words, "I can ruin your career. I've done it before," was an ever present weight heavier than any firearm, transforming me into both victim and accomplice, as fear bound me to safeguard my career over seeking justice. I attempted to justify this stance by convincing myself I was his only silent victim, yet I could never have fathomed that the same individual would extinguish my friend's spirit. However, in the depths of despair, I clung desperately to the hope that someone among his victims would find the courage we lacked to hold him accountable.

My telephone rang early Saturday morning at seven forty-five, disrupting my desire to sleep in. It was Lexi reaching out through FaceTime. I answered, my voice betraying my grogginess. As I moved slowly towards the bathroom, I caught my reflection in the mirror: shockingly beautiful, even with my hair in a tousled mane. During our call, Lexi's first question was, "Morning, Cyn, did I wake you?" That simple question, given our complicated past, filled my heart with warmth.

"No, Lex, it drives me crazy when I sleep in on a Saturday morning. Who in their right mind would ever consider…" looking at the clock, "…sleeping past seven?"

"Sarcasm?"

"Glee, coated with sugar and tempered with love."

"Gotcha. I'm calling because I miss you guys… I owe you an apology. Gina has arranged for us to video chat tomorrow at brunch, but it's not the same. "Cyn." Her voice trailed off.

"Yes, Lex?"

"I just want—need you to know that I'm very sorry for what I said to Gina in front of you guys. And for leaving, saying nothing. It was wrong. I was just hurting and needed to deal with my pain by myself and not be judged for making love—fucking—whatever you want to call it to my man. It was my choice, and I didn't need her pecking like she always does. I don't know why I let him get away with it. But we talked. He apologized—which doesn't mean shit—his ass has to prove it to me. I can promise you one thing, Cyn. If he ever pulls that shit again, he'll live to regret it. The next time, I'll let him think he's going to get some, but when he brings thing near me, I'll have a scalpel to slice it and the dangle buddies off."

I cringed. "That's rather harsh."

"Lying, cheating, and him putting his hands on my face crossed the line, Cyn. I don't give second chances. He can chase anyone he wants. But he can't just go out, hunt like a dog, and then come back, expecting to bring whatever he's picked up outside into my life. I'm not having any of that."

I knew she wouldn't hurt him physically, but she would make his life a living hell. That was the Lexi we loved—sweet as honey, obnoxious—often—but when riled up, she knew how to make life hard for you.

As my mental haze cleared, I wanted to connect the dots regarding her disclosure. I was hoping that maybe, while she was nursing Gina, she had told her the name of the rapist. I knew in my heart and soul that it was Hunter. But I couldn't let it go until it was validated. I wasn't sure why—to help me hate him more, make myself feel worse for doing nothing, or there was a glimmer of hope that it wasn't him, and I could lift the burden of guilt off my shoulders.

I asked if Gina had told her the name of her attacker. She shrugged her shoulders. "We're not going there, Cyn. It's dead and gone." *Maybe for her.* Perhaps she forgave Marcus for his deed, but I knew I would carry Hunter in my consciousness for the rest of my life, and Gina would do the same.

Lexi and I chatted for two hours about her new life. The city was young, culturally diverse, and alive with activity. Marcus believed his team was going to the Super Bowl, and he was working to be named MVP. "He's been training and dieting, up at dawn. I don't see him until six or seven at night. All he talks about now is MVP. So, I get him back from other women and lose him to his football dream. That's my life. I'll go to most of his games. I want him to hang with his teammates, not thinking he needs to answer me. I have made myself clear, and we don't go there anymore. That's my life. How have you been?"

I knew my answer would make Lexi sad, so I gave her the light version. "I just felt bad for you and Gina. We've been friends for so long—"

"Stop! I know I was wrong. I didn't mean to hurt Gina or upset everyone. But Cyn, Gina was too overwhelming; I didn't need that. She, out of everyone, should have been the most compassionate given all I had done for her when she was… you know. I needed to make my own decisions. Something like that is shocking when it happens the first time—"

"What do you mean, the first time?"

"Cyn, let me finish. Please don't be Gina. I'm speaking hypothetically about the first time it happened. It hurt me inside and out. It shocked me he would do that to me. Then you have the cheating, the other woman, or women."

She reassured me she had Marcus under control, saying, "That's the thing about men. They think they have us, women, under their thumbs. When they're giving us expensive gifts, dining, vacations, and all the other treats and the praise they give, it's all manipulations—the fakeness—though they believe it when saying it: I love you. I'll be by your side for the rest of my life. It's all bullshit. Marcus wanted me to quit my job and depend on him so that he could control me. It's not intentional. It's just how a guy's brain works. He believes what he's saying, but his selfish agenda is in the back of his mind. There's always a self-interested plan. But he doesn't. Honestly, I need you to promise me you'll tell no one. Oh my god, I can't believe I'm saying this. That's the same thing Gina said to me." I assured her it was okay. I didn't lash out in anger and say words I knew would come back and be troubling to me later.

"Let's change the subject. I don't want to go there right now. I'll be home in a couple of weeks. We can then have a heart-to-heart. I'm going to get dressed and go shopping in a couple of hours."

"I wish I was going with you."

"I wish we were all going together. It's lonely here sometimes. I have attended various social events—mostly football players and their wives. It's such a clique. I hate it. Many are just a bunch of superficial women. I miss my real friends, not being at a party with some chick glaring at you. Or giving you a fake smile while scheming with one eye on you and the other on your man, ready to drop her panties the minute your back is turned." Marcus hollered in the background, "Hey Baby, you ready? Let's go."

She yelled back, "I'm coming." She turned to the phone, "I have to go." Blowing a kiss, saying, "Goodbye. I love you beyond tomorrow."

"And I'll love you all the proceeding days until the end of time."

Chapter Nine

It was now my turn to reach out to my amour and apologize for cutting off communication so abruptly. It wasn't like me to ignore his calls, and the guilt was weighing on me. I wasn't ready to abandon the possibility of a loving relationship, yet his predictable routines, gleaned from our past conversations, haunted my thoughts.

I knew about his Friday ritual, drinks with friends at Daniel's for happy hour. The conflict within me grew—how to reconnect, or if it was even possible. I felt I owed him more than a distant apology; he deserved an explanation, and if this was to be our end, then a face-to-face farewell was the least I could offer.

I video-chatted with my girls, Gina, Courtnee, and Lexi, telling them my intentions and hoping to find support and guidance for my plan. Our sweet, timid Courtnee was the first to give her opinion. "First, you were mad at him when he went a week without calling you after your first date. Then you didn't answer any of his calls for a month. He probably figured you you're not interested."

"But I was interested," I insisted.

Courtnee asked, "What if he's there with another woman? Can you imagine how embarrassing it would be for you to go there and have him totally ignore you? Or how would you feel seeing him with another woman?" I hadn't expected Courtnee to be the one planting seeds of doubt. She's usually the cheerful one, offering support. My idea must have seemed terrible for her to say no.

Gina agreed with Courtnee. Gina asked, "What were you going to do? Just pop in and say, remember me? I'm the girl who's been ignoring your phone calls. I think you'd be invading his space."

"But…" I started to respond.

Gina replied, "I say you just leave it alone. After all, you guys didn't know each other that well. Why not just call? And if there is no answer, leave a message. If he calls back, then you can talk. If he doesn't, well, who cares? Move on."

I perceived Lexi's silence as a sign of disinterest or agreement. Deflated, I inhaled deeply, accepting my friends' advice until Lexi chimed in with her own straightforward suggestion. "Look, Cyn, why make a mountain out of a molehill? Just go see him. If he's with someone, then you know where you stand. Stop complicating things. If you care about the guy despite everything, have a talk. If he's not available, well, then you'll have your answer. Move on."

I was torn between opinions, weighing my options; I agreed that the simplest approach was a phone call. Yet, Lexi's idea was bold and assertive, which resonated with me. It was decided I was going to see him in person. Courtnee added to my doubts, suggesting, "Maybe you should just call him. Gina agrees."

Lexi pushed back, "Will you whores shut up? Cyn, see the man. If he's there with his friend and not available…" She told Gina and Courtnee, "If you're that scared for her, why don't you join her?" She rolled her eyes.

Not wanting to belabor it any longer, I tell them, "It's okay. I got this. I created the problem. I'm going to see the man in person. And if he's not where he says he is on Friday evenings or with a woman, I'll take that as a sign that it was never meant to be."

I stepped off the elevator into the lobby of Daniel's, ready to encounter the unknown. I collided with two twenty-something women, drunk, giggling, hanging onto each other, and talking about the men hitting on them. "Damn, the place is full of pervs. That old guy was fuckin' rubbing my thigh like he was expecting my pussy to appear as if he thought he was going to get laid for buying drinks." The other snorted as she laughed. "I know. Fucking losers!"

Great, just the place I wanted to be. I reluctantly walked to the entrance. It was 7:30 p.m., and the place was packed to capacity. I was so nervous. The waitress navigated through the crowd with authority, carving her path: I scooched behind her, maneuvering through the dense crowd of men and women.

A few feet in, I felt a hand glide down my ass. I twirled, looking for the errant violator. I'm not sure what kind of pleasure men receive from putting their hands on a stranger's ass. Did the idiot think I'm going to back up and ask him to do it again? *Assholes.* However, that person was not part of my mission. I didn't want to lose sight of my waitress parting the masses. *Shit.* After a painstaking effort to navigate through the dense sea of bodies once more, constantly bumping shoulders and murmuring apologies, I finally completed a full circuit of the bar, but he was nowhere to be seen.

On my way to the exit, I spied him. He was sitting at a corner table by the window. The one place I had overlooked. I could only see him from behind. I huffed in an air of disappointment. My friends were right; he was with a guy and two women. A beautiful blonde sat across from him, looking at him adoringly. She seemed more his type. As she looked up, our eyes met, and we locked gazes. She gave me a dismissive smirk, turning her attention back to him.

Oh well. There wasn't a need to make things more awkward. Once in the lobby, I texted, "Hey, remember me? I'm sorry that I flaked out on you. An old memory attacked me and sent me into hiding. I thought I to surprise you this evening, but you're with company. Anyway, enjoy your evening. Wishing all of you the best. Cyn." I felt stupid for going there. I should have listened to Gina and Courtnee. Damn, Lexi, for her bold recommendation. However, she was right. I got the facts. However, silly me, why would I expect him to wait around for me during my crisis? It's was crazy for me to even be having these reactions.

I found the place overwhelming, with its noise and throngs of people. Seeing him seated with another woman only intensified my discomfort: I didn't like this place. The elevator couldn't come fast enough to whisk me out of here. It finally arrived. I meshed in with the horde of bodies filling the lift to capacity.

As the doors began to close, shutting out the cacophony of the bar, a hand assertively stopped them. A familiar voice cut through the noise, "Hey. Remember me?" There he was, the very reason for my visit, making all my attempts at careful avoidance utterly pointless with just three words.

Oh my God, I was mortified. What was I to say? I was hoping he didn't think of me as a weird stalker. I searched for words to explain my presence. "I... I... came here to see you. But I didn't want to disturb you and your company."

From the back of the elevator, pressed against the wall, an angry lady yelled out in exasperation, "Can you let go of the damn door? We'd like to go home!" He reached for my hand, inviting me to step out. "Can we talk for a moment?"

Annoyed and cramped at the back of the elevator, the lady's impatience was palpable. "Finally, some sense," she muttered. When I stepped off with him, her irritation gave way to a sharp "Thank you!"—a biting farewell as the doors slid shut.

"It's nice to see you. How have you been?"

"It's nice to see you, too," I replied, trying to mask my discomfort. "I've been well. And I'm really sorry for how I disappeared, then just turned up. I'm not strange. It's just... an issue came up with my friends, something that dredged up difficult memories. I wouldn't have been the best company for anyone."

"I see."

My voice faltered. "I... I thought maybe..." I hesitated, then pressed the elevator button. "I'm sorry. Coming here was a mistake."

"Wait. It's too noisy here. Let's go somewhere quieter, maybe to the other side. We could use the sky bridge or just walk at street level and get some air."

"What about your friends? I don't want to take you away from them."

He gave a quick, reassuring smile. "I'll just grab my jacket and say goodbye. Won't take a moment." With that, he was off, slipping through the crowd with an ease I envied. No lingering hands for him. Why did it have to be different for women?

Crowds were swelling on this Friday night, making it tougher to find a quiet corner. "How about Bellevue Square mall?" he suggested once he returned. "We're sure to stay dry there unless there's some kind of disaster, like a downpour from the sprinkler system."

I laughed despite myself. "Don't jinx us. With my luck? It's entirely possible."

He glanced at me, a playful twinkle in his eye. "You're looking lovely tonight. Suddenly, I understood how the prince must have felt when Cinderella disappeared on him—though you didn't leave a glass slipper behind."

I lifted my phone, showing it to him. "Modern times call for modern measures, my kind prince."

"So?" he responded.

"I'm feeling uneasy. I took you away from your friends. That woman, the blonde, she seemed... well, she didn't seem happy with me. Her look, when our eyes met, was dismissive, a look of derision, as though she was saying, 'I'm better than you.'"

He met my eyes with unwavering resolve. "She'll understand. She's an old friend. It's fine."

The unease in my stomach twisted tighter. *That's not what a woman really wants to hear, buddy.* What did that mean—an old friend? Alarm bells rang in my head. Had I made a monumental error in coming here tonight?

"We've enjoyed some turbulent times. And far more joyful times, gone on many vacations together. She has always been very understanding."

"Excuse me? So you abandoned her, for now, to talk with me and intend to reconnect later? You saw nothing wrong with that?" This was not how I thought about reuniting."

"Correct. We met last week for breakfast at the Maltby Café before our hike."

"So, let me get this straight. You are trying to be... with me? I had been absent from your life, and I understood if you had moved on. But you could have told me that before we crossed the street. Did you think it was okay to see another woman? Well, buddy, you got it wrong. Way, way wrong, mister.

However, it's okay; my bad. It wasn't right for me to come here." He reached for my hand. I jerked it as I backed away, wanting to get the hell out of there. He fast-walked after me, telling me, "I understand how you feel. I'll call my sister and tell her tomorrow is off, and we shouldn't see each other anymore."

I stopped in my tracks, biting my bottom lips. I wanted to rip that smug smirk off his face. "You bastard, how could you do that to me?"

He laughed. "I wish I had a video of your expression."

"That is not funny." My nerves ease. "So that girl, that woman. She's your sister?"

He was still smiling, proud of his ruse. "Yes. She's one-hundred percent my sister. Her name is Ally. Allyson, I call her Ally. Would you like to meet her?"

I wanted to grasp the impact of my absence on our future connections. As we strolled through the mall until it closed, I found myself doing most of the talking, deliberately avoiding discussions of our past. He suggested going to the bar to continue our conversation, but I declined, realizing I had already taken up enough of his time. With an early rise ahead and the weight of uncertainty about how this evening would conclude, fatigue weighed on me. He escorted me to the parking lot, and with each step, I felt the burden of my earlier indecision slowly lifting from my chest.

He opened my door for me. I was preparing myself for the goodnight kiss I'd longed for, ready to feel his arms wrapped around my body. So, I was shocked when he motioned for me to get in and then closed the door, walking away. Wow, talk about a letdown. My mind hummed with innuendoes. Maybe he was lying about the blonde being his sister and racing back to see her. After all, he had just finished what I'm now considering a boring walk with me. I shifted into reverse. As I pulled out from my parking space, I saw him hurrying toward me in my rearview mirror.

He opened the door with his hand extended, saying, "I didn't want to appear too forward, but I'm going for it."

I exited. My body thrilled with excitement as his hands glided around my waist, pulling me close. Our lips touched. The kiss was intense but not rough. After so many interruptions, I felt a closeness I'd been missing for too long. My mind chanted, *Hold me close. I want to feel you pressed against me.* God, I loved the cologne he was wearing. After that electrifying kiss, he gazed into my eyes, his voice thick with desire as he asked, "Can we have dinner tomorrow?" he asked, his eyes searching mine.

"Ah, yes," I replied, my voice betraying a hint of nervousness. "That sounds nice."

"Great," he said, his smile warm and reassuring. "How about 7:30 tomorrow? I could pick you up."

"I don't mind meeting you," I replied, trying to maintain a sense of calm. "Where would you like to meet?"

"Aurelia's Elysium?" he suggested, and I nodded in agreement, my lips pursed to hide my delight.

I really needed to get home before I lost it. His smile was infectious and wore me down. I wasted no time driving away this time.

I had been immersed in work and various projects at home, my thoughts frequently drifting to our upcoming meeting. With every passing hour, my anticipation grew stronger. Despite the busyness, my mind kept returning to thoughts of him. It was as if he had become the focal point, and I couldn't help but wonder how our evening would unfold.

Finally, with all tasks completed and a few hours to spare before our rendezvous, I decided to take a quick nap. As I lay down, my mind, previously filled with a whirlwind of thoughts, now wandered to pleasant memories of our last meeting. My eyelids grew heavy, and I soon found myself drifting off to sleep. Sometime later, I was awakened by the ringing of my phone.

"Hey, is everything okay?" he asked with concern in his voice. I groggily replied, "Yes, why?"

He continued, "I have been trying to reach you for the past hour. I thought maybe you changed your mind." Quickly recovering from my sleep stupor, I realized the time. "Oh god, no," I exclaimed, looking at the clock, which showed that it was already 8:00 p.m. I apologized, telling him that I had taken a little nap.

His voice softened as he asked, "Are you still available for dinner?"

I replied, genuinely apologetic, "Yes. I'm so sorry."

"It's okay," he reassured me. "I can reschedule for 9:00?"

Relieved, I said, "Perfect. I'll be there. I'm so sorry."

"It's okay," he repeated. "We all need a little power nap from time to time. See you at nine." I'm glad he chose a place not too far away. With a sense of urgency, I rushed to the shower, my heart tingling with excitement like a schoolgirl thrilled with the joys of a first romance.

During my drive, my mind wandered. I asked myself, "What is it he wants from me? I'm afraid of those questions because I'm confused. I want more than I admit, but how do I balance desires with expectations of a committed relationship? Maybe I'm getting ahead of myself. Who's to say he's looking for a committed relationship? He's a blissfully beautiful man whom I find incredibly charming, and he still wants to see me after my emotional hiatus. I give him points for his patience. I focus on being positive and enjoying the evening. I'm doing too much self-talk.

Lost in my thoughts and self-talk, I continued to ponder what he might want from me, the balance between desires and expectations in a committed relationship, and whether I was getting ahead of myself. My contemplative mood remained as I entered the restaurant.

As I approached the hostess stand, I glanced around the dimly lit, cozy restaurant. The soft glow of the modern fixtures created an intimate atmosphere. The hostess led me to our table, and I noticed him sitting there, a charming smile on his face. I returned the smile as I took my seat across from him.

Our waitress arrived introducing herself, "Good evening, and welcome to Aurelia's Elysium. My name is Jacquelyn, and I'll be your server. May I get your drink orders?" Without hesitation, he ordered iced tea for me and his Macallan 15. I'm feeling more relaxed this evening, still captivated by the devilish smirk.

I inquired, "What's been occupying your thoughts lately?"

His grin widened, and his eyes locked onto mine. "You, without a doubt." I leaned in, intrigued.

"Care to share what piques your interest?"

"Well…" Jacquelyn returned, "Here are your drinks. I'll give you a few more minutes with the menu." Great, thank you for interrupting him. I relaxed, enjoying the restaurant's ambiance.

"So tell me, what are you looking for? Don't feel you have to answer, and please, don't give me a superficial bar pickup line. I don't want to mislead you or have the same done me." I spy our attentive waitress coming in our direction. Crap! I'm throwing mental daggers at her. Are waitresses programmed to know precisely when to interrupt a conversation?

"What can I get for you tonight?" She positioned herself to where she was facing him and had me more at a peripheral angle. I considered her full-on attention to him a covert disregard for me.

He placed the menu down, sitting back in his chair, bathed in the soft, ambient glow of the restaurant's low lighting. "Steak sounds good. What do you think?" I marveled at the thought of a succulent steak, my gaze shifting between him and the menu. "The prime Angus steak sounds good to me." The dimly lit surroundings seemed to enhance his magnetic presence, casting intriguing shadows across his features and deepening the allure of the evening.

"Excellent choices," She said with a wink at my date. Jacquelyn, our vivacious waitress, gathered our menus with a seductive smile and charm that she knew men found hard to resist. Her stunning blue eyes locked onto my companion as she sensually moved about the table. With a figure reminiscent of a swimsuit model and a playful demeanor, she left no doubt that she enjoyed the attention of men.

As she sauntered away to fetch our orders. Jacquelyn thrived on the attention of men, and her intentions were clear: she was there to make a memorable impression, both for the tips and to let my date know she was available if he was inclined. I couldn't deny that her flirtatious demeanor had added an intriguing layer to our evening, one I hadn't quite anticipated.

I found myself pondering whether someone with such unwavering self-assuredness truly desired a monogamous relationship. But maybe I was overthinking it once again.

Dinner arrived shortly thereafter, and we savored our meal in shared silence, the air heavy with unspoken desire. Our eyes met, and an electric tension crackled between us, a tantalizing game of cat and mouse that fueled the growing passion. His stolen glances, accompanied by sips of his drink, sent a delightful warmth coursing through me, and a blush crept across my cheeks.

As the flavors of our exquisite dinner settled, we couldn't help but exchange alluring smiles. The palpable anticipation hung in the air, and with each passing moment, my thoughts drifted to the enticing possibility of being enveloped in his arms, our hearts and desires aligned in the dance of a budding romance.

"How was dinner?" he asked, his gaze unwavering as he waited for my response.

"It was delicious," I replied, savoring the lingering taste of the meal.

"I'm glad you enjoyed it," he said, his smile intensifying, a tantalizing spark that threatened to ignite a passionate fire.

I excused myself, determined to find Jacquelyn and present my credit card. I wanted to make it clear that it's not always the man who pays the bill. Deep down, I couldn't deny the twinge of jealousy and irritation that had built up from her excessive attention towards my date.

I wanted to assert my displeasure and let her know she had misjudged which party she was working for a tip. I caught up to Jacquelyn just as she emerged from the kitchen. I introduced myself and explained that I would like the dinner to be billed to my card. Her surprise was evident, and her face flushed a light shade of red. Without wasting a moment, I headed to the ladies' room to touch up my makeup.

Returning to the table, I noticed his hand parting from Jacquelyn's, and I fixed them both with stern glares as I took my seat. He leaned in and said, "That was a nice play on your part." The tension between us simmered just beneath the surface, adding an electrifying edge to the rest of our evening.

"Nice play?" I asked, feigning innocence. Taking delight in my coup.

"Paying for dinner the way you did."

"I wanted it to be my treat. Besides, I don't want you to always pay for dinner. We hardly know each other, and it's best to share equally."

"But it was my invitation."

"So was the first date, and you paid. I find it fair that I keep things equal."

I subconsciously took issue with his hand gliding with Jacquelyn. Unable to contain my emotions, I asked, "Do you always hold hands with your waitress?" He told me, "You paid for dinner, so I took care of the tip in cash. She's a nice girl, and I wanted her to take it directly from me and not have to find it on the table. See, right there on the bill, and I wrote zero."

"Okay, that was nice of you but unnecessary. How much did you give her?"

"A hundred."

I cleared my throat, my tone tinged with unease. "A hundred dollars? That's... quite generous. But isn't it a bit much, considering our dinner and drinks only amounted to a hundred and fifty?" *Looks like her not-so-discreet flirtations worked to her advantage despite my efforts to convey I was the one paying.* I chose to let it slide. It was his money, after all. The tension between us lingered, our unspoken emotions adding complexity to the atmosphere. We decided to continue our evening on the outside deck, leaving the restaurant's interior behind.

"Thank you for dinner and for being so nice," I began, my voice softening with gratitude. "But we should finish our conversations. Okay?" I leaned against the railing, my fingers tracing the rim of my glass in a nervous rhythm. "Look... I really enjoy your company, and I feel like I owe you an explanation for my earlier behavior. It was quite bold of me to show up and take you away from your friends like that.

After flaking out on you, I was worried you'd never want to speak to me again." I took a deep breath, my gaze fixed on the city lights below. "You see, my girlfriends and I have this tradition of getting together every Sunday for brunch. But today, things got a bit out of hand. Two of them had a pretty serious disagreement, to put it mildly, about something that happened to one of them before we met. The argument brought up some surprising revelations and old wounds, and it just... it all got to me. It stirred up some painful memories, and I couldn't bring myself to talk on the phone."

"How so?"

"I knew you'd ask that... I'll share it with you another time... Let's just say I made it past the specter of my past... I didn't want to bring it into our conversation."

"Okay, got it. I was a bit concerned, though... I thought our evening was perfect, except for that sudden downpour of rain... I closed my eyes and tried to recall the events of the evening, searching for anything I might have said or done wrong... You mentioned you're an open book, right?" I broke eye contact with him, looking around at the lush greenery in the distance. "Yes, I always try to be upfront and honest."

"I find there's a lot of mystery to you." Where was he going with this? "I'm not sure if that's a good or bad thing?" He gave a polite, wry smile. "Alright, here's the truth... When I went to Daniel's and saw you with the blonde la..."

"Allyson..." My eyes fluttered in confusion at the sudden introduction of a name. "Huh?" "Allyson... Remember... That's my sister's name."

"Okay... when I saw Allyson sitting next to you... I thought you had moved on, and our brief chapter was over before it began... Though I couldn't blame you, given my departure from the conversation." "Thank you for shedding a little light on it." "Look, I don't want to confuse you or make you wonder about me."

"I wouldn't call it troubled. I was more curious, wondering what went wrong. We barely knew each other. However, we're growing to know one another. And the days in front of us matter the most to me. I'm sure, given time, we'll be less of a mystery to each other."

"Thank you for your pleasant understanding. However, I need you to know I'm not looking for a few dates and some romps in the bed."

He leaned back slightly, meeting my gaze with a warm sincerity that touched my heart. "Please, we've had time to talk, and this is our second date, the beginning of many more, if I have my way. But I'm not looking for a casual fling, either. I want something meaningful, something real. I want to love and be loved deeply. I want a partner, a woman to share my life with, and maybe even start a family someday."

His words were beautiful, and I couldn't help but smile. "Those are beautiful words, and I appreciate your honesty. My heart is fragile, and I'll protect it fiercely. I want the same things, and I'm not interested in just a casual fling."

As our conversation continued, the waitress checked to see if we wanted more drinks. He ordered his third, and I couldn't help but notice. It wasn't that I thought it was a problem, but it made me wonder. Memories of past experiences with excessive drinking crossed my mind.

"Are you planning to drive home tonight?" I asked, trying to keep the conversation light.

"Yes, I am. Does my ordering a drink bother you?"

"Responsible drinking doesn't bother me… you have had three. But I must be honest and tell you that makes me a little uncomfortable if you're driving home."

He smiled reassuringly. "Trust me, if I felt I couldn't drive, I would take a rideshare. This is just casual drinking, and I'm savoring your company."

"I've had my fair share of experiences in the emergency room, and I've seen the consequences when people thought they were 'good to go.' I shared gently. "I trust you to make responsible choices." Then, in an effort to keep our conversation on track, I redirected the topic back to him.

He spoke of growing up in Los Angeles, playing football, the beaches, and party life. He moved with his family to Seattle at sixteen to be near his mother's family. He preferred the California climate to what he considered the drab bore of Seattle and jumped at the opportunity to move back and attend UCLA. I couldn't help but inject a bit of pride, proclaiming myself as a die-hard Husky girl showcasing my allegiance to the University of Washington.

He delved into his affection for his sister, emphasizing that she held the title of his best friend. Despite being two years behind him in school, she made the choice to follow in his footsteps and attend UCLA. I found their sibling bond quite admirable. As he continued, he shared a story about her falling in love and becoming engaged during her junior year of college.

However, he didn't mince words when he confessed to disliking her fiancé upon their first meeting at their parents' house during Christmas. With a devilish smile, he recounted their encounter, mentioning an argument that took place during a brief hike on Mount Si. In that heated moment, he had expressed the family's concerns about her decision, which infuriated her. She vented her frustrations, practically sprinting up the mountain.

She was disappointed that he hadn't stood as her defender, the reliable big brother who would take her side and stand up for her against their parents' disagreement. He added, "I love her, and I always want what's best for her. In my somewhat selfish way, I'm glad she's back home..." He let his words trail off, leaving me with lingering curiosity and unanswered questions. Curiosity gnawed at me, and I couldn't help but wonder why his sister was getting divorced. His cryptic storytelling left me hanging, yearning for more details.

What happened? Why was she getting divorced? Doesn't he know he can't tease a woman with just the fringes of a story? We need to know all the details.

Shifting gears, I asked, "How has your sister's experience affected your perspective on marriage?"

He paused briefly, then replied, "I think I have learned from my sister's experience. First, I get to know the woman, taking my time to understand her needs and gaining her trust. Then, when we metaphorically decide to enter a relationship, we have established known expectations of each other."

"Expectations?" I inquired, raising a brow. My subconscious resisted the idea of a relationship built solely on expectations.

He sensed my hesitation and clarified, "All relationships have expectations. Perhaps I used the wrong word, but we expect intimacy, honesty, and trust." I nodded, realizing that what we wanted from our partners was inherent and expected, even if the term "expectations" had initially thrown me off.

The conversation continued as he shared that his parents had been married for forty years, a near-impossible feat in today's society. When I inquired why, he explained that his parents always put their children first and emphasized the importance of family.

"My youth in California was quite eventful, to say the least. We were far from the perfect family. The LAPD would occasionally visit our home due to various incidents. It was during this time that I observed my younger sister, Ally, emulating my behavior and taking even greater social risks. I began to realize that things were spiraling out of control and that my actions were contributing to her behavior. I couldn't be a hypocrite, offering her advice while continuing down the same path myself. So, I made the conscious decision to get my act together. I stopped hosting wild drinking parties when my parents were away and put an end to any abusive behavior in my relationships."

His mention of a "history of abuse" sent a shockwave through me, triggering my deepest fears. My heart raced, and a chill of dread coursed through my veins. I couldn't ignore those words, "history of abuse," as my mind conjured up haunting images of past trauma. My voice quivered with trepidation as I confronted him, my words barely escaping my trembling lips, "So, you have a history of abuse?" My past had taught me to be vigilant and ready to flee at the first sign of danger, and I was prepared to walk away if his answer confirmed my worst suspicions. But despite the fear gripping me, I needed to hear his explanation.

As I met his gaze, it felt as though he could see the fear and apprehension welling up within me. At that moment, he offered his explanation, looking deeply into my soul as he spoke, "I was more of a jerk than abusive. You know, you get caught up in the trials of dating. Maybe someone likes you more than you like them, or vice versa. But it was a growing phase, a time of learning. We all go through those phases where we create memories we want to lock away forever."

His words, spoken with empathy and sincerity, provided some relief to my anxious soul. "Touché, my amour," I responded, appreciating his understanding. "I appreciate your honesty." With that, we moved on from the delicate topic, and I felt a growing sense of comfort in his presence and a glimmer of hope for the future.

I told myself we wouldn't delve too deeply into the conversation this evening, but why not be completely open? After all, I haven't completely shied away from meaningful dialogue. Just as I was about to speak, our server, Jacquelyn, miraculously appeared. I found it rather peculiar, considering they had assigned her to tables inside the restaurant. But then again, perhaps it was part of her extended service for the generous tip she had received. She seemed overly attentive to him, and who could blame her? After a few moments of chitchat, she returned inside. "That was odd," I commented to him.

He dismissed it as if it had never happened, shifting his focus back to me. "What's your favorite hobby?"

"Well, among my numerous hobbies, I was particularly passionate about cooking. It was something I had cherished since childhood. My mom wasn't exactly a culinary genius, so I took it upon myself to master the art of cooking. I even enrolled in a local culinary class. Little did I know that it would later serve as a powerful tool to help me reconnect with my mother, rebuild our strained relationship, and learn to trust her again. I can't say my father and brother were always thrilled about being guinea pigs for our culinary experiments, especially during my early days of flat cakes and burned steaks."

The conversation reaches a standstill. My pondering drifts away, delighting in the external calm. "Despite my previous assertion that we would sidestep deep conversations this evening for fear of being too intense, here's me in a few words. I take great pride in being a dedicated woman, placing the concerns of my man ahead of my own. I give my whole heart and essence to love. I refuse to be anyone's sleeping partner. I've been there, and I will not be repeating that experience."

He stood with his back against the railing, gently rocking his head. He grinned mischievously, leaving me wanting to know what he knew. "Everything you said resonates with the way I think. I was thinking of the beauty that radiates from within. It was the appreciation of a woman from the inside out. The beauty of her love was so strong that it would last through many tomorrows, no matter what the outside world looked like. I would love her forever."

Exhaustion washed over me as I battled sudden hot flashes. Just then, with almost scripted timing, a familiar voice broke through the haze. "We're about to close. Can I get you anything else tonight?" My heart raced with irritation. *Jacquelyn!* The very thought of her meddling made me clench my fists. I up before he could end the charade. "No, thank you. We're ready to leave. I'll take the bill, please."

As she approached with the bill, I noticed the way her eyes lingered on him, glimmering with an unmistakable desire. It irked me. With a feigned casualness, I reached out and gently but firmly tugged the bill from her grasp. I gave my amour a stern glare, "I've got this," I declared, a mix of defiance and desire to escape coloring my voice.

Sitting back, I let out a breath I didn't realize I had been holding. Despite the brief tumult, the evening had been beautiful, a rare moment of tranquility in my otherwise chaotic life. Now, with the bill settled and Jacquelyn's presence fading into the background,

I could finally reflect on the serene moments we had shared before her intrusion.

The underground garage was a symphony of urban nightlife, with cars weaving in and out of the shadows, their engines a constant low thrum. We stood next to my car, an oasis of stillness amid the flickering lights and transient noises. He spoke up, his voice finding a clear path through the din. "Hey, have a business trip to Vancouver, BC, next weekend. Would you be interested in joining me?" The proposal echoed subtly in the concrete expanse, a departure from the casual ease of our previous outings.

A flicker of anxiety stirred within me, not from the proposition but from the pace at which things were progressing. *This is new territory*, I noted internally, keeping my composure. "I'm not sure… I'll have to think about it," I said, my voice steady despite the constant motion around us.

Against the backdrop of the garage's ebb and flow, he stood relaxed, his suggestion hanging between us. "I would welcome the company. I have appointments on Thursday, but you could come on Friday. We could take the weekend to get to know each other better," he offered, his voice a calm counterpoint to my inner turmoil.

The possibility of a weekend away with him was both thrilling and intimidating. As the noise of the garage swirled around us, I took a breath, letting the cool air steady my nerves. *If I do this, it has to be on my terms.* With a measured resolve, I looked him in the eyes. "I'll consider going, but only if I book my own room. I need to be clear that I'm just agreeing to hang out, nothing more," I said, my voice firm, conveying the seriousness of my condition.

Ine," he responded with an assenting nod, his smile acknowledging my need for boundaries. "I'll handle the bookings for two rooms, and you can take care of your expenses when you arrive."

He moved away, his form merging with the intermittent dance of headlights and shadows. The thought of Vancouver was now tinged with both apprehension and intrigue, a delicate balance I would need to navigate in the days to come.

Chapter Ten

Nestled in the cozy warmth of Salty's, the overcast Seattle sky seemed to press against the windows, a contrasting backdrop to the lively spirit of our table. Our brunch was alive with the thrill of shared stories, especially after my recent evening out. This weekly ritual of gathering here felt even more necessary since Lexi had relocated, a change that rippled through our group, reminding us that life was in constant flux.

As we settled in, surrounded by the hum of convivial voices. From the iPad propped among the salt and pepper shakers, Lexi's face was alight with curiosity. "C'mon, Cyn, don't leave us hanging. How was your date?" she pressed, her voice cutting through the din of surrounding conversations.

Gina leaned in, her smile wide with anticipation. "Yes, do tell. There's a certain radiance about you today that's undeniable."

A warm blush crept into my cheeks as I recalled the night. "Well, he was quite impressive," I shared, my voice carrying a hint of the happiness I felt.

Lexi, shouting from the iPad, "What? Damn, you guys. What happened?"

Gina shouted to Lexi, "Can't you not see she isn't wearing any make-up?"

I tell them, "I was out late, but it wasn't because I was with a man. I spent the night in delirium, having enjoyed a wonderful evening. So, I thought, what the hell? No make-up today."

Gina prodded me, "Come on, tell us, what happened last night? I know something happened. You're the only one with an exciting life now."

"Excuse me," Lexi cried. "I have a fascinating life."

We all respond with sarcasm, "Whoooo."

Changing the subject to Lexi, I asked, "So, what's going on with Marcus?"

Lexi looked around suspiciously as though she was afraid to talk, leaning into the camera, her eyes darting left to right. Then, finally, she whispered, "You guys have to please... promise me you won't say anything about this to anyone." The smiles of joy on our faces faded. My heart pounded, fueled by thoughts of her pending revelation. I speculated the dread of another of Marcus' ill deeds. Lexi made another emphatic plea, "Promise me."

I'm afraid of keeping secrets. "Lex, we can't keep any more promises. For God's sake, tell us what's wrong." I watched Gina tensing, but she said nothing. Anxiety was written all over her face. However, I was certain she didn't want a recreation of our last meeting. Plus, we all needed to know what he had done to our friend.

"I know, Cyn, but you have to promise me, or I can't finish telling you." Gina shook her head no. I nudged her to just relax and let Lexi talk.

"Okay. We promise," we say in unison. Thinking complicity was the only way we were going to find out what was happening in her world.

"Promise?"

Gina snorted, "We promise, we promise. What is going on? Please tell me you're okay."

"Okay, hold on," Lexi teased, taking a sip of orange juice and then taking a deep breath. Our minds raced with speculation. All my friends and I wanted to know was what he had done to her. Why was she so afraid?

"Come on, Lexi," Courtnee begged. "What is going on? Is it good? Bad? Are you coming home? Do you need help with anything?"

"Shhh, hold on, guys. Give me a second." She jumped up from her chair.

We heard doors slamming in the background. I yelled, "Lex, what is going on over there?" No response. I thought, *Dammit, Lexi, what have you gotten yourself into?* We were all fearful Marcus had done something to her again, and she was too ashamed or afraid to tell. My heart raced as I speculated about all the dangers she might be exposed to from another of Marcus' tirades.

Courtnee's voice trembled. "I don't think this is good news. She's been gone for over three minutes." She pulled out her cell phone. "I'm calling the police. What's her address?"

I looked at Courtnee, perplexed. "Address?"

Courtnee said, "Great, we don't even know our friend's address. How stupid of us. Maybe the police can use cross-referencing, radar, or cell tower searches—whatever they do to find missing people."

Gina shouted, "But, of course, she'd be dead by then."

Courtnee countered, "Do you have a better idea?"

To our relief, Lexi suddenly plopped back into her chair, brushing away an errant strand of her normally perfect hair, something she hated.

Gina cried out, "Dammit, Lexi, where in the hell were you? You had us worried to death."

"I'm fine," she smiled.

I felt relieved, but my body was still trembling with fright.

I asked, "What's going on? We heard you screaming."

"There's a spider here."

"A spider!" we yelled together, relieved that the worst of our fears was unfounded.

"Um, Lexi, can I ask where you live?" Courtnee naively inquired, her innocence evident in her gentle tone.

"Okay, you guys ready?"

"YES!" we all exclaimed in unison, bursting with excitement and readiness.

"Give me a sec. I need to turn off the lights and close the blinds." The suspense was killing us.

Lexi returned to her nearly darkened dining room table. "Okay, guys," she turned on a flashlight. "I had a hell of a time finding this thing."

Gina exclaimed, "Dammit, Lexi, you had us sitting here thinking the worst, and you were searching for a flashlight?"

Unphased, she replied, "You can never find these things when you need them. Okay, are you guys ready for this?" Then, suddenly, she thrust her hand forward, the flashlight shining on a sparkling three-carat platinum engagement ring. A tidal wave of excitement and amazement replaced our concerns. "OH MY GOD!" we shouted with joy, our voices reverberating through the restaurant. Lexi was all smiles, bouncing happily in her chair, then nipping a bite of an apple.

Gina yelled, "You bitch. You scared the shit out of us. How could you do that?"

"I know. It was fun, huh?"

Relieved, we applauded her mastery of suspense and were delighted over the ring.

"That's so beautiful," we cooed like a bunch of hens over Lexi's sparkle. Calmed, our demeanor changed to inquirings about wedding dates. I was confident we were all subconsciously wondering which of us would be the maid of honor.

Rubbing her hands together deviously, Lexi said, "Okay, now, let's talk about Cyn's man! I'm happy for you, girl. Have you met Hector?"

I yelled, "Don't change the subject. Tell us everything. How did it happen? When did it happen?"

She replied, "I'll tell you later," then asked again, "Did Gloria meet Hector?"

"NO! Oh my god, Lexi, how about—"

"Please," she said, rolling her eyes. Hector was a steganography, amongst other words, we had created in high school. When we wanted to talk about sex, we coined words for private parts. Hence, we had come up with pseudo-names: Hector for penis, Gloria for vagina, Harvey for guys who couldn't keep their hands to themselves, Albert Banner for anal sex, Oliver for oral sex, and Benson for guys who were just total idiots. I don't believe any of us had or would admit to having met Albert Banner, though, from my experience, guys would ask for it.

Lexi wasn't letting up, clapping her hands to command attention, asking, "Cyn! What are you saving it for? When the time comes, you'll have to force that thang open with a pry bar or something." Her voice screeched, "Urrrk…" as she imitated a prying motion, "That thang is," slamming her hand on the table, "tight!"

I responded, unamused, "Lexi, that is so unladylike."

Gina turned her head, frowning. "Ladylike? Where in the hell did you get that word?" She mimicked an English accent, lifting her champagne flute into the air with her baby finger extended. "Today, ladies... we are speaking of Cyn's tightly closed Gloria, some would call it a long-abandoned cavern, as we enjoy our delicious crumpets and tea. Afterward, I suggest we sally over and have a sit with the Queen?" The three of them erupted in self-indulgent laughter. What the hell. I decided to tell them everything. I spoke fast, not allowing for interruptions, holding up a halting finger each time anyone tried to interrupt me.

"I'm talking about discretion. I met a nice man. I almost lost said nice man because of some internal personal demons unleashed by two of my combative friends. After our conversation concerning how to reconnect with said gentleman, I went looking for him. We reconnected, and I now have him in my life. We had dinner at a beautifully charming restaurant in downtown Bellevue. He tipped our waitress a hundred dollars—"

"A what?" Lexi tried to interject. "I—"

"Quiet."

But there was no shutting Lexi out, even from her iPad. "Did you say a hundred dollars tip? I'd interrupt, too," she stated, her presence felt as strongly as if she were there in person.

Huffing with annoyance, I continued, "As I was saying, she kept appearing at the most inopportune moments, especially when we were about to kiss on the patio," Courtnee raised a finger. I didn't allow it. "I'm speaking. You wanted details, and I'm sharing them. Two things about him concerned me: One, there was a subtle flirtation about him that kind of irked me. I swear—but I'm uncertain—I saw him slip a note to the waitress when he handed her the tip. I said nothing because I was unsure, but a torn piece of paper was on the table.

Lexi asked, "Why speculate? Why wouldn't he talk to somebody else if you're making him think you're unavailable? That man's engine is running, vroom, vroom, and you're," she imitated a car jerking, "Urk. Urk."

"He was on a date with me, Lex." I took a deep breath, half agreeing that she wasn't wrong, but that's where it got confusing. I wasn't ready to jump into bed just for sex. But I wanted to be loved so badly that my body begged for the touch of a man's hand caressing me, peeling away my clothes button by button. Lexi disrupted my attention back to the group with her cynicism.

"Maybe you should end your love affair with Bobby Brown. Hmmm?" Lexi smiled with her eyes.

"God, Lex," I responded, my face turning red, thinking someone might have overheard her. I was pretty sure everyone knew that was our pseudonym for a dildo. We called them our always-ready-boyfriends, built to last, easy to put away without complications.

Lexi continued with her jibes, "I'm just saying, you've been single for what, three, two years? Tell us you don't have an empty packet of Costco-size batteries in your nightstand." Our rapturous laughter echoed across the restaurant, audible to everyone present. I shared with them his invitation to meet in Vancouver next weekend.

Courtnee asked, "Are you going to go? I think it would be nice."

I paused, giving the question more thought. "I'm not sure. I have work. The weekends are the only time I have for myself."

Gina asked, "You're not sure? What are you afraid of, Cyn? Why are you making things so difficult for yourself? It's just another date. Go or don't go. Stop overthinking it."

My always unfiltered friend Lexi didn't hold back, "Yeah, Cyn, what are you afraid of? We already agreed that thing is tight. Do you check to see if it's still there?" Dear God, Lexi. Please don't be so blunt. Perhaps my friends were right. I had made it far more complicated than necessary.

I informed them that I would agree to go, but on the condition that we have separate rooms. "Stop being a prude," Lexi remarked, her voice dripping with challenge as she seductively rolled her tongue over her spoon. There was no winning with this crowd.

I gave up. We discussed Lexi and Marcus further. She assured us that everything was great, mentioning their plans to marry before spring training next year. Brunch ended on a high note, and I didn't even have to drive Gina and Courtnee home.

Chapter Eleven

On Friday morning, work brought an unexpected surprise: a bouquet of roses arrived at my desk, their petals a vivid crimson, except for the two pristine whites nestled in the center. Their delicate fragrance and the thoughtful placement of the whites among the reds were clear signatures of Mr. Romantic's touch. Convinced they were an invitation to our Vancouver plans, I succumbed to the charm and phoned him in the evening, agreeing to our previously set terms. Feeling drained from the day's efforts, I declined a Friday departure, promising to arrive by 8:30 on Saturday morning.

Back at home, in the quiet of my bedroom, the vibrant roses seemed a world away. My bedside table drawer was slightly open, revealing a temptation I was all too familiar with. The stirring within me grew, but with a deep breath, I considered calling it all off — not just the night's potential escapade but the whole venture with him. Was it fair to continue this dance if I harbored doubts? My hand hovered over the drawer, contemplating.

With a sigh, I pushed the drawer shut, turning away from the solace it offered. The room remained dimly lit, a soft lamp casting shadows that danced gently across the walls. I needed to rest, to be fresh for whatever tomorrow would bring. The roses, especially the two whites, symbolized a potential for something pure amidst the passion. "Goodnight, Mr. Romantic," I whispered, allowing myself a moment to bask in the bittersweet hope they represented before slipping into the refuge of sleep.

I stepped into The Grand Sovereign Hotel at 7:50 AM, the overcast sky outside doing little to dim the unexpected elegance of the lobby. After checking into my room, a haven of luxury, I sent a message to him confirming my arrival. His reply suggested a casual tempo for our meeting, *"Great, that'll give me a chance to get in a quick jog. I'll meet you at 10:30 in the lobby."*

In the grand lobby, the atmosphere was alive with activity as a constant stream of guests flowed in and out. The space was vast and resplendent, adorned with gleaming marble floors, towering pillars, and intricate chandeliers hanging from the lofty ceilings. Elegant furnishings, including plush sofas and ornate tables, provided seating areas where patrons congregated, chatting animatedly or consulting staff. The air was filled with the soft murmur of conversations, punctuated by the occasional sound of luggage wheels rolling across the polished surface. Despite the hustle and bustle, an air of sophistication and refinement permeated the space, elevating every interaction within its grand confines.

Amidst the refined surroundings, a petite blonde woman caught my eye—a figure of elegance and confidence. She was impeccably dressed, each detail carefully chosen, and she moved with an air of self-assuredness and control that commanded attention. Our eyes connected, and in that brief moment, a chilling feeling stirred within me.

Her penetrating stare felt like a cold premonition on this morning with a mixture of sun and clouds. It was a wordless exchange that left me shaken, a mystery that seemed to herald more than just a chance sighting. As she disappeared from view, I was left with an uneasy sense of foreboding, questioning whether her presence was a bad omen.

His arrival broke through the lingering unease from moments ago, his smile a familiar comfort. "Good morning. How was the drive up?" he inquired, grounding me in the here and now.

"Quite peaceful, thank you," I found myself replying, appreciating the normalcy of the question.

"I thought we'd start the day with breakfast here," he said. "I checked earlier, and they've really outdone themselves with the spread today."

"That sounds perfect," I responded, relieved and grateful for the thoughtfulness behind his planning. Together, we headed towards the dining area, the prospect of breakfast offering a comforting bridge away from the shadows of the morning and towards the promise of a day together.

After a satisfying breakfast, he suggested we take a leisurely stroll to English Bay. As we stepped outside, the cool morning air greeted us, the sun veiled behind clouds. With each step along the path to the bay, I felt the tension melting away, replaced by a sense of ease in his company. As we walked the path, our conversation flowed. My inquiries led him to ask more about me and my past.

I hadn't intended to unpack my tenuous relationship history so soon, but the ease and trust I felt in this man's company beckoned the truth. To let him in, I realized I needed to lift the veil on my soul's hidden alcoves. I recounted my beginning with Conor, how he seemed the epitome of all I desired—fun, adventurous, and bright.

My love for his mind was instant; his passion for the outdoors, from Puget Sound adventures to impulsive canoeing trips, was infectious.

But our final year in med school marked an unforeseen shift. It was as though someone had snuck into our shared life and flipped a light switch, plunging us into darkness. Intimacy with Conor faded, leaving a hollow friendship in its wake. I turned the lens on myself, searching for reasons behind his waning desire. His attentiveness remained, but it had transformed into the care one would offer a friend or a cherished pet. I even pondered if he might be hiding his true sexuality from me. Our conversations were full, yet when it came to sharing his emotions, he would steer us back to his comfort zone—the outdoors.

The weight of my solitary emotional confinement grew daily until I could bear it no more. I remember confronting the truth like it was yesterday, seated on the deck wrapped in my robe against the morning chill, contemplating the impending heartache. As I absorbed the serenity around us, I braced myself to voice the words that had been crowding my thoughts. My resolve was firm.I knew our paths needed to part.

The relationship had crumbled, and I believed that maintaining a friendship from a distance, unburdened by the weight of romance, might foster an amicable relationship. The aroma of my coffee offered a small comfort on that cold, misty morning. Conor sat perched on the deck railing, his hands wrapped around his coffee mug, lost in contemplation of the fog-shrouded trees.

The dread of bidding him farewell weighed heavily on me; I didn't want to inflict more pain than necessary. Taking a deep breath, I prepared to speak. *Conor, we need to talk. It's important for you to know...* But as I gathered my courage, he anticipated my words and knelt abruptly, a rush of dread flooding through me. "No, please, don't—" I started, my voice a mix of fear and pleading.

"Cynthya, please," his voice was stern, a stark contrast to the detachment in his eyes. "Let me say this. It's important. Very important to me. I need you to understand how much I care about you. But I have to be honest." Ice coursed through my veins, a silent plea echoing within: *Please don't propose. This is not the time.* Yet, the words that followed struck me with an unforeseen cruelty, "This may come out wrong, but trust me, I don't say it to hurt you. But... I really do not love you. I have never loved you." Each syllable was a barb, lacing my heart with an icy sting. *I have never loved you, and* the phrase resonated in a relentless loop. "Things... We had some fun, and we grew accustomed to being around each other. But honesty is the only path I can walk now. I'm sorry." His voice, devoid of warmth, seemed to come from afar. The plan I had crafted to gently disentangle our lives was now in shambles. His emotional withdrawal was complete, his confession leaving no room for the delicate diplomacy I had hoped for. He stood, his movements robotic, informing me that he had been secretly preparing his departure for a week, timing it to avoid any upheaval in my academic pursuits.

"Conor? I don't understand," I managed to utter, my voice a fragile thread amidst the storm of my emotions.

"Cynthya, you've been a delightful companion," he continued, the word 'companion' reverberating with a hollowness that expanded the void between us.

"Companion!" The term sparked a flare of indignation within me. All this time, to him, I was nothing more than a pleasant fixture, a mere accessory to his adventures. I couldn't conceal the emptiness his casual dismissal conjured within me. "You're just walking away from everything—our life, your studies, us—just like that?"

"I had wanted to be honest with you from the beginning, to express how I truly felt. But things started off well; a glimmer of hope emerged, and I thought maybe, just maybe, with time... I might develop genuine feelings for you. I gave it my all, sincerely trying until I reached a point where I despised myself for even attempting to force those emotions.

I'm not gay, if that's what you're wondering. We're not all built for the fantasy world of love. The things you find important in life are dreadful to me. You have frequently commented on our sex life impolitely. I am not a creature devoted to my primal needs; I don't need words of affirmation, nor do I desire a champion to cheer me on." He pressed his lips together, then said, "I don't find you stimulating enough to try." His gaze shifted towards the trees. I was aghast. He continued, "Out there in the world is where I belong."

Tears streamed down my face, their flow resembling a relentless river, as a tumultuous mix of emotions ravaged my heart. Memories of times before this moment flooded my mind, a painful reminder of the love and devotion I had poured into this relationship, only to discover that he never desired me in return.

His words struck like a dagger: I was nothing more than a convenient companion, a knock-around gal chosen for the ease of early morning adventures of hiking, camping, canoeing—whatever suited his whims. We lived together, not out of love but for the sake of convenience. The weight of this realization pressed upon me, shattering the illusion I had clung to. The tears continued to flow, an outpouring of sorrow and acceptance.

"I had wanted to tell you for over a year—"

"A year!"

"However, every time we had a disagreement, and I saw tears in your eyes, I was uncomfortable, preferring to do all I could to make you smile again."

He paused, his gaze fixated on me with an expression that pleaded like a puppy dog. I waited for him to finish, seeing the discomfort etched on his face. The conversation took an even more serious turn when he disclosed his intention to leave med school. Damn, am I that repulsive? The thought that he felt the need to abandon his intended profession and leave town because of me was devastating.

"So you're leaving? Just like that? What about finishing the program and preparing for residency?" I asked, my voice tinged with bewilderment.

He took a deep breath, rolling his eyes as he shook his head. "You don't understand, do you? I'm not going into residency. I've hated my li—"

"But you're brilliant," I interjected, the shock of his confession momentarily overshadowing his previous words. At that moment, I couldn't resist falling back into my role as Suzy—the fixer, the one who believed she could coax him, champion him, and fight for him to remain tied to a vocation at which he excelled. He had sailed through his exams with ease, and I had seen so much potential and goodness within him.

However, I made a fatal mistake by glorifying his purpose of practicing medicine based on the allure of money and future material possessions once he became a full-fledged doctor.

He gazed at me, his expression devoid of emotions. He began speaking, his words hitting me with the chill of hard truth. "Cynthya, you truly are naive. You don't know me at all, do you?" He shook his head, a hint of pity flashing in his eyes. "You're so consumed with your own purpose, trying to make things work and accommodate, that you haven't taken the time to understand mine."

He let out a sigh, his voice laden with frustration. "You haven't acknowledged how I feel about you or the medical profession. I don't want to parade around in a white smock, walking sterile hospital hallways. I have enough knowledge to be effective— actually, damn good—and I don't need a degree or a wall to hang it on. I'd feel far better in Haiti, Africa, or some tropical rainforest, helping people without expecting anything in return."

Speechless, I watched as he walked away, his departure leaving me stunned. There were no parting glances, no lingering goodbyes. He simply walked off, never looking back. I remained seated, deflated and hollow.

In the distance, the engine of his Jeep roared to life, its sound reverberating in the still air. As he drove off, the tires crunched the gravel beneath them. And just like that, he vanished from my life as if he had been wiped away, leaving behind an empty space where he used to be. The memories we shared, the moments we cherished, seemed to dissolve into nothingness, as if he had never existed in my world.

Days turned into weeks and weeks into months, but I never saw or heard from him again. He became a shadow, a ghost from my past. Our paths had diverged, and I was left to rebuild, forever imprinted by the bittersweet mark he left on my heart.

It surprised me how easily I was spilling my life story to this man, my words flowing with an unexpected ease. A part of me wanted to stop, to hold back the tide of confessions, but the words just kept coming. Since Conor, I had shied away from dating. Friends tried to set me up, but their choices often seemed driven by loneliness and desire, seeking fleeting satisfaction rather than meaningful connection. After a string of letdowns, my trust in potential partners began to erode. I became wary and cautious about opening up to the procession of transient individuals driven by their egos.

We continued our walk in silence, and with each step, doubt gnawed at me. *Have I said too much? Am I pushing him away?* The fear that my candor might repel him was unsettling, and yet I found myself wanting to know his history, too. Breaking the silence, I asked about his past relationships. But he remained quiet, leaving a gap that felt like an abyss between us.

Finally, he spoke. "Anastasia was—is—her name. We had a volatile, on-again, off-again relationship. It was like a campfire, intense when fueled but quickly burning out. We'd be engulfed for three months, madly in love, until the fire dulled and disputes drove us apart. Then, after a month or two of silence, she'd reappear, reigniting the cycle all over again."

A cold chill ran down my spine as I looked at his face. There was a calmness about him as if he longed for a relationship that existed only in his mind. Doubts and insecurities flooded my thoughts, making me question whether I was misinterpreting his demeanor. Still, I couldn't help but ask defensively, "So where is she now? Where does she fit into your life?"

The image of a blonde woman leaving the lobby flashed in my mind, a memory that had inexplicably stuck with me. My curiosity grew, urging me to seek answers. However, he didn't provide a direct response, leaving me even more perplexed. Determined to understand his intentions, I changed my approach and inquired, "Where do you stand in terms of reigniting the flames of your past?"

The question hung in the air, awaiting his reply. I hoped for honesty and clarity, but deep down, I feared the potential revelations that awaited me.

He chuckled, telling me it had been six months since they were last together.

"So, is Anastasia completely out of your life, or are you two just taking a more extended hiatus? The last thing I want is to find myself caught between the two of you, fueling an inferno that should have died down," I said, my voice tinged with a mix of curiosity and concern.

He took a moment, exhaling as if deep in thought, before offering a brief description of her. Shoulder-length blonde hair, blue eyes, petite, standing at around five-four. As he spoke, a faint hum resonated in my mind, a subtle warning urging me to proceed with caution, to distance myself from any potential complications. Yet, I resisted the impulse to flee. Perhaps my mind was simply overreacting, drawing unnecessary conclusions.

The mention of Conor stirred up a wave of melancholy within me, a stark reminder of what I once mistook for love. Yet, I urged myself not to let past experiences cloud my judgment now. As I had laid bare my own history to him, fairness dictated that I offer the same courtesy and respect, allowing him the space to reveal his own.

His voice carried a blend of determination and sincerity as he met my gaze with a mix of sternness and innocence. "Listen," he began, his words laced with conviction, "If I had any intention of rekindling things with her, I wouldn't be here, pursuing a connection with you. You deserve someone who can offer you more, and that's what I want to be for you. Anastasia and I are unequivocally over. I can assure you of that. In fact, she has already moved on, starting a new chapter of her life in London with someone else."

"Someone else?"

"Yes, we had a casual conversation."

"Do you love her?" I challenged, looking him straight in the eyes.

He hesitated, his mind seemingly grappling with the complexities of his emotions and thoughts. "Hmm," he murmured, acknowledging the weight of my question. "That's a valid inquiry, and I want to be completely honest with you." As he mentioned her name, I noticed a flicker of nostalgia in his eyes, as if his mind wandered to a different time and place. London, perhaps? Six months may not seem like a significant period, considering the context of their past relationship.

The cold air embraced me, and I couldn't help but shiver, sensing the lingering tension between them. At that moment, I questioned if the door had truly been closed between them. The silence stretched on, each passing second feeling like an eternity.

Determined, I repeated my question, my arms tightly folded across my chest. Though I pretended it was for warmth, deep down, I knew it was a subconscious act of self-protection. I was prepared to face the truth, understanding that a lie would be unforgivable. I needed the raw facts to leave no room for ambiguity. And yet, he didn't provide an immediate response.

"No."

"No? Are you absolutely certain about that?" I pressed, my tone tinged with skepticism. "It seemed like you needed some time to ponder your answer. It doesn't quite reassure me."

"I never expected the question to come up, and I apologize if my hesitation made you doubt my sincerity," he responded, his voice tinged with frustration. "I want to assure you that I do not love Anastasia. Our relationship was complex, with its ups and downs. But that is all in the past now. I am here with you, a wonderful and dedicated woman whom I deeply admire. My intention is to get to know you on a deeper level, to understand your heart, mind, and soul. And I will show you my love every day, not just through words but through actions."

As we continued our walk in silence, I couldn't help but wonder if I had delved too deeply into his past, inviting him to revisit old wounds. Perhaps I had done the same for myself by bringing up Conor. It was a revelation to realize how blind I had been in that relationship and the knowledge that he had lost interest long before I did sting my heart.

The conversation left me feeling slightly disenchanted and emotionally drained. When we returned to the hotel, I requested to skip lunch. He looked at me with concern and asked, "Are you upset?"

"No." Thinking to myself, *I'm afraid. I need to lie down and collect my thoughts.* The whole of us sharing our past relationships was unsettling. We exit the elevators to our floor. He looks at me innocently, asking, "Are you sure you're okay?"

I hesitated for a moment, my emotions swirling in a state of confusion. With a forced smile, I replied, "I'm fine. I just need some time to myself. I'll see you for dinner." My words lacked conviction, and deep down, I knew that I wasn't truly fine. However, I needed space to process my thoughts and feelings before engaging in further conversation. With that, I turned and walked away, seeking solace in the solitude of my own thoughts.

Seeking comfort within the confines of my room, my mind became a battleground of swirling thoughts and doubts. The prospect of giving my heart and investing emotionally, only to witness the relationship fizzle out, loomed over me. His description of a tumultuous past romance played on my mind like a never-ending rollercoaster.

After years of embracing my independence, the idea of relinquishing it felt overwhelming. Could I find a way to safeguard my heart, keeping it locked away from potential hurt? I urged myself to let go and find some semblance of relaxation amidst the chaos of my thoughts.

Chapter Twelve

We enjoyed dinner on the rooftop at the Sandbar. As the day surrendered to evening, the sky remained cloaked in clouds while a gentle wind-kissed breeze whispered through the canal, offering a slight chill. I wrapped the wool blanket kindly offered by Ryan around my shoulders. It was clear that my amour and Ryan shared a friendly bond.

Drinks and appetizers appeared before us, unbidden — a gesture some might appreciate as thoughtful service, yet it left me feeling oddly sidelined, denied the option of choice as if my preferences were already known and accounted for from previous visits.

Internally, I chided myself for being overly critical, yet I couldn't silence the whispers of jealousy, imagining him here with other women. What did Ryan make of my presence? This silent query seemed to cast an unspoken shadow over the evening. Despite my efforts to steer my thoughts elsewhere, a sense of detachment crept in. To dispel it, I cleared my throat and asked with an edge, "So you two have known each other for a long time?"

Ryan's smile was warm. "Yes," he confirmed, glancing at my amour. "What? About five? Six years?" The exchange did little to quell the brewing sense of exclusivity I craved. As another cold breeze danced through the canal, I tightened my grasp on the blanket, a futile attempt to shield my burgeoning insecurity.

Inhaling deeply, I summoned the courage to voice the question that lingered in the back of my mind, "So... you and Anastasia used to come here often, didn't you?" The accusing words tumbled out, betraying my inner conflict. The acknowledgment that Anastasia still haunted my thoughts brought a wave of frustration. Mentally, I urged myself to release the grip of her spectral presence from our evening.

His response came swiftly, disassociating this place from any past romantic encounters. He assured me that he and Anastasia had never dined there together. This venue was precious to him for other reasons — a haven for him and his friends to escape the mundanity of their routines. He shared this space with me now, hoping I would find the same solace he did. His praise of Ryan, described as the best waiter he'd known, brushed away some of my initial concerns, offering a flicker of comfort.

Choosing to push past the jealous inklings, I resolved to be fully present, to cherish the company of the man beside me. As the evening unfolded, our laughter mingled with the night's cool embrace, and we found solace near the outdoor fireplace. The proximity, the shared warmth, and the fire's hypnotic dance seemed to draw us closer, an unspoken connection sparking in the shared silence.

Our return to the hotel was ensconced in a contemplative silence. The quiet in the car was a stark contrast to the cacophony of emotions swirling within me. I found myself aching for the faintest touch, a small reassurance that the distance I felt was just a figment of my imagination. But as the city lights streaked by, he remained lost in thought, his gaze locked on the world outside — a clear reflection, perhaps, of my own tangled emotions mirrored back at me.

There was an undeniable tension — a chasm that seemed to widen with every mile that passed. I couldn't shake off the feeling that my earlier guardedness at the restaurant, my almost territorial questions, might have pushed him into retreat. Or maybe, as I feared, he was coming to the realization that I was too much of a challenge, that my emotional barricades were too daunting for someone seeking an easy rapport.

When the Uber finally halted at our hotel, the silence that enveloped us was heavy, with the things left unsaid. The air between us was charged with the weight of our earlier conversations, and I sensed that he, too, was wrestling with the complexities of our nascent connection. Was it my defensiveness that cast this pall over us, or was it his own hesitation in the face of my intricate layers? The answer hung unsaid as we stepped out into the cool night, each lost in our own maze of thoughts.

Once on our floor, we lingered outside the elevator, the quiet hum of the hotel around us. My pulse raced with the anticipation of a kiss, an unspoken longing painted across the space between us. Instead, he pulled me into an embrace, his voice a soft murmur against my ear, "Thank you for the evening."

The warmth of his hand lingered with a gentle squeeze before he withdrew to his room. I was left pondering if my defensive posture at dinner had frustrated him or if he found my constant references to Anastasia too burdensome. Her shadow seemed to cling to my memories, an unwelcome echo of my jealousy and insecurities. I couldn't escape the feeling that I was the one holding back, that perhaps I was not ready to move past the protective walls built over two long years.

As the clock edged toward midnight, my restlessness grew. Was he lying awake as well, tormented by the same tension? Or had my erratic behavior already pushed him to resignation? My body felt electric, alive with a restless pulse that rendered sleep an impossibility. Frustration mounted as minutes ticked by fruitlessly. I lay on my side, the clock's glow the only light in the room, marking the passage of a seemingly endless half-hour.

Finally, I surrendered to the night's unrest. "Enough, Cyn," I whispered to the shadows, determination setting in. I called room service, ordering a bottle of champagne and two crystal glasses—my resolve crystallizing with the order.

The shower's cascade offered a momentary escape, but the knock on the door came all too soon. Wrapped hastily in a towel, with another twisted atop my head, I answered. The exchange was awkward, my attempt at modesty a dance of slipping fabric. The attendant's presence lingered just a moment too long, his smile a tad too familiar. I closed the door with a soft click of finality.

Adorned now in a makeshift toga, the fabric of the bedsheet transformed, I felt empowered. My friends would have cheered for this daring version of myself. Tonight, I was taking control, stepping out into the hallway with champagne in hand, my heart thudding with audacious intent. His door stood before me, my knocks hesitant at first, then growing bolder. Silence answered. A flicker of doubt crept in—had I hesitated too long? But then the door swung open, revealing him in sleep-tousled disarray, his bare chest and broad shoulders a vision that quickened my breath. I strode past him into the room, the scent of his skin enveloping me, a heady blend of man and mystery.

"Shh, no words. Just come and sit," I commanded, the cork freed from the bottle with a celebratory pop. Champagne fizzed, dampening my makeshift garb in a playful tease. I poured for us both, the ice from my glass chilling my lips as I offered him a silent toast.

I allowed it to spill over me celebration style, strategically wetting my toga. I poured him a glass and filled mine with ice. His eyes are as wide as the server that saw my wet hair, speechless. I walked to the heater, my toga wrapped tight around my ass. I turned the heater to its highest setting. He nervously cleared his throat, holding the champagne flute, still uncertain what was happening.

The heat gradually filled the room, creating a cocoon of warmth around us. I faced him, an ice chip held between my lips, my words deliberate and soft, "You've been very patient, kind." My eyebrow arched seductively as I continued, "And considerate. Perhaps I overanalyzed our earlier conversation. I might have come across as a bore—a pain, though not in the literal sense. But the truth is, I've yearned for closeness with you throughout the evening. The array of emotions I've felt since our meeting has been overwhelming, and I've struggled to just let go and revel in the pleasure of your company. Please, enjoy your champagne."

He took a sip, his expression a perfect balance of arousal and confusion. His hair was tousled, adding to the allure, and his eyes were filled with silent questions that seemed to tug at the air around us.

"I have two conditions before we have sex. Don't worry, they're easy. First, I give my body, but my heart comes with it. However, tonight, I'm making my one and only exception. I'm not afraid of intimacy. I don't want the games men believe necessary to have sex.

"Therefore, if sex is your purpose, this will be the sole opportunity that you can have my body unconditionally. Second, please understand that this is the most important condition. I ask that you be honest enough to tell me the truth about your desires." He utters to speak. I put my fingers to his lips to quiet him. "No. I don't want an answer at this moment. Tonight is all about rule number one. You need to think deeply before you can answer number two."

"Can I say something?"

"No, please don't." I'm so far outside my comfort zone that it's invigoratingly erotic. "Make love to me, then share your thoughts with me another time. Tonight is my idea, so I won't be hurt, and you need not feel an obligation to lie to me." I reach for his hand, leading him to the bed. Pushing him down. I feel the tenderness and power of his kiss. His arms are strong, and his embrace awakens long lost longings to feel the power of being in a man's embrace.

The room was getting hotter. Sweat beaded on his forehead. He requested maybe we should turn on the air conditioning. "No. I asserted softly, kissing his ear, gently blowing and nibbling his lobe. I felt emboldened, like an actress taking center stage.

Tonight, I was the architect of my own narrative, one where caution was cast aside in favor of the impulsive and the genuine. I'm in an area of sexual freedom, exploring my fantasies, enjoying my craving to make love shamelessly without fear of rejection by my partner's lackluster engagement. I moved down to his smooth chest, kissing his pecks, then rolling my tongue over his nipples while sliding my hand down his thigh. His Hector was rock-hard. I have longed for a man to love me, mind, soul, and body. I don't know what I will get, but I'll not allow that to stop my pursuit. His arms wrapped around me tightly. I stopped his wandering hand tug on my toga with a firm yet gentle touch.

I boldly asserted myself, pushing him onto his back, taking a firm but gentle grasp of his Hector, and gliding my hands up and down. I had him just where I wanted him as I tugged on his tip. I moaned my delight as I glided the whole of his rod into me, purring my thrills of having him break the forbidden seal of my Gloria. Beads of sweat streaked down my cleavage. He gently tugs my hair, his voice a whisper, "Babe, wait, please stop."

Finally, I allowed him to peel away my cloth. The room had become a sauna. It's a heavy, languid heat, the kind that makes you move slowly and speak softly as if conserving energy is suddenly paramount. Every slight shift brings a new wave of warmth, reminding me of my overzealous twist of the dial. I closed my eyes, feeling the exhilaration as I took every throbbing inch of him. I gasped as he drove the final inches of his cock inside of me. I start a slow gyration, pushing against his Hector.

I exhaled deeply, relishing the sensation of his hands, warm as the surrounding air, moving down my back, now slick with perspiration. The pressure of his touch on my heated skin created a tapestry of sensations, with each movement weaving a pattern of comfort and intimacy. The merging of our warmth, his hands on my damp back, felt like a dance of flames, intensifying the already sweltering atmosphere between us. He rolled me over to be on top.

As I gazed upward, a veil of innocence in my eyes, I found myself entranced by the palpable hunger that danced in his gaze. The intensity of his stare was a magnetic force, drawing me deeper into the moment. His eyes, alight with a raw, unspoken desire, held a depth that spoke volumes, revealing a yearning that echoed my own. In that instant, under the weight of his fervent look, I felt an exhilarating mix of vulnerability and connection.

I matched his rhythm, raising my hips to capture every inch of his thrust, exhilarating my brain. His kiss was a perfect blend of passion and sweetness. It enveloped me in a warmth that seemed to radiate from his very being. His lips moved against mine with a fervor that spoke of deep longing, yet there was a tenderness in his touch that softened the intensity, weaving a delicate balance between ardor and affection. I tried to starve away my orgasm. *No, no, no.* I felt his body tense. I was nearly there, begging, clawing his back as I shrilled, "Hard! Harder! Please give it to me."

I moaned from his intense embrace as I felt the warmth of his eruption. The heat in the room is stifling. I wrap my wet arms around his sweat-drenched body, pulling him close to me to feel his heart pounding. My climax was so powerful my body convulsed. I wasn't ready for him to pull out," Please," I whispered in a soft, pleading tone, the word barely escaping as a breathy mewl, "Don't take it away from me."

My voice carried a fragile urgency, a delicate appeal that hung in the air between us, echoing the depth of my need. The room, reminiscent of a sauna in its heated aftermath, bore witness to our earlier intensity. In this space, the echoes of our desires lingered, leaving us in a state of contented exhaustion, enveloped by the residual warmth of fulfilled passions.

He rose and walked with a sense of newfound tranquility to the sliding door leading to the deck. Gently, he slid it open, allowing the cool night air to rush into the room, a welcome contrast to the lingering warmth of our spent passions. The once stifling heat of the room began to ebb away, gradually replaced by a refreshing chill that seemed to cleanse the air.

As he stood there, a brief silhouette against the night sky, the distant sound of a siren pierced the tranquility of our cocoon. The sound, distant and fleeting, wove through the calm night, reminding us of the world that lay beyond our secluded space. But even the siren's cry faded quickly, swallowed by the serenity of the evening, leaving nothing but the peaceful quietude that enveloped us.

The world outside felt distant, almost unreal, as the siren's wail dwindled into nothingness, restoring the tranquility that had enveloped us. In our secluded haven, everything seemed to stand still, the night air a soothing balm to the intensity that had just passed.

Clutching the top sheet from the bed, I wrapped it around myself, fashioning a makeshift shawl that lightly adhered to my still-damp skin. Stepping onto the deck, I was greeted by the cool, salty breeze of the ocean, which tenderly caressed my face. Beyond the railing, the city lights twinkled in the distance, their luminance diffused by a misty haze that lent an almost mystical quality to the night.

I closed my eyes, immersing myself in the night's profound stillness, the coolness of the air enveloping me in its gentle embrace. The light moisture in the air soothed my body, a refreshing contrast to the lingering warmth from our moments of intense pleasure. I breathed deeply, the night air filled with the subtle, salty tang of the sea, and let the tranquility of the moment wash over me, a serene counterpoint to the passionate energy that had only moments ago engulfed us. Alone on the deck, I felt a deep connection to the expansive, tranquil world outside.

Minutes later, I was embraced by the strength of my amour's arms wrapping around me from behind. As I leaned back into his chest, I felt engulfed in a comforting security. His head rested gently against my hair, and his warm breath on my neck elicited a sense of serene bliss. His hug, blending strength and tenderness, washed over me, immersing me in a profound wave of contentment and tranquility.

I twisted around, throwing my arms around his neck, and our kiss transformed from tender to intense, like reigniting a smoldering fire. The gentle beginnings quickly gave way to a surge of passion, our lips moving in a fervent dance that rekindled the earlier blaze of desire.

My desires and intentions are deliberate. I was going to suck him until he came into my mouth. I hummed, feeling the firmness of his dick in my mouth, stroking and sucking. He jerks each time I suck hard on the tip. I gripped him and moved my head back and forth, creating a suction that ignited him. Swallowing his cum was a fresh experience for me.

It was a novel experience for me, being so unrestrained in making love. Now, I lay there, resting my head on his chest in the aftermath of our fervent encounter. He tenderly stroked my hair, and in these moments of shared silence, everything felt just right. A fresh gust of air swept through the open balcony door, bringing with it the coolness of the night. I closed my eyes, feeling my heart beat with a joy that was new and exhilarating.

The intensity of our passions had left the bedsheets drenched, a testament to the fervor of our connection, but they were too damp and uncomfortable for rest. I fashioned the sheet into a toga once again. My amour slipped into his PJs, and I led the way to my room, where the air was refreshingly cool. We wrapped ourselves in the cozy blankets, the day's exhaustion slowly dissipating. As I drifted into sleep, cocooned in his warm embrace, I felt a sense of peace and fulfillment that was both profound and comforting.

Chapter Thirteen

Waking up in his arms, a sudden and urgent realization hit me: I hadn't been on birth control in over two years. The stark contrast between our night of uninhibited passion and this abrupt wake-up call sent a wave of anxiety coursing through me.

I quickly made my way to the bathroom, urgency dictating my actions. After hastily washing my face and pulling my hair into a semblance of order, I gave only a fleeting glance at my anxious reflection in the mirror. The outside world was shrouded in a downpour, the rain coming down in relentless sheets. Checking my phone, I located a nearby drugstore just two blocks away. Despite the torrential rain, I knew I had to act fast.

Stepping out into the downpour, I hurried toward the drugstore, the rain soaking through my clothes, unheeded in my rush.

Returning to the hotel room, drenched and panting, his expression of concern greeted me. "Is everything okay? What was the emergency?" he asked, taking in my soaked state.

"I just had something urgent to take care of," I replied, my voice a mix of fluster and resolve. My mind was a whirlwind of emotions: the exhilaration from the previous night's liberation, the assertiveness of my 'only once' declaration, and now this jarring confrontation with reality. Was he expecting more from me? The excitement from my newfound freedom was now entangled with a tumult of conflicting feelings. While the comfort of his arms was enticing, I felt an overwhelming need for some time alone to process the morning's events and navigate the storm of emotions within me.

Setting his coffee down on the nearby table, he approached me with a look of concern. "Are you sure everything is alright? You seem a bit... shaken," he probed gently. I took a deep breath, meeting his gaze, touched by his worry. "I apologize for rushing off earlier. It's just that I realized I haven't been on birth control for some time and after last night... I needed to ensure we're safe," I explained.

There was a pause as I offered him an honest insight into my thoughts. "Last night was incredible, but it was also a wake-up call. I value love and emotional connection above physical gratification," I continued, my tone firm. "And while I'm not expecting any immediate promises, I need you to understand that my heart isn't up for grabs in a casual affair."

He absorbed my words and then found a seat on the bathroom counter as I began to brush my hair. The rhythmic strokes offered a comforting distraction from his intense gaze. "How come I feel like you're pulling away?" he asked, breaking the silence.

"I'm not trying to escape," I assured him, locking eyes with him in the mirror. "But I refuse to let physical pleasure blur my need for something deeper. Last night was physical, yes, but I'm not here for fleeting moments of passion."

The tension in the room was palpable as we both contemplated the gravity of our situation. He slid off the counter and stood close, reaching for me. My body responded to his nearness, craving the touch we'd shared, yet my mind urged caution.

"I crave the intimacy we shared, yet I'm wary," I admitted, stepping back slightly. "I need to be sure that what we have isn't just a beautiful illusion."

He nodded, understanding the complexity of my emotions. We stood there, caught in a moment of silent acknowledgment of the path that lay ahead. It was clear that this journey would be about much more than physical desire—it would be a dance of hearts and minds, a test of genuine connection and sincerity.

Pressed against the wall, I felt trapped, my escape routes narrowing as the sound of my own heartbeat reverberated in my ears. He halted in front of me, his arm casually leaning against the wall, his warm breath brushing against my face. His unwavering gaze held mine, intensifying the magnetic pull between us, eroding the façade of resistance I had constructed.

In that fleeting moment, my resolve weakened, and I found myself surrendering to the allure of his presence. The walls I had built around me crumbled under the weight of his gaze, and my heart dared to hope for something more. Despite the uncertainties and fears that linger, there is a magnetic pull that draws us together, urging me to explore the depths of this connection.

He raised me onto the counter. I savored the kiss, each hum resonating with the tentative rhythm of his caressing hand. I moaned, *oh dear god,* as I felt him slowly inching into my Gloria. I begged for more. "I want all you inside of me. Now, please." I whispered. He pulled my ass to the edge of the counter. I closed my eyes in welcome appreciation of him pressing inside of me. "Please, give me more." I moaned, locking my legs tightly around his waist, enjoying the full intensity of each thrust.

His power sent ripples though my body. The waves of emotions were intense. My body quivered. I was nearing an orgasm.

I bit my lip, fighting hard to restrain, but the exhilarating rush was like pressure building on the walls of a damn. I held tight, clawing into his back until I couldn't restrain myself. I kept working with him until I felt the throb of his eruption. *Oh, my god.* I held onto him as if he was my lifesaver, rescuing me from an ocean's swell.

As we stood at the valet stand, a palpable silence settled between us, punctuated only by the soft hum of passing cars. Our connection, like a powerful avalanche, has left me exhilarated and yet apprehensive. While our physical intimacy has ignited a passionate flame between us, my mind is already wandering down the road, contemplating what lies ahead.

My quest was never for flawlessness but for a communion steeped in the essence of love, woven with strands of trust, and bonded by an earnest partnership. The transient affections of the present, which flutter with the winds of whims and indecisions, could no longer anchor my heart. I longed, with a fervor that eclipsed mere desire, for a love that would root deep, blossom through seasons, and stand resilient against the tide of time.

He told me, "It was near lunchtime. We could talk about your declaration from last night." I liked the idea, but I told him, "Not now; we both needed time to process what we wanted. I was honest about what I said. The rest was up to you."

"But I've already told you—"

I replied, "Please… I didn't want a heat-of-the-moment answer. "If sex was your quest, you had it. There won't be any future compromises. No matter how you feel, I need some time for myself."

Once I was safely clear of the US border crossing, I decided to give Gina a call. I knew she'd be eager to hear all the juicy details of our evening together. However, luck had it that her phone went to voicemail. Part of me felt relieved that she didn't pick up. I left her a message, simply stating that I was on my way home and would catch up with her once I arrived. I wasn't quite ready for deep girlfriend chitchat, sharing every intimate detail just yet.

As I continued my journey, I rolled back the sunroof, allowing the warm sunlight of the now-clear and beautiful day and fresh air to wash over me. I hoped that the openness of the sky above and the gentle breeze would help calm my racing thoughts.

Questions swirled within me, and I began to query myself. Had I gone too far? My initial bold assertion was to give him one opportunity for a purely physical encounter, but even in those fleeting moments, I sensed that it could be more than just a casual fling. There was a connection, an intensity that reached beyond the physical realm. It stirred emotions within me that I hadn't anticipated, leaving me with a sense of both excitement and uncertainty.

As the miles passed beneath me, I delved deeper into my own thoughts, contemplating the path I'd set foot upon. Would this journey lead to a profound and lasting connection? Or had I unwittingly embarked on a path fraught with complications and heartache? Only time would reveal the answers, and I couldn't help but feel a mix of anticipation and trepidation as I navigated the uncharted territory of my own emotions.

For now, I allowed myself to embrace the open road, the freedom of movement, and the boundless possibilities that lay ahead. I trusted in the choices I'd made, and I was willing to explore the depths of this newfound connection with both excitement and a touch of apprehension.

Chapter Fourteen

After a weekend filled with the joyous company of my amour and an invigorating brunch with my girlfriends, my spirits were riding high. We had spent hours speculating about my budding romance, our laughter and conversations filling the air with excitement. As we concluded our brunch, I prepared to drop my friends off at their respective homes.

I was driving the girls home from Salty's, and as is typically the case, clouds of heavy rains obscured the Seattle landscape. I called Courtnee's husband, Stephen, speaking playfully, "Hey Stephen."

He replied cheerfully, "How are you, Cyn?"

"Well. It's another Sunday, and I'm delivering your slightly inebriated wife home. Since it's pouring, would you run out and help her inside when we arrive?"

He exhaled a long-winded sigh, responding flatly, "Yeah." under his breath. His speech was monotone. "Okay, let me know when you're outside. I'll come out and meet you." The cheerfulness that answered the phone faded. He hadn't ended the call. Instead, I heard his shocking grumble. "What else is new? I'm so sick of these goddamn worthless whores. I'm dealing with this cunt every damn Sunday, the same bullshit."

Stephen's mumbled insult caught me off guard; we were saying our goodbyes. I've just heard the truth of the man behind the mask of a loving husband. The smile he wears in my presence is now tainted by the hurtful words I overheard. It stings deeply, and I can't help but feel a mix of anger, disappointment, and betrayal. Courtnee, the timid lamb of our group, always stands faithfully by Stephen's side. Her gentle nature and reserved demeanor make her an endearing presence among our more assertive friends. So, when Stephen's disparaging words about his own wife slipped out, it was a shocking revelation.

The contrast between Courtnee's unwavering loyalty and Stephen's unkind remarks left me taken aback, questioning the true nature of their relationship. It was a stark reminder that appearances can be deceiving, and even the seemingly perfect couples may harbor hidden tensions beneath the surface.

Courtnee, with her selfless nature, has always been a master at diverting attention away from her own pains by absorbing the struggles of others. Looking back now, I can't help but recall the occasional marks and bruises I noticed on her, dismissing them as mere accidents due to her clumsiness. I never imagined they could be signs of physical abuse. After all, Courtnee's kindness and gentle nature seemed to shield her from any harm. And her partner, Stephen, always appeared to be a gentle teddy bear. She didn't fit the typical profile of an abused woman.

After having heard Stephen's words, 'I'm so sick of these goddamn whores,' echoing in my mind, everything changed. It was as if a veil had been lifted, revealing a darker reality beneath the surface. Suddenly, those marks and bruises took on a different meaning, and I couldn't ignore the possibility that Courtnee had been enduring more than we ever realized. The shock of Stephen's derogatory remarks made me question everything I thought I knew about their relationship and opened my eyes to the painful truth that abuse can hide behind even the most unexpected façades.

The deluge hadn't let up. As I neared their home, I rang Stephen to inform him I would pull into the driveway in a few seconds. He rushed out and opened the passenger front door, greeting me cheerfully with a huge smile.

"Hey, Cyn, I see you girls had a good time. Thanks for bringing my lovely one home. Thank god you don't drink." I glared, my derision tempered with a forced smile. He kept up the charade of being the attentive husband, coaxing his wife to lean on him as he helped her from the car. He didn't notice my disdainful glare... "I wanted to scream in his face: *You dirty, lying, deceitful bastard! Neither I nor my friends are bitches.'* But I envisioned Courtnee awakening in defense of him and wanting to calm the discourse, placing herself in the middle, seeking to protect and defend her husband while trying to quell my anger, wanting peace, believing her life's value is to keep others happy.

Other than this utterance, I had no proof beyond speculation… which I knew to be true. I quelled my annoyance and drove away. It pained my heart to leave Courtnee. I tried deep breathing exercises, trying to exhale the tension created by Stephen's contemptuous mutters.

I adoringly looked in the rearview mirror, watching Gina, evoking memories of the relationship she shared that broke her heart. Which I thought had made her into an overly protective friend, wanting to intervene in relationship problems on our behalf to spare us the pain she felt in her relationship. She thought Mitchell was the love of her life.

Gina and Mitchell met during the first month of med school. He was tall, with a chiseled chin and hypnotic eyes. Their attraction was instant. By the second year, they were living together as a couple. I had never seen her so happy. She worshiped Mitchell, and from outward appearances, he was madly in love with her. We trudged our way through our programs. As we neared completion, they were making plans to marry. She, like me, loved our dreary Seattle and never considered living anyplace else. Mitchell had other aspirations. He believed them to be a future power couple, destined to join the ranks of highly respected medical professionals. Thus, he wanted to move to a larger, more glamorous city where they could pay their dues and shine as they ascended the professional ladder.

Mitchell began reviewing his options for relocating. Gina assumed he knew she wanted to stay in Seattle. All their discussions were about living and raising a family in Seattle. So it caught her off guard when Mitchell began pushing her to consider moving. He had his sight set on working at Boston Massachusetts General Hospital. His sudden shift in focus led to frequent arguments.

However, all the pieces of Mitchell's behavior didn't add up. Finally, they worked out a compromise, agreeing it would be difficult, but they'd continue with their life plans and make a long-distance relationship work. However, things got worse three months before they broke up. He grew cold, blaming her for everything that appeared wrong with him, eventually ending the relationship, telling her he'd reached the end of his tolerance, saying she was impossible to be with, too damn demanding. Too damn controlling. His last words before walking out the door were, "The last damn thing I need in my life at this moment is a demanding bitch." She was experiencing behavior and using words she'd never seen or heard coming out of his mouth. The remarks shattered her heart. She explained it as being kicked in the gut, saying the physical pain would have been far less severe.

Mitch left Gina wounded and doubtful of herself. Maybe her resistance to leaving Seattle was her being inconsiderate and controlling. She concluded he was right. One evening, with tears streaming down her face, she told me how much she loved him and would do whatever it took to make the relationship work. But she would not chase him, and based on their last conversation, there weren't any reasons for her to reach out to him, fearing another verbal assault. However, as life goes on, after three weeks of sadness, depression, and remorse, he calls to tell her he missed her. He apologized for walking out the way he did, excusing his behavior related to the stress of making a life decision without texting her every day and telling her how much he loved her. They chatted on the phone for three weeks. She grew anxious, believing they were on track toward reconciliation.

She hungered to be back in his arms, enjoying his loving embrace. I accompanied her on a shopping spree for the perfect outfits and an evening number that would thrill him into bed. It pleased my heart that my friend was so happy to be reuniting with her true love. She put her plan in place. She flew to surprise him, prepared to surrender and tell him her willingness to move to wherever he wanted to practice. She'd suffer her own career if necessary and would be one hundred percent in his corner.

She shared the jitters she had in the rideshare. Having visualized and rehearsed their grand reunion. Believing Mitchell would be as overjoyed to see her as she was him. The drive to his apartment seemed eternal as they skulked through the evening traffic. She told me, "I'm so nervous and excited, Cyn. I'm about to pee my pants. No more phone sex. I will have my man tonight."

I smiled, telling her, "I'm so happy for you, Gina." I could feel her excitement over the phone. However, I had an unsettled feeling. I said nothing. I didn't want to temper her spirits. And I wanted to believe in my heart that things would work out as she planned.

"I gotta go now. I'm less than five minutes from his place."

Knocking on his door, she tingled with excitement and frustration, believing his words on the phone that the next time he saw her, he'd sweep her in his arms and passionately make love to her. Now, the prime moment was upon them. The door opened. "Gina!" he stammered. "What the hell are you doing here?" A whirlwind of emotions swept through her. Celebratory balloons burst into her mind. He corrected himself, telling her, "I'm sorry. I didn't mean it like that. I was just shocked. You should have told me you were coming. I would have been better prepared." The glee visibly returned to Gina's face as she eagerly said, "I wanted to surprise you. When you cried, telling me how different things would be if I weren't so obstinate, I realized how much you wanted this. So, I made some changes, and here I am."

Mitch stood in the doorway, his discomfort evident as he rubbed the back of his neck. Gina, with an uneasy smile, prodded, "Aren't you going to invite me in?"

Mitch's response came out in a fluster, "Well, Gina, sweetheart... Oh, my god. You should have called before coming. It's... it's kind of awkward right now."

Gina's face fell, her voice tinged with disbelief and hurt. "Awkward? I flew all the way from Seattle to surprise you, and you're saying inviting me in is inconvenient?"

Mitch lingered in silence, his internal struggle clear. "Gina, it's not that. I'm just not prepared for a visit. I miss you, love you, but—"

Interrupting, Gina's voice rose, "Mitch, you begged for us to be together!"

He exhaled heavily, "Yes, but... what about planning? I didn't expect you to just show up unannounced."

Their conversation was cut short by a voice, rich with a French accent. Nadine, elegant and composed, appeared from behind Mitch. "Mitchell? May I know who this is and why she's at our home?"

As Mitch faltered, Gina's expression turned from shock to realization. "This person's name is Gina. And Mitch, I thought we had something. You talked about love, about wishing things were different. I came here to show I was ready to compromise."

Nadine, after a brief, astute observation, introduced herself with a hint of sarcasm. "I'm Nadine. It seems we have a misunderstanding. Mitch and I have been together for a year. He came here from Seattle. Is that not true, darling?"

Gina's voice, now calm but firm, addressed Mitch. "You could've been honest. Instead, you led me to believe we could rekindle what we had. Thanks for the humiliation."

Nadine's voice was tinged with both calm and accusation as she addressed Mitch, "Well, Mitch, the lady—Gina—has a valid point. Aren't you going to answer her? Or is your silence an admission of guilt?" She paused, her gaze unwavering.

"I asked for honesty about your past, not for judgment. I wanted to know the man who called me beautiful every day. This... this is the worst kind of betrayal. Lies are an abuse of the heart, Mitch. You're an animal for what you've done, leading her on until you were secure with me. And if you could do that to her after three years, what future can I possibly believe in with you?" Her words echoed in the room, a testament to the gravity of Mitch's deceit. "I'm leaving, Mitch, and I won't be coming back. I never lie. When I leave, it's for good. Don't bother with apologies. I thought I knew you, but this? It's unforgivable." With those final words, she walked out, leaving a palpable void in her wake.

Mitch, now desperate, turned to Gina. "Gina, please, let me explain this to you." He then glanced towards the door through which Nadine had exited, his voice a mix of pleading and despair. "And Nadine, if you can hear me, I'm sorry. I need a chance to explain."

Gina stood immobilized, her eyes a turbulent blend of anger, disappointment, and deep-seated remorse. Each emotion vividly manifested across her face as she grappled with the full magnitude of Mitch's betrayal. The air seemed to thicken with the weight of his callous deceit and the humiliation it brought.

Her body trembled, not solely from sorrow but from the effort to contain the whirlwind of emotions within her, a blend of pain and revulsion. A profound sense of disgust swelled in her, directed at Mitch, who had once been a pillar in her life. Now, he appeared as nothing more than a diminished shadow, tarnished by his own lies. Her gaze, heavy with pain and disdain, pierced through him. He was no longer the man deserving of the love and trust she had once given so freely.

With a slow shake of her head, a symbol of her resignation and fading hope, she spoke. Her voice, soft yet laced with suppressed emotion, cut through the silence. "Mitch, it's too late for explanations. Goodbye." Her words, quietly resolute, signaled the end of their bond, a disavowal of the man she now viewed with contempt.

Returning home, Gina was enveloped in her grief, crying for days. Lexi, Courtnee, and I were there for her, sharing in her tears. Through her sobs, she sought understanding. "Why? Why couldn't he have been honest with me? Why paint me as a villain when all I did was love him?"

Lexi then spoke up, her words carrying the weight of weary insight. "Sweetheart, some men are akin to hunters in the woods. They engage in the chase, ensnare their prize, and once they have what they want, it's as if it's forgotten, stored away. They seem driven to pursue relentlessly, even when they're already in possession of a heart. We, in turn, become like deer – initially cherished, but eventually just another trophy on the wall."

Chapter Fifteen

My thoughts shifted from Gina's past dilemma to Stephen's haunting derogatory slur, making me suspect that there might have been more happening behind their closed doors than I had realized. Until that day, I had always seen Stephen as a nerdy yet loving guy.

Never in my life had I imagined he could be abusive. However, faint memories of bruises I had seen on her in the past began to fuel my worries. In the past, it was easy to believe that Courtnee, whom we often teased as a klutz, had simply bumped into something or hit her leg on a door. But not too long ago, I distinctly remembered seeing what looked like the outline of fingers on her arm.

After arriving home, I hesitated before calling Courtnee. The thought of her possibly being violated was deeply troubling. As I dialed her number, I gathered my thoughts, the phone ringing in the background. My intention was to initiate a conversation, to listen and to offer support without passing judgment or criticism.

She didn't answer my call. An hour later, Courtnee called back. I answered the phone with an upbeat tone, "Hey! How are you doing?" Her response came nonchalantly, "… I'm fine, Cyn. Why?"

I found myself in a tough spot. "You were pretty buzzed this afternoon. I'm just checking that you're okay."

"Cyn, you're being silly weird. I get buzzed every Sunday. Give me a break. What's buzzing in your diabolical mind?" She quickly saw through my ruse.

"Nothing," I stammered, realizing this wasn't going as I had envisioned. "I just wanted to make sure you're okay. Maybe we could talk—about anything that may be bothering you. You know, have a one-on-one conversation."

"Cyn, you would make a horrible therapist." We laughed together, and I couldn't help but admit she was right. I told her about hearing Stephen's derogatory remarks, which made me wonder about the true nature of their relationship, recalling the marks I had noticed on her in the past.

An oppressive silence hung in the air before Courtnee finally responded, her voice emerging, tinged with a mix of embarrassment and concern. "Hmm, that's kind of embarrassing. I thought I had done a good job hiding them in general. You know how Gina reacted to Lexi's situation with Marcus... I'd be mortified if she ever noticed any marks on me and jumped to similar conclusions. I don't have any dark secrets to defend myself with. Luckily, I've always been sort of an outlier in our group, so not much about me gets noticed." She fidgeted with her bracelet, a clear sign of her discomfort.

"What do you mean? You're not an outsider. You are—"

"Cyn, please don't try to counter my feelings. Look. Gina and Lexi have always dominated the spotlight. Then there's you, the well-balanced referee, the real queen bee—though Gina thinks she is—the peacekeeper, always mediating. It's always been that way. And then there's me, the skinny little redhead, always trying too hard to make everyone happy, even if it costs me because their happiness equals my acceptance."

I interjected, "That's not true. We are friends equally. I love you as much as I do, Lex or Gina."

"Maybe, but it doesn't change how things were. Actually, I'm glad you called. I need to talk. I've got a lot on my mind. Can we meet for coffee?"

"Sure. When?"

"How about at Hearth & Brew in an hour?"

As I ended the call, a knot of unease tightened in my stomach, refusing to dissipate. Courtnee's voice had been light, yes, but it was the subtle tremor beneath her words that lingered in my mind. The marks that I had occasionally noticed on her skin now took on new significance, like cryptic clues in a larger, unseen puzzle. And her reference to Gina's harsh judgment of Lexi's circumstances was a stark reminder. It underscored how quickly misunderstandings could spiral into accusations, highlighting the delicacy of the situation I was now entangled in. I realized that whatever lay ahead, it demanded careful, thoughtful navigation.

Upon entering, I was welcomed by an inviting and cozy atmosphere featuring spacious chairs encircling a fireplace fueled by crackling wood. The mix of benches and picnic tables further contributed to its rustic allure, creating an ideal environment for relaxation and unwinding.

Hearth & Brew had a unique charm that set it apart from other coffee shops. It wasn't just about the excellent coffee; it was an experience. As you entered, the rich aroma of freshly brewed coffee enveloped you, mingling with the soft hum of conversation and the gentle clinking of cups. The friendly baristas, true artisans in their craft, greeted each customer with a warm smile, adding a personal touch to every interaction.

They skillfully brewed each cup with meticulous care and precision, their passion for coffee evident in every pour. The menu was a testament to their dedication, showcasing an impressive variety of beans from different regions, each offering a unique flavor profile. The shop itself, with its cozy nooks and vibrant local art, invited patrons to linger, making it more than just a coffee stop but a cherished part of the community.

The conversations that filled the air were as rich as the coffee itself. Patrons gathered around tables, engaging in lively discussions or quietly enjoying the serenity of the surroundings. The walls, adorned with vintage coffee-related decor, and the warm lighting created an ambiance that felt both nostalgic and inviting.

Ten minutes passed before Courtnee made an appearance. With her vibrant red hair elegantly tied up in a tidy ponytail, she wore a form-fitting top and sleek black yoga pants that accentuated her slender physique. It was a striking departure from her usual style, as I had never seen her don such figure-hugging attire or pull her hair back in a ponytail.

We nestled into chairs in front of the fireplace, lulled by the crackling and popping of the blazing logs. In the mornings, the place was a flurry of activity, with the background noise of conversation and the smell of coffee drifting through the air. That evening, the hushed laughter of teenage girls filled the air as they huddled around their laptops, their faces lit by the soft light of the screens. I could tell by their youthful energy that they were students.

We sat in quietude, the air brimming with palpable anxiety and a density that seemed to mute all other sounds. I had assumed what our conversation would be about. I placed my hand on her arm, thinking maybe she was upset that I mentioned her husband's remark. "I'm sorry that I told you about Stephen—"

She gave a small shrug of her shoulders, her voice casual and unconcerned. "I'm not upset by what Stephen says on the phone." She shifted restlessly in the oversized chair, her movements reflecting a struggle to find comfort. As she turned towards me, her green eyes, usually so vibrant, now seemed soft and glistening, betraying a hint of worry beneath their surface. "I feel like I'm suffocating with everything that's going on inside me. Please don't judge me for what I'm about to tell you." I could feel the weight of her trust, and in the quiet of the room, her plea resonated deeply, urging a silent promise of understanding.

"I'm here for you, Courtnee," I replied, my tone gentle and reassuring. "You can tell me anything, and I won't judge you. I just want to support you in any way I can."

"Promise?"

"I promise," I affirmed, ensuring my sincerity was evident. "But I have to ask, how long have things been going on between you and Stephen?"

"Stephen?" she repeated, her forehead creased in a frown. "He's a decent man. He's the one who asked me to marry him, and I should be grateful for that. I've always been timid, and my self-esteem has always been low." Leaning over the side of her chair, she let out a deep sigh and hovered her hand just inches from the floor. "I don't know what to do," she said, her voice filled with uncertainty. "I don't want to hurt him, but I can't keep living a lie. Since high school, boys—even the juvenile assholes—have always preferred you, Lexi, and Gina. I've always lived in the shadows of you all.

Despite your relationship troubles, you had choices and dramas I never experienced. In college, I met Stephen. He was a safe choice." She pressed her lips together firmly. "So, when we got married, I was elated. A man wanted me to be more than a girlfriend but his wife. I finally had something that you all didn't—a devoted relationship."

She brought the cup to her lips, inhaling the fragrance before taking a sip, her train of thought pausing momentarily. "The first years of marriage were satisfactory. Not like I had anything to compare to the joys and happiness of marriage and sex. I admired his vocational ambitions, his strong will, commitment, and desire to build a family. However, after a couple of years—two, to be exact," she grimaced.

"Things turned dull. Flat. Sex wasn't great to begin with." She gave a wry half-smile. "But marriage isn't just about sexual fulfillment or fun and exciting vacations. At least, that's what I have come to realize. I've settled into the role of a dutiful wife," I reflected sadly. "Now, it feels like we're just clinging to each other out of fear. The only highlight in my life is the Sunday brunches with my girlfriends. They're always lively and full of risqué stories that make me feel alive."

I sympathetically asked. "Has he ever hurt you?"

She chuckled softly, "God no! He's not that type of man. He'd probably have to google 'how to slap your woman around.' Then afterward, he'd likely run equations before he could muster the boldness to do anything violent to me. I'd jump for joy and probably slip him a twenty if he'd just be a little rough and smack my ass during sex." She huffed, flopping back in her chair, her gaze fixed on the fireplace. "Cyn..." Her voice was bleak, barely audible as she spoke in a low tone. "I met someone... and... I love him. Wait." She snickered. "I said that incorrectly. I cherish the times spent with him."

A million questions darted through my mind. What? How? When? She's not the type to cheat on her husband. How could she keep this a secret? As an employee ambled by, adding another piece of wood to the fireplace and closing the screen, she inquired how we were doing and reminded us they would be closing in an hour. The flames flickered and latched onto the new log, the interruption giving my mind time to catch up with the conversation.

"We met last summer—"

"Last summer?" I echoed, my surprise evident.

As she continued telling her story, the log suddenly popped, causing her to flinch momentarily. However, she quickly regained her composure and went on. She explained that she, her sister, and niece Leah were visiting the U of O campus as Leah was deciding whether to attend.

She remembered how Leah's main concern was finding a school far enough from home but not too far, and U of O seemed to fit the bill perfectly. "We arrived Thursday afternoon with plans to tour the campus and leave mid-day Sunday. I've always wanted to see the track stadium. Did you know they've hosted the Olympic track and field trials?" Her eyes briefly met mine, searching for some sign of interest. "Anyway, early Saturday morning, I went to see the track, reminiscing about the days I ran track. I had dreamed of competing there but gave up running, focusing on med-school as dictated by my overbearing mother. I was happy for Leah and excited that she'd be on the track team."

I remembered her running track in high school and even some in college, but she had stopped for reasons never discussed. It made me sad to think we had overlooked something so important to her. If Gina, Lexi, or I had given up something, it would be a topic of discussion, filled with questions and encouragement. But with Courtnee, we had missed it, and I wished we had been more attentive to her dreams and passions.

She continued, "We'd gone shopping the day before. Leah urged—pestered me—to buy black yoga pants with a matching top and running shoes. I caved under the youthful pressure, wanting to be the cool aunt. Anyway, early Saturday morning, when I got there, the stadium loomed large and intimidating. It was massive. I thought about leaving—actually running away because that's more like me, but I couldn't resist the chance to put my feet on the track where some of the world's greatest sprinters have run.

So, I crept onto the field, waiting for someone to shout, "You don't belong here." But that voice never came. Without any stretching, I thought, what's the harm in a light jog? My first lap invigorated me. And since no one shooed me away, I kept going. I had forgotten how much I loved running and how it helped me cope with my frustrations. Plus, if my husband wouldn't do me, I figured I'd get my heart pumping some other way."

"Round about the eighth lap, an attractive guy with a well-built, sturdy frame entered the track and effortlessly jogged past me as though I was walking. I felt slighted. My simple jog turned into a race. I wanted to prove that I could pass him, but he was strong and overtook me again. However, for the first moment in my life, I refused to bow down. I couldn't beat him in a power run, so he would have to prove his endurance if he were to beat me. I dug in with everything I had, pulled ahead of him, and stayed in front, passing him again. He was huffing and coasting to a stop, declaring, "I surrender." Pleased, I continued with the determination to complete forty rounds, which may not have been the correct action. I hadn't prepared for such a punishing match and was going against advice I would give any patients doing the same. I started cramping and limped off the course. He came to me with the biggest smile I've ever seen. He had a nice bronze tan, which I could tell was natural. Once he got close to me, he radiated like the sun."

"That was quite a run. Are you a distance runner?" he asked, wiping sweat from his brow. His fit physique and radiant energy instantly caught my attention, sparking an unexpected attraction that I hadn't experienced in a long while.

I hesitated, catching my own breath. "No, a pent-up frustration runner," I finally admitted, my voice trembling slightly.

Still smiling, he offered, "I can help you with that."

I managed a weak smile. "I think I'm good."

He chuckled softly, the fatigue in his eyes evident. "I meant the pain. Your muscles are tightening." He extended a hand. "Oh, I'm Brandon. Brandon Jorgenson, a trainer."

I reluctantly accepted his hand, still wary. My thigh throbbed with pain, and I winced as I tried to stand steadily. After a few unsteady steps, I almost crumpled to the ground, but Brandon's quick reflexes and strong arms caught me. His undivided attention was making me feel surprisingly vulnerable. "Please, it's my job to take care of athletes," he assured me with a friendly smile.

"I don't go to school here, and I'm not an athlete," I explained, subconsciously pushing him away, my mind telling me it was taboo to allow a man to hold me the way he was, even if it felt oddly comforting. I maintained a cautious distance, torn between curiosity and the boundaries I had always observed.

"But you're still suffering," he observed, concern in his eyes.

The pain in my leg persuaded me to accept his offer. He guided me to the training room, where I was a sweaty mess. Inside the locker room, he assisted me to a bench, left briefly, and returned with a bundle of towels. He pointed me toward the showers, saying, "I'll massage your leg afterward. I can also wash your clothes and have them ready in fifteen minutes."

I hesitated, uneasy about the idea of a man handling my sweaty clothes and the prospect of being alone with him in the empty building. However, I nodded, softly whispering my agreement.

I asked, "You didn't do anything, did you?"

"No, Cyn. I wouldn't do a guy that quickly. Besides, judging from his surroundings and his good looks, I estimated he played host to far younger, more desirable bodies than mine. He pointed to a table. I initially felt scared and conflicted about being alone with him in that enormous place.

However, I accepted and hopped onto the massage table. His hands were warm and firm. His touch was so powerful and magical.

I can honestly swear I've never felt a man's touch like that on me. My suspicious tension gave way to longing for more of his touch. After he was done, he asked if I wanted to connect later. There, I drew a hard line, waving my hand with my fingers spread apart, showing my ring. He asked, "Are you trying to convince me, or yourself, that you're married?"

Actually, Cyn, I was trying to show him and remind myself. For some strange reason, I was emboldened to think about wanting something more than I had been uncomplaining. There I was, alone with this beautiful man, a curiosity of *what if* floated through my mind, but I was locked into the integrity of being a married woman. My answer had to be an emphatic 'no.'

"I wasn't asking for a date. When you're dressed," he pointed to the exit, "You can leave over there. I recommend more water and stretching next time."

He jogged away like he was running on air before I could give my retort that I'm a doctor. "I don't need your medical advice." And he was gone.

Courtnee's revelation stunned me. I took subtle deep breaths to comprehend that the person talking wasn't the Courtnee I had known for much of my life. Curiosity propelled me to ask if he left. How did they reconnect?

She continued, "To make a long story short, I stayed Sunday, telling the girls I wanted to check out the medical centers in the area and thought I'd enjoy a relaxing train ride home. Monday morning, I returned to the stadium at the same time as before, a kind of random fairytale fate thing—as if that ever happened in my life—if he was there, I'd thank him and leave. I looked around and saw three guys stretching. I thought, oh well, I'll take a last walk on the track. Midway around, I heard a very authoritative voice shout, "Come on, guys, let's not waste time! We're here early for a reason. Let's go!"

The boys took off in a trot. My heart skipped a beat. I saw Brandon jogging towards me. Standing face to face, his brown eyes looked into mine. "I'm so glad you came back. I'm sorry for my abrupt departure yesterday; I had a staff meeting. I'm the new guy on campus, and I didn't want to start off as irresponsible."

While he spoke, Cyn, I experienced an out-of-body sensation. I ached to kiss his beautiful lips. Eventually, I queried the source of his bronzed hue. He proudly proclaimed himself an Oregonian, having spent a year in Jamaica working with the country's top sprinters.

As I prepared to leave, I reached out to shake his hand and say goodbye. He glanced at me with a disappointed expression and asked if I would stay the evening and join him for dinner. I hesitated with conflict, thinking Stephen wouldn't be home for another two days. So, I thought, what the hell and agreed.

We met that evening at his suggested restaurant, a very quaint and lovely old state winery with a view so stunning it took my breath away. We saw see the rolling vineyards and the distant horizon from the hilltop. I kept reminding myself that it was just a friendly meeting. I was adamant about paying for my dinner and drinks, not wanting it to appear on a date. It's my first experience with someone other than my husband since being married. The clamor of voices was so loud that we had to sit close together to communicate with one another, which caused our faces to be in closeness. We talked non-stop about his new position and our shared love for track, and I was so lost in conversation that I didn't even notice the time passing by until I glanced at my phone, lamenting that I had an early morning departure for Seattle and needed to leave. He offered to drive me back as a way of extending our conversation. I had already ordered a ride. But he insisted, and I offered weak resistance before accepting.

Once back in the hotel, I sat uncomfortably in his car, reassuring myself each moment,each step of the way, I had done and would not do anything wrong. My delights in his company and the principles of my marriage tormented me. Taking a mental break from my commitment, I reasoned there was no harm in inviting him to my room for a few minutes.

My delights in his company and the principles of my marriage tormented me. Taking a mental break from my commitment, I reasoned there was no harm in inviting him to my room for a few minutes. As we walked the halls, I subtly reminded him of my marital status and the brief time we had for conversation. I mentioned it was merely a friendly chat, emphasizing my early departure the following morning. He acknowledged this with politeness and understanding.

However, upon entering the room, the intensity of my attraction to him became undeniable. What began as innocent chit-chat stretched into forty-five minutes, during which the tension between us built steadily. Eventually, we found ourselves caught in a moment of deep kissing, surrendering to the desires that had been smoldering like a volcano within me.

Despite torrid, grumbling thoughts of cheating in my head, my push became more of a pull until we had stripped away each other's clothes. Dear God! His body was beautiful and had solid muscles. I sat naked on his lap, kissing him, full tongue until we were on the floor going at it." She rolled her head to the ceiling, reliving the moment. Her breath shivered. He awakened every fiber in my body—"

My mouth hung open like a barn door in shock. "Courtnee! You had sex?" She looked around warily. It was near closing, and we were the only ones left.

She whispered admonishingly, "Chill, Cyn. Please don't wave the moral rattle. Yes, we had—the best sex—I ever had in my entire life! My body was begging for affection, and he gave it to me in ways I never imagined.

When Stephen and I make love, there's no heat, no emotion, just a lifeless routine. In return, he gives me a few thumps, and he groans too goddamn much. Then it's over. Brandon, he was rapturous, exploring contours of my body from head to toe." She stared into the diminishing blaze. The heat between us was just like when the girl placed the wood into the fireplace. I watched the flames, how they attached, charring the edges, slowly igniting them. Then, the blaze slowly intensified until the whole log was ablaze. That's what it was like with Brandon.

Our fire grew more powerful, leading to wild, hard, animalistic sex that lasted for two hours. Then, after my euphoric climax, our blaze gradually dwindled, and I rested, exhausted, in his firm, nurturing embrace. I had experienced the most intense orgasms in one night than I've had in my whole marriage—my entire life."

Her expression changed. She looked mournful. "Then suddenly, the emotional intoxication vanished. Anxiety and guilt raged through me like a wildfire. I needed him to leave fast so I could be alone, assuaging my mind that he hadn't spent the night if I slept and woke up alone. I took a deep breath and reminded myself that this was all a crazy dream, and as long as I kept it to myself, it would never have happened."

He seemed confused, and I could hear the uncertainty in his voice as he asked if he had upset me. I apologized for my drastic shift, reminding him and myself that being in bed together was wrong in too many ways and that we could never, ever meet again. I pleaded with him as I ushered him out the door to keep quiet and go away. I'm sure he thought I was acting irrationally.

After pushing him out, I pressed my face and hand against the door, feeling remorseful for what I had done. I looked at my hand and saw my wedding ring was gone. My body tensed with panic. I didn't remember taking them off. I frantically began searching, rushing to the bathroom.

They weren't there. I was on my hands and knees looking under the bed, on the bed, under the sofa. I must have prayed to God over a thousand times during my frenzied search. A feeling of dread washed over me. My hot, iniquitous night had resulted in me losing my rings, leaving me to believe that the man I had given my body to had an agenda to steal my jewelry and that my lover was a thief.

I snatched my phone from the drawer in the nightstand to call and demand he return them.

Next to the phone were my rings. Then I flashed back to him holding me from behind, our fingers interlaced. The pressure of his hands pressing them against my fingers had been too distracting. I was sweating with guilt until I removed the bands—something I had never done before—freeing myself from the visual reminders of my matrimonial bondage. I had removed and hid them in the drawer. I felt relieved and ashamed that my thoughts of Brandon had been darkened, believing he was a thief.

With faith restored, my mind reverberated, telling me I had been duplicitous and that I needed to put as much space as possible between me and the sordid engagement.

A single tear rolled down her cheek, leaving a wet trail in its wake. I gave her a gentle smile and murmured that it was okay. "No," she said, her voice trembling as she exhaled a shaky breath. One adulterous interlude was more than I could handle. However, I thought about—craved—him. Being home with Stephen only intensified my turmoil. A single night had thrown my life into confusion, leading me to a bitter acknowledgment: I detested life with my husband. In a vain attempt to recapture that spark, I found myself trying to mold Stephen into the image of the man who had ignited such passion in me—Brandon. I changed my clothes, bought sexy underwear, and then racier and sexier nighties. One night in bed, Stephen took offense that I begged him to fuck me hard and uncontrolled. I was trying to make him my methadone to control my addiction to the drug located in Oregon.

After several nights—not consecutive—of disappointing sex, when Stephen would lumber into bed and drift off to sleep, I'd close my eyes, allowing my thoughts to wander back to my time with Brandon. I could still feel the lingering touch of his kiss and the passionate way he explored every inch of my body. As I indulged in the memory, I couldn't help but succumb to my desires, pleasuring myself until I reached an intense climax. It frustrated me to have to stifle my moans, thereby snuffing out my ability to fully indulge in the pleasures of recalling the powerful connection I shared with Brandon.

I went another month untouched and displeased. I kept fighting my temptations to reach out to Brandon…until I couldn't hold back. I had his number in my phone and thought I should at least call him and apologize for kicking him out. Cyn, I wanted him so badly my body was throbbing.

As she cradled her now lukewarm coffee in her hands, her gaze fixed on the flickering flames, she delicately nibbled on her bottom lip before finally confessing, "It was only when he entered my life that my true emotional passions became clear to me. After reconnecting and receiving his forgiveness, our conversations grew more frequent, and before I knew it, I found myself driving to a modest hotel in Kalama, Washington, on a Friday night, seeking confirmation that the euphoria of our first encounter was not a fleeting moment.

Our second reunion surpassed all expectations, a breathtaking experience that left us both yearning for more. Cyn, I want to devour that man. He was so frickin' erotic. "Whew," she said, fanning her face with her hand.

We began meeting every other weekend, discreetly navigating the challenges posed by Stephen's work in Kansas. I was determined to maintain a façade of normalcy with all of you, believing that I could successfully balance two lives. And so, my clandestine love affair commenced, revealing profound truths about myself and leading me to make life-altering decisions. Firstly, I made the choice to leave Stephen. I officially filed for divorce last Thursday.

I listened in disbelief as she continued, "So, you're divorcing Stephen to be with Brandon?"

"Oh god, no. I'm taking a leap of faith and leaving Stephen to find my place in the world. I have discovered parts of myself that I had left dormant while I was so busy trying to be everything to everyone else instead of being true to myself. For the moment, I am feeling Brandon. But that, too, must end. I'm more about independence than rushing to be with another man or even trying to define love for me.

For too long, I have allowed the until death do us part, love, and honor shit to entrap me in a monotonous marriage. No more. If love is out there, I'll collide with it when the time is right. But not now. Not now. And if it never happens, I'll be happy knowing I took the risks. I'm also making a change — I'm leaving Seattle.

What the hell? I nodded in silent agreement as I witnessed the unseen and unknown layers of my friend being peeled back before my eyes. It was a vulnerable sight, a revelation of her true self that had remained concealed for so long. Her raw openness was astonishing, and it deepened my admiration for her courage to confront her own truth and make life-altering decisions. At that moment, I realized that I was witnessing a transformative journey, one that would shape her future and redefine our friendship in ways I couldn't yet comprehend.

"You're? You're leaving your work? Your friends?"

"Yes. I have accepted a job offer at OHSU. I start in three weeks."

"Courtnee. Aren't you being a little impulsive?"

"No. I have been planning this for months. It has nothing to do with Brandon—"

"I'll say it does. You're divorcing your husband. Leaving your job. Moving to Oregon. Leaving us." *I recognized that of everything she was saying, abandoning our group was truly what bothered me.* But I couldn't help myself. "He's there. I'd say it has a lot to do with him."

She rolled her eyes dismissively. I raised a scornful brow. "I'm not exchanging shackles here to attach myself to another relationship. Brandon was the catalyst of my liberation, and now it's me who is eager to enjoy life. I'm done with my daily burden, continually striving to mollify others, with the hope of acceptance from confidants, my sib, and my workmates. I am in the third decade of my life. But, I am akin to that of an eighty-year-old woman. I'm done."

She gazed at me with sorrowful eyes. "I hate to be the one to say this, as I feel such an intense bond with you all, but I need to grow in other directions—I'm not saying goodbye forever—we're always going to be friends. I'm just saying that I want to establish new relationships in a different environment, experience the adrenaline rush of running long-distance races, explore the world and challenge the boundaries of my previous life. I envision an exhilarating tomorrow.

I'll be truthful with Brandon and tell him when I move that he's not a component of the master plan of my life. I understand that it could come across as vain. However, I am speaking honestly, and that is the most significant factor. If he opts to stay, cognizant of the fact that I shall eventually depart—and I will—then that is fine. Nevertheless, right now, living is about me seizing control for the first time. And honestly, I don't care who doesn't love or approve of me. I shall be the pilot of my own destiny. Please do not hold any hatred towards me."

Pushing my emotions to the far corners of my mind. I wanted to take hold of her as though it was I who was drowning and needed saving. Overwhelmed by her disclosures, I assured Courtnee that I would never despise my friend no matter what and that my devotion to her was everlasting. I clasped her hand, apologizing, "I'm sorry if I ever made you feel like an inferior friend."

"It's no one's fault," she explained, highlighting how our group's dynamics had evolved naturally over time. "As we grew closer, the unique blend of our personalities began to mold the group's energy, creating an atmosphere entirely its own. That's precisely why I need you to understand my decision to leave."

As she spoke, the light around us dimmed, signaling the end of our time in that space. I tried to hold back my emotions, but a single tear escaped, tracing a path down my cheek. I then felt the warmth of her hand on my arm, the gentle touch offering a comforting reassurance. "Cyn, please don't cry," she implored, her voice soft yet full of emotion. "I love you more than words can ever convey."

We stood and hugged tightly. She pressed her lips together, a hint of a smile playing at the corners. It was a subtle gesture, but it spoke volumes about the strength and confidence she had found within herself, saying nonchalantly, "Whew. I really needed this talk. I'm going home now." She left as though her disclosures to me were the confessional release of her burdens.

The pressure she had been keeping inside her had reached its peak, and she burst forth. In the blink of an eye, I witnessed her transforming into her new self. I comprehended all of Courtnee's words. Often, we humble ourselves so that others may rise beyond us. I just never realized how much we had taken her for granted. It took me a few moments to digest what she said before I ambled out the door. *I'm happy for her.* But sad that another member of our group is leaving, changing the dynamic of our band of sisters.

Chapter Sixteen

As I navigated my way home, Courtnee's revelation continued to echo in my mind, leaving me deeply shaken. How could someone so integral to our lives have concealed such profound secrets? A wave of sadness washed over me as I thought about how she must have felt so unnoticed, so peripheral in our intertwined lives.

The truths she revealed bounced around in my mind, each one striking with the unexpected force of a stray bullet. I empathized with her complex emotions, yet I found myself paralyzed by shock. She had been hiding an affair, a secret life unfolding stealthily right under our noses, and we, her supposed confidants, were completely unaware.

The signs I had noticed, which had led me to suspect something amiss, now pointed to a reality entirely different from the abuse I had imagined. The thought that Courtnee, always seen as the most unlikely person for such actions, was involved in an affair hit me like a thunderbolt.

Courtnee's story struck me with its stark truth. It was a moment that forced me to confront my own naivety and the understanding that those closest to us can harbor the most surprising secrets. It was a profound blow, reminding me of the intricate, often hidden layers of emotion and experience that shape our relationships.

I felt an urgent need to see my amour, to look into his eyes and find reassurance that I wasn't making a mistake by allowing myself to be vulnerable. I longed to feel the warmth of his presence, a longing that had become a tangible ache in my chest.

So, I called him to inquire if he would appreciate some company. His gleeful response of "Yes!" set my heart fluttering, filled with a blend of joy and nervous anticipation. I was keen to cast aside my somber reflections and dive wholeheartedly into his presence, to surrender to the enigma and charm of this budding romance. The journey from Sammamish to Magnolia lasted forty-five minutes, each passing minute amplifying the adrenaline surging through me.

Upon arriving, he warmly welcomed me into his living room, his demeanor always polite and kind, even during my most turbulent episodes. In his company, I found not just warmth and comfort but also a thrilling sense of adventure and the unknown.

His living room boasted an unobstructed view of Puget Sound, a sight that was nothing short of breathtaking. The floor-to-ceiling windows led out onto a spacious deck, presenting a picturesque view of lush green trees and the expansive water beyond. It was a serene vista that contrasted sharply with the whirlwind of emotions within me. As I stood there, admiring the beauty surrounding him, I couldn't help but wonder about the mysteries he might be hiding behind his kind eyes and warm smile. The beauty of the place mirrored the complexity and depth of our burgeoning relationship, each view and each moment with him revealing layers I was only beginning to explore.

He thanked me for coming and offered to show me around. Guiding me from the living room to the guest room and then downstairs to his home theatre, his hospitality was evident. The large television in the room hinted at his fondness for screen time. It's my game and playroom, he said, a devilish tone in his voice. I couldn't help but wonder, *What games do you really play down here? What sort of films are watched in this secluded spot?*

"Nice. Do you entertain often?" I asked, my curiosity slightly veiled.

"I wouldn't say often. But I do enjoy having people over for sporting events. Or watching a good movie with a lovely woman," he replied with a casual ease.

I gave him a skeptical, raised brow. *I see.* He showed me to his bedroom. The view surpassed all expectations. I stepped out onto the deck, inhaling the crisp, moist night air. Before me lay a mysterious world, the trees standing tall like sentinels in the darkness, their shadows concealing the ocean just beyond.

"I'm okay here. I can trust you, right?"

"Yes… you can trust me. Do you feel you can't?"

I studied his response. I knew I didn't need to answer him. "Look, I have some things on my mind." The salsa sound ringtone interrupted his cell phone, distracting my well-rehearsed thoughts. "Excuse me, I have to take this call. Make yourself comfortable." I was still adjusting to being here, feeling slightly ill at ease being left alone in his bedroom while he spoke on the phone. So, I went downstairs, overhearing him on the phone. "Yes, I have a guest. I'll call you later. It's okay. I promise. I'll call you back."

I stood midway down the stairs as he turned and headed back up. "Something important? I can leave if you like."

"No, please don't go. It was my sister, Allyson. She wanted to make plans for later."

"Ah, I see. I'm sorry to have interrupted your conversation."

"It's okay. She understands. I had today open, and we were going to discuss some things."

"I remember you telling me she was going through a divorce."

"True. She's in the middle of a conflict concerning their California home. Other than that, it's going okay. I do what I can to keep her spirits up. You know, the protective big brother. It endears me to him that he's close to his sister."

"Great, I've stolen away her brother twice now. She's going to hate me."

"She's nothing like that. Is everything okay with you?"

"Yes, I'm fine. I felt it was strange to be sitting in your room alone."

He apologized, suggesting we go back and finish our conversation. I hesitate, partly aroused, wanting to say yes, then apprehensively thinking we shouldn't. But I relent, believing I have the self-control to ensure we only talk. I sat on the sofa. He sat on the end of the bed. He looks at me inquisitively. I'll tell him I want to talk about Vancouver. He responded," Finally, we get to have that conversation."

"I'm sorry if my hasty departure caused you concern, but... please," I pat the space next to me. "Sit next to me, please." My face was burning. I was a confluence of emotions. My desire for intimacy clashed with my determination to abstain from another sexual encounter.

"Let me talk for a minute." He said. "I have done nothing but to think about you since we met. I consider myself a lucky man to have the opportunity to go out with you. Since the first night and all times in between, I have thought deeply about you and everything we discussed since I first held you in my arms. I found you to be a powerful woman of intrigue: intelligent, fun-loving, kind, devoted, and passionate. Correct me if I was wrong." I was too distracted by the surge of desire building inside me. "I can promise you I won't play with your heart." *That's what Gina thought about Mitchell initially and believed until the end.* My thoughts of her and Mitchell are clouding my mind. He continued, "Though I enjoy my home, it feels empty. I'm lonely."

I couldn't believe him. He's a handsome man, and many women would be happy to be with him. I resolved to be upfront and said, "Let me be direct with you. I don't give away my heart easily. There are so many valleys of disappointment in my past that I'm fearful of giving all of myself. I hunger to have a man love me with the whole of his heart as much as I will love him with the total of mine. You say pleasant words—and I've met many men—using kind words with an agenda in mind. Given our recent history, you may find me a contradiction. However, I was honest. That was the only time we'd have unconditional sex. To be blunt, I am not into fucking to release tension."

"I know—"

"Please let me finish. It's important to me you listen. I want true love. I don't want my man to make me doubtful about myself. I've had that before. While I don't hold any person responsible for my happiness, I hold them accountable for being a part of my journey. Love is always exciting in the beginning. It's an all-consuming blaze, fueling great sex, filled with jubilation that consumes you daily.

"However, six months down the road, things dwindle. Love's heated blaze becomes a flickering flame struggling for survival as its fire nears exhaustion. Then, one is left wondering what happened?" I blow air in exasperation as though I'm having an epiphany that what I want may not exist. Thoughts?"

He sat back, his form sinking into the cushions of the sofa, his eyes intently focused on me. The room was enveloped in a quiet tension, punctuated only by the rustling of the wind outside, whispering secrets to the night. It seemed as if even the wind was waiting for his response. His usually playful eyes now held a contemplative depth, silently dissecting every word I had said. The atmosphere was thick with unvoiced thoughts and emotions. As the wind caressed the window panes, he took a moment, deeply inhaling as if to gather his thoughts, before he finally broke the silence.

He said, "We've both traveled a journey in life and have our wounds from previous relationships. You're right. A relationship is an adventure. I see it as finding the right woman and giving her one hundred percent of me. I don't think about tomorrow. I take today as the reference point of my accomplishment in pleasing my lady and doing my best to make tomorrow better. I can't say when our journey would end, but if it were to end, it would conclude with us both knowing I gave one hundred percent of my heart. We distort the meaning of love, lost in the allure of Hollywood's love stories and fairytales. There's no forever after, only as long as we're blessed with living our life's timeline.

People who live with purpose and dedication to mutual happiness leap over all distractions and enjoy fulfillment until God's call." His words intrigued my heart.

Having moved back downstairs from his bedroom, I found myself resisting the allure of returning to the comfort of the bedroom, enticed by the mystic calls to feel his love. The wind howled savagely outside, battering the branches and stripping leaves, some of which spiraled down into the yard. Others were swept aloft, only to land nearby. Briefly, the gusts subsided, bringing a moment of peace and tranquility. The trees stood resilient, having withstood the windstorm's wrath.

Lost in thought, I reflected on how life mimics the patterns of nature: the days of radiant sunshine, the overcast periods, and stormy times like these. The true test, I realized, is in how we stand strong against life's gusty challenges. My contemplation was interrupted by his offer to grab dinner. I snapped out of my reverie and declined, saying that I should head home.

"I have guest rooms you're welcome to stay in," he offered.

"Thank you, but I have an early morning meeting," I replied. At the door, we stood face to face, caught in a moment of magnetic appeal. His hand glided over my waist, gently pulling me into his embrace. His kiss was a sweet indulgence, and I closed my eyes, losing myself in its warmth. A wave of sensation surged through me, reminding me of the need to call it a night. Reluctantly, I tore myself away, taking deep breaths. *Wow!* The desire to make love was overwhelming, but I knew now wasn't the right time.

"When can I see you next?" he asked, his voice a soft murmur.

"My schedule is pretty light this week."

"I'll align my schedule with yours. How about we talk on Tuesday?"

"That works for me."

We lingered in the open doorway, the rain outside pouring onto the pavement, the sound of a rhythmic companion to our own tumultuous emotions. My body ached to be held; a furnace of desire burned within me. I told him I had to go. "You sure you have to go?" he questioned, his voice tinged with longing.

"No," I began, my breath betraying my arousal, "I mean, yes. Trust me, I need to go." He offered me a jacket, but I declined, craving the rain's cool touch to quell the fire raging inside me. As I turned to leave, he pulled me back into his arms. We kissed instinctively, a raw, passionate connection that spoke volumes. My body yearned for him, crying out silently, *Make love to me.* But I resisted, answering myself, *Not now, I'm not ready.* With a final push, I broke free and dashed outside, welcoming the pelting rain as it washed over me, soothing the tempest within.

As I hastily ran from his house to my car, the rain was blowing sideways, a tempestuous torrent that seemed to mirror my inner turmoil. Gusts of wind blew my hair into a wild dance, creating an uncontrolled whirl around my face. Reaching my car, I paused amidst the torrential downpour, the wind lashing against me relentlessly. Thoughts raced through my mind at a million miles a second in this chaotic tempest.

It was cold, and there I was, fleeing the warmth and comfort of a kind and caring man. Standing there, soaked and shivering, I realized I was on the brink of abandoning what could potentially be a good relationship. But true understanding would only come if I genuinely engaged with him.

With a sudden surge of determination, I slammed the car door shut without getting in and turned back towards his house. The rain pelted me mercilessly, but it now felt almost invigorating, echoing the tumultuous emotions I was wrestling with. It was time for me to confront these feelings, to make a choice—either to commit to exploring this relationship or to walk away for good. The storm outside was a vivid reflection of the storm within me, and as I made my way back to his door, a newfound sense of resolve coursed through me amidst the chaos.

Chapter Seventeen

Rain pelted down as I turned back to his house, the winds whipping around me, urging me forward as if fate itself was pushing me toward what I had almost left behind. I knocked on the door, my heart thudding against my ribs, the tumultuous weather a stark contrast to the storm of emotions inside me. When he opened the door, the phone was still in his hand, his surprise evident.

"You came back," he noted, stepping aside to let me in from the cold.

"I did," I said, brushing past him, the warmth of the house wrapping around me like a much-needed embrace. We resettled into the living room, where I had spent many contemplative moments. I shifted in my seat, my eyes drifting to the television, the fireplace, and out the window where the world seemed to be washed clean by the downpour. "Can I be honest—totally—with you?" I asked, my voice barely above a whisper.

"Of course, you can tell me anything," he replied, setting his phone aside.

"Will I get the same degrees of honesty from you?" My question was direct, searching.

He smirked slightly. "You don't trust me?"

"No," I confessed, and it was the raw truth.

"Okay, very blunt. I respect that." There was a note of admiration in his voice.

"Please, I don't mean to offend you. I came back because..." I hesitated, my internal monologue racing. *Shit, why did I come back here?* "I believe you care about me, and I am intensely intrigued by you. When I say I don't trust you, it's because I have barriers, and they're crumbling, and I keep running away for fear of being hurt. The whole relationship, the love thing from my perspective, doesn't do me well. It scares me. I'm afraid of giving my heart to a man only to have him break it down the road."

"As I have told you, I am a hundred percent all-in kind of person. I don't give parts of me; I give my all. I'm sorry if I appear to be a complicated mess. However, I'm at a place in my life where I want a solid relationship. You have been very charming, and perhaps I'm looking too far down the future road, fearing that the intensity and luster might wear off and the river of romance could run dry. I want a love that can withstand the challenges of life."

"Do you remember what I said in Vancouver?" I asked him. He nodded. "I meant it. You intrigue me. You make me feel desired and appreciated. However, that's today. My mind always thinks about tomorrow. Keeping true to our Vancouver conversation, I'm going to tell you about my past so that you will know and understand me."

I questioned internally if I was pushing for too much commitment too soon, but then I realized that I wasn't.

"So here goes," I said with newfound determination. He cleared his throat, signaling he was prepared for whatever I had to share. "Are you sure you want to hear everything?" I asked, my anxiety palpable.

"I do," he said, and there was a quiet strength in his affirmation.

Taking a deep breath, I clasped my hands together, my fingers nervously tracing my lips. Then I broke the silence, "If you don't mind, I would like a cup of coffee."

"Sure. Mine needs a little warming as well," he said, perhaps sensing my need for a brief respite.

His absence gave me a moment to compose myself, to gather the fragmented pieces of my story.

When he returned with the coffee, I started to unveil the layers of my life. "I'm like a rag doll that's been torn apart and pieced back together. But today, I stand before you, a woman reconstructed. As I've shared, I don't drink because I'm an alcoholic," I revealed, meeting his eyes, which were now filled with a mixture of concern and understanding. "I started drinking at thirteen," I admitted, my voice steady despite the tremor I felt within.

He looked at me with astonishment. "Thirteen? How is that possible? How does a thirteen-year-old get alcohol?"

I mused at his naivety, a bittersweet smile crossing my face. "When you're a young girl, and people want to do something to you, it's easy," I explained, my tone carrying the weight of those early experiences.

Lauren and I spent countless scorching summer days and chilly winter nights hanging around the local 7-11, haggling with strangers to buy booze for us. That came with its own set of dangers, especially when you handed over the only money you had—money usually pilfered from mom's purse—to some creepy guy who insisted you meet him around the corner so he wouldn't get caught distributing alcohol to minors.

Their indifference to our safety was evident. Holding our money, they used it as leverage, manipulating us into favors in exchange for the alcohol. Each transaction was never just a straightforward exchange; it came with unspoken expectations and a subtle, yet palpable, sense of coercion.

It was a risky game we played, one that seemed thrilling and rebellious at the time. In hindsight, it was a dance with danger, a gamble that could have easily spiraled into disaster. Each time we did it, we were trusting our fates to the hands of those who saw us not as children but as opportunities.

Now, as I look back on that chapter of my life, I am struck by a mix of regret and disbelief. I'm amazed at how I navigated through those times, believing I had come through unscathed. It's only with the passage of time that I've come to realize the true extent of the risks we took and the lasting impact of those early choices.

My amour sat looking at me like an amazed child.

"So… so, how, what happened?"

Telling my story launched me back in real-time, reliving the moments as I told him. *I'm scared now. Why did I insist on doing this to myself?* "I never had the best home life. My life has been one of sexual violation. My friend Lauren was experiencing the same dread at home as me. We clung to each other for dear life. Everyone who crossed my path wanted to fuck me. My father—I still love him with all my heart, but he violated me, my brother, and his friends, and for the love of God, even my mother.

His eyes nearly popped out of their sockets. His mouth was open, aghast. I asked, "Are you sure you want to know all this?"

"I'm here for you. However, if it's too much for you, I understand. But to answer your question, yes, I want to know everything about you." I was uncertain if he appreciated my story for the insights it provided about me or if he was merely entertained by its shock value.

I continued my nightmarish revisitation of my past. "As I was saying, guys—and some women—were very willing to help us in exchange for us doing them favors. Sometimes, we'd be stuck on the store side, and they wanted to see us undressed or to take things a little further. It didn't matter to them. We were thirteen, then fourteen. All they wanted was sexual gratification. And before you knew it, we were in the back seat of someone's car, and they were trying to stick their fingers or other things in side of us. One evening, this is when we were fourteen. This well-dressed man, a lawyer-looking type in a luxury silver Mercedes, offered us a case of beer, a carton of smokes, and a ride to Discovery Park if he could see me and Lauren kiss.

During the drive to Discovery, he pulled into a dark parking lot. We didn't know what to do other than do as he asked. In the past, we gave each other little smooches, like kisses on the cheek or picks on the lips, so kissing her was innocent. But he wanted more than our customary quick smooches."

"Real kissing," he said. He wanted to see us deep kiss each other, share tongues, and kiss to turn each other on. It felt like a game, so we tongue-kissed. While we were kissing, he was getting aroused. He then coaxed us until he got us to open each other's pants. "Now, take them off." He was sweating profusely. We're both novices, so we didn't know the extent of turning each other on with our fingers. At first, I found it repulsive and wanted to stop. Lauren whispered, "Come on, he's going to give us two hundred dollars, not to mention cigs and a rack of beer. We could hang out a couple of nights and have beer and smoke without having to bum. Plus, if we had money, we'd be able to eat."

"Fuck her," he said to Lauren. She obliged, deep-tonguing me as she pulled away my jeans and panties, and then I helped her do the same, sticking her tongue in my mouth. Her hands glided over my nipples. Beads of nervous sweat dripped from my hair.

Suddenly, we were all over each other, her fingers inside me and mine in her. Lauren got more turned on and moved her head down to my vagina. I was in the back seat of a man's car, on the verge of my first sexual encounter with a girl, my friend. I trembled with uncertainty until she shocked me to reality, sliding her tongue inside me. I swallowed hard and gave into the moment. I held her head when she hit the right spot. Our moans got him excited. He was in the front seat, jerking off. I pushed Lauren to lie down. We sixty-nine each other, and our tongues teased each other's clit until we were jerking and moaning. Despite my nervousness, I screamed at the thrill of my first orgasm. Moments later, he was grunting from ejaculating.

"Afterward, he gave us a hundred dollars each and dropped us off at Discovery Park with our beer and smokes. We found a safe area in the trees where we built a small shelter from the rain. We clung to each other for warmth and sipped beer. Lauren boasted with excitement, "Was that crazy or fuckin' what?"

"What do you mean?" My mind rattled. I was despondent and confused by what we had just done.

"Bae, I totally licked your pussy until you screamed."

"I'm sorry. I didn't know what to do."

"So, you liked it?" Lauren asked with a sense of self-satisfaction.

"I don't know," I said, feeling unsettled from the experience.

"Will we do it again?"

"I'm not sure. Maybe if I was super drunk, and you wanted me to."

"I don't think I'd want to do it again. I mean, it felt good but weird at the same time. I was having sex with my best friend. Talking about it makes it worse."

"It's not a big deal. It's not like we came on to each other. We got paid money to kiss and makeout."

"Yeah, don't say that, please. It grosses me out."

We left it alone. We didn't see each other as sex partners. However, until that night, she was the only person who had sex and cared about me.

As the days progressed, two things changed. First, we met up with a group of guys who had access to a flophouse, an abandoned house near Green Lake. Second, Lauren became a lot more daring with drugs and ventured further out on a limb with sex than I was ready for. Most of the guys were older than us and could gain access to drugs and alcohol. I felt like my friend was pushing me away, freely having sex and experimenting with different drugs. We hung out daily, but it was not just her and me anymore. She was hooked up with Cameron, a tall, skinny kid with dusty blonde hair, a Ballard high school dropout. Lauren had grown an appetite for drugs and sex and would sleep with guys to get them. They thought since I was her friend, I too should put out."

I took a break from my story to see if my amour was okay. *I felt chilling ice running through my veins as I watched him. He hasn't turned away.* I thought maybe I should stop. I lowered my head. I'm reliving my hell from my teens. "I'm sorry. I shouldn't have spoken to you about this. I don't know where my head is."

His eyes keenly attached to me. His voice was compassionate. "It's okay... I'm here for you." His eyes were nurturing. He encouraged me to continue.

"I learned I was a blackout drunk during a night of power drinking. Lauren boasted to the other teens about our initial encounter. Talking and laughing as she told them, "She, she," uncontrollable laugher, "liked it so much she was screaming." More laughter. My face was red with humiliation. I went to one of the vacant rooms, bare except for a well-worn mattress on the floor. The next morning, I awoke with a throbbing headache and a queasy stomach, my mouth dry and my mind clouded with a mix of regret and fragmented memories, a stark contrast to the reckless abandon of the night before; I craved coffee.

As I got off the bed, my panties and pants were on the floor. My heart was pounding. I had a vague recollection of falling out on the mattress, fully dressed. I wondered to myself, *what did I do last night?* It had embarrassed me, thinking I had done something reprehensible. I scrounged up my clothes and got dressed. I sneaked to the bedroom where Lauren was sleeping. She and Cameron were passed out. In the other room were three guys left over from that night. With only a light jacket, I went out into the cold mist of rain, headed to get coffee.

Through the head fog, phantom images revealed faded in and out. From what I could grasp, Lauren's tongue was in my mouth. Then her hand snaked down my pants, working down to my vagina, her fingers working inside of me. Then I felt the tugging of my jeans being pulled away.

I feebly whimpered for her to stop, yet I couldn't assert any control over what was happening, as I was too out of it. She didn't relent until she was done and satisfied with her deed. Then, as though I was looking through a foggy lens, I saw her take a bag from a kid. Everyone left the room, leaving him and me alone.

Having returned from the coffee shop, I pulled Lauren aside, seeking clarification about the events of the previous evening. She dismissed my annoyance, telling me, "Don't make a big deal of it. You just have a hangover. Nothing happened last night."

"Are you sure? Promise me nothing happened last night." I asked, pinching her, determined to understand what had happened.

"Stop pinching me, bitch. I told you we were partying. You had too much to drink. Now you're imagining shit."

"Did you have sex with me? We held a confrontational stare."

Her bottom lip trembled. She glared at me, huffing, "Yes! I did. Okay. No big deal. It's not like we haven't done it before." I gained glimpses of memory as my mind fog cleared images of two others taking advantage of me while Lauren looked on, justifying the encounter.

"Before! We experimented once and said we'd never do it again. You're supposed to be my best friend. If the tables were turned, I'd protect you with my soul."

She looked at the two edgy guys. Pulling me aside, whispering, "Just chill out, dude. It's not like you're thinking. You were all over them earlier. I—we thought you wanted to be alone. I'm sorry. It's not that big of a deal."

"Lauren, it is a big deal." They violated me and you and took part.

"Look, I'm sorry. No harm. We can find another place to flop or go back to the park. Either way, it's okay with me."

I was angered by her indifference and betrayal. I stormed out of the house crying, wondering how the person—the only person in my life I trusted—could abuse and abandon me and say it wasn't a big deal. Lauren caught up with me after I had walked two blocks in the freezing cold. "I'm really sorry. We are all drunk and fucked up on coke. But you were just as fucked up. So, I thought you wanted it to happen." We walked in silence. With nowhere to go, the flop was the best option. I promised myself not to get that messed up again.

It was a Friday evening. Lauren and I went with the guys to score coke. We took the bus with them to the Seattle Center and hung out. Brady, a tall, skinny kid, stole off with a six-pack from the 7-11. The guy with the coke wasn't to meet with us until ten that evening when everything in the city was quiet. With nothing but time on our hands, we did random crap to keep us busy until we made our way to the market. We navigated the cobblestone streets outside the market. The place felt eerie and dark to me.

Despite Lauren begging me to come with them, I refused, still feeling the sting of her previous betrayal. I didn't want to take any additional risks of doing lines in dark corners. Lauren said to the boys, "It's okay. She's scared." Cameron looked at me with a fiendish grin. That made me even more uncomfortable. I only hung around them because I needed Lauren in my life. Finally, unable to get me to join them, they walked off into the night with Lauren sharing a cigarette. I waited at street level, pressed against the cold brick wall underneath an awning, seeking warmth and shelter from the rain. I grew impatient, wanting to find Lauren.

As I took my first steps, the most horrific scream pierced the air. Instantly, I realized that something terrible had happened. Fright engulfed me, and without a second thought, I took off running, fearing they might come back for me.

I ran from the market to Myrtle Edwards Park and hid behind a boulder. I pushed my body as close to the rock and ground as possible, shivering from cold and fraught with fright the whole night.

When they found Lauren's body the next morning, it was said she had been strangled and sexually assaulted. Later, rumors spread that she had been injected with heroin and subjected to unspeakable horrors.

As I reflected on these horrifying details, everything that had seemed strange at the party started to make sense. My friend had spiraled from one drug to an even more dangerous one, and it seemed like she was trying to drag me into that dark, morbid world.

"After three days of hiding out, my stomach was growling, and I needed a shower, so I had no choice but to brave the streets, my eyes darting around for any sign of danger and my body tense, ready to flee at the slightest touch from a stranger. Beneath the heavy, gray skies of Seattle, I trudged along the city streets, my mind as foggy as the morning mist.

The clamor of the waking city couldn't drown out the gnawing in my stomach or the fear twisting in my chest, leaving me feeling hopelessly lost and alone. My first encounter was with a street newbie named Hillary, who advised me that two guys were asking around about me. "Your friend is dead, right?"

Word got around fast on the street. The revelation that Hillary possessed knowledge of the night with Lauren—a night that remained shrouded in mystery even to me—heightened my distress. How she came to know such intimate details, which were absent from my own memory, deepened the sense of vulnerability that already haunted me. She told me that Lauren and I were bargained as part of an exchange for sex and drugs.

"The guys that killed your friend are laying low, but they have it out for you. You're not safe anymore. You need to get to the police before they pay someone a bag to kill you."

"I could feel an intense sense of dread as my anxieties increased a thousandfold. I surveyed the area, feeling a chill run down my spine as I wondered where I could go. My head was spinning, my limbs felt like lead, and my stomach growled with hunger, making it impossible to search for a safe haven.

I asked if she had any food. She looked around the surroundings suspiciously, wary of all eyes and voices of the people and faces moving about. She grabbed my flimsy leather jacket that provided me with a little warmth from the cold and pulled me against the wall. Her eyes were like icy pools, piercing and severe, as she shoved a twenty-dollar bill into my palm. "Here, take this. Get food, and stay away from shelters. I hate to say this, but you should go to the police."

Twenty dollars can be hard to come by on the streets, so I thought maybe to see if she had just enough for a meal and coffee.

"Don't worry about me. I got money, but I don't want anyone to know."

The cold was biting into me, and I wanted to know why, of all the people I knew on the streets, she, unknown to me, was offering to help. I asked, "Who are you? Why are you trusting me?"

She bit down on her lip. Her cheeks redden from the cold. "Because I can feel that you are a good person. You need to understand that the guys that killed your friend are going to hurt you... bad. Everybody knows you, and she went to score. The dudes with the drugs did it to her. They were furious at Brady and Cameron for having left you behind."

To shield themselves from the consequences, Brady and Cameron had to find you. They're asking and threatening everyone, telling them they need to help find you. She removed her ski cap, slapping it on my head. Long, clean blonde strands of silks—permed hair—unfurled down her shoulders, a striking contrast to the grime and dishevelment of the surrounding homeless community. It was clear that she was attempting to blend in, but her appearance and demeanor set her apart from those around her. "Here. Tuck in your hair." My hair was long, frizzy, and frayed. "Get a bite at Mc D's. Then go to the police before dark. Okay?" she pleaded with her eyes.

My throat was so tight I could barely force the word okay out. I can't say if it was a gift from God or if I was just fortunate that she showed up that day. I could tell she was a newbie to the streets—she had an aura of naivety about her, as if she didn't quite belong. Meaning she had a nice home to go back to if she wanted. She was undoubtedly pushing the boundaries of living in the cold or doing it as an act of revenge on her parents,

"Now go, goodbye." She pushed me away and ran to catch a departing metro bus. After my conversation with Hillary, I crept inside McDonald's and merged with the breakfast crowd. I ordered a breakfast meal, trying to maintain a low profile. The restaurant buzzed with morning chatter, against which I strained to eavesdrop for any useful tidbits.

My attempts to remain inconspicuous faltered, however, as two boys by the door, holding skateboards, caught sight of me. They began to snicker, whispering to each other while their eyes remained fixed on me, adding a layer of discomfort to my already heightened sense of exposure. One of them slipped out the door while the other lingered inside. Stuck at a crossroads, I trusted my instincts and fled as fast as I could. The sound of my pursuer's footsteps grew closer and closer as I blindly ran for my life. Going to the police was my last resort. In my world, the code was to avoid law enforcement at all costs. The cops didn't like us, and we didn't like them.

The police were always on our tails: to bring us back to our parents, assuming they cared; for stealing food, beer, or anything else they deemed valuable; or for catching us doing drugs. Glancing back, I saw the kid chasing after me, sending a surge of fear coursing through my veins. I dashed across Third and Pike Street, narrowly avoiding colliding with a bus and several cars as the wind whipped past me. Unbeknownst to me, my panicked flight for survival caught the attention of a nearby motorcycle cop. It wasn't until he blared his siren that I realized I was being pursued. I refused to stop, triggering a full-blown police response. They cornered me outside the Fifth Avenue Theatre, guns drawn and aimed at my trembling body. "Hands up! Get on the ground!" they shouted. My heart pounded in my chest as I shut my eyes, bracing for the impact of bullets. I collapsed to the pavement, my sobs echoing off the surrounding walls. Once in the police car, the cop questioned me. "What the hell were you running from?"

"Barely able to speak, my chest heaved as I struggled for air, and with a trembling voice, I managed to whisper the chilling words. "I... I think they're going to kill me." The terror that had engulfed me moments ago still lingers, intensified by the knowledge that I'm now headed to juvie. As I was being taken into custody, the police car became my uneasy refuge, surrounded by an overwhelming sense of fear and uncertainty. My heart raced, my breaths came in short bursts, and I could feel the tears welling up in my eyes. The reality of my situation sank in as I contemplated the unknown world of juvenile detention.

"Who's going to kill you?" The officer commanded with authority.

I spoke in a frenzied tone, gasping for air between my words. "Those guys and boys back there... they killed my friend, Lauren McCluskie."

The officer spoke into his radio, using jargon that I couldn't decipher. With that, the other cars sped off, their lights flashing and sirens blaring. The burly officer drove me to the police station. There, I was interviewed by a detective who wanted to know everything about me, from my past as a runaway to my struggles with drugs, alcohol, and sex, and finally to my friend's death. I refused to divulge anything about the flophouses, but the detective wouldn't let up. He demanded to know every detail, from the locations of the houses to the people I knew and how we gained entry.

When I lied, he called me out on it, saying, "Let's start over from where the truth dropped off." Then he asked about Lauren. I was traumatized and just sat there reliving that night. I gave them the details about Brady and Cameron, how they all disappeared into the night by the market. I didn't feel comfortable going into the darkness and stayed behind. When I heard Lauren's horrific scream, it scared me so badly; I knew something cruel had happened. I ran and hid. After telling them everything I knew, they sent me to juvie for protection. My days on the streets—at least in Seattle—were over.

I cried the whole night, my body still shaking violently, thinking I never got to say goodbye to Lauren, sad that they had taken her from my life. A month later, a social worker reconnected my parents and me.

My mother promised me a better home life. It felt weird being back in this house of secret sexual abuse. No one in the family was in jail or had been questioned about the sexual manipulation, so they were pretty sure I hadn't told on any of them. I was older and could put up a fight if anyone tried. Slowly, we repaired our family connection. I forgave them, and we all focused on living everyday life. We started therapy, but there was so much I couldn't—wouldn't—tell her.

"I cannot even believe I'm sharing this with you. I suppressed those years as deep within my psyche as possible. If they were coal, they'd be diamonds by now. I figured if I loved my family three times more than they loved me, we'd all be happy, and they'd forgive me for whatever I did to make them use me for sex.

"After returning to school, I had the good fortune of meeting a dynamic and loving group of friends whom I bonded with immediately. Their support was instrumental in aiding my recovery, and I learned the true meaning of genuine friendships. My therapist suggested that I enroll in AA, and I was able to leave behind all the self-destructive behaviors of my past, including cigarettes, booze, and drugs. The school became my sanctuary, and I poured my heart and soul into making up for lost time. I excelled in all my classes, graduated with honors, and eventually pursued higher education in college and medical school."

This is a story I have never shared with anyone, not even my closest friends. But for some inexplicable reason, I felt compelled to share it with him. "I understand that this may be a lot to handle, and I will completely respect your decision if we never speak again," I said to him.

He nodded, saying he understood. I responded defiantly, as though he couldn't possibly understand. He hadn't suffered and survived the way I had. "No, you don't. You can't understand unless you've lived on that block. So please don't believe you need to appease me."

"Hey. I'm not saying I understand the pains inside, but I understand your emotions. However, you can't capitalize on trauma as though you're the only person to have experienced it. Your life experiences, though painful, are not unique to you. We all know pain, and this isn't a competition. I'm not running away from your past. It's you pushing me away because of it. How do you plan to live or love if you're wearing it around your neck, allowing it to drag you down, or keep you from letting someone else care for you?" As he spoke, I realized he was right and that my response had been overly harsh.

I guess I came on far too heavy. *Time to go.* "I'm sorry to have burdened you this evening. Thank you for your hospitality. You're a charming man, *But I should go*," I thought, chastising myself for the outpouring of words, fearing I had already said too much and irreparably frayed the evening's gentle weave.

"No. No, no, no, please. Please relax. I just need to get a refill. Would you like me to warm yours?"

I realized the whole time speaking that I was gripping the cup so tightly that I had to pry my fingers away. I declined the refresher and worked to relax my grip. He returned with a hot cup of coffee. "Okay, sorry, I'd like to share my perspective with you. Thank you for being so open with me. I respected your courage and how you not only rehabilitated your life but excelled. You are a truly remarkable woman. Though I knew you lost your friend, you lived and overcame your obstacles. I admired you for trusting me with so much of your backstory. I don't know about tomorrow. I live each day of my life with passion and perspective on what can be.

You said you are an iceberg. Through my lens, I see life as a majestic river flowing at a smooth pace. However, I know before it got to that place, the waters were tumultuous and heartbreaking upstream. You mentioned love, romance, and honesty. Let me address them from my vantage point:

Love is a destination. Many people say they want to journey, but they seldom equip themselves to make it beyond the adversity of the first year. I have learned that to make love's destination. You commit to faith: belief in your partner and always be honest about your feelings, desires, and ambitions, leaving nothing to the chance of miscommunication, to be one hundred percent dedicated to a long life of love and happiness. And when there are turbulent times, we grab each other and come out on the other side together. If you allow me into your life, I'll be vigilant to protect your heart. I can't guarantee I will never hurt you. But if I do, I'll do everything I can to learn and never do it again."

I absorbed his words. They touched my soul. The hours have finally taken a toll on me. It's 2:30 in the morning. He extends his hand. "Would you like to come to bed?" Saying yes sends energy surging through my veins. I follow him to his bedroom. I undress to my bra and panties, crawling into bed, telling him, "I don't want to be a tease, but would you mind just holding me this evening? I'm feeling emotionally humiliated after our talk."

He pulls me into his arms. "I do not mind."

This gave me a great appreciation for him. That evening was the beginning of our tomorrow. For the first time in a long time—perhaps in my life — I felt the reassuring warmth of love and compassion.

My amour had become the reliable, supportive partner I had always dreamed of. For the next six months of our relationship, I spent the majority of my evenings snuggled up with him at his place. His job required him to be constantly on the move, hopping from one destination to the next. He was generally away from home three to four days every other week. I found myself missing him and anxiously awaiting his return home.

Chapter Eighteen

I have been basking in the glow of romantic bliss for an entire year, utterly captivated by the love I share with my amour. He has always been the epitome of perfection, showering me with affection and adoration. However, recently, a subtle shift has taken place in our relationship. I can't quite put my finger on it, but his behavior has become somewhat altered.

The once passionate and attentive man I knew now appears distracted and distant, especially after his business trips. There's an unspoken tension that lingers in the air, leaving me with a sense of unease. I can't help but wonder what might be causing this change. Could there be someone else occupying his thoughts, a shadowy presence in the background? Despite these doubts creeping in, my love for him remains unwavering, and I'm determined to navigate this uncertain phase and reclaim the deep connection we once shared.

Two nights ago, I was looking forward to him coming home. I'd been lonely and missed him for the days he was gone. After he got settled, he went and sat on the lounge in front of the television. Ignoring that, I had dinner prepared and the table set. I understood that he probably had a long, stressful trip and needed some time to himself. But I frowned at the fact that he showed no interest in my presence other than hello. I tried to make him feel good, telling him I missed him and I'm glad he's home. All I got was a grunt. "Missed you too."

This is not my man, thinking to myself. So, I gave him his space. Finally, after an hour, I asked him if he planned to have dinner. "No, I'm fine. I only want to relax."

Very well, thanks for letting me know. Another dinner to be put in the fridge. Great. I lost my appetite after the disappointing shut down of expecting to have an intimate evening with my man.

I sat next to him on the sofa. He wasn't really watching television but using it to ignore me. I asked him if there was something bothering him. "Can I get you anything? Is everything okay?" His reply was a dry, "All is well. I'm just taking it easy." Talk about having a door slammed in your face. I realized I wasn't a part of his evening. So, I told him, "Sweetheart, I know you're appearing to be stressed and obviously don't want to talk to me. I'm going to give you space and go take a bath. You're welcome to join me."

His disinterested dismissal irritated me. I'm left wondering what the hell was happening with him. I sat on the ottoman where he had his feet propped up, rubbing his leg, telling him, "I'm sorry that you had an unpleasant trip. I recognize something is troubling you. But please understand that when you're behaving unexpectedly, I'm concerned, and I'd appreciate you at least recognizing me enough to say you care about how I'm feeling when you're just shutting me out. You totally ignored the fact that I made dinner and didn't even say thank you."

He rolled his eyes, telling me he was not one of my goddamn patients; so much for the compassionate approach. Things got progressively worse, as I responded, "I'm not trying to be your doctor. I'm your woman. Remember the person you profess to love?"

"I don't feel like dealing with this shit tonight." He huffed a sigh of exasperation, got up, grabbed his shoes, and left. I was left home wondering, what lit his fuse this evening? Why was he so bothered by my concerns? I would have called Gina to lament. However, I was miserable enough. I don't want her overly critical opinion denouncing my man, adding to my concerns. I explored the regions of my brain, replaying the event prior to his leaving and return home. Nothing resonated. I dismissed it, thinking he must have had a horrible trip and would talk about it later. However, I didn't appreciate him leaving so abruptly. I thought about calling him, but given his departure mood, I didn't want to perpetuate an argument over the phone.

He arrived home at 2:45 a.m. He rambles around in the bathroom, showering, then he eases in bed. I'm filled with curiosity. Where has he been? I can deduce he hasn't been in a bar with one of his buddies. I'm lying there, wanting him to show me affection. Finally, his hand slides on me around my waist.

My tense body relaxes, imploring him to explain his condition before leaving and returning home, giving no acknowledgment of his last blowup. However, I preferred the affection over igniting a powder keg that would end with me going to work with baggy and bloodshot eyes and wanting to cry all day. I allowed him to pull me close. If he wanted sex, he had to work for it. And he did.

The next morning, we didn't discuss the evening and his time of arrival home. Another matter tucked away in my memory. If he thinks sex cured the problem, he's morbidly wrong. In the meantime, I'll keep trying to provide justification for his behavior, a way for me to process it as acceptable so that it does not bog us down in futile disagreements and I can forgive him.

My conclusion, since we've merged our lives, perhaps we are both feeling overwhelmed with the multitude of changes in new financial and social adjustments, joint mortgage, new neighbors, new cars, and different commutes to work. Our work schedules have been hectic. I'm working more, and he travels—a lot.

I shouldn't complain. We are financially healthy. It's been said that hard work gives you success—and it affords you a glorious life with high incomes—but they never put an emotional dollar price on it. Allow me to tell you, it's very pricey: Loneliness—even when he's home, he's working or preoccupied with work—long separation, starved for attention, sexual frustration, distractions. I could go on.

Would I rather be poor? Hmm, a very contemplative question. I guess it depends on how you define the poor. In the beginning, I loved the idea of the enormous home, the new car, and being financially secure. However, in my heart I think I'd be happy with a small cottage, two kids, and a less emotionally demanding professional life, regular nine-to-five work weeks.

Chapter Nineteen

The time had finally arrived. We had been navigating the intricate dance of our busy lives, adjusting to the stresses that often come with melding two worlds. Our journey had begun with the excitement of a budding relationship, but as time passed, it felt like some of the seams holding us together had eroded. It was time to regain that lost traction, to recreate moments of uninterrupted togetherness.

As the plane took off from the tarmac, I reclined my seat and reached for my amour's hand, feeling a sense of relief wash over me. With every breath, I exhaled the accumulated stress that had burdened us in the weeks leading up to this moment. Fatigue enveloped me, and I surrendered to a deep slumber, awakening only when prompted to adjust my seat to an upright position.

Stepping off the plane, the humidity instantly embraced us, a stark contrast to the chilly and rainy climate we had left behind in Seattle. Beads of perspiration formed on my skin, dotting my pink cotton tank top. The change in weather was a refreshing welcome, a tangible manifestation of the vibrant tropical paradise that awaited us. In my mind's eye, I could already picture the blissful scenes that lay ahead. Our villa, a haven of relaxation, awaited our arrival. I envisioned myself reclining by the pool, lounging on a comfortable chaise lounge, and indulging in the breathtaking view of the ocean from our secluded haven. The anticipation grew as I imagined strolling along the beach under the starry night sky, the soothing sound of waves serenading our steps. The thought of these experiences fueled my excitement, and a smile danced upon my lips. This beautiful, sun-kissed destination held the promise of unforgettable moments and cherished memories. We had finally escaped the gray skies and rain, trading them for a slice of paradise that had captivated our dreams.

With renewed energy and a sense of adventure, we set forth, eager to immerse ourselves in the wonders that Zihuantanejo had to offer. I was excited. I'd give serious consideration to fuck him in the taxi if he asked me. I know it would be awkward for our driver, Jesus, but I'm aching to make love. The cab isn't air-conditioned; the humidity has me soaking wet, heightening my arousal. The hot air swirls around us. I want to be intimate so badly. My breasts were moist with perspiration, and my nipples were hard and aching. I slid my eyes to my amour.

Thinking how badly I wanted him last night. But rousing him was like waking the dead. I couldn't even get the satisfaction of giving him a blowjob. But today is all different. I spy Jesus out of the corner of my eye, adjusting his mirror as I lean to kiss my amour. Okay, buster, you want a show. At first, I was only going to give him a little tease, but my man pulled me onto him, and I couldn't resist wrapping my arms around him, sucking in his tongue, and giving him mine. I turned so Jesus couldn't see me grab my man's cock. It was rock-hard. I ached to get on top and grind the hell out of it.

Thoughts fluttered in my mind, the things I wanted to do with him as soon as we were in the hotel room. I kindled my stimulated thoughts, realizing there was a little too much display of affection.

Dear God, I was so horny. We hadn't had sex in a week, and his touch would be like throwing a burning match onto the forest floor's dry tinder. I drew in air through my teeth, grabbing it firmly. My mind was running crazy. I entertained the desire of jerking him off in the back seat. *Shit, I need to contain myself until we're in the room.* I found myself gasping while delicate droplets of perspiration cascaded along the contours of my back. With an ardent jolt, I retracted myself from the profound abyss of yearnings. *Whew. Okay, Jesus, the show is over.* I returned to sitting on my side of the seat, settling for holding my Amour's hand.

I asked Jesus, "Ah," Trying to regain my composure, "Excuse me." *I'm so flustered I can't wait to get there*, "How far would you say, are we from Villa El Ensueño?" He replied in broken English, "It's ah, I say maybe six more minutes." *Very exacting.* However, twenty torturous minutes elapsed before we coasted to a halt at our hotel.

Dear God, finally. I enjoyed the change in elements, but it's going to take me a few days to get acclimated. Right now, I wanted the air conditioning to pee, shower, and have sex. Then, sleep and do it all over again.

The last five days have been glorious. We sat on the beach, a distance from the lights of nearby restaurants. In the darkness, the glowing moon hung in the sky like a large orb. The stars higher above shimmering against the canvas of the universe's blackness were our audience twinkling cheers. The ocean, our orchestra, the cadence of waves roaring to shore with voluminous force. Our feet were just away from the rolling swash, followed by the susurration of retreating waters returning to unite in the next mythical surge.

The wind blew softly and warmly, enveloping us in a cocoon of solitude. It was as if we were the sole inhabitants of this planet. This night belonged exclusively to us. I was in love with every aspect of this man. We sat there, relishing nature's recital. He spoke, his voice distant, as if detached from his own body, mentioning, "This is a perfect night, an incredible vacation. I'll be forever grateful to have you in my life. I know I've been somewhat preoccupied lately, and—" *That was putting it lightly.* "However, I felt something was missing." My mind was ablaze with curiosity. What could possibly be missing? He had just described the night as perfect. I twirled around to face him, half-expecting a shooting star to streak across the sky. Given the way I had been feeling, I wouldn't have been surprised if one did.

He smiled gently and said, "I can see the stars in your eyes. They're beautiful."

"That's what's wrong? My eyes?" He shook his head.

"Then what is it?" He knelt in the sand, pulling a ring box out of his pocket. *Oh my god! Oh my god! Finally, the ice wall is starting to thaw, and the man is stooping before me.*

"Cyn, I love you with all my heart. You're the most loving, compassionate, and loving woman I have ever known… will you marry me?" Dear God, I cried puddles of tears. He took my hand, waiting. I tackled him.

"How dare you scare the hell out of me? Yes! I love you!" I straddled him, helping him slide it onto my finger. I couldn't have asked for a better moment. I lowered my head to greet his kiss. His tongue rolled across my lips. My mouth was open to receive it. I'm consuming every portion of my man. I want the wonderment of everything tonight. I kissed him, gripping his dick. It's hard and unbendable. I pump it.

I work down, kissing until I have it in my mouth, sucking his rock-hard cock until I feel him ready to come. I hum from the sensation, stroking it hard, until he moans, "Oh god, Cyn, babe, please." I felt his come squirting into my mouth. He pulled me up. He strokes my hair. "Babe, I love you so much." I rest my head on his chest, listening to the thumping beats of his heart. Suddenly overcome by a burst of desire, he exclaimed, "We should get married here tomorrow night, in this same serene place, in the glow and prosperity of the full moon. Let's seize the moment with all this beauty around us. Just look at the brilliance of the moonlight. This vast, beautiful ocean stretched out before us, its shimmering waves glistening in the moonlight. I want to go home with you as my wife."

Oh god. I wasn't ready for that response. *Just because I sucked his cock here doesn't mean I want to get married in the same spot.* On this beautiful night, the evening had been fascinating until now. I didn't want it to take a turn into yet another dispute, fearing that he might sense my hesitation as rejection and the night would deteriorate into a hellish experience. I paused for a few dramatic, uncomfortable moments, trying my best to appease and preserve the romantic connection between us.

"I love you, and I will be your wife. I can't think of a more splendid location. *How to I absolve this…* I plan to be with you forever. However, I couldn't marry you without my family and friends present. Please understand," I explained. *The truth was I needed my audience to champion and support me in my happiness. I longed for my girlfriends' admiration, knowing they would support my joy. I had come a long way in my life to reach this moment, and I wanted to bask in its splendor.*

He exhaled an exasperated sigh, and my body tensed. I had derailed his spontaneous proposal. "I'm sorry," I whispered, but he said nothing, staring out into the sea without responding. I sensed his disappointment, and even the ocean seemed to have fallen silent. I softly touched his arm, leaning into him. "Hold me. Please understand that I love you with all my heart," I implored. "I want us to have the important people in our lives present. What about your sister? Your friends? I want our day to be perfect. I will always be by your side and promise to love you with every fiber in my body."

"Hold me. Please understand that I love you with all my heart," I implored. "I want us to have the important people in our lives present. What about your sister? Your friends? I want our day to be perfect. I will always be by your side and promise to love you with every fiber in my body."

Though asking about his sister's presence probably wasn't a good mention, given her past divorce traumas, I was confident she wouldn't give an enthusiastic blessing. I had met his sister on occasion, and I didn't get the impression that we would become best friends or that she would wholeheartedly champion her brother's marriage.

Finally, he turned, pulling me into his arms. His voice sounded somber and detached. "...it was an impulsive moment. I understand. We can do it your way... discuss dates when we return home."

We sat together on the moonlit beach, the warm night air carrying the salty scent of the ocean. The gentle sounds of waves caressing the shore filled the atmosphere with a soothing melody. A slight chill ran through me, and I instinctively nestled closer into his comforting arms.

The night embraced us with the enchantment of the ocean, creating the ideal setting for our romantic moment. His hands slid across my breast. I closed my eyes, welcoming the sensation of his kiss. He pulled my shorts off, and I tugged the button off his pants vigorously.

I enjoyed being on top of him, looking down at his face. *Oh God, I was so wet* it felt incredible as I pushed down. Hard. Panting as I worked my ass, clenching my teeth, enjoying the exhilarating shocks of his cock jamming inside me until I was nearing the ecstasy of climax, biting my lower lip, clawing his chest. Holding my breath, doing all I could to starve off my orgasm. I delight from the firm grip on my ass. My mind cries, *fuck me, hard babe, I love you. Fuck me.*

I gyrated harder, ramming my Gloria down his shaft, shocking my senses with a delightful jolt. His body tenses as he tries to hold his ejaculate, grunting until he can't control it. I absorb his hot release, triggering mine. I struggled to stifle my screams of exhilaration, crying, murmuring through my clenched teeth. My body is drenching sweat from the heat of my aerobic fuck. Winded, I collapsed on top of him, breathing deeply, pulling in the night air and his sweet musk, purring, "I love you so much."

Following our beach adventure and the shared moments of ecstasy, we strolled back to our villa hand in hand. Upon our return, we indulged in a soothing shower together, followed by an intimate encore of lovemaking. Afterward, he succumbed to slumber within an hour, but my veins still pulsed with lingering energy. I decided to retrieve my trusted diary, which had been untouched for some time, to document the whirlwind of thoughts racing through my mind.

Dear Diary,

I've been away from you for a while; my life has been moving fast, and it's moving faster.

The night air is warm and tranquil here in Zihuatanejo. The gentle sound of the ocean waves soothes my restless mind. I look up at the sky and see the stars twinkling in the darkness. It's a sight that steals your breath away, leaving you in awe of its stunning beauty. The view is nothing short of magnificent. I wish I could capture this moment forever. I'm enveloped by the gentle caress of the night, like a loving embrace that cradles my soul. The air carries the sweet fragrance of blooming flowers mingled with the salty sea breeze, creating an enchanting atmosphere. This night is nothing short of magical, a moment when time itself seems to stand still, and I long to be suspended in its beauty eternally. Yet, my thoughts persistently return to the proposal, tugging at the corners of my mind like an unanswered melody. I know he loves me, but I need more time to plan the wedding of my dreams.

I want him to understand that it's not about the size or the cost of the wedding but about the meaning and symbolism behind it. I want to start our life together with a beautiful and meaningful ceremony, surrounded by the people we love.

As I sit here, lost in thought, excitement fills me at the prospect of announcing our news back home. I believe the reception will be filled with warmth and joy, just like this evening. There were some initial concerns among my parents and friends, but I know they'll come around to support us. I cherish the days when we were celebrated as a great couple, and I'm confident that they'll see the love and happiness in our relationship. This vacation has reaffirmed our love, and I'm certain about the path we're on. I stand by my man, knowing that our bond is strong, and I'm eager to share our joy with our loved ones. Tonight, I'll fall asleep beside my love, and in the days to come, we'll plan our wedding. After all, I've always been a 100% kind of girl, and I can't wait to embark on this new chapter with him.

Reflectively, Cyn

We returned home from our retreat, our hearts filled with the deep conversations and rekindled love we had shared. Just in time for the holiday celebrations, my family had a tradition of celebrating the eight days leading up to Christmas. On the first day, as we arrived home from the airport, I couldn't help but wonder how to approach announcing our engagement. Should I keep it quiet for a couple of days, or perhaps make the declaration after Christmas dinner when everyone would be in good spirits? I decided to keep it low-key and say nothing.

Once at my mother's house, I pressed the doorbell button with my left hand, making certain my amour noticed, thinking it would register in his mind that I was wearing it upon our arrival and would pay little attention if I kept my hands from view. My intentions were to start by telling Mom and Dad on a separate occasion, and they'd make the proclamation to the rest of the family.

My mom greeted us at the door. Gave me a big hug. She and my amour were cordial. They are warm and friendly but not excited to see each other. I discreetly took the brilliantly sparkling ring off my finger and tucked it in my jeans pocket. Doing it ripped my heart apart because I was proud that we were engaged and wanted everyone to be happy for us. However, my calculations were that grudges would be forgiven by the third night, and I could show off my beauty.

We filled the night with great conversations. My aunt and her husband, my brother, sister-in-law, two nieces, and three nephews were there to share in the merriments. The evening was filled with laughter and talk of the upcoming holidays. It was a wonderful evening; questions abound about our vacation. Which I was happy to share, omitting certain activities.

Finally, we left at midnight. I was totally exhausted. I was basking in the joys and festivities of holiday spirits. I wanted us to hurry home so I could take a hot shower and we snuggle in our own bed together. As soon as we got in the car, I kissed him with lots of tongues. "Take me home so I can ravish your body." He was quiet. *Shit. Shit. Shit. My ring.* I tried distracting him on the drive, talking enthusiastically about going back to work as I discreetly worked my diamond onto my hand. "Yes, we're back to reality," he said flatly. Fear raced through my body. I don't want an argument tonight. *Dear God, what do I say?* With my finger properly adorned, I placed my hand on his thigh. I felt his leg tense. He moved my hand, telling me not to touch him.

My mind is perplexed, I thought to explain why I didn't wear it. However, I knew I could say nothing that would calm his anger. Things could only deteriorate. I knew he'd pick up on my rejection of eloping in Mexico because of my parents. And tonight, I hid my ring. There was no rational way out of it. I could only hope he didn't explode on the drive home.

So, we were silent for the forty-five minutes it took us to get home. By this time, I was truly exhausted and knew the moment of intimacy was gone. On the fourth night, he refused to go any other evening and vehemently stated that he was not attending my family's New Year's Eve gathering. It worsened when he told me to go alone. That meant he was okay, with or without me. Great way to make a woman feel loved. I told him, "It's not my desire to be away from my fiancé on New Year's. Where will you spend New Year's without me?"

"I have friends and other places I'd like to go other than being cooped up with your mind-numbing parents—whom I hate, by the way. It's your choice if you want to go."

I glared with intense anger. "You hate my parents? What are you saying to me? We're engaged, about to get married, and you don't want to be around my parents? I've made an effort to support your choices and do what you want, and now you're using such offensive words. Go to hell. Go wherever you want."

In the middle of our disagreement, his phone rings. It's that fucking antagonizing ringtone that had become familiar. I fell silent, gritting my teeth, my eyes glaring. "Are you going to answer it?" I huffed, my frustration tempting me to grab the damn thing and throw it out the window. "Who was it? And why was that ringtone so different from all your others?"

"I have ringtones for various people, so I know who's calling without having to look at my phone," I say nothing as he's driving. I discreetly dial his number to see what my ringtone is. Figures the standard default, and he ignores it. So, I suppose my ringtone must signify that I am an insignificant woman. I feel dejected and tell him I'll be on call in the ER on New Year's Eve if that makes things better for planning his festivities. I may as well be of benefit to someone since I'm not needed at home.

Chapter Twenty

Four large scented candles on tiered pillars illuminate the bathroom. I slip into the soothing spa, seeking solace. The hot water brings a momentary comfort to my sullen spirits. I find myself trapped in a heart-wrenching quandary after this morning's conversation.

Disappointment fills my heart as I reflect on my participation in what I try to justify as a mutual agreement. Deep down, I know I yielded to his logic, not ready to embrace the prospect of having a child. The weight of my decision weighs heavily upon me, compounded by the fact that this is my second abortion in just two months' time. I can't help but feel an overwhelming sense of despair. Adding to my distress was the knowledge that I couldn't confide in my friends or family.

The thought of revealing my situation fills me with intense humiliation. How can I possibly say, *"Hey, remember last month when I underwent an abortion? Well, here I am, facing another one."* The mere thought of their judgment makes me cringe with shame. So, I bear this burden alone, suppressing my emotions and stifling my pain. It's not only the fear of sharing my struggles with others; it goes against the very core of who I am. I have always staunchly supported a woman's right to choose, but when it comes to my personal beliefs, I can't fathom extinguishing the life growing within me. I saw it as a divine blessing, a precious gift from God. Especially for me, it would have been a chance to experience the boundless love that came from nurturing a life that was a part of me, regardless of whether it was a boy or a girl.

My amour doesn't know the torment I feel inside. I yearn to confide in him, but I restrain myself, fearing it might ignite an argument. Why must we wait until after marriage to consider starting a family? Our baby was already taking shape within me. He'll ask about birth control. *Yes, absolutely, a thousand times, yes, I am meticulous with my birth control.* Yet, here we are, falling into the unfortunate one percent twice over.

The comforting warmth of the water envelops me, and my mind drifts back to memories of my friend Kayleigh Marie Jansen, a fellow classmate during my final year of med school. Kayleigh, an extraordinary figure, stood tall at 6'0" with a radiant beauty that captivated men's hearts. They eagerly vied for her attention, willing to do anything to be seen by her side, walking proudly next to the stunning, statuesque blonde. Throughout our journey from high school to med school, Kayleigh faced the painful decision of undergoing seven abortions. The frequency of these procedures left me deeply unsettled, to the point where I gradually distanced myself from her, unable to confront her about the moral implications of her contraceptive choices.

One evening my phone's income call screen lit up, Kayleigh Levenson's name displayed. I hadn't spoken to her in over a year. I sent the call to voice mail. Given our last interaction, I didn't have the desires to hear about her latest gift or her current best fuck ever, and how he showered her with gifts, or the latest trip to wherever.

The last time she called, she wanted to boast about her newest gift, a thirty-thousand-dollar tennis bracelet given to her by Tarek. Her newest lover was living in Dubai. I recalled rolling my eyes, part resentment, part jealousy. My greatest elation in the past was a handmade necklace from my last boyfriend, purchased at Pike Place Market—it's the thought that counts, right?

I listened to Kayleigh's message in the afternoon two days later. "Cyn." She bawls, trying to catch her breath. "It's me. Kayleigh. I know you think I'm a horrible person, and you probably hate me. But I always thought of you as my most trusted friend. Someone— actually the only one—who always listened to me and I could share my deepest secrets with and not be judged. Do you remember that old black guy who used to always approach us in a red square where we studied? Haddock was his name, right? Yes. How did his poem go?"

"Never have I ever seen two beings as breathtaking as you. One adorned with locks of golden radiance, the other adorned with locks as dark as the night sky. Together, you bring a heightened splendor to the day and embody the essence of the nocturnal. Fortunate is the person who basks in the brilliance of either of you. Blessed am I to revel in your magnificence as I pass by, a simple and humble servant of God. I send a tender kiss to the heavens above, for I am one of the privileged souls bestowed with the gift of sight to behold two of His most exquisite creations."

Her reflection on Haddock seemed to brighten her tone. I, too, loved Haddock's verse. Her message continued, "Back then, I thought he was just a creepy old weirdo. Now, I feel he was the only person whose praise was true…. Cyn… I'm hurting, and I thought I'd feel better if I heard your voice and words of encouragement. However, fate rules this evening, and I take this as a sign that I'm doing the right thing, saying goodbye to you all. Your friend, or should I say ex-friend?" she said with a sarcastic laugh.

"However, the least... the least you could have done was tell me to my face that you didn't want to be friends anymore. Yes, I am pregnant—again. That's why I'm calling you because I need a friend. But you hate me. Don't you? I don't blame you. I'm tired of guys thinking they can just knock me up, throw their fucking money in my lap, telling me to deal with it. How would a man feel if someone snatched off their cock and then said to deal with it? I have come to realize that I could never give a child the love it needs. I have too many needs of my own to take on the burdens of giving life. Here's something you don't know. I have tried birth control, but my body reacts negatively to all the preventative measures. Yea me. That includes IUDs. Guys never want to take responsibility for birth control. All they care about is sticking their cocks inside of me for their greedy ass gratifications. Though condoms gave me a negative reaction, I insisted on using them. But men being boys, used rubbers maybe once, twice—three times max in the beginning. But! Concerned for their own sexual sensations, it becomes all about excuses."

"We don't need condoms if we're in a committed relationship."

"Lying to me, pointing suspicious fingers, accusing me of being a cheat because of a simple request to wear a goddamn prophylactic. I'm so fucking, fucking, fucking, stupid. I let them abandon the practice and put the burden on me. Maybe when you become a prominent doctor, you can invent a drug that helps fucked up people like me. I know in my heart of hearts that abortions are wrong. Well... I can promise you it will never happen again. Guaranteed. Anyway, I'm going to go away, Cynthya. Thank you for once, being my friend."

My heart raced with panic. What did she mean by going away? Was she finally going to be with one of her boyfriends? Her Dubai man? Athens? Rome! Sadly, I received my answer later that evening.

An acquaintance named Nicole called, asking if I had heard the news that Kayleigh was dead.

"Dead?" I asked, bombarding her with questions to which she had no answers. All she knew was that Kayleigh had jumped from the Aurora Street bridge. That seemed impossible to me. Kayleigh was far too self-absorbed to take her own life. A broken nail would send her spiraling into a frenzy, let alone the hassle of jumping off a fenced bridge. Nicole must have been mistaken. I decided to follow up with the Seattle Police Department to obtain their report. As I read it, my heart sank. Her message to me was at 7:08 PM. The police report stated that a concerned motorist had called in, reporting the sighting of a young lady attempting to breach the suicide barrier on the Aurora Bridge at 7:20 PM.

Officers arrived on the scene at 7:28 p.m. It is recorded that she had navigated the fence and jumped as the patrol cars were rolling to a stop. They recovered her body an hour later. *Dear God, how could life be so cruel?* To think I was the last person she called. If only I hadn't been a judgmental bitch and answered her call, I could have saved her life. How will I live that down?

Chapter Twenty-One

My mournful discontent extended to Kayleigh's memorial service. Afterward, I visited her family's home, a place I had frequented when we were closer. Her mother, Margaret Levinson, was always sweet and doting on me. She believed our friendship positively influenced Kayleigh, keeping her focused.

"I know it's a terrible burden, but please keep an eye on her. You guys are going to be wonderful doctors," she would often say. In the kitchen, Margaret was surrounded by Kayleigh's two younger sisters and many other mourners. I crept in, greeting her with, "Hello, Mrs. Levinson." She looked at me, almost as if seeing me for the first time, and dabbed away tears.

"Cynthya?"

"Yes, ma'am."

"Oh dear lord, come here, sweetheart." Her arms flung open, pulling me into a crushing, motherly embrace. I knew she was holding me as a representative of Kayleigh's spirit. "It's so good to see you. Please, come to my study so we can chat. Sorry about the bear hug."

"It's okay. I always loved your mama's hugs."

She closed the doors to her study. "It's ungodly rude of me to sneak away from so many people, but I want to speak to you. I'm so glad you came." I sat on the leather sofa; she took a seat beside me. "I understand that you and Kayleigh had stopped talking." Another layer of bricks seemed to fall on top of me. Tears welled in my eyes.

I lowered my head, ashamed, "I wouldn't say we stopped speaking… school just got really busy and—"

"Dear lord, my child, please don't think I'm about to blame you," she reassured, wrapping her arms around me. "Heaven's no. I understand she had her priorities and could push people away who interfered with them. She was a strong, self-willed girl with a penchant for men: the gifts, the cars, the trips. They were distractions for my baby. I'd like to share something with you to better explain how she felt. I'm sure you're wondering yourself." She patted me on the leg. "Stay here a moment; I'll be right back." She returned with Kayleigh's journal, handing it to me. "Are you sure you want me to read this?"

"Yes, I've bound all the other pages except for the few that matter."

Holding Kayleigh's diary, a testament to her most private thoughts and experiences, felt like a delicate transgression, yet an invitation I couldn't refuse. As I opened it, the first sentence immediately captured my attention, sparking a deep curiosity about the revelations to come.

This was no ordinary book; it was a sacred confidante of her innermost feelings, a treasure trove of her life's story, previously shared with no one else. With a sense of honor and a tinge of apprehension, I began to delve into the pages, eager to connect with the essence of her being:

I'm a fucking breeding machine. Seven abortions cut to the core of my soul. But here I am once again, two months pregnant. But this one I planned to keep. It's mine and Dr. Colin Hightower's — he's 45 and handsome. Oh my god, I am so captivated by this man. We met at Harbor View's community medical day. I was doing my volunteer work, providing medical care to the homeless. Colin was the physician leading our team. I spent the day treating a plethora of ills. He was excellent and compassionate with each person. I couldn't help but admire his command and depth of knowledge in aiding discarded people labeled homeless or societal blights. Watching him gave me a sense of purpose and helped me realize how vital my pursuit of becoming a doctor is. By the end of our twelve hours shift, we were exhausted. All I could think of was going home, taking a shower, and curling up in bed. I assumed he would be heading home as well. But he asked me to dinner. And voila, the rest is history, or I should say, the beginning of our story.

Though a bit of a bad influence, he loves me—constantly stealing me away on the weekends, telling me he'll help me with my studies. I swoon. I can't say no to this man... My friends are annoyed—more like jealous bitches.

Sorry, Cyn, I've seen your sneers as well. But you take love when it kisses you and let it grow like a tree. Last week, we stayed at a cabin on Crystal Mountain. It was so frickin romantic! And the sex, OMG! It was awesome. We lit a fire Friday evening, sat, talked, and made love. We got up Saturday morning. The rousing flames died to flickers. Colin got dressed and went outside, picking up an ax. I watched him chop and stack wood for the fireplace in the falling snow through the window. It thrilled me to see this medical whiz with delicate surgical hands trade in his white smock and transform into a roughed outdoorsman. After chopping wood for the weekend, we made passionate love in the shower. I denied none of his sexual requests. None. He was a sex-starved mad man who rammed me hard, pushing me against the wall. His command and voracious hunger for my body made my orgasms the most intense I have ever experienced. After the third round, I could barely stand; my legs wobbled as I stood up. I am proud that I can give him such passionate pleasures.

We spent the day hiking. The undisturbed snow was glistening white. The tree branches hung low from the weight of the snow. Back at the cabin, he fueled the fire. I have never been alone in this kind of seclusion before. I even protested

219

when he surprised me on the drive-up. My initial thoughts were skeptical: What can one possibly do in a cabin for an entire week? With no television, no nearby shops, and no heat, I had braced myself for a miserable weekend. But, boy, was I wrong. He transformed what I anticipated to be a mundane experience into one of the most enjoyable moments of my life. In the evening, my love, Dr. Colin Hightower, prepared a scrumptious dinner that we savored under the soft glow of candlelight. Not only is he a brilliant doctor and a passionate lover, but I've now discovered his prowess in the kitchen as well. He truly is a fantastic man. Each dish he created was a delightful surprise, a testament to his culinary skills and his desire to make our time special. As we dined, the cabin's seclusion felt like our own little world, where the hustle of everyday life faded into a distant memory. In those moments, with the flickering candles casting a warm light on his face, I saw not just the skilled doctor or the ardent lover but the genuine, multifaceted person he truly is.

We made love in front of the roaring blaze of the fireplace until we exhausted each other falling asleep. The weekend at Crystal Mountain was fa-bu-lous. I hope this feeling never ends. After a life of superficial admiration from men who valued me only for my beauty, Colin's genuine love has been a revelation. He cherishes me for the person I truly am, not just as an ornament on his arm. This profound connection makes me confident in a way I've never been before — I can definitely see myself settling down and marrying him.

Dear Diary,

My birthday brought an unexpected surprise that perfectly encapsulates why Colin is everything I've ever wanted in a man. He's incredibly supportive, clear in his intentions, and deeply loving. And he has this way of easing my worries, like how he addressed my concerns about money and transportation. Imagine my shock and joy when he presented me with a brand-new Mercedes-Benz SLC convertible! The excitement was so overwhelming that I nearly lost my composure — a moment that, in hindsight, is both hilarious and endearing. Knowing Colin, he would've turned even that into a moment of laughter and intimacy. His thoughtfulness and ability to make every situation special, whether grand or awkward, only deepen my affection for him.

He also purchased me a two-bedroom condo near the university, explaining that he didn't want the stress of rent to distract me from my studies. He tells me to focus on becoming the amazing doctor he knows I can be. I expressed my concerns about him taking care of my expenses; it feels like too much. Yet, he is adamant, saying he wants to ensure his future partner isn't weighed down by financial burdens. He believes in us, in a future where we both support each other.

He constantly remarks on my beauty, convinced my patients will be as taken with me as he is. I remind him that my intellect and care are what will endear me to my patients, not just my looks. The fixation on my appearance over my capabilities has always been a sore point for me. However, Colin has a way of blending his admiration for both my mind and body that's endearing. He reassures me with a kiss, half-joking that he hopes the care I offer him will always be just as good as what I offer my patients. I respond with an embrace, the kind that speaks volumes more than words ever could. My affection for him grows deeper by the day.

The thrill of imagining myself as his wife sends waves of joy through me, but Colin's impulsive nature often tests my resolve. His spontaneity is charming yet it can unsettle the rigorous schedule of a med student like me. Last week's impromptu trip proposal is a perfect example. I had to muster all my willpower to tell him that I couldn't afford to be whisked away, not with my studies demanding my attention and a nagging feeling of unwellness. "I have to get caught up on my studies. Plus, I'm not feeling well. I have an appointment this afternoon," I inform him, albeit reluctantly. He's quick to offer his own medical services, but some matters are too private, too close to the heart. I prefer the anonymity of my regular doctor, especially given the intimate nature of my concerns.

With the amount of physical affection we share, the thought of discussing the details with anyone makes my cheeks burn. The possible reasons for my ailment are clear in my mind; the medical school has equipped me well to recognize the signs. Yet there's a part of me that wants to remain in the dark a little longer to delay the confirmation. The knowledge of what this could mean, an unplanned turn in my carefully plotted journey, is daunting. It's not just about my plans; it's about us, about not wanting to divert Colin's focus from our relationship. For now, ignorance is my chosen bliss.

The knowledge weighs on me, but I try to dismiss it, to will it away as if, by sheer force of mind, I could undo reality. I'm no longer the naïve girl of my past; I'm nearly a doctor now, and my partner is one. We've been careless, relying on timing rather than protection, confident in our understanding of my cycles. Yet, here I am, sitting in the familiar examination room, awaiting confirmation of what I already know deep down.

Dr. Sheila Leary enters, her hands casually tucked into her pockets, her demeanor gentle but somber. Her voice, usually encouraging, now holds a tone that reminds me of a mother bracing to deliver unwelcome news. "You're eight weeks pregnant, sweetheart," she says, and the room seems to stand still for a moment.

She has been more than my physician since I was twelve—she's been my mentor, the one who inspired my medical aspirations. Now, she stands before me, once again delivering news of a pregnancy. There's a pause, a knowing look in her eyes as she asks about our plans, anticipating the cascade of reasons I've recited before. The excuses come to mind readily: I can't be a mother right now—not in the midst of high school, college, and now med school. I must establish my career and ensure stability, love from a partner, and the opportunity to travel. The thought of marriage, especially to the last person I was involved with, feels like a trap.

She listens, her expression unreadable, perhaps recalling the many times we've been here before. She knows my history, the pattern of my choices, and likely even the recommendations she's about to make. It's a cycle we've both become all too familiar with.

This time, my answer surprised us both. With a smile that feels like it's opening a new chapter, I embrace the unexpected with acceptance. "I think I'm going to enjoy being a mother," I tell her, and the words feel right. The shock is evident in Dr. Leary's eyes, a brief flicker behind her professional facade. She recovers quickly, though, her congratulations wrapping around me in a warm, sincere hug.

Dear Diary,

The anticipation for the weekend at Salish Lodge with Colin is evident. When I arrive alone, informed of his delay due to an emergency, the quiet that greets me isn't unwelcome. It grants me a moment of calm to relax and perhaps even catch up on some study. Being here, surrounded by the tranquility of nature, I feel a sense of well-being. There's a comfort in knowing that Colin's arrival will soon complete the picture.

Colin calls me at 8:45 PM, his voice tired yet still able to convey warmth over the phone. He's wrapped up at work and has some business matters to attend to with his partner. "I'm pretty bushed. You like the room?" he asks.

"Yes, it's beautiful," I respond, even as a tinge of disappointment creeps in. "It's getting late. Is everything okay?"

"Everything's fine. But look, there's been an emergency—nothing too serious—but it means I won't make it there until tomorrow afternoon," he explains. His words carry the promise of togetherness, a hike, and dinner at Snoqualmie lodge to make up for the lost evening.

"That's a bummer. I had plans for you tonight," I say, a playful note in my voice hinting at the news I'm eager to share.

He chuckles, that familiar sound that always seems to lessen the distance. "Hmm, I bet you did. Save it all for me tomorrow. You can use this time to study," he suggests, showing that blend of practicality and thoughtfulness that defines him.

With a soft 'Mwah' and an 'I love you,' we end the call. I'm left with my thoughts and the quiet rustle of pages. I had hoped to reveal my secret tonight, but it seems the universe has other plans. The waterfall's steady cadence eventually lulls me into a restful slumber, a temporary retreat from the rush of emotions and the weight of tomorrow's revelation.

Dear Diary,

On Saturday, Colin's arrival was later than I had anticipated, stirring a mix of frustration and disappointment in me, and he sensed it immediately. He explained that our frequent weekend getaways had caused him to neglect some aspects of his work, resulting in an overwhelming pile-up of tasks. The earnest appeal in his limpid blue eyes sought my understanding, tempering my initial annoyance. I reminded myself to be reasonable, especially considering the lethargy I'd been experiencing, likely an effect of the pregnancy, which had me sleeping most of the day.

However, my understanding was tested when he mentioned he could only stay the night. He had preparations to make on Sunday for a hectic week of appointments starting Monday. This revelation draped over me like a heavy, damp shroud, casting a pall over our time together. Despite the luxurious setting of our hotel room above the falls, the knowledge of his imminent departure loomed large, overshadowing the brief joy of our reunion.

I had imagined a different scenario: languishing in his arms until the sun climbed high, sharing whispered dreams and laughter. Instead, I'm caught in a tangle of sheets and emotions, grappling with a mix of contentment from our closeness and a simmering disappointment. The pregnancy, still a secret nestled within me, seems to amplify every feeling.

I try to steady my heart to be understanding of his responsibilities. He does so much and cares so deeply, and yet, there's an ache in holding back the news of the 'little Pixie' we've created. It's not just the anticipation of his reaction that has me on edge—it's the need to connect with him on this new, profound level before he steps back into the whirlwind of his work life.

As always, it seemed, we made love, although, this time, it was like a punishing fuck. He was thrusting inside me, Hard! I begged him to stop. He didn't until he was satisfied. I rushed to the bathroom. I was bleeding, and it scared the shit out of me. Did he know I was pregnant? Why was he being such a cruel asshole? I showered, rubbing my stomach, asking Lil Pixie for forgiveness.

"It's okay, my little one. Daddy doesn't know you're in here yet. Mommy will protect you. I love you."

Colin knocked on the door, asking if I was okay. "Yes, I'm fine! I'm just putting on my make-up."

"You mind if I come in?"

"No! I want to get dressed. I'm starved. Or have you already had dinner?"

"No, Sweetheart. That's why I want my gorgeous angel to hurry."

"You know you hurt me. What the fuck was that all about, Colin?"

"Baby, I'm sorry. I thought you liked it."

"I actually like it, gentle and sweet. You like it rough, and I let you do it. But this time, you were brutal, and I didn't like any of it. So maybe you should go back home tonight."

"I'm sorry, babes. It was insensitive of me. I'm going to step outside for a breather. You think you'll be ready in ten minutes?"

"I'll meet you outside in thirty minutes."

"Okay, I love you." He double-tapped on the door with the knuckle. He always did that when he was leaving.

I felt lethargic at dinner; my glow of excitement melted away, triggering Colin's inquiries. "You're not being your normal self. Are you angry with me?" I frowned. He reached across the table for my hand, looking me in the eye, "Sweetheart. Look, I am so sorry. I didn't mean to be so aggressive; we have sex that way all the time.

That's the problem, Colin. Are we just having sex? Is that all I am to you, a sex puppet satisfying all your wicked sexual fantasies?"

"No, love, no." He said, rubbing my hand with his thumb. "It's just that I have been so stressed and needed you last night. I drove well over the speed limit to get here. If I was too rough, please forgive me." I told him I understood. It was a combination of bottling up my emotions and the vaginal pounding I took from him that made me doubtful. "So, are we okay?" His lips pressed together in a slight smile. Heavy sigh, I assured him I was okay. Though I said I forgave him, I couldn't let go of my anger as quickly. We ate dinner in relative silence. I didn't

225

feel comfortable sharing the news with him. This wasn't turning out to be anything like I had rehearsed: I told him I was pregnant, and he would excitedly take me in his arms, sweeping me off my feet.

It was freezing outside, but the stiff wind felt good on my face as we walked to our room. Colin immediately turned on the fireplace. I wrapped a blanket around myself, sitting next to him on the sofa. My heart was pounding. My thoughts conflicted. Should I tell him? Of course, I have to. "Colin... "

"Yes, sweetheart?" He answered, staring absorbedly into the blaze.

"Do... Do you love me? Truly love me?" He was quiet, absent. My heart sank, waiting for him to spark it back to life with his answer. But it did not come. I thought, what the hell? He has been telling me he loves me, and now when I ask him directly, he's silent. Finally, he tells me, "Of course. I love you, Kayleigh. Look, I'm sorry about this weekend. Things have been chaotic lately, and I'm just trying to reorganize them again. I promise I'll plan our next weekend better."

"... Colin. It's not about this weekend. I understand I must share my time with the demands of running your practice." His shoulders dropped as he leaned back, pulling me with him. My long record with men has taught me one thing: when there's a long pause to an important question, there's something amiss, and they're telling me a lie. I blurted out, "Colin, I'm pregnant." Fuck! That's not how I planned to say it. He leaped forward, nearly launching himself off the sofa. "You're what?" His reaction was one of shock rather than the delight I had pictured in my mind's vision. "You? Are you pregnant? How? How many days or weeks? Months? How? Oh my God, Kayleigh."

"Three. I'm three months." He inhaled deeply. "Th, th, three months? Are you kidding me? This has been happening for three months, and you're just now telling me? How is this even possible? You're entering the medical profession, you have books and journals, and you should know... everything about pregnancy at this point and certainly should know how to keep these things from happening. What were you thinking? Dammit."

Talk about plans falling apart. The joy I thought I would experience sharing with Colin our good news disintegrated into oblivion. So far, it's all about *him, and he hasn't shown an iota of compassion or joy. He sat on the edge of the sofa with his head down, massaging his forehead. "Okay, let's calm down and think this through." He had seemingly morphed into the kind of man I'm more accustomed to — the one-track-male-mind, where they tend to focus solely on themselves and seek single, straightforward solutions to their problems.*

"You have your residency to look forward to. I have my practice keeping me occupied more and more each day. It seems the sensible thing for us...." I was waiting for the shoe to fall "... is an abortion." I would have felt better had he punched me in the stomach. Instead, I felt numb and hollow, like someone had thrown a hand grenade into the room and exploded, knocking me senseless.

I looked at him in shock, wanting to scream my head off, but opted to remain composed. I would not allow him to drag me down. I inhaled deeply, telling him, "Colin... this is my baby. I'm keeping him or her." I swallowed my words, proud that I hadn't referred to it as 'it.' Why do people refer to their unborn child as 'it?'

"What?" he shouted.

"Colin, I have thought this through a thousand times. Though I had expected a different and more caring reaction from you, I have considered the challenges of having a baby and completing my residency. I can and will do it. We have had a beautiful relationship, and our child will be happy. I promise you. Don't worry, it won't be a burden. This I can promise you." I try to ease the convergence of emotions in the room. I joked, "Don't worry, I promise to stay beautiful for you."

"No," he said, with no hesitation. "A child is not a part of any plans we discussed. We don't have room in our lives for any more children." A whoa moment flashed before me like lightning streaking across the blackened sky. My brow rose. "What do you mean, any more children? This is our first."

"I meant it in the plural sense of the word. There's only one child, right?"

"Yes, Colin, there's only one child... between you and me. Tell me about the other children in our lives." It was then I knew I'd only been seeing the tip of his iceberg, and I had a chilling feeling our ship was about to sink. Colin massaged his face with his hands.

"Look, there are no other children, just us, and we're not ready to have a baby. For Christ's sake, I can't believe you're even making this an issue. I give you everything you want, stuttering: a home, a car, and now you want to ruin it all with a child. Goddamn. What? You looking for an insurance policy?" My eyes opened wide with anger.

"You fucking asshole! What are you saying to me?" I looked at him defiantly with my arms folded. Shaking my head in disbelief. Thinking, "What an asshole."

"Look, I didn't mean it." He deflates the air from his lungs, "This is all shocking and overwhelming to me. Let's just let calmer minds prevail. You know, and so do I, that having a kid between us is more of a burden than something to be thrilled about. Abortion is your—our only option."

"Colin, I've had seven abortions in my lifetime. My friends hate me, saying I use it as birth control."

"Then number eight shouldn't be a problem." I shivered at the coldness of his statement. The blood drained from my body. It was then I knew the truth that had been present the whole time. I prepared myself for what I knew was the truth, calmly asking, "What's your wife's name, Colin? How many children will we have between the three of us?" His face turned ten shades of red. Then I'm hit with the harsh—dumb blonde—reality. I've been a kept-woman. I honestly thought I had a life with this man, believing he truly loved me.

Boy, I register high on the stupid chart. I thought he was being sweet, buying a place we could share while I was attending school. It never dawned on me. I didn't even know where he lived. The reality of it all was the condo was his secret hideaway. This bastard was just like all the others before him. He wanted me in a position where he could control me to ensure that I wasn't seeing other guys and was available at his convenience. Evidenced by his random unannounced visits to 'Check on me.' Great, stupid me. But kudos to him. He's a smooth son-of-a-bitch. The man who told me minutes ago that he loved me turned into a cold and heartless son of a bitch. Having a baby would threaten his dual life: me, beautiful 'dumb' blonde, audacious in the sack, willing to let him slam his cock inside me whenever he wants. Her sweet, I'm sure: sedate and conservative, a *loving stay-at-home mother taking care of the kids. I now realize it's not his work that's been piling up from his absence. I wonder how she feels about his disappearance. Or is she as blind as I have been? How did I not know that he was married? It's all been so obvious, and I choose to ignore it.*

His unavailability via conflicting meetings. He doesn't want to be an all-night distraction, coming to fuck me and play house, always leaving by 9:45 pm, as if on schedule, telling me how critical my studies were. Constantly swooped me out of town when he wanted overnight time with me. I genuinely wish I could explain my feelings, but I can't. So much is happening inside of me at the moment. I only know I will not give him the satisfaction of crying, telling him, "You can go home tonight. I think I need to be alone."

"Listen, this doesn't seem to make sense for either of us. You're the last person I expected to want to bring a child into this world."

"What does that mean, Colin? Am I not fit to be a mother? Just good enough for your sexual debauchery?"

"No! That's not what I meant. You've always been concerned about your figure. When we once joked about children, the conversation repulsed you. And for God's sake, you're behaving like this is some big fucking moral dilemma for you. You've already admitted to having seven abortions; why am I the unlucky number eight? It's mind-boggling." He slapped the side of his head. I was growing angrier by the second, looking at him with disgust and saying, "You call yourself a doctor, you fucking predator." Before I knew it, I was recovering from his backhand. I rolled my tongue across my bloody lip. He immediately tried to comfort me. I pushed him away. My disdain for him grew in nanoseconds.

I felt the throbbing swelling of my lip. But I'm not backing down. Fucker thinks I should hop on a table as if I'm hopping on a horse with my legs spread open and say, "Let err rip doc." Then, when all is said and done, he'd be ready for me to screw him again. Instead, he tried to embrace me. I push him away, demanding that he not touch me. He softens, pleading,

"Sweetheart. I'm so sorry. I, I, I can't tell you how horrified I am. Please forgive me." He held my face in his hands, trying to kiss me. I pushed at him with all my might. "Are you crazy?" He held up his hands.

"You know what is stupid, Colin? I truly believed you loved me: that you had a modicum of decency in you and saw me as a person—a woman—not a delightful piece of ass for your leisure. You bastard. You're no different from any of the other motherfuckers out there, and I've met many. Yes, you fucking jerk. I have had seven abortions. Do you know what that does to a woman's heart? Her soul? No, we don't dwell on it every day. But it lingers in the back of our minds, invading our consciousness at inopportune moments. You feel remorse, or when you see a mother with a child, you salute her for having the courage you lacked to give life. I'm not telling you I want to have this baby to wreck your marriage—that I knew nothing about.

You've made me care more about my body. I thought you loved me because I was a smart woman, not a beautiful piece of trophy-ass. I don't need you. I don't need your fucking money. I don't need your goddamn car. If I were driving it now, I'd drive it off the road. You… are… the epitome of slime." He shushes me. Heaven forbids one of the neighbors to recognize the great Dr. Hightower.

"Let's lower our voices and speak calmly. I'm sorry… I have lied to you about Elise."

"Elise?" He finally humanized her by name and made her presence in our conversation.

"My wife's na—her name is Elise. We have three… children: six, five, and three. I meant everything I said to you. But if I left her, she'd take me to the cleaners, and I'd have nothing. We'd have nothing. You're in med school, and I thought I'd be in a different space by the time you finished. I love you so—"

"Don't you dare! Don't you dare say that to me! You do not have the right to lie to me and then tell me you love me. How stupid do you think I am? My light may take a moment to shine, but when it does, I'm brilliant."

He sat on the sofa with his hands clasped together, contemplative. He inhaled deeply to relax. "Kayleigh, I am sorry about the deception. The truth remains, even if I weren't married, we wouldn't have a child together. It's not right for either of us. Why don't you put your school back into the forefront of your behaviors and forget about this child thing? Then, once we calm down, we can get back on track."

I shook my head in utter disbelief. I keep asking myself, "Is he not listening to me?" Then I realize I'm not correctly translating male speech. He's hoping to quell the situation, fearful that his wife may find out about his secret woman. Once the anger of abortion is clear and the baby is gone. He can talk to me about getting my tubes tied and continuing what I can officially term "fuck me" jaunts. Finally, I've had enough of his bullshit and asked him to leave. He agrees, saying maybe we should spend some time thinking about the choices we need to make.

"Choices?" I asked.

He stammers, "You know, the future of us and things we need to do in our lives." He bit down on his bottom lip for a pause. He tilted his head in the air. "Look, Kayleigh, there are kids involved. I can't just go home and make a declaration that I want a divorce. I can't leave the kids. We shouldn't be complicating our lives like this."

He asks if he can call me on Monday evening. I tell him no, "Please stay away. I don't want you in my life anymore." His head lowered like a sniveling child. He turned before exiting. Tears sparkled in his blue eyes. "Baby, I love you. We just need time." I remained committed to wanting him to leave. I walked to the door. "Colin, you need to leave. Now." He glared at me as though he was looking for pity. I was not caving, telling him, "Bye." I felt a sense of empowerment, closing the door behind him.

I thought long and hard, realizing what a horrible person I have been. Maybe he was right. Previously, I had been overly concerned about the disfigurement of my body to consider having a child. The superficial me transformed into a compassionate woman who truly cared about the life inside of me rather than being overly concerned about what I looked like on the outside.

Dear Diary,

I now realize there's more to me than expensive jewelry, exotic vacations, make up—or, oh god—I have makeup and perfumes from all over the world. I've been so caught up being arm candy that I lost my identity—lost in a world of men fighting over me like mad dogs with their wallets open. Giving myself to the highest bidder. God, what a whore I've been. I am a woman, not an ornament to dangle from a man's arm who's trying to impress his friends. So that he can say to them, "look at what I got" Man speak translation, "Look at this beautiful bitch I'm fucking."

When Colin came into my life, he seemed genuine, loving, and caring. I thought he was the man of my dreams, and he had been until moments ago. I have had enough of male manipulations. I will not get an abortion.

It's final. If my lil Pixie's life goes, then I go with him. So, fuck all of you, Bensons. The only person who knows all my history is Cynthya. She's annoyed with me since she started accompanying me on some of my abortions. The last time, her face was riddled with disgust. She said nothing since number four, just faded out of my life. To quote Steven Wallace, "… the world is ugly, and people are sad." How true, Steven. My world is ugly, and I am miserable.

Dear Diary,

It's been two weeks since I kicked Colin's ass out of the hotel room. He's been calling incessantly, leaving messages that we need to talk. I'm feeling depressed and lonely today. I can feel my body changing as my—I hope it's a boy—baby takes form. But it doesn't matter either way, and I'll be happy. I can't believe I will be a mother; the acceptance of the word "mother" has me scared.

I haven't told Margaret. Though we have a strained relationship, I should try to be closer to her now that she's going to be a grandmother. Maybe she'll be less bearish to her grandchild.

Perhaps it's wrong of me to feel so much anger towards her. I know she loves me and always wants the best for me. I just hated her trying to dictate my choices, telling me what was right, or wrong, as though getting divorced and exiling my father from my life was her right choice. However, I must appreciate all her well-meant good intentions. I want to call her now, but she'll blow her stack if I tell her I'm pregnant. My first abortion was at her behest in my junior year of high school. She suggested I wasn't ready to be a mother and should put higher achievements at the forefront of my life rather than a boy's cocks inside me. I got the abortion. She cried the whole time and weeks afterward begging God for forgiveness, fearing that her soul would be in hell. Now I'm in one hell of a pickle. I need her, but I don't want her to be ashamed of me. Sigh, "Bury the hatch, Kayleigh."

How do I tell mother I've been a kept woman by a married man—and others for most of my life — and oh, he has three children. Dear God, it would break her heart. Therefore, I ruled out turning to Mom for emotional support. All my friends hate me. I can't blame them; I've been a royal bitch over the years. I sat on my sofa, rubbing my hands over my stomach. I giggle. I felt a small rumble. Okay, time to think, K. How do you manage school and a baby without a father?

This was all too consuming. I'll definitely have my tubes tied after this delivery, that's for sure. Sorry, Pix, you're destined to be an only child. I have to study and survive for you and me. I love. I love. I love. I love my lil Pixie.

Love mom.

Mom! — oh my God! I just referred to myself as a mother. I felt so happy. For once in my life, I don't feel a need to be some man's token. I finally have taken control of myself, and it's so liberating.

Dear Diary,

Colin came by this evening unannounced—nothing new about that, banging on the door like a madman. His ultra-stick-up-his-ass professional charisma appears to be crumbling. I was feeling comfortable enough to sneak out on the wife. I hoped he had faded away back to his family. I have come to know men's controlling behavior well; when things with me start unraveling and I have grown outside of their manipulation, they become total obsessive borderline psychopaths. It drives me crazy. In an ideal world, everything would end at goodbye. But the men in my life are arrogant, controlling—predictable—jerks, thinking that pampering me with treats will forever pacify me.

I've heard more than once: "Why do you have aspirations to become a doctor? Are you sure?" Translation: are you smart enough? Let me fuck you some more. You should stay a model and allow people to admire your beauty. Stay with me. My dick is all you need. I can give you everything you want.

Translation, be my Lil puppy -dog-showpiece and let me parade around so people can admire me for having your hot ass attached to my arm. Memories of my life sicken me. I allowed so many misogynic thieves to steal away my integrity. Adorning me like a goddamn Christmas tree, not giving a shit about my heart. However, I finally have clarity, and here's Colin, the latest and greatest asshole, to enter and exit my life under protest.

Why can't he stay home and be happy with his wife? At least he gave her the title of "Mrs. Hightower." I reluctantly opened the door in frustration to see Colin disheveled. He hadn't shaven in days, giving him a rugged look that reminded me of our weekend at Crystal Mountain... Rolling my eyes, "Colin, why are you here?" The first thing he noticed was that I wasn't wearing make-up. "No, I'm not. You better sell all your Chanel and other glamor care stocks before word hits the street that I won't be buying volumes of make-up."

He smirked and started sniveling, like a sad dog, "Kayleigh, sweetheart, please listen to me. I just need to talk. Please, don't do this to us."

"Us?"

"Look, I can understand that you're upse—"

"Upset doesn't even describe how I feel. Colin, You're drunk." I could barely understand his hoarse, "Yes, I know."

My heart and mind are at war, the rational mind saying, "Send him packing." Then there's the portion of my heart that tingled with invading memories of happier times says let him in." The heart wins. I invite him in. He walked in and plopped down on the sofa, leaning forward with his head down, rubbing his hands over his face. Please sit down and talk to me, baby." I said no, asking him again why he was here. He stuttered, "I, I, I, I just needed to see you. Look at me; I'm a fucking wreck." I stood with my arms folded, telling myself no. He pleaded with his eyes. I finally relented and sat next to him. After eternal moments of silence, he threw himself back, shifting to me, slightly nodding his head, apologizing for slapping me. "I'm a doctor, and, and, and… hitting a woman — it—goes against the core of my being. I've never been so in love with someone before, trying to manage my life… and us having a kid, and trying to figure out how to love—and I truly love you. I want. I want for us. You and me. There's no excuse for it, and please—I beg you—please forgive me."

"I'm pregnant, Colin. There is no longer just me. I'm a mother and damn proud of it. Now, what do you want?"

I will not lie. Despite my anger, I wanted to feel his touch, to be held. He told me he's been unable to sleep. I think to myself, Join the club, buddy. He told me he took a week off work to sort things out. "Sort things out? What does that mean?" He gently placed his hand on my thigh. I wanted to push it away, but his sadness disarmed me.

Finally, he said, "Let's just relax together, and we can work things out. I know you won't believe anything I say... and... and—I probably don't deserve your trust." His hand crept towards my gift. He tells me, "I can't live without you." I stopped his hand just as he tugged my panty line. I had an uncomfortable desire to control my emotions, and despite my stopping him, I didn't turn him away. He told me he understood. Looking into my eyes, his hand tried to creep more. I was aroused and too weak in my desire for affection to stop him. Allowing his fingers to crawl into my vagina. I'm saying in my mind, "I will not fuck you, Colin." It wasn't long before he had shed my black nightie, and I tore away his shirt, helping him get out of his pants. Kissing me like we had done so many before, I learned the horrible news that he had a wife. I closed my eyes tight to push that image to the back of my mind.

He took me to the bedroom, laid me on the bed, and kissed me. I moaned in his ear. He kissed my lips and moved down my neck until he was where he wanted to be. I purred from the sensation of his tongue loving my clit. The feeling traversed my body. Closing my eyes and enjoying the titillation. "Oh god, Colin." My breast rises and falls as I inhale the air of satisfaction. "Oh, baby," I groan. He stops as I'm nearing my climax, rising to insert his penis. It felt like an eternity since last we were together. We moved in a slow but powerful rhythm. He got close to his peak and then stopped. Saying he wanted me from behind. I said no. I didn't feel comfortable giving him that freedom. "Honey, it's okay. I promise to be gentle with you." I looked at him doe-eyed, unable to say no. I got on my knees with my ass in the air. "Please don't be rough," I told him. He massaged and lubed my anal promising to take care of me. I clawed at the sheets in pain as I felt his shaft inside me. Oh my god, it hurt and brought me to tears. I tensed up. Colin coaxed me, "Just relax, baby, it's okay," he reassured me. He pulled out to reposition himself. Then back in. I whined, "Colin, it hurts."

"It's okay, baby. Just relax for me." He said in a hurried breath, tightening his grip on my ass like a vise. He pushed hard.

"Colin!" I cried through halting breaths. "Please, don't go so fast." The rush of dopamine intoxicated him to his brain, driven by his own desires. The more excited he got, the more forceful he became, pushing HARDER and harder. "OW!" I cried. "Colin, you're hurting me. You promised you wouldn't." He wasn't thinking about me, only his sensation, pounding my ass repeatedly. "Please, Colin, please," Gritting my teeth, suffering his pain, I begged him to stop. Brutal thrashes met each of my screams. Finally, I said, "Colin, just cum. Please! Please cum and stop." His grip tensed, and he pushed his ejaculate thrust inside of me. Finally, he had his release. He collapsed on me, winded and moaning, his achievement of punishing me. I yelled for him to get the fuck off of me. I hopped from the bed and ran to the shower to wash the spew out of my ass. He said. "I'll join you."

"No, you will not. We are done, Colin. You insensitive bastard. No more of this, whatever you call it. What do you think I am? Some whore you can trash with your sadistic fucks at will?" Looking at him made me sick. Any vestiges of emotion I had for him instantly vaporized. To think he's a doctor I once regarded as a compassionate man. The throbbing pain fueled my rage. "You can shower after I'm done. Or go home to your wife. But you, mister, are done here. I promise you." He rolls off the bed with his hands raised, surrendering, "Okay, baby. It's okay. It's nothing like that." He inched closer, thinking he could lessen my rage. Then, extending his arms, beckoning me toward him. "You touch me, you son of a bitch, and I'll scream rape."

"Rape?" He jumped back, astonished.

"I am not playing with you."

"Why would you say something so horrible? I have never forced myself on you." I shook my head, thinking, you pathetic loser. I rushed to the toilet, puking

out my guts. Here I was with my face planted in the bathroom, crying, questioning how I got here. Colin skulked in, kneeling, "Baby, are you okay? Let me help you." I held up my pointer finger for him to halt, speaking into the toilet, "Do. Not. Touch me." I got myself into the shower.

I was sitting on the sofa with my knees pulled to my chest. Colin's hair was still wet from showering; he sat down as though he hadn't violated me. Now, he wanted to congratulate me on finishing med school. "So, what's next? You'll be placed in residency, which is not always your choice. Suppose you end up in another state. What should I do with this place?" I couldn't believe this asshole.

"I'll rent it," I said with finality.

He stammered. "Y, y, you'll what?"

"I will rent it. It's my place. Right?"

"It was your place as long as you are here, and we're together. I never said you owned it."

I huffed. "I will be after tomorrow. I think you should have your attorney draw up a deed, giving me full ownership."

He laughed dismissive, "You expect me to quitclaim a property that I own to you? Why in the hell would I do that? If you're not using it—"

"You mean if you're not allowed to come here for your heartless pleasures?"

His face grimaced. "I'm saying it's only fair that I sell it."

"You won't be doing that, Colin. Remember, you purchased this place for me. When I said it was too much, you insisted, saying you wanted me to have my home. Naturally, it came with the fringe benefits for you: control, deception, and stalking—I was too stupid then to realize it. I believed you loved me. But tonight. I have come to terms with the fact that you are the most heartless, self-serving asshole I have ever known. So, you got your last fuck here, mister. I hope you enjoyed it. I'd appreciate the quitclaim deed by five o'clock tomorrow."

"The hell you say, you're insane."

"Look, I will not sweat you for child support. The least you can do is relinquish the home to me. And it's not a request."

"Oh?"

"It's a demand. Fuck with me and see Colin."

"So do as you say, or you'll blackmail me?"

"It's a small price to pay, considering what I could ask for in support payments from you and the honorable Mrs. Hightower. However, she's an innocent bystander in your world of deceit and trickery. However, you have choices. Choose wisely, doctor."

"Bitch." he murmured. "Thank you. After all I've gone through and just finished doing with you. I take that as a compliment."

"So, I give you this place."

"And the car." His eyes glowed. What the fuck do you take me for?" I stood firm in place, unyielding, shaking my head, thinking how pathetic. "Please, Colin, you don't want me to answer that."

"What do you plan to put on the birth ce —"

"Immaculate conception, huh?" He chuckled and sneered.

"I'm to be written out of the picture? What was tonight about?"

"As it's always been, I allowed you to snake your way in here and fuck me. Were you thinking that if we had sex, everything would be back to normal? Do you believe for one second that your dominating-fucking me in the ass gave you back your power over me? It only reaffirmed that you need me to give you the sick, perverted sex your wife, the noble, Mrs. Elise Hightower, won't give you. You fucking prick. For the first time in my life, I finally have someone other than me to care about.

Let me write what I need from you before you leave. I wrote: One sign over the condo to me—two, pay the taxes and maintenance until I sell it- so plan on thirty years. Three sign the car over to me—all by five o'clock tomorrow. I held the note, waiting for him to take it. His eyes narrowed. He scrunched his lips, speaking through closed teeth, "You're a total bitch."I saw a look of evil I had never seen before in his eyes. His bottom lip quivered involuntarily. I stood resolute, refusing to yield to his intimidating scowl. I hated him more each second; he stood in front of me.

"You're getting off cheap, asshole. You screw with me on this, and I'll purchase billboard space down by the courthouse, announcing your despicable deceptions." He stood helpless, saying nothing. Finally, he snatched the demand and walked toward the door. With the door half-open, he said, "Fine. You're nothing but a fucking slut, anyway."

"That's fine, Colin. Maybe your spineless wife will let you bang her in the ass or do all the other kinky shit you like. Maybe she'll agree to the threesome you keep trying to get me to do. Or better yet, find your next med school mark, you goddamn predator." The door slammed so hard I thought it had shattered from the hinges.

Colin's right hand was clamped around my throat, squeezing, speaking with menacing evil vigor, "You listen here cunt, you don't know who you're fucking with." I was struggling to breathe, trying to pry away his hand, telling him that he was hurting me through my deprived of air of breath. He finally let go. I dropped to my knees, coughing for air. He stood there, trembling, his fingers curled into fists. He's gone to a whole new level of <u>depravity</u>. His true character was on full display, fearful that I would disturb his hidden perfect life.

I watched his face as he recognized how his actions would affect his life. I spoke so angrily that spit came out of my mouth, yelling, "No. No goddamn man on this earth has ever dared to touch me. And you've done it twice, you loathsome son of a bitch. Get out of here now, or you better kill me because I'll have the cops at your house before you know it. Go!" I backed The cheater into a corner, his secret life of sexual convenience over.

I inhaled confidently, calming my vehemence. "One word from you, just one speck of a word, Doctor Hightower, and I'll scream so loud, I won't need to dial 911. Cops from here to the Canadian border will hear me. So, I strongly advise you to leave." I walked past him and opened the door. There would be no coming back. He humbles, reaching apologetically for my hand as he walks toward the door. "Don't! You worthless asshole, do not touch me." Then, raising the inflection in my voice, "I'm out of patience and desire for you. I mean it."

"Fine, you'll need me soon."

"To hell with you, Benson." He sulked out the door with his head lowered like a pathetic dog with his tail between his legs. I collapsed on the sofa. Colin's assault was the final straw. The vile swing in accepting his apologetic outreach, *sexual pummeling, and fight with him sapped what strength I had left in me. The surges of humiliation and emotional conflict had taken its toll on me. Why was I so stupid and weak, allowing him to come into my home and give in to his sexual domination? My heart hurts. I'm so tired I need to sleep. But Pix is demanding more energy than I have available.*

I need my mother now, but I can't go to her and let her see me this way. I can't tell her what has been happening with Colin. I could picture her storming into Colin's office, demanding he take responsibility for his foray with me. It would create more problems than I care to deal with. I desire no more drama. I curl up in a ball, crying myself to sleep. I woke up this morning believing everything with Colin was a nightmare. But my aching body reminded me it was not. I'm aching and heartbroken. My Lil Pix ripples in my tummy. I coo, saying mommy understands.

Tears cascaded down my face as I closed the pages of my friend's harrowing journal, revealing the depths of Kayleigh's despair and the shocking revelation of her pregnancy. The weight of her burden and the unknowns that unfolded left me troubled and overwhelmed.

I mustered the courage to ask if I could keep Kayleigh's diary. Her eyes, brimming with tears, traced a path down her grief-stricken face.

Embracing me tightly, she whispered, her voice laden with sorrow, "Yes, my dear, for I fear that I would only immerse myself in the depths of despair, questioning where I went wrong. I loved her with all my heart, and I cannot comprehend why such a young and beautiful soul chose to depart from this world. You were her friend. Please, tell me, did she perceive me as an inadequate mother, unworthy of her trust? I would have supported her and her unborn child unconditionally."

The room fell into an eerie silence as the realization of her pain and self-doubt washed over me. How could I have been so blind to her struggles? I had failed as a friend, unable to provide the comfort and understanding she needed. Guilt and regret consumed me, leaving me unable to find the right words to console Mrs. Levinson in her grief.

With a trembling hand, she pressed the diary into mine, a poignant offering of remembrance and closure. In that solemn exchange, she guided me to the door, her frail figure consumed by grief. The weight of guilt settled upon me as if I had held Kayleigh's lifeline within my grasp. Each heartbeat resonated with a piercing ache, a constant reminder of the void left by her untimely departure.

Chapter Twenty-two

I suffered from the haunting thoughts of the voicemail. Guilt hung around my neck like a weight, and I was suffocating. The one time I could have made a difference, I ignored the phone call because of my critical denunciations of her behavior regarding abortion. It's easy to have an opinion of another when they're doing something I would never do... Today, I realize how hypocrisy is. In need of support, I called my friends for a girls' night dinner.

Hoping our bonds of cheer and laughter would help ease my depressed spirit. Instead, Kayleigh's words hung in my mind like dead bodies suspended from the rafters. Gina, as always, was the first to notice something wrong, her frown denoting her concern, asking, "Cyn, you're behaving strangely. What's wrong with you?" Kayleigh's diary, a book with botanical flowers on a black background, personalized gold lettering, Kayleigh J. Levinson Notes and Thoughts lay on the table between us. The message playing in my head distracted me. I lowered my head, looking at the diary, thinking I could have made a difference had I not been such a bitch, and ignored her call. A tear escaped from my eye. I quickly brushed it away, hoping they didn't notice—as if I could get anything past the three.

I pointed to the book. That's all I could do before breaking down. They sandwiched me between them. I turned my head into Gina, holding on to her for dear life, hoping that she, Lexi, and Courtnee could help ease my remorse. Lexi's voice quivered with concern as she asked, "Made a difference? What do you mean? What kind of difference?" Lexi held the diary in her hands, examining the cover and flipping through the pages.

Together, we sat in stunned silence, the weight of Kayleigh's story hanging heavily in the air. The room felt suffocating, filled with the harsh realization that we had misjudged her struggles. How could we have missed the signs? We had labeled her as self-absorbed, never imagining the depths of her pain and despair. The revelation of her tragic end shook us to the core, leaving us grappling with a profound sense of loss and bewilderment.

As Lexi closed the book, her eyes mirrored the shared disbelief and confusion that we all felt. She sank back onto the sofa, her body sinking into its embrace as if seeking solace from the overwhelming emotions that flooded the room. There were no words that could capture the magnitude of what we had just discovered. It was an unraveling of illusions, exposing the fractures beneath the surface of our perceptions.

At that moment, the unspoken vow to understand and support one another seemed inadequate and hollow. We were at a loss, grappling with the weight of our own limitations and the heavy burden of guilt for failing to see Kayleigh's pain. The air was heavy with unanswered questions, leaving us adrift in a sea of confusion and sorrow.

As we sat in silence, the room became a sanctuary of shared vulnerability. We clung to one another, seeking solace and a glimmer of understanding in the midst of the incomprehensible. In that solemn space, we began to grasp the depth of our own fallibility and the importance of compassion, even when faced with the unexpected and inexplicable.

Courtnee, in her meek, innocent, quiet voice, "That's very sad." Gina shook her head in agreement.

Lexi was fuming. "What an asshole. You know she was right. He'll just find a new piece of ass and forget that she was alive. He'd probably put that bitch up in the same apartment and give her the car. He'll keep living with his happy family and women on the side. Never give a shit that your friend and baby are dead."

The three of them finished a bottle of red wine. With heavy hearts and distracted minds, we turned our attention to studying to complete our assignment due the coming Monday. Suddenly, Lexi exclaims, "No." Our heads raise, looking at her questioningly. "We can't let him get away with her just dying like that—with a baby inside her. That's murder." Courtnee answers, "Lexi, he didn't kill her. He just made her hate herself. He didn't tell her to go jump off the bridge."

Gina said, "Yeah, but he assaulted her." I could feel the thoughts of vengeance brewing in their minds. I encouraged them to let it go, asking, "What can we do? Go tell his wife?"

Lex responded, "Yes! Let's take the book to her as a present for her lame-ass husband's deceitfulness. She needs to know the truth. A woman died because of his ass. She doesn't know he had Kayleigh housed in his little fuck-condo, lying, telling her she owns it until she refuses to have sex with him anymore. That asshole needs to pay." We sat silently for the next five minutes. The three of them sipped wine. Though I thought it a good idea, I didn't feel comfortable confronting a man's wife.

Why not just leave it alone? Finally, Courtnee broke the silence. "It's so sad that he treated her like that. She was a beautiful person. And she had a child. I agree with Lexi. I don't think he should just walk away from it." We looked at each other, then at Courtnee in astonishment, disbelieving she'd be the one endorsing a vengeance. They waited for me to respond. After all, it was to be my decision that would guide us.

I wanted something done but was uncomfortable, uncertain it would be right, challenging the doctor and his wife. Finally, after bantering back and forth, we agreed to gift-wrap the diary in an 8.5 x 11.5 box with black paper, white and yellow ribbons, and a purple bow and deliver it to Dr. Hightower's wife.

Two weeks later, we skipped brunch and headed to the Hightower's residence in the Montlake area, a charming, colonial-style house in a quiet, wealthy residential neighborhood in central Seattle. An area close to the University of Washington campus, one of the unique Seattle areas, is home to Portage Bay, a part of Lake Washington, and is bordered on one side by the Washington Park Arboretum. We arrived just as the doctor and his family came out the door for what appeared to be a family outing.

Their house was a captivating brick abode that appears to have been constructed in the early 1950s and kept in pristine condition through the decades, likely passed down through generations. Our rehearsed plan had been to ring the doorbell asking to speak to Mrs. Hightower, then hand her the gift and leave without interaction. But preconceived plans don't always play out as expected. The whole family was exiting.

After conducting thorough research on every aspect of Doctor Hightower and his wife, Elise, we were taken aback by the vibrant presence of a woman in her mid-forties. Our gaze fell upon Elise as she walked out of the house, accompanied by her two young boys, forming a gleeful family unit. We had delved into the depths of her life, discovering that she had resigned from her esteemed position as a superior court judge to prioritize her family. Her attractive figure, lean and toned, was accentuated by her attire: a white hoodie paired with black yoga pants adorned with the University of Washington W near the ankle. Her short brown hair added a touch of sophistication to her appearance.

As they filed out of the house, we prepared ourselves to present the well-decorated gift to Elise, symbolizing our intention to expose the lies Doctor Hightower had told Kayleigh.

As we approached, Dr. Hightower, clad in a charcoal waist jacket with the Princeton logo and jeans, greeted us with an uneasy smile. His eyes betrayed a hint of discomfort and questioning as if wondering why we were there. Deep in the recesses of his mind, I sensed a flicker of alarm, as if the ghosts of his past were resurfacing.

He subtly shifted his weight, betraying a nervous energy as he blocked our path. Meanwhile, Elise's voice floated in the air, gently guiding the kids toward the car. Holding Kayleigh's diary close to my chest, its weight a constant reminder of the truth we sought, I approached the vehicle cautiously.

Dr. Hightower's facade of confidence wavered as he clasped his hands together, rubbing them anxiously. His voice, though attempting to maintain composure, carried a subtle tremor as he spoke, "Hello, ladies, how can I help you?" The forced cheerfulness in his tone only deepened the sense of unease that hung in the air. It was evident that our presence had unsettled him, triggering a cascade of memories and fears he had hoped to keep buried.

His presence was intimidating, and we hadn't plan to be face-to-face with him. It was hard to look him in the eyes. I stuttered, "Are you Mister Hightower—Doctor Colin Hightower?"

"Yes, you caught me. I am he, Dr. Colin Hightower," he admitted his broad smile now a deceptive facade. Behind it, I sensed a man harboring countless secrets. His expression transformed from confusion to a calculated curiosity as he tried to unravel the purpose behind four women approaching his home. The gray sky loomed above, and the drizzling rain seemed to mirror the unease that settled within us.

Summoning every ounce of courage, I proceeded with my intentions, knowing full well the deceit that lay within this man. "I have something..." My voice quivered, betraying my nervousness and the weight of the perceived confrontation. "I'd like to speak briefly with your wife."

Skepticism etched deep lines on his face, and his eyes gleamed with a cunning awareness. The disquieting ambiance of the gray sky and the persistent drizzle intensified the atmosphere as if the very elements conspired to magnify the treachery that surrounded us.

"I'm sorry. Why would you like to speak to my wife? I'm more than happy to deliver your message to her—do I—do we know you?"" He asked with a scowl on his face. I read on his face that he was crafting a base story. "Is this some kind of college prank? If it is, we don't have time for it."

"Sir, Mr. Hightower, this is not a prank," said Gina. "We have a package for your wife." Elise was creeping up behind him. Taking hold of his hand. He instructed her to wait for him in the car, but she remained questioning our presence. Finally, with a frown of apprehension, she asked, "Colin. Sweetheart, is everything alright?"

"Yeah. Yeah, honey. Please go back to the car. I'll be right there. I think these ladies appear to have the wrong house."

"Okay, but please hurry. You'll all be soaked," Elise responded, her voice carrying a hint of impatience. The fine droplets drifted down gently, enveloping us in a hazy curtain of moisture.

I exchanged a quick glance with my companions, the mist of rain creating an atmosphere of mystery and anticipation. It was as if nature itself had joined our quest, casting a veil of ambiguity over our encounter with Dr. Colin Hightower. With each step we took towards the car, the mist of rain dampened our skin, adding a chilling touch to the disquietude that enveloped our encounter.

"I'll be right behind you." He replied to her adoringly.

As I worked up the courage, my throat was tight, reaffirming, "You? You're Colin Hightower, right?"

"Yes." His smile widened, revealing a set of gleaming white teeth. "Again, I am Dr. Colin Hightower… and as you can see," he said, rubbing his hands together, "My family and I are on our way out. If you have something for my wife, you can give it to me." He extended his hand to receive the box. I took a step back, hesitating, but he beckoned me once more.

"Very well, suit yourself. If you will not hand it to me, you need to depart my property. I'd hate to get the police involved." He behaved as though he knew the package in my arms was incendiary. And he wanted to thwart us before our news erupted into a flame that he could not extinguish.

"Dr. Hightower, we're all medical students, and we don't mean to offend you or intrude on the sanctity of your family. However, a friend of ours—okay, mine—left something that I think your wife should have." His eyes bugged wide. His chest rose.

The veins in his throat erupted to the surface. Elise, having grown impatient that he hasn't waved us away, returns, clearing her throat to make her presence known. This time, she looks at us questioningly and says, "Colin, what is going on? Who are these people? Ladies."

Through clenched teeth, he said, "Elise, please go wait in the car with the kids. The guys at the hospital are playing a joke on me. Isn't that right, ladies?" His stare was searing.

Elise interjected, "Four well-dressed women greeting you on our front lawn, embracing a gift box. That's an odd joke. I think I'll stay and listen." She folded her arms tightly, emphasizing her stern speech.

He continued, "Now, listen to me. I'm not into practical jokes or games. I must remind you that you are intruding on our family time. This prank you're attempting to pull off is not amusing in the slightest. It's raining, and you're upsetting my wife and kids. You have two choices: leave now, or I will call the police." And trust me, I have the power to get you dropped from your program for harassment. He asked again, his voice filled with intimidation, nodding his head, emphasizing his warning as he asked, "Do I make myself clear?"

Elise, seeking to dismiss our presence and move on with their plans, tugged at his arm. "Colin, we need to leave," she said, looking at us. "Please respect my husband's request and leave our home. Now." Colin gloated with satisfaction, bolstered by his wife's reinforcement. He took her hand and walked back to their black BMW SUV. A child's voice cried, "God, Mom, Dad. We're going to be late." Elise responded as she opened the door, "Janna, we are leaving now. Don't be impolite by yelling out the window." Colin hopped into the driver's seat.

Lexi took the package. "This is silly. My hair is getting wet. You let him run you away. We are giving this box to her." She walked to the car, tapping on the passenger window, raising Elise's ire. Elise rolled down the window. Colin shouted, "I told you to get out of here, dammit!"

"Colin!" Elise barked.

"This will only take a moment, ma'am. My name is Lexi. These are my friends: Cynthya, Gina, and Courtnee. Regarding your husband calling the police, I highly encourage him to do so."

Colin exited the car slamming the door, storming towards Lexi like a raging bull. Lexi continued, "This package is—" The quick swipe startled Lexi, and she screamed. This disturbed his wife. She exited the car. "What the hell is happening here? What is so important about this box? Give it to me."

"I've had enough. I didn't appreciate your presence. My wife is a judge, and we will have you arrested." Lexi remained undeterred, "Yes, I know. I read about her."

Colin huffed, his eyes glowing with livid anger as he tried to remain inconspicuous, "You go tell whoever sent you I don't have time for sorority pranks." The kids cried out impatiently. "Dad. Come on, let's go already." Elise got out of the car once again.

"Elise, sweetheart, please get back to the kids. We are not accepting anything from you…ladies. For all we know, it could be a bomb."

Elise said, "I'll take it if this will bring an end to this intrusion. Give it to me. I can assure you there can be severe repercussions for your prank. I do not appreciate you upsetting my family."

Colin snatched the package away. "What are you thinking of taking gifts from mischief-makers? This could be a bomb, for all you know. Get in the car with the kids, and let me handle this." She hesitated. "Elise Please!"

"Colin, give me the box." As she stepped forth to grab the box, he stiff-armed her, twisting his body to keep it from her. She slipped and upended into the grass. He turned to me angrily, "Look at what you made happen." He told us firmly, the veins in his neck clearly visible; he commanded, "You get off my property. Now!"

He dropped instantly to his knees, cuddling and helping her to her feet, kissing her copiously, apologizing. She pushed his hand away, simultaneously snatching the box. He tried grabbing it back.

She looked at him with a fierce warning glare, twisting her body to keep the box. "Don't you dare ever touch me that way again!" She looked sternly at Colin then to us. "This day is ruined. Thank you all very much. Please take my kids into the house." He stood like a rabid dog, ready to rip us to shreds. Elise spoke in measured calm, "Colin? I said, take the kids into the house. Please."

"Elsie, I said I will handle this."

"No, darling, I allowed you to handle it, yet my clothes are wet, and these women are still here. And it doesn't appear to be a joke. I aim to find out what's so important about this goddamn present they brought." Her calm authority was that of a woman used to having her words obeyed by complicity or authoritative might. She looked at me. Her crystal blue eyes were like glacier lakes, enticing to look into but freezing. "So, again, take the children inside." Defeated, his face grim, he made a final plea. "Elise, these women…. They…there is no truthful reason for them to be here. Give them back their little trick, and let's go."

"I will say once more. And final. Take my kids inside." The children stood in the background, solicitous. He sulked away, ushering the kids into the house, glaring over his shoulder. His fate was sealed.

"Ladies, now that you have intruded on my plans and upset my family's peace, and since I don't want to give my neighbors any additional fodder for gossip than they've already witnessed. Let's get this little gambit over with. Which of you is he sleeping with?"

"Neither."

"I didn't imagine it to be so. I am proud of my husband's integrity and dedication to his family. Why did you come?"

Looking skyward, noting the drizzle of rain as if we hadn't previously existed. "… he was sleeping with a friend… of, of mine."

"So, this… friend of yours is sleeping—or was—sleeping with my husband. She tasked the four of you to come out him?"

My eyes could not meet hers. "I guess you can say that. But mainly because she can't." She examined our faces with curiosity. "Hmm, an acute case of nerves."

"No... she's not here because she jumped off the Aurora bridge." Her face paled as she heard the shocking news. The words hit her like a physical blow, making her gasp for air. Instinctively, wrapping her arm around her stomach as a mother would, feeling the death of a child. "You mean...the young lady who jumped from the bridge two weeks ago?"

"Yes. Yes, ma'am."

"She was your friend? And from what you're saying, was a friend of my husband as well?"

"Yes."

"The news reported they believed her to be in her second trimester of pregnancy. She had to be very motivated to negotiate the fence and jump."

"Yes, and yes, from what I have learned."

"...that's a tragedy. No one deserves to die that way. And take a child's life with her." I could see wisps of steam seeping from her head. I looked over at Colin standing at the doorway, snarling like a dog wearing a shock collar, unable to leave the imposed boundary of the door frame.

The mist had turned to a drizzle. Water beaded on the wax paper as Elise examined the box. Her voice was like a ghost, speaking out of the deathly silence of the graveyard. My friends were like silent sentinels, standing motionless on either side of me. We felt the cool drizzle slowly soaking our clothes. "I assume this package, which my husband so viciously defended, is going to change my marital status....very well." No matter how hard she tried to be apathetic, her face twitched from the strain.

I saw the smoldering anger and wavering hurt that only a woman who has felt the indignation of betrayal would understand. She closed her eyes, lowered her head and inhaled deeply, taking in one last scent of the idyllic life that was now over.

"Nice touch with the black wrapping, so... appropriate, yet so inappropriate. But I assume you had your motivations. I can't say it's been pleasurable; however, I request that you leave my lawn."

She swiftly turned on her heels, her thoughts undoubtedly consumed by the impending despair awaiting her children as they faced the harsh reality of their shattered family. Each step she took toward the house echoed the weight of the situation, and as Elise walked past Colin, who stood silently in the doorway, it was as if she had left behind the aftermath of his deception.

At that moment, I could sense the overwhelming sadness and uncertainty gripping her heart. The image of her retreating form etched itself in my mind, a poignant symbol of the pain and upheaval that now plagued their lives.

Feeling the heaviness of the situation, Gina, Lexi, Courtnee, and I held hands, a silent gesture of support and solidarity, as we meandered back to my car. Tears welled up in my eyes, and my heart ached with sorrow at the sight of Elise and her children. They had begun the day with hope and optimism, only to have their world shattered by Colin's deceit.

Our role as messengers had come at a great cost, as we had demolished the notion of an ideal family—the embodiment of a mother's faith and unconditional love and a father's supposed faithfulness. The aftermath of Colin's betrayal left a wake of destruction, leaving five lives devastated and forever changed.

As we drove away, the weight of our actions settled upon us, a profound sense of responsibility and empathy for the pain we had uncovered. The image of Colin standing in the doorway, like a specter of broken trust, lingered in our minds, a haunting reminder of the consequences of deceit and the power of truth.

As I step back into my world today, I can't help but feel remorseful for the abortion choices I made in the past. I was aware of my ability to take control of the situation and make the final decision. I was constantly torn between the feelings of right and wrong.

Even when life was difficult, I tried to find the rainbow in the storm, having faith that beyond every storm, there was a glimmer of hope. One only needed to possess the fortitude to survive the typhoons. God had blessed me with the chance to become a mother twice, but I derided them both. In the depths of my soul, I was perpetually regretful that I did not possess the bravery to be as resilient as Kayleigh. Because of my transgressions, I resolved to never again be reliant on a man to make my choices, and I vowed never to bear a child. It wouldn't be appropriate for the first two. The smoldering embers of my regret would linger in my conscience until the end of my days.

Chapter Twenty-three

Valentine's Day falls on a Friday this year, and the excitement is electric. My friends and I try to act nonchalant as if it's just another day. But deep down, we're all secretly thrilled about the romantic plans our partners have in store for us. As for me, I've meticulously chosen my outfit—a sleek black cocktail dress, a sultry red lace cage bra, and a garter—hoping to set my man's heart on fire when he lays eyes on me. The day has been a whirlwind, and I've missed a couple of his calls. When I finally find a moment to reach out, it goes straight to voicemail. I leave a message, hoping he'll catch me during my lunch break at 1:00 PM.

In the breakroom, I join my friend Gina, who's radiating with joy, gushing about her new boyfriend, Vincent. She describes the thrill of their blossoming relationship, the spark in every interaction. While I'm genuinely happy for her, a pang of envy and sadness washes over me. I can't help but compare her excitement to the growing distance I feel in my own relationship.

Our conversation gets interrupted by an intercom page asking me to call the nurse's station. Intrigued, I inquired for more details. Claire, one of the nurses, suggests I come and see for myself. We make our way to the nurse's station, and there, I see a breathtaking vase of flowers awaiting me.

It's a touching gesture, and I can't help but appreciate the thoughtfulness behind it. I thank Claire and tuck the note away, savoring the mystery of what awaits me later.

The rest of the day is a blur, with a steady stream of patients needing my attention. As the clock inches closer to my lunch break at 3:00 PM, I can't help but feel a sense of anticipation. I yearn for a moment of quiet solitude to open the card and soak in my man's words. Finally, as I close my office door, I'm met with a brief moment of respite.

But just as I'm about to open the envelope, my cell phone rings—it's Gina. She asks if I've had a chance to read the card yet. I admit that I've been swamped with patients and haven't had the opportunity. We exchanged small talk, and she shared snippets of her own Valentine's Day plans with Vincent. Her enthusiasm is infectious, and for a moment, I forget about my own worries.

As I hung up the phone, I was alone in my office, the anticipation building. I took a deep breath and finally opened the envelope, ready to immerse myself in the romantic words penned by my beloved.

Sweetheart, I love you dearly and was hoping to be home by eight. Unfortunately, I'm stopping in San Francisco to meet a client that's only available today. Otherwise, I'd miss out on a vital opportunity. I apologize with all my heart. Love you now and forever, from yesterday and all the days to come.

The joyous feeling that had filled my heart and mind quickly faded away. I'm grateful that I avoided the awkwardness of reading it with my friends around. I sink back into my chair, the life and enthusiasm drained out of me.

All he had to do was pick up the phone and call me. What's wrong with a quick call, like, "Hey baby, I won't make it home in time for our Valentine's celebration." But I decide not to dwell on it.

My stomach churns, and I'm not sure why. I'm not a teenager. Gina calls again, her curiosity getting the best of her. I suggest we meet for coffee around 4:00 PM.

When I arrive at the lunchroom, Gina and Courtnee are already seated. I try to conceal my disappointment and feign happiness, but after being friends for so long, we can read each other like open books. I take a seat and inhale deeply, and they both immediately spot the disappointment on my face.

I settled in for my Valentine's Day with a gourmet meal, top ramen for dinner, and Netflix. I scanned the options for a good movie—definitely nothing romantic. I felt tension swelling in my chest. I hated this morbid feeling of disappointment. At 3:48 AM, I was awakened by him easing into bed. Glancing at the clock, it was. "Welcome home," I said in my sleepy voice with my back to him. He whispered, "I'm sorry. I was trying not to wake you." Sure, why wake me? I had only been here alone all night.

"I did everything I could to get home earlier." I was livid, that's for certain. My anger dissipated as I ached for his tender arms to envelop me, to reassure me of his love. "I don't care. Just hold me, please."

I was so horny all I could think was *I want to feel cared about tonight.* I pulled him to me as I stripped away his pjs. The sex was wild. I was putting all my frustration into achieving an intense, powerful orgasm. I rode him until I reached the peak of my rapture, and my body trembled with pleasure until I was screaming my fulfillment at the top of my lungs. Winded, I melted into his arms, feeling the warmth of his embrace as I drifted off to sleep.

Chapter Twenty-Four

We enjoyed a perfect weekend in Vancouver, BC. We laughed like old friends while enjoying dinner at Joe Forte's. My mind relaxed, and the tension from work and relationship troubles seemed to seep away from my shoulders. I mentioned that I'd like to spend a weekend in Whistler one day, nestled in his arms, enjoying a body-revitalizing hot tub. "I like that idea," he said. "Why not tomorrow?" His swift reply took me by surprise.

I backtracked, my voice sounding hollow as I told him I hadn't brought enough for more than the weekend. His alluring smile sent a thrill through me as he spoke. "I'm only asking for one extra night. It's a beautiful suggestion, and I love Whistler." I twisted my mouth, contemplating my work schedule. I treasured the idea of us extending our weekend. After some coaxing, I rearranged my schedule and got Gina to cover for me. I felt guilty for making last-minute changes, but I wanted the extra day of togetherness sans work. We reconnected after our Whistler weekend, and I felt good about us—except for a few of his business trips.

He had gone on two to three overnight trips, mainly on the west coast. However, I was most bothered by the week he had to travel to Portland, Maine, in September for a business conference. During that trip, I started considering his pattern of phone absence during all trips.

He called me on his first day there and then went silent. I was home alone, and he did little to maintain a connection. I didn't know why it was so damned hard for him to pick up the phone. Just a quick "I love you" would have gone a long way. Since he was gone for a week, I envisioned him calling me from his hotel room in the evening, telling me how much he missed me, and cajoling me to at least have phone sex. Instead, despite giving him hints of my arousal, the most I got was a fifteen-minute conversation. It took a week before we were on good terms again.

When he returned home, all I could think of was being in his arms and making love, seeking affirmations of reassurance that he loved me. He arrived home late on a Sunday night. I dressed provocatively, wearing a white nightie with a garter belt and white stockings. When he entered the bedroom, I lay in bed waiting for him to want me. I was starved for affection and knew this outfit would have him hard as soon as he saw me. I didn't want to ask him questions about not calling me. I wanted him to make love to me again.

"Wow," he exclaimed, his eyes widening with delight, "you're absolutely stunning."

"I'm thrilled that you appreciate it," I replied with a warm smile, my heart fluttering at his compliment and craving him more than ever. Inviting him to join me on the bed.

"I need to take a shower." *A shower? Your woman is lying in bed, ready for copulation, and you want to shower first?*

"Babe, forget the shower. I want you now."

"Sweetheart, I been traveling all day. I need to get freshen up. Trust me, I'll be right back." My roaring sexual desire was diminished to a flickering flame. Dammit. The twenty minutes spent in the bathroom seemed eternal. He finally came to me. I pulled him between my legs onto the bed, and we began to kiss. I teased his lips with my tongue, rolling it across the top and bottom, pushing into his mouth, inhaling his scent, heating my burning arousal. His arms wrapped firmly around me, locked in my kiss. I'm panting from the exhilaration, moaning, "I love you. I love you with all my heart." He pulled at my garter, unsnapping each one and peeling away my stockings, tearing away my panties.

His fingers part Gloria's lips the sensation explodes in my brain. I guided his head down to kiss my Gloria and work me close to an orgasm. He sucked my tits, moving down between my legs. His tongue rolled over my clit. I buried my head in the pillow, absorbing the joys of his explorations. As I neared climax, I called, "I want to come with you inside of me." I bit my lips, pulling his head away. He slowly kissed his way back up to my breast, plying my legs further apart. I was horny and anxious to have this cock. I helped him insert it, clawing his back as I felt full of his shaft. The thumbing sensation felt so good. I gyrated on his dick. "Push hard inside me, babe. I want it all. Give it to me."

I wanted a simultaneous orgasm. He started to push vigorously until we were both near the top. I kept asking, telling him. No. No. No, until I can no longer withhold, screaming my joy, coaxing his warm lava. My Gloria was throbbing. He laid limp on top of me. I held him tightly, not ready to abandon our closeness.

I fell asleep in the comforts of his arms. It's where I find our greatest connection. He's not defensive, and when we make passionate love, I feel that I have all of him. He's at peace, and I feel proud of our love. I only wish at times that I could peer into his mind and find out what causes him to pull me close one day and push me away days later.

Last night, after making love, memories of my past surfaced, revealing a pattern I was hesitant to acknowledge in my present life. Once more, I found myself repeating familiar behaviors, seeking acceptance in ways that echoed past exploitations. Yet, these thoughts I steadfastly pushed aside, unwilling to admit that my current relationship might mirror those old dynamics of one-sided affection. In my moments alone, while I tried to distract myself and focus on anything but the turmoil these memories stirred, tears would often silently stream down my face. Despite my attempts to ignore these echoes from the past, a nagging doubt remained—a fear that the shadows of previous experiences were casting a pall over what I had once believed to be a uniquely beautiful relationship.

In the waning days of September, he became increasingly cold and distant, just as he was finalizing plans for his traditional boys' trip to Las Vegas set for the first weekend of October. Our recent months had been a tapestry of joy, yet this sudden shift left me bewildered. Maybe it was the green-eyed monster of jealousy whispering doubts as the date of his departure neared.

His cell phone, once an inanimate fixture on our coffee table, had become an extension of his palm, and he now requested that I steer clear of it. Silent questions haunted me, their shadows darkening with each secretive glance he cast toward the device. I was still seething from the argument last week when he had thrown that piercing label of 'a meddling bitch' at me, a barb that had lodged itself deep within, fracturing something fragile.

I had yet to confront him about it, but the desire for him to understand the pain he inflicted was fierce. To consider that the man I loved, the one I had devoted my life to, could conjure such a harsh word as a descriptor for me was devastating. I detested the extreme fluctuations in our emotions, and there were moments when I pondered which one of us was truly at the mercy of tumultuous tides.

I longed for the return of my lover, for the shared joy found in the laughter that would bubble up when he spoke with his friends, Bronson, Naveen, and Miles, about their Las Vegas escapade. In the week prior, their hours-long phone calls filled our home with mirth and memories of trips past, their excitement reminiscent of schoolboys anticipating a grand sleepover. He regaled them with plans of gambling, feasting, and merry drinking.

During one animated debate, he rejected the idea of staying at the Paris with a laugh, recalling some mysterious incident from last year. That moment, lighthearted as it seemed, planted seeds of insecurity in me—seeds that grew into towering oaks of uncertainty.

I didn't want to begrudge him on this adventure. Yet the thought of him leaving filled me with an impending sense of solitude. I strove to embrace his travels, wishing him the joy of camaraderie with his friends. I hoped for a morsel of appreciation, a token acknowledgment in his absence. But he had become the antithesis of my desires.

Where I saw friendship and support, he saw insidious influence. His resentment toward my own gatherings with the girls had become palpable. He accused us of corrupting our relationship with our chats, dismissing my friends as conniving and declaring them a coven of chaos. His words about them were harsher than just 'women'—words that stung and resonated with disdain. He made it clear: He neither appreciated nor liked the company I kept.

His words had been razor-sharp, slicing through the soft fabric of my heart. In an attempt to mollify him, I had become the one offering apologies, the one to break our longstanding tradition of sacred brunches. I ought to have been relieved about his upcoming trip, viewing it as a chance to reconnect with Gina and Courtnee.

Once, we four had shared unbridled happiness, but even Lexi had receded into the margins of our circle, absorbed by her new life with Marcus. Our pact, forged at eighteen to prioritize our union above all else, was fraying at the edges—men and their unwitting capacity to drive wedges among us had not been part of our youthful calculations. Still, I held onto the hope of seeing Lexi's face on the iPad, craving the spark of her indomitable spirit.

Forty-five minutes after he had sequestered himself in the study, he emerged. "Is everything okay?" I inquired, to which he responded with a tone devoid of warmth, "Yeah, things are fine. We're just hashing out the travel details." "Have you naughty boys settled on a hotel?" I prodded playfully. "Yeah, the Venetian," he confirmed. Leaving the safety of the kitchen counter, I wrapped my arms around him, my whisper barely audible, "I love you so much." My body ached for his affection, yearning for him to enfold me, to reaffirm our bond before his departure. But he remained silent.

I pressed closer, seeking the rhythm of his heart, proof that the man I cherished was still present, that he hadn't morphed into the unrecognizable monster he sometimes became. His embrace was devoid of passion, devoid of the desire I so desperately sought. I reiterated, "Did you hear me? I said I love you." He drew a deep breath, one tinged with annoyance, and his words fell like boulders, "You should love another." Those words sent tremors through me. I reeled back, my mind scrambling to deny the harsh reality of his utterance.

The confrontation I had been dreading unfurled before me. Fury took hold, "What the hell did you just say to me? Did you actually tell me to love someone else?" I stood there, arms crossed, my stance as rigid as my disbelief. "Why would you utter such cruelty? Is your boys' trip so thrilling that you can so easily discard me? Why are you being so goddamn heartless?"

My voice rose with each word, a crescendo of hurt and bewilderment. "What have I done to deserve such a turn from you? I've given you everything a woman can offer a man. And you, you cold-hearted brute, fling those callous words at me. What more do you want? Just say it—if it's not with me, I'll find it for you. That's how deep my love runs. You don't tell someone you 'care about' to find love elsewhere, you fucking jerk!" My chest heaved with each breath as I fought to calm the storm within.

After what felt like an eternity, he muttered an apology, "That was wrong of me." I battled to keep the tears at bay. "What's wrong? I can't grasp what's tearing at the seams of our bond." He closed his eyes, shaking his head, and only after my emotional outpour did he draw me close. "Look. I do love you," he said, wrapping his arms around my waist, though his words and touch were devoid of conviction. "I've been tense, and yes, I've been looking forward to this weekend. We only see each other once a year, and I got carried away. But you're right, and it was a foolish thing to say."

"Why are you driving us to this brink? It's as if you want me to end things." He retreated to the entertainment room, sinking into a chair as if weighed down by thoughts. I followed, bracing for some terrible confession. Could he possibly reveal that he no longer loved me just as he was about to leave?

"Let's drop it for now. We'll talk when I get back," he suggested, as though distance could mend the fissure between us.

"What is 'it' that we're dropping? You're always away; the only thing that's alone here is me. Even when you're here, I'm alone competing with your goddamn cell phone. I wish I was the phone because it gets a hell-of-a-lot more attention than I do."

He lets out a weary sigh and gestures for me to take a seat. "Please, sit down," he says. "After this weekend, I promise things will go back to normal. I've just been so overwhelmed with work lately, and this weekend with the guys is my way of resetting and taking a break. I'm truly sorry if my words hurt you just now. I didn't mean it."

The alarm's shrill call pierced the morning quiet, and with a gentle extraction of his arm from beneath me, the day began. "No, it's too early," I groaned, my voice heavy with sleep and a silent plea for him to take a later flight. But our truce from last night's skirmish still held a delicate peace.

He whispered back, the plans with his friends set in stone, not wanting to miss the flight they had all coordinated. With that, he rolled out of bed and disappeared into the bathroom rituals of the morning. Meanwhile, I shuffled to the kitchen, driven by the knowledge that he wouldn't face the day without the warmth of a homemade breakfast. His upcoming days would be a whirlwind where meals might be forgotten amidst the Las Vegas spectacle.

When he entered the kitchen, I handed him a cup of coffee, the rich aroma a silent testament to the mornings we had shared. "Sit down, sweetheart, and I'll bring your breakfast over," I said, placing his plate before him as I settled across, cradling my own hot cup. The chill from outside seemed to press against the windows, justifying my choice of warm flannel PJs.

"Are you excited?" I asked, searching for a glimpse into his thoughts.

He hummed a response that spoke more of routine than thrill, "It's a trip I'm used to. I wouldn't say excited, but I am looking forward to reconnecting with my buddies."

I couldn't help but tease him lightly, "No strip bars," as I rose, drawn to him by an invisible force, wrapping my arms around his neck, my touch laden with the emotions coursing through me. "I'll miss you for the next seventy-two hours, mister."

His reply was dry, and the smile that had begun to form on my lips withered at the edge. The uncertainty of his hot-and-cold demeanor left me troubled. I wanted to probe further, yet I held back, honoring the space he seemed to need.

"Please call when you land, just to let me know you're safe," I implored softly.

He shrugged off my concern with a lighthearted jest about his friend Bryson's drunken escapade, "Come on, baby, don't bog me down with worries. We've done this before and come back fine—well, except that one time with Bryson."

In a playful, seductive maneuver, I pressed against him, hoping to kindle a flame of desire, "Why search for excitement elsewhere when all the pleasure you need is right here?" I whispered.

A kiss was his reply, a fleeting token of affection that was abruptly severed by the incessant ring of his phone. He brushed it aside, promising me a wife-free return.

I joked with a hint of seriousness, "You better remember, you've got someone who loves you waiting right here." But the phone persisted, its ringtone slicing through our last moments together. "Why not answer it? They seem insistent," I remarked, masking my irritation.

"I'm trying to savor this morning with you," he said, attempting to dismiss the interruption.

But the calls were incessant, a chain of confirmations for their planned rendezvous in Vegas. As the notification for his ride pinged, he hurried away, promising he'd be at the Bellagio by noon. He offered a kiss to my forehead—a perfunctory gesture—as he dashed out, leaving me to echo an 'I love you' into the empty space where he once stood. The silence that followed closed around me as I shut the door, enveloped by a sinking feeling of neglect. It was his time with his friends; of course, he was excited. Yet, I couldn't shake off the mope that clung stubbornly to my heart.

Saturday morning arrived without a message from him. The absence of a simple "I'm safe" text left a hollow pit in my stomach. I wavered between calling him and chastising myself for being overly insecure. In an effort to distract my mind, I turned to cleaning with fervor, hoping that order in the house might lend order to my thoughts. It was during this frenzy that I stumbled upon an old briefcase, forgotten and gathering dust on the top shelf of the closet. Curiosity piqued, I wondered at its contents, its past significance, and why he had kept it locked away.

My inquisitiveness and the challenge of seeing if I can open it propel me to snoop. After a few tries to manipulate the lock, it opens. Okay, I used a screwdriver. Once open, I scan the contents of files, letters, and a few older generations of iPhones. Curiosity got the best of me. I charged the most current version, thinking it's probably broken. But to my surprise, the Apple welcome logo appeared after a few minutes. At least it works.

My heart is thumping with suspense like an old horror movie with ominous music in the background. I try guessing the passcode. Attempt one failed. I query my mind, wondering what I know about this man who would inspire his passcode.

I try, again, birthday. Fail. License plate. Fail. Huh. I think about everything we've done or seen together. If I fail this attempt, then I'm out of options. Perhaps he just uses a series of random numbers that come to mind. I take a wild guess, raking the history of our conversation about places he's traveled in the world or foods he likes that would inspire a passcode. As I tamper with obtaining access to his cell phone, I question my purpose. The answer is I don't know. Though I think it's wrong, I can't control my concern. Even if it opened, the memory has probably been erased.

This is insanity. There are thousands of variations of numbers. I decide to make one last wild random guess. If it fails, it's a sign that I should give up and leave it alone. One last combination comes to mind: Two. Eight. Four. Four. Six. Six. Six. Avignon, his sacred travel, is the center of many stories he shared of past journeys. The home screen displayed, to my astonishment. I felt deceitful, but my feminine curiosity got the better of me, and I sneaked a peek. I did a fast scroll, scanning thousands of texts.

Nothing glaring jumped out at me. I felt naked with shame and embarrassment. I thought to myself, *This is wrong, Cyn. Put the silly thing away.* As I'd convinced myself to return the phone to storage, my thumb landed on a text exchange with Anastasia. Below her was Jaelyn. Katie. Lana. *Don't read any of them*, I said to myself, acknowledging this was his personal business. But having come this far, I couldn't resist. There were thousands of exchanges between him and them. However, my focus narrowed to Anastasia. I had promised myself to read only the last few exchanges from three months before we met. It was there I learned his truth through contemptuous texts that oscillated between declarations of love and biting exchanges:

Him: "Go fuck yourself, you stupid bitch."

Her: "I'm leaving your ass."

Him: "Believe it or not, go fuck yourself is absolute, meaning I don't care where you go. I hear hell would be a great place for you."

Her: "Go to hell, bastard."

Him: "Been there, spent the weekend with you."

I was saddened to discover that my man had engaged in such exchanges with his then-girlfriend. This revelation took me back to the day of our conversation at Stanley Park, where things had ended on a far more volatile note than he had led me to believe.

The texts showed they had only been apart for three months before he and I met. I knew I needed to delve deeper into the phone. What else was hidden or misconstrued? Looking in the briefcase pocket, I found a letter from Jaylen. I thumbed through its pages — five pages of neat, handwritten text.

"*I'm doing my best to keep from crying as I write this letter. You're so hard to get through to, so I thought maybe you'd take a moment to read my words. Hopefully, some part of what I'm feeling will touch your soul. You are so perplexing. At times, you're the most loving man I've known, and I have loved you with all my heart.*

My days are lonely when we're apart at work, and I can't help but rush home to be with you. However, everything has changed recently, and I've been struggling to understand why. Just last evening, as you were preparing to go out, I expressed my desire to spend the evening together. But you ignored me and left, making me feel as though I didn't matter. It's taken me weeks to uncover the truth behind your behavior, and frankly, you've shattered my heart. I can't believe you're ending things with me for someone you've just met. How did she become so significant in such a short time? We've been together for a year and a half. Doesn't our life together mean anything to you? I know you might say I pushed you away. That was never my intention, and for that, I am deeply sorry.

Why does everything with you have to be all or nothing? Have you ever considered my feelings? Perhaps I was scared, scared of giving you my entire heart without the reassurance that it was safe with you. There were days when my love for you was so overwhelming it frightened me. Yet, the thought of building the life we discussed always outweighed my fears.

I have given you my heart and supported you, but you only give back when it suits you. You've made me feel worthless in your pursuit of that little blonde as if I mean nothing. I wish you could experience just a fraction of my pain. Tonight, I am engulfed in misery. Despite the hurt you've caused, I... I wish you and Ana—no, just have a good life...

Always, JJ."

The letter boggled my mind. I'm shaking my head to regain my senses. My heart is pounding with anxiety. The closet is stifling. It's as though the air is being sucked out of the room. The ceiling is lowering, and the walls are closing in. I'm feeling faint. Yet, I can't help myself from reading more of this treasure trove of untold secrets of his past. Communications we would never discuss. I see a blazing image of a stop sign with red lights flashing in my mind. I'm telling myself, *leave it alone. Drop the damn thing, Cyn!* But my curiosity is overwhelming.

Despite my suffocation and the need to run outside for fresh air, I read one last message from Katie a couple of days before Jaylyn's text: *Hey, I stopped by last night thinking maybe you wanted company. However, I went down to the club and saw you with a new chick. I wonder how long you've been seeing her? I won't get into all the other mess between us. Like we agreed, 'Don't ask, don't tell.' So, all is well between us. We got what we needed from each other. Over the past decade, I hadn't quite figured it out, but I loved how I felt when we were together. Perhaps it was my way of punishing myself. But what the hell? We did it for the sex, and tonight, I felt I wanted to be with you. Heart sign.* It continued, *"But anyway, some other time, enjoy yourself. By the way, where is the other chick you said you were building a committed relationship with?"* I was aghast. Ten! They've been having casual sex for ten years? The burning question lingered: Was he still seeing her?

Oh my god, who in the hell were these women?" Alarm bells blared in my mind. What could he possibly have been doing in Vegas? The lack of phone calls heightened my suspicions. Maybe he was there with his drop-by chick or any one of the others. Emotions drained from my body like water from a dry riverbed, leaving me with thoughts I didn't want to consider.

I read enough. The phone in my hands felt like scorching coal, burning with the weight of its revelations. I struggled to hold back tears and steady my rapid breaths, panic rising within me. Adrenaline coursed through my veins, its icy shards tearing at my flesh. I reached for solace, desperate for something to calm the storm within. *Yes! I surrender.*

I reached for a Klonopin, seeking refuge in its embrace. I made my way to the sofa, sitting with my knees drawn to my chest, staring at the blank television screen, rocking back and forth, coaching myself, *breathing deep... Relax. Breathe, Cyn. Breathe. Relax. Relax. Relax.*

Chapter Twenty-Five

In the abyss of my soul, emotions waged war, each wave of feeling crashing into me with merciless force before retreating, leaving me hollow and gasping for air. The rideshare's arrival at ten-thirty on Sunday evening was like a punctuated echo of my swirling thoughts. I was nettled—had I even flickered across his mind while he was away? A cocktail of anger and relief brewed within me as I heard him return. In bed, book in hand, I did not mask my discontent. "Welcome home, lover," I said, my smile a brittle veneer.

His smirk was the only greeting he offered before escaping to the shower, void of any endearments or signs of missing me. When he finally joined me in bed, I cloaked my disillusionment, my voice a soft purr, "I hope you saved some energy for me," even as I nibbled his ear and warred with my doubts.

The urge to confront him about the secrets I had unearthed was a fire within me, yet I feared the explosion that might follow. He had woven a web of lies, and I had stumbled into it. To voice what I knew would invite scrutiny over how I came to such knowledge.

Yet in that moment, a raw, searing desire overtook me—I wanted him to consume me with his passion, to erase the uncertainties that clawed at me. But his kisses were devoid of the warmth I craved. He was as distant in his touch as he was in his spirit, a chilling echo of the man who had left days before. Desperate for a flicker of connection, I attempted to coax details of his trip, only to be met with detached brevity. "It was alright," he said, and to my further probing, "Yeah, it was fun." The simplicity of his answers grated on me.

"What did you guys get up to?" I pressed.

His shrug was noncommittal. "The usual—gamble, hang out, drink, talk about old times. Just the usual crap we do."

I prodded a hint of sarcasm in my tone, "Sounds enthralling. No strippers, then?"

He laughed it off, "Nah, pretty low-key this time." But 'low-key' was hardly the term I'd use for his escapades. I pondered the bright lights of Vegas, the shows, the throngs of people, the sumptuous meals—experiences that would have left me with stories to share.

Yet, all I received was his silence. His indifference to my need for affection, for connection, was growing unbearable. It echoed past disappointments, the ghost of a distant relationship flickering in the back of my mind. My patience frayed, I confronted him, my voice thick with exasperation,

What in God's name is going on with you? Did something happen? I thought you'd be eager to come home, but you act as if you can't stand the sight of me. Have I become so insignificant to you?"

His frown deepened. "What truths do you think you're owed the moment I walk through the door? I was with my friends. Do I need to give you an hourly update?"

I wasn't demanding constant attention, I explained. But was it too much to ask for a mere hint of thoughtfulness? A simple message or call to reassure that the distance hadn't severed the thread between us? The unspoken words and texts from his past spun in my head, a maelstrom threatening to burst forth.

The words burst forth, propelled by a frustration that had been simmering beneath my calm facade. "You know what? I would've appreciated some consideration. My life, my whole being, is dedicated to you, and what do I get? Crumbs. You carelessly hand out crumbs when I offer you my heart and soul. I'm meant to be your rock, not a stepping stone. I'm sick of this aloofness. If something's eating at you, spit it out. I can't stand this cryptic nonsense anymore.

You're away so often, and here I am, missing you before you've even reached the end of the driveway. Is it too much to ask for a little bit of that to be reciprocated, mister?" My voice trembled with the force of unspoken words, the weight of what I had found hidden away, fueling a rage that I struggled to contain within my thoughts.

Today's brunch felt markedly different, tinged with a melancholy that seemed to hang in the air like the heavy clouds outside. Courtnee had driven up from Oregon to join us, her presence a reminder of change. She was brimming with stories of her new life, a stark contrast to the subdued mood that otherwise enveloped us. The joy and laughter that once defined our gatherings seemed to be on hiatus, replaced by perfunctory chit-chat about our weeks and work.

Gina asked half-heartedly about things at home, her lack of genuine interest palpable. I let the question hang unanswered, a silent acknowledgment of the disinterest that seemed mutual. The atmosphere was more reflective of obligation than the desire that once drew us together.

Our bond, once resilient against the intrusion of relationships—the one thing we swore would never come between us—now felt weakened. Its vibrancy diminished without Lexi's fiery sarcasm to ignite our conversations.

Courtnee, meanwhile, seemed unaffected by the somber tone, her spirits lifted by the new chapter she was living. Her updates were a bright spot in the gathering, yet they also underscored the distance that had grown between us. The Mimosa remained untouched by her; she no longer needed the lift it provided.

Sitting there amidst the disconnection, I felt adrift. A growing sense of unease tugged at my heart, a lingering uncertainty about my relationship that refused to be ignored. The fragments of life's events swirled through my mind, and I yearned for clarity amidst the conflicting emotions pulling me in different directions. Was the stability and excitement Courtnee found in her new life possible for me as well?

Could I find the same happiness and certainty within my own heart and my future with the man I loved? These questions and the shadows they cast left me yearning for answers amidst the mists of a rainy afternoon.

Courtnee, bless her, brought a momentary lift to our spirits, her face flushed with embarrassment as she recounted the audacious story of her ninety-year-old patient, Mr. W. Heinze. In his bold attempts to charm her, he had regaled her with tales of his youthful sexual conquests and the three wives who had shared his bed over the years. His latest, and quite possibly his last request, was both shocking and comically tragic—he wanted Viagra and a partner to relive his glory days. She imitated him, his voice raspy with age; his final living request was for her to prescribe him Viagra and have sex. He reached under the covers grabbing his penis, telling her, "It's sleeping right now, but if you give me a couple of those blue bombs and jump-start it with a few good jerks, it'll become a hard-on son of a bitch in no time." She retorted, "Mr. Heinze, I have seen you naked. How about I order you sleep medication? That way, you and your little too-soft friend that's very unlikely to ever regain consciousness can rest peacefully." With that, we adjourned to go home.

Driving home, my mood was reflective, weighed down by the complexities of my emotions. The argument with my partner, though partially resolved, had left a lingering unease. His recent attentiveness, a stark contrast to our previous discord, added layers to my inner conflict. I recognized this clash of past grievances and present efforts as the source of my turmoil.

The day's brunch with my friends, usually a source of joy and rejuvenation, had mirrored the internal chaos I felt. Our interactions lacked their usual vibrancy, further highlighting the sense of disconnection I grappled with.

As I navigated the roads, I pondered over these contrasting elements—his promises and the long conversations we'd had against the backdrop of our heated argument. It was this unresolved tension, juxtaposed with his sudden showering of affection, that left me in a state of emotional limbo. I longed for harmony between my heart's lingering doubts and the present reassurances from my partner.

In the quiet of my car, I sought solace, a yearning for understanding and clarity to navigate through this complex emotional landscape. "Please, God, help me," I whispered, a plea for guidance amidst the swirling thoughts, hoping for the strength to reconcile the tumultuous currents of my life and find a path to inner peace.

Chapter Twenty-Six

Morning always comes sooner than I wish for. Lying there, I struggled with the thought of leaving our bed's warm embrace. I purred contentedly, snuggling closer to my amour, holding onto him and spooning until the very last possible second. In these moments of quiet intimacy, I found a comforting sanctuary, a fleeting respite from the uncertainties and complexities that awaited us beyond the bedroom.

Clinging to these precious seconds, I cherished the feeling of his body against mine, a silent exchange of affection that said more than words could. It was in these quiet, early hours, with the soft light of dawn creeping in, that I found a simple yet profound connection, a reminder of the tenderness that still existed between us despite everything.

Finally, I pulled myself away from the warmth of our bed, whispering "I love you" into his ear with a sense of yearning for just a few more minutes. The temptation to remain, to make passionate love before the day began, lingered heavily, but practicality overruled desire with the awareness of time pressing against me.

Today's schedule was non-negotiable—an early meeting demanded my presence, followed by a series of patient appointments that couldn't be delayed. I allowed myself one final, tender kiss, an attempt to carry the sweetness of our connection into the day ahead before I stepped briskly away from our bedroom sanctuary.

With a final glance back, I reminded him about the car service as I grabbed his keys. I dashed out, slipping into his car and pulling out of the garage, the familiar hum of the engine marking the transition from our private world to the responsibilities waiting in the world beyond.

The day greeted me with a sky painted in hues of hopeful blues, the sun a radiant orb that seemed to promise a fresh start. A wave of cautious optimism washed over me as I pondered the possibility that the pieces of our relationship were slowly knitting back together.

However, the serenity of the morning shattered in an instant. As I reached into the car's overhead sunglass storage for what I presumed would be his sunglasses, my fingers stumbled upon a silky texture. Drawing it out, the realization struck with a visceral force. The delicate fabric I held was not a cleaning cloth but a woman's lacy underwear, the 'VS' emblem glaring at me accusingly. Time felt suspended as shock and betrayal coiled tightly around my heart.

In a reflex of disgust, I tried to cast the garment away, but a stubborn thread caught on my engagement ring. I shook my hand frantically, desperate to rid myself of the vile evidence of infidelity. But the distraction was costly. My gaze, too late, snapped up to the road just as I collided with the car ahead at fifty miles an hour.

The airbag deployed with a force that both protected and stunned me, muffling the world into silence. A chilling wave of realization crashed over me, then a tide of horror and disbelief. As the airbag deflated, a sense of nausea engulfed me. There, on the floor, lay the black panties, a stark symbol of my shattered illusions.

Visions of betrayal swirled in my mind, a tumultuous sea of emotions that left me feeling utterly sick to my core.

The driver of the car I rear-ended was tapping on my window, and concern etched into his features. "Ma'am. Are you okay?" I barely registered his words, gripping the steering wheel with a fierce intensity, my gaze fixed straight ahead.

Another loud tap, a more insistent "Ma'am! Ma'am, are you okay?" jarred me into action. Fumbling with the lever, I tried to open the door, only to find it jammed. The driver, now joined by several bystanders, worked to pry the door open. With a collective effort, it finally gave way under the force of three men.

The victim of my inattention, a gentleman in his seventies named Carl Hendrix, extended his hand to help me out of the car. "Don't worry about it, ma'am. They're only cars, and we—we're both fine," he reassured me with a gentle smile and a comforting pat on the shoulder. If only he knew the damage to my heart far exceeded the physical wreckage around us. "What's your name?" he asked gently.

My reply was a slurred whisper, "Cynthya. My friends…they call me Cyn."

"Okay, Cyn, listen to me. Everything's going to be okay," he tried to assure me. But deep down, I knew nothing would be the same again. The beauty of my morning had been irrevocably altered.

Carl's kindness was a small solace as my face started to show signs of bruising, a line of blood trickling from my nose, courtesy of the airbag's impact. The distant wail of sirens heralded the arrival of emergency services, and soon enough, two state troopers were directing the scene. A young blonde officer approached me, his voice cutting through the cacophony, "Do you have your driver's license, ma'am?"

Time seemed to slow down, my thoughts echoing loudly as I struggled to make sense of the whirlwind of events. "…yes, it's in my car. Do you mind if I go get it?" The trooper nodded and signaled for his partner as Carl interjected about the need for an ambulance.

In a daze of adrenaline and confusion, I rambled through my purse, hands shaking. With a haphazard motion, I upended it, spilling its contents like scattered pieces of a disjointed puzzle across the seat. Amid the chaos, my fingers found the familiar plastic edge of my driver's license, which I clutched and presented to the waiting trooper. The wailing sirens grew louder, and soon, the medical unit loomed into view, its arrival a blur of urgency.

The medic, a figure of calm amidst the disarray, stepped forward with a reassuring presence. Her hair, tied back in a no-nonsense ponytail, swayed as she guided me with a gentle firmness into the haven of the ambulance.

Inside, the world narrowed to the bench I was seated on and the focused attention of my temporary caretaker. She worked swiftly, treating my visible wounds, while the blood pressure cuff on my arm whispered of hidden injuries with its inflated squeeze and the high numbers that followed.

The decision was swift and non-negotiable; my condition warranted immediate hospital care. As the ambulance doors closed, sealing me away from the scene of twisted metal and broken glass, I surrendered to the professionals' care. The sirens cut through the cacophony of morning traffic, a clear path carved to the emergency room.

Emerging from the haze, the sterile white of the hospital room enveloped me, a stark departure from the accident's turmoil. Doctors hovered, their faces etched with concern as they monitored my vital signs, their grave expressions speaking volumes of the threat they feared—a potential heart attack. Nurses circulated, efficient and silent as they drew blood and recorded data, their tasks punctuated by the occasional hushed consultation about providing samples to the state patrol. In the midst of their meticulous care, the implications of inattention or driving under the influence hung in the air, an unspoken query amidst the beeps and murmurs of hospital machinery.

When asked about my next of kin, I hesitated. Before today, I would have immediately mentioned my amour, but now the thought of him only brought visions of betrayal. I couldn't face Gina and her inevitable inquisition, not with her already dim view of him. Yet, since it was his car involved in the accident, he would be wondering about me, and I didn't want to invite more drama into my life. Taking a deep breath, I decided to give the hospital my amour's name and number, trying to steady my mind against the mental images of him with the owner of the black lace underwear.

I reached out to the physician scheduler, my voice a mix of firmness and fatigue, to notify them of the accident. "Please reschedule my appointments for the day," I requested, hoping the disruption would be minimal. I knew Gina, always attuned to any ripple in my routine, would hear of this. She'd be concerned, so I decided to get ahead of it to alleviate her worry before the sedative could dull my senses.

Her voicemail greeted me instead of her voice, and I left a brief message, trying to sound less shaken than I felt. "Hey Gina, it's Cyn. I've had a small car accident. I'm fine, no need to worry. I'll fill you in later." I ended the call, feeling a twinge of guilt for downplaying the truth.

The nurse soon administered the sedative, and as its soothing tendrils wrapped around my consciousness, the sharp edges of pain and betrayal began to soften. The world slipped away, and I succumbed to the drug's promise of escape, however temporary.

As I blinked away the remnants of the sedative's grip, I found myself at the intersection of competing concerns. On one side, my amour, his presence a steady beacon of support. Across from him, Gina, embodying a tension that belied her worry. Despite their mutual disdain, it was evident that my well-being had momentarily bridged the chasm between them, each vying to express their concern in the wake of my awakening.

My amour's smile was a study in tenderness, but my newfound knowledge painted it in a different light. "How are you feeling, sweetheart?" he asked. I offered a smile back, but it was a hollow performance.

Gina's question, tinged with skepticism, sought the narrative hidden beneath the surface of my accident. "So, what really happened?" she pressed, her gaze searching mine for any flicker of evasion. "It was an accident," I insisted, my response a blend of truth shadowed by the complexities unspoken. The words felt heavy, laden with the reality of the event and the nuances that lay untold.

The tension in the room was intense, a current of unspoken suspicions. When my amour requested privacy, Gina's reluctance was clear. Her quiet utterance, "I hate you," as she passed him was a testament to her feelings about the situation.

As she left, I clutched his hand, trying to divert his attention from Gina's parting words. His query was gentle, filled with concern. "Honey, are you okay?" So many responses jostled for release, yet I remained silent, knowing that this was neither the time nor the place for such revelations.

"What happened?" His question hung in the air, his concern apparent. I held back my words, fighting to keep my voice even, to hide the bitterness that threatened to spill. As he leaned in for a kiss, I instinctively turned away, a silent plea resonating within me—*no...please don't touch me*. He paused, his act of concern unconvincing. "What's wrong, sweetheart? Are you in pain?" he prodded gently.

No, not pain—at least not the kind he could understand. I had just had my world turned inside out, the discovery in his car tearing through the fabric of my trust. The irony of the 'VS' emblem wasn't lost on me— 'Very Stupid' indeed, a crude but fitting rebranding in my current state of mind.

He settled into the chair beside my hospital bed, promising to stay. But his words were hollow, the sentiment failing to touch the cold space between us. "I'll stay with you until you're ready to go home," he said, unaware of the finality that had settled in my heart.

Tears welled up, not just from sorrow but also from the dawning realization of what must come next. With a voice firmer than I felt, I urged him, "Go check on your car." It was a small, spiteful wish that he'd find the lace evidence, that piece of betrayal I'd so unexpectedly held in my hands.

As he hesitated, likely puzzled by my insistence, I knew it was the only way for him to understand the gravity of what he'd done. That forgotten trophy of infidelity was the catalyst of this heartache, and I needed him to confront it, to see the chaos his carelessness had wrought. It was over for us, and the sooner he realized it, the sooner I could start to mend.

I asked him to please leave. I couldn't maintain the facade that all was well, not when I felt like everything was crumbling inside. He looked at me, his expression morphing into one of confusion. "Sweetheart?"

"I need to speak to Gina alone," I insisted. "I'll be off work for a couple of days. We can talk… some other time." My voice was steady, but inside, I was a storm of emotions.

"Some other time?" he repeated, his face wrinkling with perplexity. His inability to grasp the situation only fueled my inner turmoil.

"Yes, some other time, as in not now," I responded, trying to keep my voice calm. His ignorance was infuriating, but I didn't want to reveal the depth of my emotions to him.

He started to say something, "Cynthya—" but I cut him off immediately. "Don't call me Cynthya."

"Okay, Cyn. Why are you asking me to leave? What's going on, babe?" His voice was laced with concern, but I couldn't deal with it right now.

I was sharp in my response. "Please, just go take care of the car. I don't want to talk right now." I wanted him to discover the truth himself. To find the black lace and understand the depth of his infidelity.

"So, you don't want to talk to me? What is going on?" he asked, his voice tinged with frustration.

I sighed heavily, a mix of anger, hurt, and a sudden, overwhelming feeling of disgust for his presence enveloping me. "Nothing I care to discuss right now. Just leave it alone and go check on the car. I need to know the extent of the damage—and no, it can't wait."

He stood there for a moment, looking completely baffled. Was he really that oblivious? Eventually, with a confused look, he left the room.

After spending two weeks at Gina's place, deep in contemplation about my life and future, I finally mustered the courage to turn on my phone. A flood of notifications greeted me - messages and voicemails from him. With a heavy heart, I tossed the phone aside, not ready to face his attempts to connect.

On the final night at Gina's, as I lay upon the borrowed bed, sleep eluded me, evading my grasp like a slippery shadow. The air was heavy with the weight of impending departure, and my mind churned with restless thoughts. Outside, the full moon hung in the sky, its eerie glow casting elongated shadows that danced across the room.

Despite my restlessness, the rhythmic dance of the moon's shadows and the distant, soothing sounds of the night began to weave a spell of drowsiness over me. My eyelids grew heavy, fluttering against the pull of an unseen slumber. The world around me seemed to blur, the edges of reality softly fraying as the grip of wakefulness loosened. In this twilight of consciousness, where the tangible and the ethereal merge, my thoughts drifted into a realm of shadow and moonlight.

It was here, in this ethereal atmosphere, amidst the whispered farewells of the night, that the boundaries between wakefulness and sleep dissolved entirely. Surrendering to the embrace of dreams, I found myself transported beyond the confines of the room and into the depths of an ominous dreamscape.

In the depths of my dream, a haunting scene unfolded. Beneath the ominous glow of the full moon, I found myself entrapped, powerless against the relentless advance of a sleek black panther. Its fur glistened with an eerie sheen, each muscle highlighted by the moon's pale light as it moved with a grace born of lethal intent. The panther's gaze, sharp and calculating, pierced the night, each step deliberate as it circled ever nearer. The moon, casting an eerie brilliance, intensified the dread of the moment, weaving sinister shadows around the prowling beast.With every movement, the panther's presence grew more menacing, its intentions clear yet chillingly mysterious. Its tail swished with a sinister rhythm, a silent harbinger of impending doom. Paralyzed by fear, I remained captive to the unfolding nightmare, unable to move or call for help.

As the predator closed in, driven by instinct under the ominous moonlight, it lunged forward with savage determination. Its powerful jaws seized my chest, ripping through flesh and bone in a brutal display of dominance, snatching my heart from its cavity.

With a start, I awoke, consumed by a primal scream that shattered the silence of the night. The visceral terror of the dream lingered, clawing at the edges of my consciousness, as if the darkness itself had tainted my very soul.

Gina burst into the room at the sound of my distress, her movements swift and purposeful. Without hesitation, she enveloped me in her arms, holding me tightly against her chest as if to shield me from the looming specters of my nightmares.

"Cyn, honey," she murmured, her voice a soothing melody, "Cyn, my dear, you're safe now." With each repetition of my name, her words carried a deeper assurance, her embrace a fortress against the encroaching darkness.

"You're alright, Cyn. I've got you," she whispered fiercely, her presence a steadfast guardian in the midst of my turmoil.

But I wasn't alright. The dream felt too real, too symbolic of the heartache I was experiencing.

"No! It's not alright," I cried, caught in the grip of my anguish. Gina, tears in her eyes, held me close, trying to assure me that I was safe, that my heart was still intact.

In that moment, I realized that the panther in my dream was a manifestation of him - a creature that had consumed my love, my devotion, and now, in my dream, my very heart. As I lay there in

Gina's arms, I understood that no matter how much I gave, he would always seek more from others.

I found a new place to live, a fresh start, a place where echoes of the past could not reach. My final task was to return to our shared home, now solely his domain, was made with a heavy heart. It was a necessary step, an act of closure. I had carefully chosen a time when he would be away, ensuring the process would be as painless as possible. As I stood before the house, a surge of emotions washed over me. Despite the turmoil, I reminded myself of the strength that had carried me this far. Today was about moving forward.

The moment I crossed the threshold, the absence of warmth was striking. The home that once buzzed with shared dreams and laughter now felt foreign, a stark reminder of the distance that had grown between us. Yet, my focus was clear. I was here to reclaim what was mine, to pack my belongings and close this the chapter of us.

In the bedroom, where our lives had intertwined the most, the memories were the strongest. I allowed myself a moment to acknowledge them, to feel their weight, before pushing them aside. This wasn't a time for dwelling; it was a time for action.

With my heart pounding and a mix of fear and curiosity driving me, I returned to the closet, taking a deep breath as I gathered the courage to pick up the phone again. My trembling hand reached for it, and I opened the photo app. The screen filled with a myriad of images, each a potential harbinger of more heartache.

Despite my inner voice cautioning me, I scrolled through the gallery. The world around me receded into a hushed silence, and then, without warning, one particular image stopped me cold. It was like a jolt of electricity, a visual scream that pierced through the ordinary and catapulted me into a realm of disbelief. My breath hitched, and my fingers trembled as they hovered over the screen, afraid to make contact with the reality now glaring back at me. The shock rooted me to the spot, making me a statue amidst the flow of life that continued unaware around me.

It was her—the woman from the hotel in Vancouver, the missing piece of the puzzle that brought everything full circle. The reality of the black garment, the mood swings, the changes in our relationship—it all made sense now. The on-again, off-again affair between my amour and Anastasia had been rekindled, a secret dance that destroyed the beauty of what I thought we had. Pain and horror washed over me, leaving me doubled over, clutching my stomach in agony.

The room felt heavy and suffocating, as if my soul had already withered away, leaving only an empty shell behind. Tears and sorrow wouldn't change anything. If I had any doubts about leaving, they were now completely extinguished. I wrote a letter intended for her but meant for him, pouring out my heart, my pain, and my final goodbye.

Dear Anastasia,

Congratulations, he's all yours. It never had to be a game of secrets. I don't know why he left your world to come into mine only to secretly re-enter yours. I don't understand why he couldn't be honest with me. Now I see you knew about us, a willing accomplice in this deception.

I remember the day our eyes met in the hotel lobby. Your glare was resentful, powerful. You knew, yet you said nothing. Were you having one last rendezvous before I entered the picture? How could you walk away, knowing he was meeting me? Maybe he broke your heart too, as he has mine.

He said he loved me, and I believed him, even in his rejection. I thought it was just a struggle we had to overcome. Did he say the same to you?

I don't understand why I had to be involved, but now I know the truth. I've been a fool right from the start. I wish you both the happiness you deserve. You were both deceitful, and he won't have to hide you anymore.

But I've been foolish to tolerate this for so long. Today, I've found myself again. I hope you find your self-respect too. I wish you both the best,
Cynthya

With the letter penned and carefully placed atop the briefcase, I positioned his old iPhone beside it, its contents a dark portal to the lies he had woven into our lives.

Resting ominously on the kitchen counter, the phone stood as a silent witness to the deceit that had slowly dismantled what we once cherished. This deliberate arrangement marked my final act, sealing the end of a chapter marred by betrayal. As I turned the key to lock the door behind me for the last time, I felt a profound sense of release. This moment was more than reclaiming my possessions; it was a resolute closure to 'he and I,' a definitive step towards a future free from the shadows of his duplicity.

Epilogue

Deception Unveiled: A Journey of Redemption and Self-Discovery

Walking the path around Green Lake, I find myself enveloped by a curtain of snow, each flake silently contributing to the winter's quietude. This scene, so starkly different from the lively warmth of summer, mirrors the change within me—a transition from tumult to tranquility.

The path stretches ahead, an untouched canvas, echoing the new beginning unfolding in my soul. Here at the lake's edge, the world seems to pause, with snowflakes falling gracefully, embodying nature's patient endurance.

Drawing in a breath filled with the day's crispness and a resolve forged from the trials I've faced, I open my hand. The ring, with its platinum band and the brilliance of its diamond, once a symbol of a bond now broken, is released. It arcs through the air, a transient spark against the white, and touches the lake with the barest whisper of a splash. The ripples it creates are small and quick to fade, much like the lingering traces of a past I'm ready to leave behind.

The chill in the air brings a refreshing clarity, sweeping away the remnants of doubt. Each step I take on this journey etches a new path, one that is entirely my own. The snowfall, no longer a shroud over what was, now lays the groundwork for what will be.

Now, on this path freshly laid with snow, my footprints chart a course of resilience and newfound purpose. Ahead lies a clean expanse, a space where the legacy I build with each step is one of strength, wisdom, and empowerment.

FYESBIII